Date: 11/26/19

FIC GRANT
Grant, Dan
Thirteen across : a thriller /

THIRTEEN
ACROSS

A Thriller

Dan Grant

Mindscape Press

Cover art by MindScape Press, Inc.

Identifiers: ISBN: 978-1-7325040-4-2 (hardcover)
ISBN: 978-1-7325040-5-9 (trade paperback)
ISBN: 978-1-7325040-6-6 (e-book)
ISBN: 978-1-7325040-7-3 (audio book)

Subjects: fiction | thrillers | mystery | suspense fiction |
science fiction | adventure fiction | FBI thrillers |
illegal human research-fiction | human cloning fiction |
super soldier fiction | puzzle fiction | crossword puzzle fiction

To learn more, see author notes, and read background material,
go to www.DanGrantBooks.com

Publisher: MindScape Press, Inc.
www.MindScapePress.com

ALSO BY DAN GRANT

The Singularity Witness

THIRTEEN ACROSS

1
MORNING COMMUTE

Monday, 7:40 AM, East Falls Church Metro Station, Virginia

Katherine Morgan hated inquisitions. The congressional hearing on her Monday calendar torpedoed the buzz of a tropical vacation. The summons had greeted her two days earlier, in the form of a stiff in a suit, as she deplaned from a Grand Caymans flight at Dulles International Airport.

The nation's capital was a place where the stars were aligned against her, a place where federal law enforcement and beltway political hacks waited to pile it on.

Standing on an outdoor platform, Kate wedged herself into the fluid mass of morning commuters. An eastbound Orange line train arrived. Doors opened. People crowded inside. Navigating the throng of bodies, she found a vacant vinyl seat and did her best not to stare. But it was impossible to ignore the gray-haired woman beside her. The woman's face was buried in the Bible. The page header noted the Book of Revelation. Gold bracelets clanked on her wrists when she turned a page and her lips moved in an animated fashion, as if she were a TV evangelist preaching to an unseen congregation and someone had muted her with the remote.

Kate rolled her eyes. *Reading about the end of the world?*

Forcing her attention to *The Washington Post* in her hands, she skimmed a story on the bizarre murder of an Oklahoma senator. Secret research programs. Human experimentation. Tabloid news. And Congress wanted to hear her version of it. She flipped to the entertainment section and the day's crossword puzzle. For her, the childhood addiction passed the time.

The train jolted into motion. Clicks and clacks of steel wheels on rails filled the air with white noise as the commute found a hypnotic routine. Minutes passed as the Metro train made stops.

"Foggy Bottom GWU," an automated voice said over the intercom.

Kate ignored the announcement. Not her stop.

Biting her lip, she studied the puzzle and scratched her scalp with the end of a pencil, digging under the barrette that held her hair. 12 DOWN. A twelve-letter word for ARCHAEOLOGIST'S TIME MEASURING-TECHNIQUE. The word started with C. D was the seventh letter. It ended with—

An explosion rocked the train.

Its shockwave reverberated like thunder accompanying a flash of lightning. The train shuddered and dropped several inches, causing Kate's feet to lift from the floor. The unrestrained creaking and moaning of metal made her ears throb. More thunder cracked as the train rocked off its rails.

Gasping for breath, Kate slung the paper aside and grabbed at the bottom of her seat for a handhold.

Passenger screams competed with the sounds of tortured metal.

"We're going to die!" someone yelled.

Kate lifted her chin with a jolt and locked eyes with the woman beside her.

The woman broke her silence and chanted like a falsetto monk on speed, her words running together as indecipherable noise. "Holy Father...!"

Sparks streamed past windows. Cabin lights blinked off. Outside, brilliant fireworks cascaded in the blackness of a railway tunnel.

Fearing death, she thought of Thomas Parker. Their spontaneous trip to the Caribbean had come after surviving a deadly ordeal in Princeton. Kate yearned to return to the sugar white sand and sail under amber sunsets, and she prayed that she'd see the professor and neurologist again.

Lights streaked past the train car's windows.

Off its rails and on the concrete underlayment between tracks, the train's lead car skidded into a concrete side wall. The passenger cars in tow buckled under a change in momentum and the train pitched forward. Plexiglas windows imploded, showering passengers with jagged bits of plastic.

Kate lost her grip on the seat. A chorus of screams erupted as bodies tumbled through the air like rag dolls in a clothes dryer. The clatter of metal was deafening before the crescendo diminished as the train stopped its motion.

Wisps of haze clouded dim lights.

Forcing her mind to focus, Kate realized that her car, the second in the train, rested on its side. She faced the ceiling. A faint glow broke through smoky darkness as emergency lights replaced inoperative cabin lights. Unable to budge, she gagged on air saturated with metallic silt, and a caustic taste pasted the inside of her mouth.

Kate felt the pressure of people pinning her. The drumming of her own heartbeat overtook the ringing in her ears. She discovered she was buried among other passengers, and lay atop a man who hung out a shattered window. His lifeless torso, crushed between the side of the passenger car and the tracks below, had broken her fall and kept her from flying out when the train rolled onto its side.

"Oh, thank you, Father!" proclaimed the chanting woman.

"I second that," Kate mumbled, assessing her condition. Nothing felt broken, although she'd have a few bumps and bruises—small prices to pay for survival.

Screams, lots of them, stifled any elation. Wrenching her head around, she couldn't make out what the panic was all about, until she heard a shriek: "Fire!"

"Get off!" Kate snapped, imagining the passengers above her swimming in a sea of molasses as they unpiled. Realizing she was a floor mat, she jammed her fists into the dead man and pushed. The muscles in her arms quivered and her heart raged as she wrestled free from the entangled mass of bodies. Nudging others aside, Kate gained enough room to stand.

Her eyes flashed wide at the sight of fire.

At the rear of her compartment, flames licked the edges of the twisted metal. Smoke smelling of soot, grease, and melting plastic flooded the space, stinging her eyes before trickling out the shattered windows.

The immediate threat wasn't death by suffocation, it was by incineration.

The panic-stricken faces surrounding her all shared an orange glow of desperation and a "fend for yourself" hysteria.

The scene was a coffin of wreckage. Debris and bodies littered the tipped-over train. Moans from the injured competed for attention as panicked passengers climbed out and fled to safety above.

Lightheadedness swept over her as she sucked in shallow breaths of soiled air. When her head finally cleared, she discovered she was standing on the Bible. Her neighbor, the monkish woman, had vanished—as if a guardian angel had swooped down from heaven and whisked her away from tragedy.

An answered prayer. Who would have thought?

As the crackling of sparks and fire devoured more of the passenger car, Kate grew mesmerized by the splashes of heat touching her face. She felt the presence of death, its fingers of fire claiming the fallen.

The fire wanted her next.

2
LET THERE BE LIFE

Foggy Bottom—GWU Metro Station, Washington, DC

Phillip Barnes checked his watch as the railway platform shook. The thunderous vibrations felt as if an earthquake had just rocked the nation's capital. The sounds of explosions and mechanical chaos emanating from the west tunnels seemed otherworldly.

Better than he ever expected.

Commuters around him gasped and migrated to the edge of the tracks as steel and concrete rumbled before something large ground to a halt. A grit-laden wave of air swooshed into the faces of those craning their heads for a view. Hands clutching cell phones jolted up to record the tragedy and post it online.

Barnes beamed. The whole world had paused.

A fiery luster materialized from a darkened tunnel and led a distant wave of screams.

Nothing was visible from the platform, but the tragedy was clear—a train wreck.

Two uniformed Army soldiers hopped around the platform gates and disappeared down the tunnel. WMATA transit cops followed, carrying flashlights.

"This is awful," a woman said over the crowd's chatter.

"Yes, it is," Barnes said, standing indistinguishable from a hundred onlookers. His carefully selected attire included no dramatic colors: a gray suit with matching overcoat and collared shirt. His normally blond hair and eyebrows had been dyed black. Coal black. Thick-rimmed glasses perched on his long, Grecian nose. To the surrounding crowd, Barnes was nothing more than another commuter—perhaps a mid-level bureaucrat, a government lawyer, or accountant. Nobody important.

But hardly nobody, having just graduated to the ranks of mass murderers. Oh, he had killed before, but not like this. The grandeur of his malice had altered hundreds of lives, forever.

Barnes strained for a view, hoping to catch a glimpse of FBI Special Agent Katherine Morgan.

His calculations for the quantity and placement of explosives had been imprecise, yet it was important that she survived. He expected ten to twenty percent fatalities, all told, leaving a possibility that Katherine Morgan could be among the unlucky twenty percent.

During the months of planning, he had fantasized about, dreamt about seeing her distressed, crawling on all fours across the tracks and begging for someone to rescue her.

Either way—life or death—this was payback for murdering his family.

A challenge was cast in motion. All the FBI agent had to do was survive her first ordeal.

The excitement caused his hands to sweat and reminded him of the briefcase he clutched—a leave-behind present for the first stop on this journey to hell.

Panic-stricken voices bellowed out of the tunnel as onlookers surged even closer to the platform's edge.

Barnes allowed the curiosity seekers to swell past him, while he receded to a concrete bench in the center of the platform. His footwork was methodical, moving behind a diamond-shaped speaker tower that obscured his movements from security cameras.

He let the briefcase drop to the floor. After pushing up his glasses, he dabbed his eyes with a handkerchief, careful not to be melodramatic. This was no time for an Oscar performance. Using his shoe, he slid the briefcase across the terra cotta-colored, hexagonal tiles and nudged it beneath the edge of the bench, out of sight.

The first wave of terrified passengers hit the platform. A frantic woman with gold bracelets on her wrists broke through the crowd, collapsed at his feet, and vomited.

Barnes frowned. This poor, poor woman was not his target.

He had spent a year watching from a careful distance and knew Kate Morgan intimately, like a painter who had captured a model's essence on canvas time and time again. He could reproduce her portrait while immersed in darkness.

A thousand times at least.

No, this woman was not responsible for the death of his family.

After a deadpanned breath, Barnes wiped his shoe off with a handkerchief.

The morning commute had gone almost perfectly.

3
FIRE

Kate spun away from a tentacle of flames that lashed forward at alarming speed. Fumes churned in the confined space, making it difficult to breathe. She hacked and listened to moans, like those that lurked in nightmares. Hunching close to the floor of the overturned train, she peered into haze. Bodies and debris made walking difficult. Years of medical training instilled a sense of Hippocratic duty—an obligation to help those less fortunate.

Yet she didn't have to be a physician to identify the most common injury of the fallen: severe head trauma. And the overwhelming carnage was more than one person could handle.

She felt helpless. Even with time to search for survivors, she had no idea where to begin.

Compulsion, more than compassion, forced her to feel the carotid artery of a man buried amidst an entanglement of arms and legs. Closing her eyes, she knew that he was one of many... corpses. She felt the neck of another. Shaking her head, she pressed on, moving away from the pulsing heat at her back, which felt like a thousand pinpricks burying themselves in her flesh.

Her brow beaded with sweat, and she brushed it away with her hand.

A raspy cough announced, "Help."

Kate cocked her head as new sounds emerged.

"Please," a weak voice said in a world of gray.

She zeroed in and dislodged baggage to find a hand, then a face.

"Hold on," Kate said, locking eyes with a scared pair staring back at her.

A woman lay beneath entwined bodies. The lifeless condition of the first was obvious—near decapitation. Kate pushed fingertips into the neck of the second. Nothing.

A voice yelled from somewhere above her, "Start climbing. Come on."

Kate glanced up into the intense gaze of a dark-faced woman, an Army soldier, peering down from a shattered window frame.

Kate pointed. "This woman's alive!"

"Let's get you out first," the soldier said.

Kate shook her head. "No. Get in here. Help me."

The soldier—no, officer, Kate could tell from her insignia—assessed the advancing fire before dropping into the smoke-filled passenger car. Dressed in fatigues, she maneuvered awkwardly in the confined space, seeking a better place to stand, while her chocolate brown eyes drilled down on Kate. The officer's face remained neutral, but her eyes carried a mixture of concern and animosity, all of which seemed directed at Kate.

"There's not much time," Kate said, trying to redirect the officer's concentration.

The officer held her gaze, unfazed by the impending threat of fire, before turning to the entangled mass of bodies. Together they pulled away the dead and located a terrified mother clutching an infant swaddled in a blanket. The child struggled for breaths and the woman's right arm was grossly distorted at the elbow, fractured and dislocated.

The officer studied the woman. "We need to move ya. It'll hurt. A lot. But we'll get you out of here. Both of you."

The woman offered a fearful nod of understanding.

Kate peeled the infant away, and was about to provide medical directions before being waved off by the determined warrior, who seemed like the type who never left another soldier behind. The take-charge Army officer directed the woman to take a full breath, before shifting her distorted arm to the center of her chest.

A primal scream filled the car as the woman fought the pain.

The officer gestured upward. "Ladies, if you don't mind, we're out of this hellhole."

Kate climbed, grasping seat backs with one arm and clutching a crying infant with the other. At the shattered window, she slid the child out first before climbing through.

The train's stainless steel skin was almost hot to the touch, and she whisked the baby back into her arms as the infant gasped in clearer air. Plumes of gray swirled past them. Kate did her best to shush the baby, finally noticing the child was a girl. Around them, others emerged from their metal coffins and sought refuge. The tunnel's air was thick and rancid, but cooler. Its domed shape pulsed in orange from the illumination of scattered fires.

A distant brilliance grabbed Kate's attention. On the horizon, the Foggy Bottom station landing looked as bright as heaven.

Approaching flashlight beams bobbed up and down as more first responders signaled the cavalry was coming.

Grunting and grappling for handholds, the Army officer popped through the window, struggling to carry the woman. Kate dropped low, pushed her heels against a bracket to steady herself, and latched onto the woman's good arm. Boiling heat penetrated her skirt. She shrugged off the nightmarish memory of being scalded with steam a bit more than a month earlier—another ordeal she didn't need to relive.

The officer shoved the woman clear, then followed her out.

They all rolled together in a clump, their bodies lying on the train's heated skin.

Tears filled the woman's eyes at the sight of her child safely tucked in Kate's arms.

Taking turns, they slid down to the tracks. Kate went first, then the infant. Other rattled passengers came to their aid as the woman in fatigues lowered the mother, who did her best to fight through pain-filled breaths and a mangled arm.

Kate's gaze took in the twisted, metallic confines painted over by smoke and patches of fire. It looked like an underground war zone.

4
THE PLATFORM

Orange Line Transit Tunnel, Foggy Bottom—GWU Metro Station, Washington, DC

Carrying the infant, Kate trudged toward the light with the disoriented survivors. Beside her, paramedics carried the child's mother on a stretcher. The Army officer had remained behind with first responders.

Drained, Kate felt only grateful to be alive. The derailment had left her senses numb. She tried to push the faces of those less fortunate out of her mind. In their wake, a world of orange glowed as fire devoured the mangled commuter train.

Greasy smoke churned in the stale air of the tunnel.

Time seemed fractured, clouded.

A subpoena required her to testify before Congress. Well, that wasn't happening today.

"Stay clear of the power rail," a WMATA engineer said, waving his hands and pointing the beam of his flashlight in the only direction that made sense.

Kate watched haggard strangers, their faces painted with surreal masks of survival: men, women, and school-aged children in matching t-shirts. Some covered in blood, others helping the injured who could walk. Approaching footsteps announced a band of firefighters with masks and respirators, jogging past with stretchers and medical supplies.

She hated being the victim, helpless, dependent on anyone. Those cookie cutter labels dug at her psyche. Yet there was no escaping what had happened, and the migration to safety gave her time to think. Thoughts drifted to Thomas Parker.

They'd returned to the States after a month sailing the Grand Caymans. Their impromptu escape seemed to heal wounds that each needed tended. Thomas was unlike most men she'd dated during her time at the bureau and was definitely not the law enforcement sort. When would he hear about the disaster? Would he worry about her safety? She yearned to call him and tell him she was okay.

But that call would have to wait.

Through disheveled hair hanging in her face, Kate looked past the child in her arms to assess her dress-up clothes. She grimaced. What was the penalty for skipping out on a congressional subpoena? Bad, probably. Gone was her jacket, shredded to form a makeshift sling for the child's mother's arm. Her soot-covered blouse was torn, exposing her bra underneath.

I'm a freakin' mess.

The infant cried again, shaking Kate out of her reverie.

Kate soothed the baby. In the meager light, she became aware of blood splattered on the child's swaddling blanket. "It'll be all right, little lady."

That was probably a lie, but what else could she say?

The sound of mechanical engagement sparked above her. Squinting, she saw a chain of lights flash on and cast pale light onto the tracks. Somewhere out of sight, high in an arched, pocketed ceiling, exhaust fans kicked in to siphon off smoke and fumes.

Ahead, she spotted Washington DC transit police officers clearing people from the Foggy Bottom platform.

A WMATA station manager holding a permanent marker approached. Her uniform patch identified her as Marie, and she wore a painted-on smile. Marie wrote a number on back of Kate's hand: 1236. The numeric tag would help authorities with victim identification and track potential witnesses to a crime. Separating the injured from the merely panic-stricken, passengers were sent in different directions. On the platform, medical workers managed a frantic triage scene. Those less fortunate were laid perpendicular to the westbound tracks, and the row of sheet-covered corpses formed a growing line.

Kate watched Marie mark 1237 on the baby's hand as a nurse joined them.

"You the mother?" the nurse asked.

Kate pointed to the woman on a stretcher, who'd received 1238.

"We'll take care of them," the nurse said, whisking the child away before she could reply.

Kate watched the nurse rejoin the mother and child, before letting her vision drift across the platform between the Vienna westbound and New Carrollton eastbound transit runs. High in the arched ceiling, an ominous stratification of haze loomed in the matrix of rectangular concrete pockets. Pale lighting filtered down to illuminate the hexagonal tiles of the station's floor. Brown placards read Foggy Bottom—GWU. Electronic status boards had been updated to announce OUT OF SERVICE runs.

Familiar jargon vied for her attention. "No chest sounds on the right." "Get me an ET tube." "Let's start a central line." It sounded like her medical residency all over again. For a long moment, Kate watched the George Washington University Hospital staff performing triage on mass casualties.

Dread overwhelmed her. Horror-filled images formed unwanted reflections in her mind, like ripples in a dark, ominous pond. A coal mine explosion. A train yard accident. A one-gas station West Virginia town called Elk Pass. The injured and dead under her care had been numerous. The Johns Hopkins rural clinic outreach program had turned into the worst night of her life.

She stood motionless.

A nurse approached her. "Ma'am, do you need medical attention?"

Kate shook her head. A faint ringing lingered in her ears, but she was fine except for aches and bruises. She straightened her soot-covered blouse to hide her exposed bra and glanced over at a man being treated for a laceration on his forehead.

"I'm a doctor," she said, clearing her throat. "I work for the FBI. How can I help?"

5
THE SCENE

8:20 AM, I Street Northwest Pedestrian Plaza at the Foggy Bottom—GWU Station, Washington, DC

Dix Martinez with the Federal Bureau of Investigation's (FBI's) Critical Incident Response Group (CIRG) stepped to the curb along 23rd Street NW and studied the urban landscape. Behind him, special agents carrying Heckler & Koch MP5 submachine guns piled out of mine-resistant ambush vehicles (MRAPs). Via headset communications, Martinez marshalled teams into strategic locations. Traumatized passengers milled about and talked with DC cops. White SUVs with flashing lights screeched to a halt behind him and more agents joined the chorus. Agency leads from the ATF and NTSB flanked him in blue windbreakers and khaki trousers, relaying communications to their own teams.

"MPDC works the perimeter," Martinez said, using the Washington Metropolitan Police Department's acronym. His hands rested on the assault rifle clipped to his bulletproof vest. "Close streets two blocks out to traffic. No media is permitted past those boundaries. And close GWU," he said of George Washington University Hospital, "to non-essential services. Lockdown adjacent and intersecting buildings. The FBI will secure surveillance feeds to all public and private entities. Set up emergency response tents in this plaza to process witnesses." He turned to the National Transportation &

Safety Board (NTSB) lead. "ATF and FBI K9 teams will sweep the tracks and the station. We need to know what happened to that train. And if this is an act of terrorism."

Martinez sighed and scrutinized the chaos. From a public perspective, this tragedy looked like mayhem.

Not for long.

FBI CIRG trained for such scenarios, and this was his moment in the spotlight.

His second-in-command approached carrying a tablet. She spun the device around so he could see the image on screen. It was from a helmet-mounted camera on an agent performing an initial sweep of the platform. At the center of the frame was a briefcase tucked below a bench. A luggage tag read: PROPERTY OF KATHERINE MORGAN, FEDERAL BUREAU OF INVESTIGATION, WASHINGTON FIELD OFFICE.

Martinez frowned. "Who the hell is Katherine Morgan?"

6
EMERGENCE

Ten minutes later, an FBI agent in a green field uniform and helmet, carrying a submachine gun, extracted Kate from tending to the injured.

"I was helping people who need medical attention," Kate said, as the agent escorted her to the street level and a white tent in line with a myriad of others that dotted the I Street NW pedestrian mall. "If this stupidity is about the congressional subpoena, it can wait."

The all-business agent wrenched back the flap to the tent.

Kate struggled to imagine what was so damn important and peered inside.

The eyes of a dead man met hers.

Her bureau escort took up a station outside as she went inside.

The words shot out of her mouth like an indictment. "The last time I saw you, you were—"

"Dead," Special Agent Jack Wright said, finishing her sentence with a faint smile forming at the corner of his lips. "Yeah, I know. Hey, you missed my funeral."

"There wasn't one," she said, uncertain of what she was seeing. A miracle? There was no rational explanation for it. Gunned down in Princeton. Point blank shots to the chest. Another to his shoulder. Jack Wright had no pulse. There was not one thing she could do to save him.

But somehow Jack had survived.

His mystical resurrection looked like it came at a cost: less handsomely rugged than normal, more road weary and trampled. He'd aged ten years in a span of a month. Now Jack resembled an apparition more than the man she'd once loved.

"I'm under orders. DNC," he said for do not contact. "I wanted to tell you. Earlier. But we couldn't risk it." He cleared his throat. "Kate, thank God, you're all right."

"We?" Kate launched into full stride and swung with an open palm, the strike spinning Jack's face ninety degrees.

His eyes watered as he grimaced.

Her breath shuddered coming out of her lungs. "This is impossible. You died."

"You have to hit me?" he asked, shaking his head to clear his vision.

"Damn right," she said, throwing her arms around him. Her heart skipped a beat as it thundered in her chest. She could feel his warmth and breath against her neck. Jack was no apparition.

He groaned. "Don't squeeze too tight. My ribs are still mending."

Kate took an uncertain breath and shoved him back to arm's length. His tired eyes looked unusually vulnerable, revealing how much he still cared.

"How?"

His face fell solemn. "Long story."

"What does that mean?"

He hid something. Jack was good at compartmentalizing life, keeping secrets. Deceit and cheating had ended their romance. His Princeton murder had proved another example of that, yet his return showed her love's flame still lingered. And she hated herself for it.

"I have to stay dead… a while longer. It's need-to-know."

"Need-to-know?"

His tone went calculated casual. "Kate, I don't have time to explain. This derailment, this explosion was no accident."

"What?"

"Mortal limitations, my untimely encounter with death, prohibit me from intervening. Director's orders. Kate, I'm afraid you're on your own. Don't trust anyone."

She rolled her eyes. "Last time you said that, you abandoned me, got shot, and died. What part of your brain says 'trust no one?'"

Wright feigned understanding as the tent flap swung open.

Two people entered: an armed agent in FBI-branded fatigues and the Army officer who had magically shown up at Kate's passenger car.

No introductions were made, and their attention was solely on her.

Kate did a double take, her gaze ignoring the man and gravitating to the woman.

"What are you doing here?" Kate asked, unable to take her eyes off the posterchild for the U.S. Army. Earlier, she'd paid little attention to the woman's uniform, which bore the rank of captain with a black two-bar and carried a Ranger insignia. Layers of filth and grime on her fatigues nearly matched her mahogany-colored skin.

"You Katherine Morgan?" the Army captain asked.

She glanced from the woman to Jack. "How do I respond to that?"

The accompanying FBI agent spoke into a microphone linked to an earpiece.

A second later, a bureau crime scene technician entered, his blue-gloved hands cradling a soft-sided briefcase. Blue plastic gloves were passed out. The case was set on a table. Before departing, the technician said that it had been properly field processed: x-rayed, no chemical or biologic or explosive traces had been detected.

"That was on the platform," the Ranger told Kate. "And your name is on it. Oddly, you hadn't arrived at the station yet. When I pulled you from the train, you had no briefcase in your possession. Coincidence?"

"What the hell is going on?" Kate asked.

The soldier's dark eyes drilled in on her. "Unlock the briefcase, Agent Morgan."

From the corner of her eye, she spotted Jack Wright nodding to the obvious agent in charge and ducking out without even a glance her way.

As the tent flap closed, she said, "Not again?"

Jack Wright had just pawned her off like an unwanted possession.

"Morgan," the agent in charge said, "can I call you Kate?" He didn't wait for a reply. "I'm Dix Martinez, the CIRG Section Chief. NTSB's initial assessment is that this was an act of terrorism. Captain Rachel Pratt here is from the Pentagon. She's the DoD liaison on this case. Your train was bombed. Well, technically the tracks were sabotaged. An IED took out the tracks. The Orange line might have been bombed because you were on it."

Kate's face flushed. "What? Why?"

"Why indeed?" With the tip of a gloved finger, Pratt flipped over the plastic luggage tag. A generic nametag. It was obvious who was intended to own the case. Her name and employer were clearly spelled out.

Kate's heart fluttered with fear.

"It's locked," Pratt said, indifferently. "A four-digit combination code."

Kate hesitated. "That's not mine. Never saw it before. And I don't know anything about it or its combination. I was on the train."

Pratt and Martinez exchanged a look. An unspoken secret.

The Army captain eyed her suspiciously. "The number on your wrist."

"Huh?" Kate fought to keep up with the conversation and turned over her wrist. Four random digits had been scrawled out on her flesh. 1236. It was the number the WMATA worker assigned her on the platform. "This is insane."

Pratt's voice hardened. "Open the case, Agent Morgan."

Kate took a breath, released it, then another before sliding on blue plastic gloves and reaching for the case. It had a four-digit tumbler. She had four digits. The first dial moved easily, as did the other three.

1236.

THIRTEEN ACROSS

A torrent of anxiety surged through Kate as she leaned closer and snapped up the briefcase's two outer clasps.

7
COMMUNICATIONS

Carrying a backpack bearing an FBI logo, Phillip Barnes entered the FBI mobile command center parked on 23rd Street NW without incident. His change of attire to a navy blue logoed shirt, white khakis, ball cap, and sunglasses matched the two technicians manning stations in the truck.

He flashed a set of credentials and located the terminal marked "Communications."

"I have a work order," Barnes said. "Your antenna array is down."

"It failed to come online when we arrived," said the active scene manager, who faced a bank of monitors and choreographed inter-agency deployment and responsibilities. "The damn thing telescoped up, but we can't activate outbound communications."

Barnes scanned the interior of the million-dollar tactical operations center. Impressive, this bus—one of the many nicknames the state-of-the-art vehicle carried. Eight stations, four on each side around the perimeter. Two spots were occupied. That wouldn't be the case for long. A red digital clock displayed the time. Screens and monitors covered walls where token windows didn't exist. A larger screen posted a satellite map of the area highlighted by four red dots—drones.

"Give me five minutes," Barnes said as he moved to the rear of the vehicle. Fixing previously sabotaged actions wouldn't take long. Grinning, he understood that he was behind enemy lines, in the heart of the Orwellian beast. He studied the technicians at their assigned consoles. Each wore headphones, tuned into the tasks before them. They had barely noticed him, believing he was part of their tribe. One of the good guys.

He listened to the technicians coordinate logistics and felt the constant thrum of the vehicle's diesel generator reverberate through the soles of his shoes.

Exhilaration warmed his blood. He could kill them. Right where they sat. Their murders would be easy to pull off. But the game afoot served a higher cause, with little time for sidebars or distractions.

He fought the temptation and focused on a closet next to the bus's toilet. He swung the server rack's door open and slid out the top blade server, the dedicated communications interface to the vehicle's 24-foot, multi-frequency antenna out back.

From his backpack, he took out a laptop and patched it to the server. The prescribed passcodes worked like a charm. The out-of-band and in-band network streams were reset to defaults. Wrapping up, he plugged a custom interface module into the rack and slid it back into place. From his laptop he downloaded group IDs, network validation scripts, and dependent communication targets. Lights on the front of the server flashed from red to green.

"Antennas online," Barnes said with a hint of amusement. "Now you're free to shout at the world."

"Primary communications protocols confirmed," the second technician announced. "Fleet synch-check is initiating. SIOC engaged. Outstanding job, and in record time."

"It's what I do." He broke a careful smile and stowed his laptop.

As he grasped the door of the vehicle to leave, Barnes caught sight of an image. A face on one of the screens.

He wheeled toward the monitor and fell hypnotized by a photo crammed in a mass of others. The caption identified FBI Special Agent Katherine Morgan. A bio accompanied her picture, as did the highlighted number 1236.

A thrill worked its way up his spine. Veins flexed and blood coursed through his body. Anxiety flushed his face and a bead of sweat formed on his brow.

It's her! Katherine Morgan had survived.

The active scene manager caught the focus of his gaze. "Can I help you?"

"No." Barnes flashed a sheepish expression and fell silent for a long moment. "She looks familiar. Someone I thought I recognized from a long time ago."

The agent spun back to his station in a dismissive "I've got to get back to work" manner.

He enjoyed the moment and cracked a slight grin. She survived her first trial. This challenge held layers, yet its core exposed dark secrets and tormented FBI Special Agent Kate Morgan most of all.

Barnes left the mobile command center, allowing his grin to broaden.

It was time to prepare for the next stop.

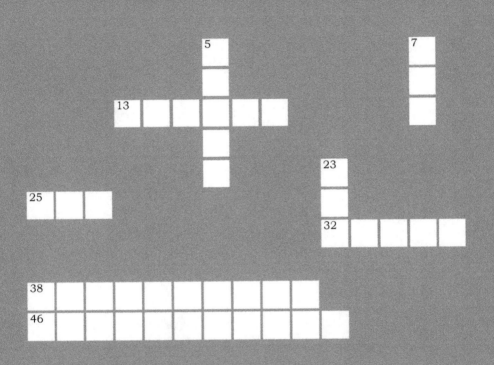

8
THE MESSAGE

Kate's heart pulsed wildly as she drew frantic breaths.

She could only stare at the single object occupying the briefcase.

A chill surged through her, causing her mind to momentarily reject what she was seeing. As a fornsics investigator she worked with troubling artifacts almost daily. The object before her was different.

She glanced to the others in the tent, their eyes fixed on her as much as the contents of the briefcase. The Army officer gestured for her to pick it up.

Stepping beside her, Dix Martinez clicked on a penlight to better illuminate the message scrawled on a leather-like material.

"What is this?" Martinez asked.

Kate shrugged off the sudden chill freezing her muscles and anchoring her inaction. Hesitantly, she retrieved the flat object and felt its weight in her gloved hands. Slowly, a forensics mindset kicked in and she caressed a protected finger over the material. Less rigid than cow's hide. Not rawhide. Not paper-thin, either. Flipping it over, she found no markings on the back.

"The writing appears inked on," she said. "All capitals. The perpetrator didn't want authorities to profile a handwriting sample."

Army Captain Pratt leaned in. "What does the message say?"

"How would I know?"

Kate focused on the parchment as its significance hit her.

It was addressed to her.

SOLVE THIS, AGENT MORGAN. ONE OF THE CLUES DEPENDS ON IT.

ACROSS
13 GROUP OF CROWS
25 JEKYLL'S PLACE
32 WORLD WONDERS
38 PAIR OF LAST TUDOR MONARCHS
46 CHRONICLE AN ARTICLE'S JOURNEY

DOWN
5 EVE'S SUCCESSOR
7 ABBR: LEGAL DEMAND LETTER
23 POSSESSION TO 32

Pratt exhaled, flaring her nostrils. "One of the clues depends on it?"

"Carbon dating," Kate said, anticipating the direction of the conversation.

"Huh?" Martinez asked.

"The *Post's* twelve-letter answer to twelve down." Fractured moments on the train flashed through her consciousness. A woman wearing gold bracelets next to her. The *Post's* morning crossword puzzle. The eruption enveloping the train. More images, faster, pinged inside her brain like repeated ripples on the surface of a pond. "This is a nightmare."

"What's that symbol?" Pratt snatched away the message and tugged at a brownish, circular contour that contrasted with the material itself. It had mole-like characteristics—rough compared the rest of the parchment. "This smear looks like dried gum."

The floodlights came on and Kate dropped to her knees, weighted down by her new understanding as oxygen seemed to squeeze from her body.

Unable to take a breath, she choked out, "It's taken from a breast."

Pratt looked uncertain. "What?"

Kate gasped, "Tattooed human skin. The pectoralis major. The ink wound wasn't healed when the skin was cut off the victim's chest."

Pratt's face paled almost to white. "Human—?"

Martinez clicked his radio and fired off a rapid stream of orders.

As an FBI forensic pathologist, Kate was familiar with death, working with bones, bodies, and parts of bodies dismembered or burnt beyond recognition. Blood and gore came with her job description. But this was the first time she'd felt apprehensive about evidence. This evil was different. Personal. Frightening. A byproduct of unabashed, premeditated malice. The bomber wanted her not only to survive the train attack, but to find his cryptic message.

The killer sought to involve her somehow.

Horrors overwhelmed her. Mangled train. Bodies. Death. A mother and child. A Bible-reading woman.

Pratt eyed her wearily. "What's this symbol about? These clues? What does it mean?"

Sweat formed on Kate's forehead, and her hands felt drenched beneath the gloves. "I don't..."

Martinez liberated the tattooed patch from Pratt, returned it to the briefcase, and snapped photos of it with his cell phone. He closed the case's lid.

After several breaths, Kate staggered to her feet and reflected on the characteristics of bombers. Academy training drilled agents on the basics. It wasn't too hard to see the investigation evolving into a mammoth nationwide case. The pressure on authorities to catch the bomber, the terrorists responsible, would be enormous.

She was square in the middle of the chaos.

And the bombing was meant to be personal. Why else taunt her with crossword clues?

More would die, and a mass murderer dared her to stop him.

She swallowed hard. "The unsub's tasted blood this morning," she said, using a term for an unidentified suspect, a perpetrator of a crime. Since neither Martinez nor Pratt voiced the obvious, she said it: "He'll strike again."

Stunned silence was the response.

The crime scene tech returned and collected the briefcase.

Martinez pointed to the evidence in the man's gloved hands. "I want a receipt and the identity to everyone who's assigned to its chain of custody."

Kate understood the dig, the personal criticism. On her last case, a laptop loaded with incriminating evidence had been removed from the crime lab. She'd been the mule who took it to Princeton. After several deaths, the laptop had ended up in the hands of the Department of Justice.

Martinez turned to Pratt. "Captain, I need a few minutes with Morgan. Alone."

The Ranger grunted and left the tent on the heels of the crime scene technician, but not before casting an unsympathetic gaze at Kate.

Martinez crossed his arms and arched an eyebrow. "You know, surviving a train bombing is an extreme way to escape testifying before Congress."

She mustered a cautious flat smile. He was trying to lighten the mood.

Martinez held out the cell phone where she could see it.

"I read your file. You're a doc and forensic pathologist. No performance issues until Senator Samuel Ford's missing person's case and its related fiasco in Princeton. What a botched investigation. Something to be proud of, I bet. The Office of Professional Responsibility, our internal affairs group, has cited you for professional and criminal misconduct. That means you're suspended without pay while OPR completes its investigation." He took a solemn breath. "Criminal misconduct sounds serious."

Kate shrugged. His broad-brush statements were close enough, minus her exposure to illegal human research trials and out-of-control top secret research. To add to matters, the White House had pressed the U.S. Attorney General to lock her up for destroying scientific initiatives related to national security interests.

Something clicked inside her brain. "Why is the Pentagon involved in a domestic terrorism case? What is Captain Pratt's involvement here?"

"Don't know," Martinez said. "Her DoD work is classified. Above my pay grade. Her uniform says she's a graduate from Army Rangers training. Rare for women. And that makes her a badass soldier. Because she's a Ranger, the Pentagon gets some latitude in my book. At oh-six hundred this morning, Captain Pratt received a text message and a picture of you. She was told to search for you on the Orange line at the Foggy Bottom station. The text included the underlined words 'Thirteen Across' and told her you'd have a number."

Kate snatched the cell phone from his hands and thumbed to the photo taken of the marked-up patch of skin.

GROUP OF CROWS.

Kate felt flustered. "Thirteen across spells MURDER. A group of crows ties to Edgar Allen Poe's *Murders in the Rue Morgue*. The perps are showing off, trying to manipulate authorities. Clues set the ground rules."

"Clues? Like crossword puzzle clues?"

She shrugged. "I don't know how else this reads."

"This is an act of terrorism." Martinez shot her an odd look. "Morgan, you need to help us riddle this out."

She didn't blink. "I'm suspended, remember?"

He bared his teeth. "Not for long."

Kate nodded apprehensively and took a breath. "Okay. Eight clues. THIRTEEN ACROSS expresses intent." She scanned the remaining clues. "Get ahold of the *Post*, the *Times*, *USA Today*. They have a stable of enigmatologists and cruciverbalists."

He eyed her skeptically. "Cruci—who?"

"Puzzle masters. Crossword puzzle geeks."

"I'll start with the *Washington Post*," he said, taking back his phone and shooting a series of rapid orders into the device.

"No. No. Call the *New York Times*. That's the guy we want."

Kate considered the tapestry of clues. A message from a cold-blooded killer or killers— clues—a symbol.

"What's the black circle with three white triangles in it?" she asked.

"It's a symbol for a fallout shelter. DC has a couple of signs around town."

"Fallout shelter? Maybe that's where we're supposed to find him."

"Holed up underground?" Martinez shook his head. "Doubtful. I bet he's planning more Metro bombings."

9
MEANINGS

Kate lingered in the doorway of the FBI mobile command center. Chatter from technicians coordinated active site logistics. Consoles, high and low, radiated streams of information. Satellite maps framed the George Washington University Hospital (GWU) campus. Real-time video patched in the bureau's Strategic Information and Operations Center (SIOC). Martinez's snapshot of the tattooed patch of skin was well represented on several monitors.

Agents and techs in FBI apparel turned toward her, their collective expressions revealing impatience, if not hostility. Kate sensed she'd walked straight into a conversation where she wasn't welcome.

"Morgan, we got off on the wrong foot," Pratt said, as if under orders. She rose from a station and blocked Kate's path into the rig. "Apologies for being forward. I'm just seeking answers only you seem to possess."

The Army Ranger offered a handshake: strong, measuring. A stern gaze grilled Kate, summing her up. Pratt left little doubt that she felt physically superior to Kate in every way measurable.

Kate mustered a cautious smile. "You risked your own life to save others. Thanks."

Pratt almost smiled through a rigid façade. Almost.

Martinez pushed past them, pointing to a vacant console. "Morgan, we're on the clock."

"Any luck tracking down fallout shelters?" she asked.

Martinez snapped his fingers. A technician brought up a map of DC and expanded the view around the George Washington University campus. Blue dots tagged the urban landscape.

"How many are there?" she asked, scanning the screen.

Martinez laughed. "Too many. A website called 'District Fallout' gives a Google map and links to a 1965 Cold War Community Shelter Plan. Two hundred twenty-five possible fallout shelters listed in black and white. Nearly fifty are in a three-block radius of the Foggy Bottom Metro station. And those are the ones we know about."

Martinez's eyes followed Kate as she touched the screen. A blue pin at the intersection of I Street NW & 23rd Street NW led to a side bar that revealed an address: 901 23rd St NW.

Kate's mind buzzed with incoherent thoughts. "Fallout shelters. Bomb shelters. Places of refuge. We're directed someplace."

Martinez spoke into a phone. "Call out city engineers to inspect underground shelters immediate to the university. Pair them up with bureau resources, ATF, and K9 teams." He turned to Kate. "Logistically, law enforcement doesn't have enough resources to search all 225 bunker locations. And we don't even know if all these bunkers still exist."

Pratt chimed in. "Maybe this hide and seek is a diversion, deception to spread law enforcement thin while another location is bombed."

Martinez nodded. "Point taken."

Kate shrugged. "My hunch is that MURDER discloses intent. It's not an arbitrary act." On a computer, she typed up logical answers to the clues and selected a random fifteen-by-fifteen grid for a placeholder, knowing a puzzle's solution could free-form into a variety of symbolic arrangements. 13 ACROSS went horizontally in the upper quarter of the grid.

Pratt spoke up from the console next to her. "Who's EVE'S SUCCESSOR?"

Kate bit her lip. "It's not a person. Just EVE'S SUCCESSOR."

Pratt typed. Her monitor displayed the top answer, via another crossword puzzle website: TODAY. "EVE'S SUCCESSOR is TODAY."

Kate nodded. "Okay. Run with TODAY." She took a long breath. "This entire effort is about wordplay. Themes. Associations."

Martinez stated the obvious. "Six to go."

A technician at the other end of the row called out "The Seven Wonders of the Ancient World are the Great Pyramid of Giza, Hanging Gardens of Babylon, statue of Zeus in Greece, temple of Artemis, Mausoleum at Halicarnassus, Colossus of Rhodes, and the lighthouse of Alexandria. The only historical site that still exists is the Great Pyramid of Giza."

Kate leaned back in her chair to study the clues again. "23 DOWN is POSSESSION TO 32. POSSESSION implies control or ownership."

The technician asked, "Control over the wonders of the world?"

"No," Pratt said. "Controls, owns, the quantity of SEVEN."

Kate wrinkled her forehead. "The answer could be as simple as HAS SEVEN."

Martinez peered over their shoulders and watched Kate fill in random squares with HAS and SEVEN. "Has seven what? Seven more bombings? Seven more attacks?"

Kate nodded. "POSSESSION is the key."

Pratt frowned. "POSSESSION as in people? Things?"

Technicians kept potential answers coming. "The LAST TUDOR MONARCH," one of them announced, "was Elizabeth the first, daughter of Henry the Eighth and Anne Boleyn. Never married. Never named a successor. Wouldn't a pair of them imply ELIZABETHS?"

She logged the entry. "Well done."

Pratt moved onto Jekyll. "JEKYLL'S PLACE? The story of Jekyll and Hyde takes place in London."

Kate anticipated where the captain's thoughts were heading. "It's double entendre. A statement to dual meanings. Jekyll and his alter ego Hyde represents duality. Good. Evil. The two faces of Janus. Janus is the two-faced Roman God of beginnings and transitions. In one myth, Janus plays a prominent role—Romulus, one of the founders of Rome, and his henchmen kidnapped the Sabine women. Janus saved the women by creating a volcanic hot spring that erupts and buries the assailants in boiling water and volcanic ash."

Pratt's expression darkened. "That's apocalyptic." She thought for a long moment. "Morgan, how do you know all this stuff?"

Kate smiled thinly. "I loved books, puzzles, history as a child."

"And JEKYLL'S PLACE?"

Martinez interrupted. "It's Jekyll. Doctors work in hospitals and labs."

She raised an eyebrow. "The place is the centerpiece of his profession: hospital or lab." Kate turned to Martinez, who seemed to be thinking along the same lines. "Narrow the search down to hospitals and labs?"

"That's a destination we can work with." Martinez made another call.

Two terminals down, a technician called out, "I'm not finding abbreviations to a LEGAL DEMAND LETTER. Will LDL work?"

"Keep searching." She shook her head. "Okay. Who has 46 ACROSS?"

10
CLARITY

Rachel Pratt bailed on ineffective attempts at 46 ACROSS, careful not to reveal diverging interests. Her vision panned the monitors displaying clues and answers that mocked authorities. The time squandered solving the spoon-fed nonsense felt like having a searing knife blade on an exposed patch of flesh. This episodic challenge delivered only pain.

Her mind sparked with ideas until the next stop was absolute: ELIZABETH'S LAB.

It would take Morgan and the others longer to decipher the destination.

And that offered her an advantage.

Without a word, Pratt rose from her station and stepped outside. Morning air frosted her cheeks and fostered a deeper sense of clarity. She couldn't explain the resolve rising inside her, as if destiny tugged at her.

The display of force—law enforcement personnel in fatigues, carrying assault rifles in response to an act of terrorism—was reassuring. Barricades and emergency vehicles lined 23rd Street in both directions and tents populated the plaza between the hospital and the Himmelfard Health Sciences Library.

A mass murderer had injured the nation she loved, tainting its stars and stripes.

Her path ahead was clear.

Pratt hit an auto dial number on her cell phone.

A gravelly voice answered. There was no greeting, no exchange of names. "Report?"

"St. Elizabeths Hospital." She took a confident breath. "If you intend to move on this, the window of opportunity is small. The FBI won't be far behind."

11
DESTINATIONS

Dix Martinez watched Pratt as she left the mobile command center. Leaning against Morgan's workstation, he let his mind process his directives. A high-level call from the Pentagon to the Director of the FBI had delivered more of an order than a request—U.S. Army Captain Rachel Pratt would assist with the investigation.

The directive meant the Defense Department had skin in the game, and somehow the bombing was connected to national security initiatives.

But that didn't mean he had to trust Pratt, the Pentagon, or the FBI agent beside him.

A month ago, the news broke on government-sponsored, illegal human research trials. Those events had put the entire intelligence community on edge, with the White House at the center of the controversy. Now both the White House and the Pentagon were inserting themselves into his investigation.

"Why do you think I was targeted?" Kate asked.

"No idea." He watched Morgan study words on a computer screen. Non-puzzle related questions percolated in his mind as a hunch took root and germinated.

What if the terrorist knew both the FBI agent and Captain Pratt?

A disturbing thought.

Martinez spun to a satellite map dotted with fallout shelters within the boundaries of Washington, DC.

Fallout shelters?

Martinez's instincts bristled. The locations were important, not coincidence or accidental.

Moving to Pratt's computer, he swiped his common access card (CAC) with an embedded chip across the machine's sensor pad and launched its Internet browser. He typed CTRL+H to bring up the machine's recent history sessions.

He saw the unexpected.

St. Elizabeths Hospital, Washington, DC.

ELIZABETH'S LAB. "X" marked the damn location.

"Mobilize HRT," Martinez said to the incident's logistics manager, using the acronym for the bureau's hostage rescue team. "Contact the GSA and Coast Guard. Notify them we require immediate access to St. Elizabeths Hospital. Direct the GSA historian to meet us on site." He considered his orders, then added, "Do this quiet-like, without fanfare. And get Morgan outfitted. She's deploying with us."

12
GROUND ZERO

Kate ignored the driver's heavy foot on the accelerator, their FBI-marked Ford Explorer racing dead center in a parade of lights and sirens. Nationals Park streaked past. The rumble of tires on the Frederick Douglass Memorial Bridge announced the crossing of the Anacostia River. Next to her in the rear seat, Martinez progressed through conversations on his cell phone. The non-stop chatter in the earpiece she wore delivered radio play from the unfolding FBI field operations.

Ignoring the chatter, she worked on a laptop to home in on the last two clues.

"How's the fit?" Martinez asked, tugging on her camo helmet.

"Fine." She glanced at her field attire: FBI-branded fatigues and bullet-resistant vest. Two major differences marked her different from the rest of her FBI detail. The first was the black lettered patch on her chest that read OBSERVER, and the second was that she was weaponless. But the new clothes were an improvement over the tattered and soot-covered clothes she'd ridden out the train bombing in.

She grinned, thinking she hadn't suited up like this since Quantico.

"Fifty-five confirmed dead," Martinez announced. "And it's growing."

Her grin disappeared. Not what she wanted to hear.

"NTSB confirmed the train's rate of speed: a whopping ninety miles an hour. Seventy-five is the design limit. The speed parameters were overridden before the tracks were taken out beneath it." He rattled off the NTSB's preliminary findings. "You and a whole lot of other people are damn lucky to be alive."

Kate shrugged off the thought. Bombing a train was incomprehensible.

13 ACROSS was cold-blooded mass MURDER.

A chill swept through her body, causing a shiver. A terrorist knew how to over-speed commuter trains; knew that she'd be on that Orange line train. Innocent people had died because she boarded a particular train at a particular time. Their deaths were on her.

13 ACROSS. A GROUP OF CROWS. This was just the beginning. More innocent people would be targeted. Why else make a game out of death? Until leads could be developed, deciphering the sick and twisted clues was her way to hunt down the perpetrator.

An internal-to-the-bureau instant chat message popped up on her computer screen. 7 DOWN. A lawyer from the General Counsel's office flagged the acronym. LEGAL DEMAND LETTER. Notice of Intent. NOI. The declaration of a lien concept was like a demand letter, warning that if payment was not made, the claimant would file a mechanic's lien.

"What's a mechanic's lien?" she typed on the computer.

The response came back. "A claim against a property title for the benefit of those who provided labor or material that improved said property."

Kate closed the laptop.

A half-mile from their destination, the sirens on their convoy went silent.

"Is St. Elizabeths Hospital still a hospital?" she asked.

"It's remaining psychiatric care has moved elsewhere," Martinez said. "The old grounds are now split between Homeland Security, the Coast Guard, and community redevelopment efforts."

Martinez ran through the quick facts on St. Elizabeths, once called the Government Hospital for the Insane. The site predates the Civil War. Lincoln once wrote about it in a letter to Mary Todd. Over the years, the 346-acre campus had served many functions, including as boarding stables for the Smithsonian for its animals that were captured from overseas expeditions. Before deinstitutionalization, it had been the size of a small town, with 7,000 patients and 4,000 staff. It had shrunk over the years, and the repurposed campus was partially assigned to the newly formed Department of Homeland Security in the mid-2000s. Most patients lived in obscurity with its most notable residents being the would-be Presidential assassins to Andrew Jackson and Ronald Reagan.

"Does the site have fallout shelters?" Kate asked.

"Sixty-eight, give or take a couple." Martinez passed her a tablet displaying a satellite image. "Hardened bunkers were constructed during the Cold War, one on the east side and one on the west."

Their motorcade swung south down Martin Luther King Jr. Avenue.

Kate thought about 46 ACROSS. CHRONICLE AN ARTICLE'S JOURNEY. She initially translated CHRONICLE to RECORD and JOURNEY to STOPS, thinking everything circled back to the metro bombing. RECORD STOPS.

That was her task from a terrorist. RECORD THE STOPS.

A requirement to pay attention, document his madness.

How did a killer's notice of intent apply to an old insane asylum?

It had to be more than a place on a map. The location had relevance.

Their caravan came to a stop. Gate 1 to the west campus was blocked by white cars with flashing lights. Uniformed officers carrying assault rifles patrolled its perimeter. An electronic sign read THREATCON CHARLIE.

"The GSA," Martinez said of the General Services Agency, "manages construction efforts for Homeland on their new operations center."

St. Elizabeths, East Campus, Washington, DC

Army Captain Rachel Pratt reconfirmed her mission with a Pentagon two-star via an encrypted satellite phone. The general's orders were precise:

Find the threat.

Eliminate it.

Secure their asset.

Troubled, Pratt clicked off the phone. The directives broke from normal operating procedures. Her mission had a limited hierarchy—she reported directly to a general in the U.S. Army Intelligence and Security Command (INSCOM), no one else.

Apprehension swept through her.

This unsanctioned domestic op fell outside the purview of U.S. Armed Forces, and she knew what that meant to the tactical strike Ranger team.

Don't fail.

Don't get caught.

Execute the mission without incident.

Her gaze panned the six men huddled around a truck parked in front of a group of abandoned buildings. Each one's expression reflected their motto: "Rangers lead the way!" They collectively studied old, hand-drawn plans—the mission's map to the Holy Grail.

The weathered drawings showed how Martin Luther King Jr Ave SE divided St. Elizabeths into west and east. In government fashion, buildings were tagged with numbers rather than official names. The secured perimeters of the U.S. Coast Guard and Department of Homeland Security occupied the west site. The east side redevelopment master plan divided the 183-acre historic property into revitalization sectors, a collection of affordable housing, mixed-use, and education innovation hubs. Abandoned underground tunnels linked the two sites together.

"We enter 90," the squad leader said of a building once called the W.W. Eldridge Medical and Surgical Building. "We clear the first bunker, then access the second. A reminder, gents—stay out of the U.S. Coast Guard boundaries and the power house. Coast Guardsmen are friendlies. So try not to shoot them." The six Rangers turned to her. "Confirmation of orders, Captain?"

Pratt appraised each pair of eyes. "Top-secret ops are at risk and cannot be made public. Intel suggests one of our own is held captive on the premises. Our mission: find the threat, eliminate it, and secure our asset. Show no quarter," she said, meaning "take no prisoners." "There's limited power on this side of the property. So once we're in, we're on night vision and flashlights. Stay tight, disciplined. Get in, get out. Any questions?"

"No, Captain," they said in unison.

"Homeless might be squatting in some of the east buildings. Don't draw them into our business." She snatched up her M4A1 carbine and adjusted the enhanced night vision goggles affixed to her helmet. "We're a go."

The squad leader snapped his fingers and the soldiers broke into a field formation. They ignored the NO TRESPASSING signs and breached Building 90's main doors.

Thermal imaging showed only darkness. No civilians. No homeless.

The squad leader issued directions over linked intercoms as flashlight beams led the way.

A fallout shelter sign marked the trailhead. A stairwell led to a basement and the central plant for the east campus. Night vision tech was useless in the absence of light, so the LED flashlights attached to their assault rifles made the difference navigating the stairs.

Through her weapon's scope, Pratt's vision raked the cavernous, decrepit mechanical space. Silent machines, pumps and piping, conduits, and electrical equipment sat in various stages of disarray. The trash-laden facility showed years of neglect.

"You see those?" one of the soldiers called out over comms.

They were impossible to miss. Rats damn near the size of Chihuahuas scurried about. Their fat bodies, carried by stubby legs, glowed yellow in night vision.

"We're not here to hunt rodents," the squad leader said. "Stay focused."

Systematically, the mechanical spaces were cleared and they located another set of stairs leading further below grade.

Descending, the squad passed markers for SUBLEVEL 1.

At SUBLEVEL 2, they intercepted underground brick-lined passages, a T-intersection that split off in two directions. A musty smell filled Pratt's nostrils and she noticed a thin film of water on the tunnel's floor. Above and beside her in the confined space, endless runs of piping and conduits lined walls and ceiling.

In the next quadrant, stenciled graffiti greeted them, highlighted in their night vision.

The wall art was luminescent. It was a face. A woman's face.

Pratt stopped in her tracks.

"Hey, Cap," one of the soldiers joked, "that looks like you."

It sure did. It was the kind of poster art peddled by street vendors.

She stepped closer, her eyes probing the artwork. It was her spitting image. In the artistic reflection, she looked sad, remorseful.

A thought hit her. The terrorist knew she would come for him.

St. Elizabeths, West Campus, Washington, DC

Kate raked her gaze across the old campus as déjà vu flashed through her mind. Its dirt drives, topped with asphalt, would once have received passengers in horse and buggy. Green parkland surrounded red brick structures, which were either abandoned or under some kind of renovation. Scaffolding enveloped the closest buildings. The semi-derelict insane asylum was picturesque, the perfect setting for a horror movie. All they needed was the cloak of darkness, menacing evils, demented ghosts, possessed clowns, and the typical carnival lot of chainsaw-carrying madmen.

Her comms crackled with conversations as FBI agents formed a perimeter. A K9 agent readied a harnessed Belgian Malinois.

Martinez turned to her. "Special Agent Morgan, you're support here. Nothing more. Under no circumstances are you to engage any threats."

From his bullet-resistant vest, he retrieved two letters.

Kate scanned the documents. Both carried the signatures of the Director. The first announced the rescinding of her suspension with provisional reinstatement. Effective immediately, she'd been reassigned as field support to Dix Martinez's CIRG team. The second letter was addressed to the Senate Subcommittee of Science, Technology and Space. It notified Congress that she would not be testifying on any ongoing investigations.

Martinez chuckled. "I told the Director to lock you away... for your own protection. He considered that extreme and counterproductive, given your personal involvement in matters."

The letters were *bona fide* get-out-of-jail free cards if she ever saw them: pass go, collect your $200, and avoid testifying in front of Congress. She thought about her conversation with Jack Wright. Someway, somehow, her reassignment had his fingerprints all over it.

What was the catch? Nothing like this came free.

Martinez returned her badge and semi-automatic, a Glock. She clipped her badge to her belt and felt the weapon's weight in her hand.

"You're not giving me a choice?" she asked. Reassignment was better than the alternatives: congressional sequestration or secured confinement.

"A round is already chambered," he said, while handing her a new badge on a lanyard. "Do not leave my sight. That is an order."

Her keeper seemed like a dangerous man to cross.

Martinez pivoted back to her. "One last requirement. No communications with Thomas Parker. He's on a federal watch list. So do not contact."

She blinked hard. "Thomas is on a watch list?"

His false smile was not an apology. "I know you two spent time together. But this mandate comes directly from the U.S. Attorney General. Steer clear of the professor. It's not negotiable."

An autonomous, driverless black Ford Transit van stopped at the curb of Martin Luther King Jr Ave SE just outside St. Elizabeths West Campus Gate 2. Hazard lights clicked on as a signal to other traffic. The satellite-linked antenna inside the top of the van did not require line of sight for the planned surveillance activities.

East of the Washington Navy Yard, Washington, DC

In a secure, private complex on the Navy Yard Channel boundary, less than two miles northeast of St. Elizabeths, Phillip Barnes scrutinized monitors and intercepted communications.

He leaned forward on his elbows and closer to the screens.

Ultra-high resolution satellite video showed two individuals in combat apparel standing outside St. Elizabeths' original structures. The audio from the autonomous van forwarded the conversation between FBI special agents Katherine Morgan and Dix Martinez.

Barnes beamed. Events were getting interesting.

He pivoted in his chair to face more screens and satellite images.

Rachel Pratt and her six-man squad of Rangers had just entered a shuttered building on St. Elizabeths' East Campus.

He clicked on a digital clock to chronicle the duration of their incursion.

It had been a long time since he'd thought like a Ranger. Rangers were a predictable lot. All you had to know was their tactics.

Ground zero was squeezed on two very different fronts.

His enhanced eyes-in-the-sky surveillance was complements of the U.S. National Reconnaissance Office (NRO) and its NROL-71 Vandenberg-launched payload six weeks earlier. The latest in sophisticated Keyhole-type, the real-time tracking, electro-optical imaging satellite delivered clarity enough to decipher license plate numbers from outer space. The four billion dollar platform, codenamed SpaceKey, had dual capabilities. Besides tracking and surveillance, the 24-ton, multi-channel, orbiting reconnaissance platform could actively manage autonomous assets, like vehicles, planes, and military defense systems.

Barnes' advanced security systems and signals intelligence company, SkySource, specialized in scalable future imaging architectures (SFIA) and controlled the game changing satellite. To the NRO, SpaceKey was a failed asset that had become terminal after launch. And SkySource's task order was to engage and revive the dead rock floating in space. Barnes exclusive contract gave him total control of the spy satellite for another four weeks.

FBI Special Agent Kate Morgan and Army Captain Rachel Pratt would both be dead well before that time expired.

13
DARK ORIGINS

St. Elizabeths, West Campus, Washington, DC

Kate hung close to the GSA historian as he rattled off facts about the former hospital. Its history was a matter of interpretation. She understood the dark side of involuntarily locking people away and mass institutionalizations. Muckraking journalism and movies like *One Flew Over the Cuckoo's Nest* had spotlighted systemic abuses and shaped public perception during an era of growing civil and individual rights.

The public recoiled from stories about barbaric medical practices and indigent held at the mercy of their captives. Extreme cases involved horrendous acts—physical and sexual mutilation, electric shock, water immersion, frontal lobotomies. The combination of snake oil remedies under the guise of patient care, a flawed mental health system, changing public opinion, and cuts to federal funding had cast many with severe mental illness (SMI) out into the margins of society.

As a doctor, she recognized that modern medicine had lost its way in serving the five to ten percent of the population with long-term mental illness needs. Extended mental health support systems were a lesser fiscal priority in for-profit, corporate healthcare marketplaces.

The carcass of St. Elizabeths was a sign of changing times and mindsets. What remained were ghostly shells reminiscent of an abandoned past.

The scene in front of Kate reminded her of a B-grade horror movie. She frowned, realizing that the characters who entered ruins like these rarely made it out alive.

At least they were armed, everyone except the historian.

The man led them across a treed landscape. "What you see here," he said, gesturing to the rear of the largest structures, "is an Italian Renaissance Revival-style. Force protection measures required us to gut the inner structures, so all we've managed to salvage is their outside skin. Over half a mile of tunnels are documented. Since we started construction, ground-penetrating radar has revealed more passageways."

"How many more?" Martinez asked.

"It totals just under a linear mile." He pointed to two brick smokestacks rising like goal posts past the adjacent buildings. "The tunnels originate at the power house and route through the boiler plant." He took a right along a concrete path and cut into a three-story red building with bricked-over windows. "Tunnels served as the conduits for power, steam, water and waste water. Overhead rails and carts facilitated laundry and food service transport during winter weather conditions."

"What about fallout and bomb shelters?" Kate asked.

The historian led them through vacant and utilitarian-style storerooms, bakery and kitchen areas. Decades-old white paint flaked off encrusted walls. Kate's nose smelled a mix of dirt and mold. Dusted brick and tiled floors spanned every direction.

The man kept a methodical pace. "Most buildings have basements that function as places of refuge. When the buildings were constructed, it was social placation really—the delusional reassurance that people could survive a nuclear strike on Washington. On the other hand, our hardened bomb shelters were kept secret from the Library of Congress for fear that the Soviets might learn of them."

The historian gestured to a pair of wooden doors. The K9 agent and his dog took the lead as Martinez wrenched open the doors. A cool mustiness greeted them like an apparition fleeing its entrapment, as air pressure equalized. Somewhere deep underground, building spaces were pressurized.

Cold air splashed Kate's face in a way she'd never experienced. Hairs on the back of her neck tingled, warning of danger.

The windowless confines ahead were dark, devoid of sunlight.

The CIRG team clicked on flashlights to illuminate their way and methodically pushed ahead, entering another set of doors leading downward.

Kate let a hand drift to the semi-automatic at her side, unable to shrug off the irrational expectation of encountering some kind of revenant—a tormented, dead patient unable to take their soul into an afterlife.

She hastened her steps to stay with the tail end of the group. Her earpiece crackled with conversation.

A stairway headed down and she passed to take in a SUBLEVEL 1 landmark.

Martinez's voice echoed in her comms. "Hold your position."

Stairs diverged to an arched concrete tunnel marked SUBLEVEL 2.

"We're fifty feet below ground," the historian announced. "The five-foot thick reinforced concrete walls, self-contained water treatment and power plant, and bunker were sized to hold two hundred people for a year. Congress designated this shelter as their Plan B. It was never intended to house patients or staff, only government dignitaries."

On the wall, neon stenciled artwork read ABI LAB.

The markings glowed green in the beams of their flashlights. The marquee looked newer than other dated landmarks.

The Belgian Malinois began to bark and pulled against its handler, sensing something humans couldn't.

Evil was coming.

An invisible sensation swallowed Kate whole. Pain sparked inside her skull and pinpricks scorched her temples. The phenomenon caused her to crumple to her knees. Her brain was on fire, as if burning from inside out.

The dog's agitation and barking confronted something unseen.

Martinez touched her shoulder as she closed her eyes and screamed.

"What's wrong?"

Kate heard only garbled words before a new voice overrode Martinez's concerns. "FBI Special Agent Katherine Morgan."

Distorted shapes flashed through a battered consciousness: a swarm of zombie-like patients clawed at her flesh. It was impossible to discern if these were real or delusions. Her understanding of mental illnesses, disorders like schizophrenia, bipolar, and deteriorations in the neurochemistry and neurological plasticity, did nothing to calm primal, uncontrollable fears.

The voice inside her head blocked out her comms. Its god-like mental intrusion caused her to teeter on the edge of sanity.

Her lungs felt filled with sand, her entire body weighed down.

Grimacing, Kate clutched her scalp and gasped for air, barely remembering how to breathe.

Martinez was still talking, but she could no longer hear him.

"Do you hear him?" she yelled.

"Who—?" she read from his lips. Shaking his head, he took a knee beside her.

The voice in her head returned. "I wasn't sure you'd survive."

The pain storming through her brain was insufferable, and keeping a fragile hold of consciousness was near impossible.

The historian hunched over and watched her.

"Get out of my head," she snapped. Her eyes filled with tears and she turned to Martinez. "Do you—?"

"Your FBI colleagues can't hear me," the voice continued.

She ripped out the comms out of her ear, thinking that would help.

The K9 continued to fight against its handler.

"Katherine, you're a killer."

The terrorist, the bomber, knew her beyond just a name.

She gasped for air and forced herself to concentrate on the voice. Male. Confident. Chiding. Vaguely, she remembered a news article about U.S. Cuban and Chinese diplomats being targeted by sonic warfare. "Acute auditory or sensory phenomena" was the official term. Sonic cannons had targeted consulate staff. The CIA had explored similar tactics, both as torture and a way to generate subversive telepathic communications.

"Who are you?" she asked, scanning the underground concrete landscape. It wasn't magic, it was technology. The master magician needed equipment to pull off his grand entrance.

"You won't remember me. But soon you will."

Under the meager illumination of flashlights, Martinez squared up to her. His distorted face looked skeletal-like, misshapen. Glowing eyes searched hers for a hint of what was happening.

Fighting through the pain, she pointed to her lips, then her head, and mocked an exploding skull. It was a bad mime act, but Martinez got the picture. At least she hoped he did.

"Cowardly figureheads will label me a terrorist," the voice inhabiting her mind said. "That's far from the truth. I'm a patriot. A pure-bred soldier."

Soldier? Gasping in short breaths, she tried to keep up.

"You destroyed my life when you murdered my family."

What? The lunatic wasn't making any sense.

"Katherine, you must atone for your sins."

The vise grip crushing her brain intensified, causing more tears to flood her eyes.

Sins?

She screamed, "Stop!"

"Listen. Log the tour. Seek the truth. Earn my rewards. Save those you can. Lose my tools and people die."

"I'm not—"

She caught sight of movement. Martinez and his agents had located an array of devices mounted up high in the concrete ceiling of the tunnel, above piping and conduits.

Martinez raised his M4A1 and took aim.

She yelled, "Not yet!"

"Keep your mind clear—"

Martinez fired. The flash of his weapon ended her enslavement. The telepathic rope was cut, and the demonic spell lifted.

Weakened and drained, Kate collapsed to the cold concrete floor and vomited.

14
FAMILY HISTORY

St. Elizabeths, East Campus, Washington, DC

Pratt's Rangers entered the east's hardened bomb shelter. The air in the dome was cool and musty. Yellow placards with black triangles identified its purpose.

Not what she expected.

Taped-together sheet plastic formed a pocket at the center of a vacant concrete cavern. The plastic envelope sharply contrasted the bunker—white, heaven-like and bright. Cables snaked across a grunge-covered floor and disappeared up an airshaft.

"Secure entries and exits." The squad leader's scrutiny panned the barren room. "Cap, what's this all about?"

"Not sure." It was true.

She stepped closer. The thin, semi-translucent shield diffused electronically generated images that pierced the confines of a sterile, plastic world.

Pratt used the nose of her M4A1 to part a curtain-like divider.

Inside, monitors flashed a sequence of pictures. Personal photographs: her as a child playing softball, her playing board games with her parents and two older brothers, her chopping firewood. The glimpse of a distant childhood was a past she sought to forget.

Those days carried scars. Her family was dead. All dead.

She fought the emergence of memories. In a single night, a mining accident had claimed the men in her family: father, brother, uncle. A year later, her mother had died.

Her family, each and every one of them, needed to stay dead and forgotten.

The Army was her family now.

New photos appeared on the screens, different from the others.

She was hanging from a tree, playing with a boy.

"Power and communications come from the surface," a solder said.

The stroll down memory lane paralyzed her and fueled indecision.

"Premises are secured," another soldier said, returning to the group. "Whoever set up this roadshow is long gone."

"Maybe they're in the other bunker?" The squad leader turned to her. "Your orders, Cap?"

Pratt thought for a long moment. "Tag your route every one hundred yards."

The squad leader's response was sharp, challenging. "We function as a unit, not as individuals."

Pratt hefted her M4A1 and gave him a cold stare. "Our mission hasn't changed, not one iota. Proceed to the next bunker. Eliminate threats. Rescue the hostage."

"Look, Cap," the squad leader said. "I'm a simple fella just following orders, and even I can see this freak show is all for you. Someone wanted us to traipse straight into Mr. Rogers' neighborhood. Okay. Bingo. We've arrived. Now you're aware as much as I am that we're fish in a barrel down here without backup."

"Complete the mission. That is paramount."

He grunted. "Fine. But someone remains behind to watch your back."

"No. Keep the squad together. I'll catch up."

The squad leader swore, reconfirmed his directives with his men and led them out.

When she was alone, a man's voice came across a pair of speakers.

"Rachel?" The voice sounded vaguely familiar, like that of an old friend talking to her in a dream.

Her gaze gravitated to the photograph of her and a boy in a tree. "Identify yourself."

She loathed her childhood, her family. Childhood memories weren't suppressed for her protection; instead, the deep recesses of her mind locked away memories she couldn't bear to relive. Out of tragedy, she'd evolved to become a warrior, a phoenix.

"You don't remember me?" he asked, sounding hurt.

Flustered, she grasped for a truth that she didn't want to acknowledge.

Her gaze swept the plastic bubble, searching for a camera.

She was being watched.

"We were supposed to be the future of humanity."

Pratt shook her head. His words were like battering rams, breach poles slamming against her castle's portcullis, trying to penetrate her mind. "You don't know me."

"I do, Rachel. We were childhood friends long before being lovers."

Her castle's barbican cracked.

Memories flooded her mind. A whitewashed skin of a wall melted away to expose the blanched out, forgotten truths beneath. People. Places. Family. She hated rediscovering her past.

"I've always known you," the man said, his voice laden with sentiment.

The words came fast out of her mouth. A name came to her. "Phillip. I used to call you Logan the Wolverine."

"Yes." He paused. "Before ABI transformed us into monsters."

ABI? The acronym seemed vaguely familiar.

She pinched her eyebrows together, thinking harder, afraid of her walled off memories. "Phillip, you bombed a train. You're a coward who murdered innocent people."

A kaleidoscope of fractured recollections shifted into focus: a small mining town, her family, a neighbor boy. He reappeared to her as an adult. Before her training as an Army Ranger, they were paired together in covert training exercises. They kissed. It was wet and passionate. Intimate moments were shared as his skin touched hers. Their bodies pressed against one another. They made love.

Fraternization and intimacy broke rules. Serious rules.

Participation in their covert program came with restrictions.

Her face flushed as flickers of a forbidden romance exposed more dormant memories.

She had loved him. Once.

"Yes, I bombed a train. For that I stand accused. But my actions are justified. I don't expect you to understand now, but soon you will."

"You're right," she said, fighting rising uncertainty. "I don't understand,"

"Rachel, clarity will come after dark facts are illuminated. Be mindful of your past and search your heart. If you are worthy, we will be reunited."

She drew a startled breath. "Phillip, my mission is to hunt you down and execute you."

"Take heart, Rachel. You have a new mission now—one that will release your demons and set you free forever."

Covert ops had given the Ranger squad leader field-earned instincts and antennae that crackled when things didn't add up. Something about their op gnawed at him, beyond the legal jurisdictions and conducting a mission on U.S. soil. As a soldier, he followed orders and was trained to address outcomes as they materialized.

He took point, leading his team through the service tunnel connecting to the site's power house. Radio comms were silent. No one spoke. Under flashlight illumination, their red-bricked tunnel looked no different from other passageways, its walls and ceiling lined with old stream lines, plumbing and pipes, and electrical conduits.

Something caught the tip of his boot. It twanged.

His mind sparked with alarm, and there was no time to react.

The trip wire set off synchronized explosions, ahead and to the rear. The bottom half of concrete walls disintegrated and a torrent of movement spread into the tunnel.

A raging spray engulfed them, filling their nostrils with the scent of ammonia.

"Back! Back! Back!" he yelled over the rumbling, thick churn seizing their feet.

Retreating, the team trudged in unison through a rising mixture of earth and sewage. The sloshing mass engulfing them had the consistency of liquid quicksand.

"The tunnel's blocked," a soldier shouted, pushing against a caved in section of tunnel. He struck the logjam with the butt of his M4A1 assault rifle.

Nothing moved.

Both ends of the tunnel were sealed.

The squad leader cursed. They had nowhere to run. Fear seized him as he understood he'd led them straight into a trap.

"Dig!" he yelled, slogging through the quagmire swallowing them up. "Dig, damn it, dig!"

St. Elizabeths, West Campus, Washington, DC

A gentle out-of-body nudge rocked Kate as blue brilliance flashed across her optic nerves, like the sensation of standing on rumbling train tracks and staring down an oncoming locomotive in the dead of night. Jolting awake, she was greeted by two companions—a splitting headache and a man lying naked on the cold, hard concrete floor beside her. Someone had covered the man's midsection with a blue FBI windbreaker, leaving bare legs and torso exposed.

She pushed herself upright and fought the gnawing pain inside her skull. Her pulse quickened.

What happened?

Closing her eyes, she tried to remember the attack.

The assault had been telepathic. The terrorist knew her, somehow.

She glanced around. An arched ceiling spanned the full length of the bomb shelter, which had been transformed into modular lab spaces.

ELIZABETH'S LAB.

The killer's words broke through the fog in her mind: *keep your mind clear, sins to pay for, murdered my family.*

None of the insanity made sense.

Fighting through the haze occupying her mind, Kate watched FBI agents secure the bunker. She took shallow breaths and turned her head, trying to work out the kinks. Her tired gaze landed on the half-naked man beside her. Unconscious, his breathing was shallow. Something about him didn't look right. The skin over his left breast had been replaced.

The donor of the tattooed skin?

Lose my tools, people die.

Foreboding words meant for her.

She let her fingers drift across the stranger's bare chest, tenderly feeling, exploring the softness of fused joints where artificial and real skins merged. The seam was barely noticeable. The nippleless replacement patch was near perfect, in a hue complementary to nature's original version one breast over.

Why abduct a person, tattoo them, and remove their skin?

Then go to the trouble to replace the skin once you've removed it?

She knew medical researchers had the ability to grow replacement skin grafts from modified stem cells in fibrin substrates, for burn victims and for people with rare skin diseases, but medicine still struggled with wholesale, seamless, multi-layered skin transplants.

Until now?

In certain parts of the world, drug cartels used human mules to smuggle drugs inside their bodies. Seamless skin replacement would make it easier to conceal those wounds.

She caressed the patch. Hairless. Baby bottom soft. Softer than the original. She guessed the victim's age was somewhere north of mid-forties.

"Kate," a voice asked, "you okay?"

She jerked her hand away and turned to find Dix Martinez kneeling beside her.

"What happened?" she asked over a dry throat.

He handed her a small tubular gadget with a clear lens. It looked like a camera.

"Sonic communicator. Military-grade. My bet, CIA."

Questions flooded her tender mind.

"I've never seen anything like it," he said. "But we'll track down its manufacturer and squeeze them to disclose their buyers. Don't worry, we'll nail this bastard."

She tugged on each earlobe, trying to clear the ringing that accompanied her headache.

He sighed. "You remember anything before passing out?"

Kate shook her head, not wanting to tip her hand so quickly. She needed to process her telepathic interaction a bit longer. Cocking her head, she asked, "Who's this guy?"

Martinez's expression darkened. "Frederick Lock. A bioengineer. He's a civilian with the Defense Department. His work is classified. Need to know. Imagine that." He sighed. "Mr. Lock went missing two weeks ago after failing to return home from work. And we've had no luck waking him."

A shiver streaked down her spine as she leaned across the man to flip up each eyelid.

Martinez seemed to know where she was headed and passed her a penlight.

Pupillary responses were sluggishly reactive. "Well, he's not brain dead."

Kate felt through his patch of replacement skin for a pulse, strong and normal, then checked his extremities for needle marks. Nothing dotted the usual locations.

The unconscious man conjured up memories of illegal human test subjects. She had almost died in Princeton. A thought of Thomas Parker comforted her. Their Caribbean trip seemed like months ago.

Thomas's forbidden companionship would go a long way toward soothing her aches.

Without asking, Martinez took her hand and pulled her to her feet. "Come this way. I need your assistance."

Kate frowned. "What about that guy?"

"Med evac is five minutes out. They'll transport him to George Washington."

"Martinez," she said, "get him a full body MRI. Let's rule out that he's not a mule and make sure there's nothing stashed inside him. Have brain scans run to check for neurological abnormalities." She glanced back at the near naked man and wondered what a killer, a terrorist, had done to him. "And for your information, never ever ask me to take an MRI."

An eyebrow on his forehead shot up. "Sounds like there's a story there."

"Not much of one."

Martinez was already steps ahead of her. Catching up, she panned her gaze along the white paneled walls that formed a labyrinth of kit-built rooms. Placards on walls announced the functions of the clinical spaces: observation, patient hold, performance assessment, enhanced testing, cognitive analysis, surgery, hematology, histology, transfusion, procedure, imaging, and pharmaceutical.

The bomb shelter under an abandoned insane asylum housed a covert research lab.

Who would've guessed?

They entered a room numbered 1236, identified as CYTOGENETICS. Workstations with slate counters sat empty. The lab was equipped with the usual microscopes, centrifuges and cyclers, incubators, hoods, refrigerators and freezers, and scientific glassware. Two most interesting things were missing: lab-coated scientists and their genetic research.

Kate remembered the Advanced Neurological and Cybernetic Research Institute in Princeton. That place had lots of labs.

Martinez sighed. "The users cleared out fast, loading up records and computers. In their haste, millions of dollars in research equipment was abandoned. I'm guessing that Frederick Lock is connected to this lab somehow."

"Is someone ratting him out?"

Martinez shrugged, then pointed.

Kate's eyes followed the direction of his finger to a clear Plexiglas case framed neatly under a spotlight. Her blood ran cold. The case's contents brought back flickers of her migraine, and her heart pounded as she absorbed the macabre sight.

Another parchment of flesh mimicked the one left for her at the Foggy Bottom Metro station.

15
SOME CHOICE

St. Elizabeths, East Campus, Washington, DC

Pratt felt marbles beneath her feet. The concrete floor she stood on was unsteady. Phillip seemed to be asking her to commit treason, forsake a sworn commitment and sacrifice other soldiers for a selfish purpose. Some long-sealed off memory tingled.

Sua Sponte, on their own accord, Rangers lead the way. The creed was available only to a select few, earned with blood and sweat.

Pratt spun away from the monitors and clutched her M4A1 tight. Neurons sparked. Dots connected. Disjointed thoughts spanned a broken childhood to Virginia Tech Army ROTC recruitment to being a female graduate of the male-dominated U.S. Army Ranger School.

As suppressed memories surfaced, a gap remained, a black hole of time and place: her life after college and before Ranger training.

Phillip had called it ABI.

The Advanced Biogenetics Initiative.

A block of time and place in her mind was repressed, and for good reason.

Evolution. Reconditioning. Reprogramming of the human psyche.

Under the supervision of the Department of Defense, ABI sponsored applied research far beyond chemistry bottle genetics.

Its mission statement: *the scientific quest to build the perfect solder through advancing human evolution (AHE).*

Memories percolated behind a veil in her mind, like a swarm of lightning bugs buzzing in the night air behind of a bedsheet pinned to the backyard clothes line.

Her youth had been a placeholder until the science was mature enough for her to complete an evolutionary journey. Sights and sounds flashed in her mind. Her Virginia home, the deaths of her family, her foster family.

Pratt gripped the assault rifle tighter and brought it up to her face, allowing the cold steel to press against her cheek. Her breath shuddered in her chest.

Life was different from what she had pretended it to be.

Faces from a sterile world emerged from the recesses of her mind.

ABI had engineered twelve lab rats, eleven others just like her. Relentless testing, day and night. Surgeries. Cognitive enhancements. Foreign language immersion. Drug regimens. Life-altering blood transfusions. Extreme physical conditioning. Combat training.

Four bred-alike companions had died during medical procedures. Two more during combat training. Another didn't survive the rigorous gauntlet of the Human Replication & Enhancement Technologies Protocols (HRETP).

Phillip had saved her from certain death, sacrificing himself instead.

Love, fraternization, and failure trimmed survivors down to three.

But his death had been a lie, as was the transience of his love for her.

A flood of childhood fireflies sparked through the bedsheet and lit up her psyche.

Phillip Barnes' reemergence posed a threat to ABI, a threat to their Perfect People endeavor.

The Pentagon two-star had wanted her and the squad of Rangers to execute Barnes before he exposed more government secrets. Her dark secrets.

Pratt took a breath and knew what needed to be done.

Army Rangers took care of their own, and the men accompanying her were as much family as any she had ever known.

It was time for her to act like a Ranger and save her family.

16
CALL OF DUTY

LaGuardia Airport, New York

Will Shortz had experienced a morning of firsts, starting with FBI agents arriving at his Tudor-style home, giving him fifteen minutes to pack, and a helicopter hop to LaGuardia. This initial surge of cloak-and-dagger adrenaline had drained into the churn of aircraft noise and flight turbulence. The helicopter banked. He craned his neck to look out the window.

A business class jet sat off the flight line, near the Port Authority side of the airport.

His federal escorts had come short on specifics, only that his enigmatic skillset was vital to national security or something along those lines.

His immediate presence was required in Washington, DC.

An aptitude for creating and deciphering puzzles didn't translate to solving crimes.

Without clues, he guessed this had something to do with the Washington Metro bombing investigation—the horrific attack dominated the morning news. It was the only answer that made sense.

His career had afforded him brief moments in the public spotlight: film, television, radio. People recognized his byline. An Indiana upbringing kept him grounded, humble, and he never considered himself a much of a celebrity. His social recognition came with no glossy biography, certainly not to the level of being summoned to the nation's capital.

Indeed, it was a morning of firsts.

Rousted earlier than normal, his night owl habits rarely supported a day starting too early. He mustered a tired chuckle and peered through a window as LaGuardia drew closer. This unplanned diversion required him to shift his commitments with *The New York Times* and NPR's Weekend Edition and still find a way to maintain his streak of more than six consecutive years of daily table tennis.

At least DC had a table tennis center.

The helicopter jostled as the pilot feathered the rotors and cut engine speed. The aircraft's descent grew more rapid and it touched down twenty yards from the private jet. His federal escorts popped open the aircraft's side door and transferred his bags. On the tarmac, Shortz cupped his face with his hand in a vain effort to keep swirling dust and air out of his eyes.

"Thank you for coming," shouted an anxious-looking man. "FBI Special Agent Sam Loyd." Over the dying whine of the helicopter's rotors, he asked, "I trust your flight was okay?"

Shortz shrugged. "What's all the secrecy about?"

"I'll explain on the way," Loyd said.

Shortz followed Loyd aboard the jet. The aircraft's interior and the beige leather seats were luxurious—and empty. Shortz frowned. Loyd conversed with the pilot and copilot as they completed flight checks.

He ran his hands along soft leather armrests of empty seats.

"How do I get one of these?" he asked as he took a seat.

The mechanical hum of the jet's twin Rolls-Royce engines grew louder as it taxied for takeoff. A smile stretched across his face. No intercom announcements required seatbacks and tray tables to be returned to full upright positions. No security screens. No migration through crowded passenger lines. No quart-bag limits for liquids stashed in carry-ons.

This skip-the-line, taxpayer-funded ride was traveling in style.

"Mr. Shortz," Loyd said, handing him a tablet and taking a seat, "sorry about the limited disclosure of information. Law enforcement couldn't risk saying anything until now. You've undoubtedly seen the news."

Shortz nodded. "It's tragic."

"The Federal Bureau of Investigation needs your assistance."

Shortz scrutinized the image on the portable device. As a word-play artist, words and quips rarely escaped him. "Is this—?"

The agent frowned. "Afraid so."

Comprised of block lettering, the inscription appeared to be methodically inked onto a patch of skin. The engraved wording was tattooed, making it permanent. An epigraph led a short list of five down clues and three across clues. A symbol anchored the lower left-hand corner of the parchment. A mole-like, ringed circular shape balanced out the lower right. The skin was from someone's chest. If the clues mated to a standard crossword puzzle, the grid was withheld, thus adding to the message's challenge.

It was addressed to someone.

SOLVE THIS, AGENT MORGAN. ONE OF THE CLUES DEPENDS ON IT.

A cascade of words zinged unrestrained through his thoughts, like rapid fire associations. Shortz suspected he wasn't the first to rack his brain on the clues. Several were elementary, although he struggled to qualify an overall theme.

"13 ACROSS is MURDER. 4 DOWN is TODAY." He glanced up to find Loyd watching him intently. "This isn't the only set of clues, is it?"

The man shook his head. "We believe there could be as many as seven."

"Seven?" Shortz returned his focus to the screen as his gaze panned to the objects. He recognized the on the left as a warning sign. A circle with black triangles. Radioactivity? No. A fallout shelter symbol. He returned to the clues. "37 ACROSS is SEVEN. 22 DOWN is HAS. As in HAS SEVEN? The bomber has seven bombings planned?"

"We don't know that. It could refer to more bombings or victims."

He could not look away from the screen. "Besides murdering people on trains, who are the victims?"

"We haven't figured out everything."

Wordplay had evolved beyond a casual pastime. Customary challenges adhered to accepted conventions. In most crosswords, solutions populated a fixed grid.

Shortz scratched his forehead. "Is there a grid to place the answers against?"

Loyd leaned closer to tap the tablet and reveal the remainder of the clues. "That's precisely where your expertise comes in. A mass murderer bombed a commuter train. Is it an act of domestic or international terrorism? We don't know. Teams are studying the crime scene and tracking down every lead possible. For some reason, this murderer or murderers made the attack personal." He took a breath. "Help us solve clues before they appear. Figure out themes so we can get ahead of potential revelations."

A chill tingled Shortz's skin like the surface of a Pleasantville pond freezing over.

Shortz pondered the limited clues.

13 ACROSS spelled MURDER.

Much like double clues or an anagram, MURDER wouldn't be the only theme in play.

A GROUP OF CROWS. Simple wordplay, used many times before.

But this challenge was like none he'd ever solved, and clearly another first.

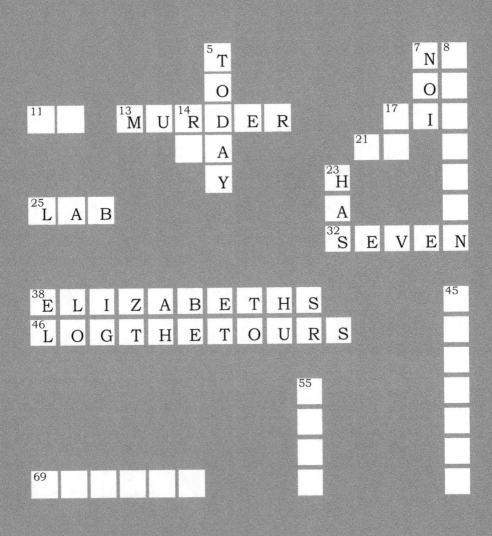

17
DISCLOSURES

St. Elizabeths, West Campus, Washington, DC

Knowing what lay before her did nothing to dispel the rising nausea. Kate drew closer to the illuminated Plexiglas case. The sequel of skin spoke to her, like someone else's voice inhabiting her mind.

Martinez handed her plastic gloves as she read the inscriptions branded on flesh and studyied the trophy.

That's what it was: a trophy on display.

KATHERINE BE MINDFUL OF ORIGINS AND THE CLOCK. THE PUZZLE IS GREATER THAN RIDDLES AND PAIN. THE QUEST FOR TRUTH IS NOT FOR THE FAINT AT HEART. SURVIVE IF YOU CAN.

ACROSS
11 ABBR: SYMBOL PORTRAYAL
17 LATIN 12
21 LATIN 2 (ADD TO 16 ACROSS)
69 BRAND OF DISGRACE

DOWN
8   MERGE ABSTRACT IDEAS
14 ABBR: INITIALISM GENUINE EXISTENCE
17 EXTREME INTEGRITY
45 BAD WEATHER LAIR
55 SHORT MON'S FOLLOWER

Skipping the foreplay, Kate homed in on the freckles splashing across the precisely cut patch of human skin, which stretched as if it had been torn from the breast of a woman rather than another man. The tattoo disclosed a host of new clues.

She fought the urge to run as cold crept down her spine.

This madness and cruelty were beyond comprehension.

The killer's accusations rattled her mind. *Katherine, you have so many sins to pay for.* What sins? How had she ever murdered anyone's family?

The last thing she wanted was to solve this kind of wickedness.

BE MINDFUL OF ORIGINS AND THE CLOCK. It was an order. Directions.

Martinez stepped beside her as she slid on protective gloves.

"How long was I out?" she asked, her gaze not leaving the patch of skin.

"About five minutes." He cleared his throat. "Sorry you had to endure the torture."

"Don't be." RIDDLES AND PAIN. She got the pain part, all right. "Any luck tracking down our enigmatologist?"

"You mean that crossword puzzle fella?" He watched Kate unlatch the clear plastic container and retrieve the scripted message before answering. "He's landing at National. We have a car waiting."

She pinched her eyebrows together and studied the skin under better light. "For the record, I solved THIRTEEN ACROSS, not Will Shortz. Wanted that stated in advance."

St. Elizabeths, East Campus, Washington, DC

Pratt sprinted through the underground tunnel linking St. Elizabeths' east and west campuses. Her flashlight beam sliced through darkness under the glow of her night vision, and she skidded to a halt in a pool of reeking water.

Her heart pounded as she caught her breath.

Chunks of jagged concrete and mangled rebar angled down from the tunnel ceiling to her feet. Instinct told her the blockage hid a watery grave, its stench-filled liquid trickling between gaps in the rubble.

Rank air made it smell like she was standing in the bottom of a latrine.

Phillip had sabotaged the tunnel in order to trap if not kill her fellow soldiers. He had purposely separated her from the others. They should've stayed together, as a team.

She spoke into her comms again. Nothing. Her sense of dread rose. Time meant everything, if she wasn't already too late.

Searching for tools, Pratt scanned the collapsed tunnel. Abandoned pipes and conduits were anchored to the walls and ceiling of the concrete steam tunnel.

She had a knife, flashlight, an assault rifle—and an idea.

Cold steel greeted her fingertips as she felt the surface of electrical conduits. The abandoned raceways ran from the power plant or peripheral buildings. She struck the thin-walled steel hard with the butt of her rifle—not to break them, which seemed impossible, but to send a message. The metal piping rang hollow upon each blow.

"How alive?" she asked, the rifle vibrating in her grip as she rhythmically struck steel against steel.

Seconds passed. No response. She repeated the phrase in Morse code.

The response was slower than expected, but it came. "Water… rising. No time."

The butt of her rifle went back to work. "Shoot large conduits. Shoot conduits."

Pratt took a steadying breath, stepped back, and switched her weapon to full auto.

She pushed the thought of ricochets in a confined space out of her mind—she'd worry about that when a rebounding bullet struck her.

She aimed and let her trigger finger snap in spurts.

Flames spat from her M4A1 carbine. Lead punctured holes through cylindrical steel. The challenge was keeping the weapon steady enough to make a rough cut. Shards of concrete, conduit and steel fragments, sparks, and dust filled the air. Thirty rounds cleared the weapon. She discarded an empty magazine and inserted a fresh one. Thirty more rounds erupted. The hollow raceways shook and she broke them loose of their wall mounts with the heel of her boot.

The four lowest run conduits sagged out their parallel routing, showing significant gashes.

Her end of the equation had worked.

Ringing filled her ears and she choked on dust-laden air.

What was happening on the other side of the blocked tunnel? Pratt lowered her weapon and let shoulders dip. Had the squad drowned?

Damn you, Phillip!

The conduits clattered, slightly at first, then robustly.

She stepped back with an inkling of what might be coming.

An inch of movement preceded a blast of air and a gush of sewage-filled water. The spray from the sheered conduits seemed to cut through the clouds of dust.

She grunted a "booya" and turned her attention to the tunnel blockage.

St. Elizabeths, West Campus, Washington, DC

Troubled on many levels, Dix Martinez watched Kate Morgan flip over the parchment. Its backside was unremarkable, blank. She returned to the inscriptions and noted that the substrate contained feminine features. A woman's. He'd guess her forensics investigator instincts would spot those details when others could not.

Martinez tried to focus. "Any clues on who the victim is?"

Kate shook her head.

HAS SEVEN? It was only the first of many questions. Did this second victim, too, have connections to the secret lab residing beneath an abandoned insane asylum? If these relics were trophies, what achievement did they reward?

A mass murderer goaded authorities, first with a train bombing and then with these exemplars of madness. And why had a psychopath picked Kate Morgan as his mode of communication? What made her special?

The unanswered questions gnawed at him.

Martinez raised his cell phone and frowned. No bars. The underground fallout shelter blocked cell coverage. He clicked several photos with its camera.

"Come on." He placed a hand on Kate's shoulder. "We're passing on these clues to command. And you're not staying behind."

"What does this look like?" She shrugged off his hand and pointed to the dark circle encapsulating two intersecting double-ended arrows. "Last time we were given a symbol to a fallout shelter. That led us here."

Martinez moved closer. "You think crossing arrows lead us to the next stop?"

St. Elizabeths, East Campus, Washington, DC

Hip-high in sewage, Rachel Pratt broke through the crest of the collapsed tunnel and found the face of a grinning squad leader on the other side.

"Thanks, Cap," the commando said. "Quick thinking on your part, and not a moment too soon. I was starting to think you forgot about us."

"Everyone accounted for?" She cast a flashlight beam through the basketball-sized hole and into the void. Five grizzled veterans standing in chest-high water nodded in appreciation. She reached through and locked arms with the squad leader. "Rangers lead the way."

"Booya!" resounded back at her.

"Damn right," she said, inhaling the wave of fetid air that greeted her. She glanced over to the severed conduits draining the swamp, satisfied. "How 'bout we get ya boys out of the latrine."

Pratt and the Rangers excavated a cavity in the debris large enough for the men to slither through one at a time. Once clear, the team waded through the down current of sewage to the east campus central plant and up into daylight.

Outside, the rank crew reconvened around their vehicles, stowing weapons and gear. Their cheerful demeanors showed no sign of trauma from near-drowning. Any soldier who spent time in battle eventually developed a twisted brand of survivalist humor. The men cracked jokes about missions to past shitholes. And St. Elizabeths had just been added to their passports.

But the men had nearly died and she was the one who'd put their lives at risk.

The mission failed because of her personal involvement.

That would not happen again.

Rage simmered as she stepped away for some privacy and used her encrypted sat phone to dial the Pentagon. Fumes rose almost visibly from her clothes, which reeked like she'd been rolling around in pig manure.

A voice she didn't recognize interrupted her thoughts of a hot shower.

"Captain Pratt, mission update?"

"We were unable to secure the target and were forced to fall back because of a tunnel blockage." She waited for a response, but none came. "I know the identity of the man responsible for the WMATA Metro bombing."

"Phillip Logan Barnes. Yes. But his identity was never your concern. Your mission was explicit: find him, eliminate him, and retain our asset. That was the totality of your operation."

She forced calm into her voice. "Barnes was never present. Of course, you probably knew that before you sent us in. This was a trap. Barnes baited us. Knew the U.S. Army would come to silence him." Something clicked in her mind and she cleared her throat. "My team reports directly to General Davidson, no others. Who am I speaking to?"

"My identity is irrelevant. However, your unsanctioned actions are not. The general exceeded his authority to initiate a domestic military operation. As a result, he has been relieved of duty. You and your team are hereby ordered to return to Ft. Benning for debriefing and reassignment. Cease and desist. Stand down. Is that clear, Captain Pratt?"

She recalled Phillip's words to her: "Take heart, Rachel. You have a new mission now—one that will release your demons and set you free forever." He had returned from the dead to remind her of where she came from, who she was at her very core.

Yet Phillip needed something from her, which had nothing to do with love or intimacy.

Something deeper was in play.

Bombing a commuter train was a reprehensible, public attack that left the United States government with no way to play it down, cover it up, or sweep dark secrets and multi-agency criminal investigations under the proverbial rug. Not after recent events in Princeton. Public and congressional outcries still raged from the revelation of illegal, government-sponsored human research trials. Which made Phillip's targeting of an FBI agent clever; her association with matters before Congress meant greater exposure for his cause.

Phillip had thrown gasoline on an already raging fire. And the whole world was watching.

She imagined the political appointees inside the command structure at the Pentagon conducting full-out damage control. *ABI.* The quest for a perfect soldier was threatened.

Years of research hung in the balance.

"Captain, confirm your orders."

She clicked off her phone and terminated the call without replying.

In the U.S. armed forces, relief of command operated under strict protocols. She reported to a two-star general. Superseding standing orders required established channels and a chain of command. And those in command would never fail to identify themselves to the soldiers beneath them.

From the corner of her eye, Pratt spotted a caravan of unmarked white Ford Expeditions streaking south along Martin Luther King Jr.

Boulevard. Tinted windows obscured the occupants, but she guessed it was Martinez and Morgan, heading to their next destination.

She glowered. It was time for her to get reacquainted with the FBI agent.

Phillip's actions had threatened her very existence—who she was and what she'd become—eroding everything she had worked so hard to achieve after his death. His vengeance threatened to expose truths that were never meant to see the light of day.

Phillip was going to die by her hands, and no one else's.

And if FBI Special Agent Katherine Morgan got in her way, she'd be eliminated, too.

"Command ordered you back to Ft. Benning for debriefing," she announced, returning to the squad of Rangers. She shook each man's hand and offered her thanks. "Hey, you pretty boys smell like—"

"Roses!" one of the Rangers shouted.

"That's so true, Juliet," the squad leader added.

"We'll catch this bastard," she said, climbing behind the wheel of her SUV and pushed the ignition button. "Next time."

Something was wrong. Her vehicle failed to start.

She pushed it again. Nothing.

In the SUV next to hers, the squad leader slid on a black Ranger ballcap and offered a grateful nod as his men piled into their vehicle.

A sudden flash and fiery explosion blinded her. Windows shattered under a shockwave.

Heat painted Pratt's face as her world turned white hot, her ears concussed by sound. The blast slammed her against the driver's door, and she blacked out.

18
THE SAND IN AN HOURGLASS

Washington, DC

Will Shortz absorbed the features of the second object displayed on his tablet.

Human parchment. Nine fresh clues. A cross.

In ancient sailing times, cartographers had favored inking valued maps and secret trade routes on hide over papyrus. Paper proved fragile. Hide offered durability. Animal skin was common. For wealthy merchants, royalty, and sometimes pirates on the high seas, an alternative foundation was the hide of slaves or even your enemy's back.

This tattooed substrate served as a troubling guidebook, an embodiment of evil.

The skin represented the price paid in the exchange for knowledge.

A bump in the road caused Shortz to lift his eyes and glance out the window of his chauffeured vehicle. To his left, Thomas Jefferson stood inside his memorial and peered across the waters of the Tidal Basin, his bronze statue aligned so he could take in the Washington Monument on the horizon. Shortz had visited the nation's capital numerous times and preferred a more practical building carrying Jefferson's name, the Library of Congress.

None of his prior trips had come with flashing lights, a private three-vehicle parade, or human maps. He turned back to the clues.

BE MINDFUL OF ORIGINS AND THE CLOCK.

The reference constrained the dark and ominous game. It had a beginning and an end.

Time was of the essence.

Pencil in hand, he jotted down words and phrases on a notepad, a habit the technological age hadn't cured him of.

55 down for SHORT MON'S FOLLOWER yielded TUES. A trivial answer, even without parameters of a grid. His mind sounded an alarm. Did Tuesday represent a boundary of time limits? Perhaps LATIN 12 and LATIN 2 were simply numbers: XII and II. Their sum was fourteen. Fourteen hours?

He glanced at his phone to check the time. It was after 11 A.M. in fourteen hours it would be an hour into Tuesday.

Shortz reread the clues as he felt a knot form in his stomach.

When the figurative CLOCK struck midnight, did that mean the killer's murderous game was over?

KNOW THAT THE PUZZLE IS GREATER THAN RIDDLES AND PAIN.

The PUZZLE was a literal treasure map—a "catch me if you can" dare.

He took a ragged breath and spied the Washington Monument rising above the DC landscape to the north of his caravan.

What happened after midnight?

It'd be nice to know no nuclear weapons went off when the hourglass ran down. Escaping Armageddon's wrath seemed unlikely when working at its epicenter.

He cracked a thin smile. It might have been smarter to stay in New York and teleconference with the FBI. Starting a long distance relationship seemed like the perfect alternative.

The nation's capital was ground zero.

He returned to the challenge.

All he had to do was riddle it out, word by word, answer by answer.

Before midnight.

Easy enough. The crosswords and puzzles he edited daily, hosted on his weekly NPR radio show, or in the American Crossword Puzzle Tournament came with predictable rules and structure. Nothing ever translated into life or death situations.

But being a full-time puzzle master meant that his brain was trained to solve dilemmas and saturated with seldom known, arcane facts. So what was the meaning of intersecting double-ended twin arrows? A symbol of friendship, intimacy. The enclosed circle translated as bounded, contained. The Cross Barbée, the arrow cross, symbolized the followers of Christ, their mission being the "fishers of men." White supremacists used similar icons as their Crosstar. It was hardly farfetched to see the bounded Crosstar, white against black, as a morphed swastika.

A scary thought.

Cocking his head, he saw the intersection of lines as the figure of an hourglass, or as simple as X marking the spot.

He leaned forward toward Sam Loyd, who sat next to the driver. "The first clues showed a fallout shelter symbol. Did that lead to a location?"

The agent turned to face him. "St. Elizabeths Hospital. An abandoned insane asylum. Homeland is relocating there. That's where we got the—"

"So the location proved relevant?"

Loyd's eyes narrowed. "Absolutely."

Shortz took an excited breath. "If your killer stays true to his symbology, this cross barbée represents a church."

"Cross... what?"

"Barbée. Fish hooks." He held up intersecting fingers. "Crossing doubled-ended spears. You know, 'I will make you fishers of men'? Think of it like a Christian crest on a coat of arms. The Cross Barbée represents a location. The LATIN connection in 17 and 21 ACROSS might link to Catholic churches."

19
A QUEST FOR TRUTH

Washington, DC

Kate didn't ask where they were driving but guessed they were returning to Foggy Bottom, the ORIGIN of the morning's insanity. Beside her, Martinez made one cell call after another before finally debriefing the FBI Director.

She tried to expand her thoughts, riddle out a mass murderer's grand cipher, but her brain was overstimulated. Where was the next destination? She wasn't sure if she wanted that location unveiled. Not at the moment. Martinez had transmitted crime scene images from St. Elizabeths to the bureau's Strategic Information and Operations Center (SIOC), where agents and technicians coordinated operations and examined the data in granular detail.

Even with the added manpower, the next stop remained elusive. THE QUEST FOR THE TRUTH IS NOT FOR THE FAINT OF HEART.

Her lungs felt tight, short on air. Melding minds with a psychopath gave her an inescapable headache. She closed her eyes in a vain effort to forget the world. A collage of solved and unsolved puzzle clues lurked in her conscious and demanded attention. Her mind raged, overwhelmed with fragmented memories: the morning commute, the bombing, the dead and wounded, the appearance of Jack Wright, Army Captain Pratt, a Bible-reading woman with gold bracelets sitting next to her on the Orange line. Kate wondered how that woman had spent the rest of her day.

In the front seat, an agent's jingling phone interrupted her thoughts. The agent answered, then said, "Agent Morgan, you need to take this call."

Martinez ended his discussion with the Director.

The device was placed between them and the speaker icon was activated.

"Will Shortz," a voice announced through the phone. "You brought me in to assist with the investigation." They exchanged greetings and he offered a synopsis of what he'd learned so far. 55 ACROSS translated to TUES. His assessment emphasized the possible relevance of Tuesday's association with the clock and the summation of Roman numerals to equal fourteen. The stroke of midnight seemed to be implied. The puzzle's treasure map symbolized the QUEST FOR TRUTH. "The piecemeal wordplay doesn't indicate whether the killer considers his fantastical mayhem a universal or spiritual journey. I'll have to defer to others on that assessment."

The words rolled out of Kate's mouth before she could stop them. "It's a journey of enlightenment."

Martinez clicked on his phone to conference in the SIOC team.

Shortz continued as urgency filled his voice. "Puzzles often exhibit themes, deeper cross-associations. Much like that fallout shelter symbol led to St. ELIZABETHS, the LATIN connection of the Cross Barbée translates to a church. Catholic, probably."

Kate's voice fell distant. "I forgot I have sins to atone for." She exchanged a nervous glance with Martinez.

He arched an eyebrow. "Something I should know about?"

"No."

He gave a shrug. "SIOC, track down Catholic churches inside the beltway."

"Besides supporting a theme," Shortz added, "17 and 21 ACROSS act as fillers. Words that exist to complete other portions of the puzzle. Added together they're fourteen."

"Fourteen?" Kate asked. An eerie horror seeped into her mind as she postulated on possibilities. Fourteen more victims? Fourteen locations? Fourteen could mean anything. She leaned closer to the phone. "Is it associated with 14 DOWN?"

"INITIALISM, GENUINE EXISTENCE?" Shortz cleared his throat. "I thought of that. INITIALISM is a semi-clever way of saying abbreviation. Initials. Another filler word or phrase. Traditional crossword standards don't allow two letter words. It could be something as simple as REAL LIFE. RL perhaps?"

Kate suspected REAL LIFE led to a different clue rather than a destination. She caught Martinez's gaze; they were thinking along the same lines.

REAL LOCATION? Another fallout shelter?

She nodded. "District Fallout lists 225 locations. St. Elizabeths had several shelters." Clicking on her laptop, her eyes gravitated to 45 DOWN. BAD WEATHER LAIR. "Narrow the search to DC churches that have fallout shelters?"

Martinez held up a hand as he gathered his thoughts. "The document breaks up the District of Columbia into quadrants. Northwest, northeast, etcetera. Addresses are indexed with numbers. Bring up those locations tagged as fourteen. There should be four total."

A technician spoke through the speaker, "Real-time satellite maps are active. Cross referencing locations. Wait. We have a deviation. Fourteen locations are chronicled as fourteen: apartments at 1114 F Street Northeast; Smothers Elementary School, 44th and Brooks Street Northeast; Congress Heights Methodist Church at 421 Alabama Ave Southeast; the Franciscan Monastery at 1340 Quincy Street Northeast; the Argyle Condos—"

Martinez cut her off. "It's the monastery."

"Sir, several other sites are listed, including Janney Elementary and St. Ann's Schools, which is attached to… a Catholic church."

Kate's face hardened as she said to Martinez, "Run with your instincts."

20
ON HALLOWED GROUND

12:10 AM, Franciscan Monastery of the Holy Land in America, Washington, DC

Kate's fears multiplied knowing that a symbol for the fishers of men had led authorities to the Franciscan Monastery of the Holy Land in America. A grand cathedral greeted the promenade of vehicles that rumbled through gated arches. Crosses affixed high above, similar to the Cross Barbée, overlooked immaculate grounds. Tires screeched as vehicles ground to a halt in a turnaround drive, scaring the hell out of tourists milling about.

Kate had nothing but questions. Was the monastery the killer's next stop? Who or what awaited them—a band of rogue and murderous friars? More sonic traps and mind-penetrating messages? Another disfigured, comatose victim?

And what was the twisted connection between a mass murderer and a band of friars?

SIOC agents schooled them on the difference between monks and friars: the Franciscans (Friars Minor) were the oldest of the friar sects within the Catholic Church, receiving their oral papal approval in 1209 and adhering to the teachings of Saint Francis of Assisi. As servants, the brethren took vows of poverty, chastity, and obedience with lives centered on prayer, communal living, and ministry.

The beautiful monastery sure looked like a place to atone for her sins, Kate thought. Part of the killer's plan.

Vehicle doors swung open and camo-clad agents bolted out, carrying automatic weapons. Kate fell in behind CIRG's agents, never allowing her hand to leave the sidearm holstered on her belt.

Three friars dressed in traditional brown with white waist ropes appeared, palms out to protest the intrusion. Kate studied the men's calm expressions, which conveyed a blend of reverent-like tolerance and passive resistance.

Someone had tipped them off.

"FBI." Dix Martinez raised both hands, to reveal a digital warrant on his phone in one and his badge in another. "We have a warrant to search the premises."

An odd look flashed across the old men's faces and the centermost man stepped ahead of his brothers. The man's frosted hair and weathered face showed a life of service, but his steel blue eyes radiated defiance.

"I am Brother Nicholas Padua," the man said. "Our monastery is a place of reverence. It's an international house of God. I presume you've consulted the U.S. State Department. Our mission operates with a diplomatic distinction."

Martinez drew a long breath and squared up to the friar.

It was a common misconception that places of worship operated with diplomatic distinctions or could be used as sanctuaries. The U.S. State Department recognized the Holy See, the ruling authority of the Catholic Church based in Vatican City, but that distinction did not translate into legal protections of its properties within the United States. What latitude was informally given to religious and sensitive locations was merely common courtesy between law enforcement communities and places of worship. Nothing in the law allowed churches or other places of worship to aid, abet, or provide refuge to individuals who had committed crimes.

Yet Kate knew Martinez's digital warrant was unenforceable. Only the actual writ carrying the signature of a United States Magistrate Judge from the District of Columbia was valid. That version had a ten-minute delay due to the intense, closed-Metro-syndrome snarl of DC traffic. And if the friars protested that the monastery was diplomatic property, sovereign church soil, their argument could force a delay and a hearing in District Court for final resolution.

The friar's eyes narrowed. The bureau's show of force didn't intimidate him.

CIRG's agents glanced to Martinez, waiting for his cue.

Two more friars appeared.

A chartered bus pulled to a stop outside the property's paired arches and a horde of tourists piled out.

Kate grinned. It was almost comical. Men of God seemed prepared to defend 21 ACROSS and a throng of tourists were about to complicate things.

She scanned the immaculate grounds. The tan-colored structures with salmon-colored roof tile were well preserved. The distinctive architecture reminded her vaguely of St. Elizabeths. Two U.S. flags flew half-mast. During the drive over, she'd digested facts about the monastery from its website. Forty-two acres. An oasis of peace. Church. Shrines. Gardens. It was internationally recognized for fundraising efforts, travel agent-like pilgrimages, and the preparation of friars for service in the Holy Land.

Nothing suggested a link to a cold-blooded killer.

The FBI had come up short on tracking down public records and building permits for a fallout shelter. But the monastery did have a basement and catacombs dating back well before building permits were ever issued.

Catacombs. Fallout shelters. Close enough.

The progression of tourists drew closer.

This is an awkward moment, Kate thought. Bumping Martinez aside, she extended her hand. "Brother Padua, may I have a word with you—alone? Please."

The elder statesman gave her an inquisitive look. His handshake was strong, receptive.

She guided him to the courtyard overlooked by the grand cathedral's Cross Barbée. A statue of St. Francis with a boy was in line with the cross and the cathedral's secondary door. Its granite plaque read "Saint Francis and the Turtle Doves."

"My name is Katherine Morgan."

The man prompted her to continue, content to listen.

She tossed a nod toward the closest of the half-mast flags. "I was aboard the train this morning. The bombing… the death… was horrible."

The friar's face softened. "We prayed when we heard about the tragedy. That kind of evil resides in a hardened heart." He thought for a long moment. "*For where one's treasure is, there will your heart be also. A corrupted heart and mind can possess a great deal of evil.*"

It resonated. The point of removing the flesh over the victims' hearts—to reveal a treasure.

She nodded. "For reasons I'm not at liberty to share, we believe the person responsible for the bombing has left clues inside your monastery. And we need your help to find them."

The friar folded his hands and pondered her statement.

From the corner of her eye, she caught Martinez's impatient frown and the odd mix of concerned friars, anxious agents, and massing tourists.

She forced her attention to the expansive courtyard, a work of art in itself. Weathered statues, shrines, and planters dotted sculptured paths. With a little imagination, it wouldn't be too hard to believe it was an escape to Italy or the Holy Land.

A small stone church with old-looking arched doors sat offset to the main cathedral caught her attention. The unpretentious structure with its little bell tower and simple cross offered a humble contrast to its neighboring buildings.

They'd been brought to the monastery for a reason.

Kate faced the friar and smiled politely. "Brother Padua, take us to your catacombs."

Martinez felt the pressure of time, its crushing vise-like grip torturing him as old men blocked their path. He grumbled beneath his breath. Perhaps Kate's diplomatic approach could defuse the situation and bypass the need for a warrant. He directed agents to permit the busload of tourists to pass. Their troubled expressions were certainly photo-worthy—come to church and watch law enforcement take down unarmed holy men in brown bathrobes.

Martinez surveyed the compound, enclosed by red-tile roofed breezeways that formed a perimeter around a courtyard and citadel-style entrance.

Intuition whispered to him. The Franciscan Monastery of the Holy Land in America was the next stop. A place where they'd find the owner of another patch of skin, another victim.

No telling what lay in wait within the earthen bunkers of an old church.

Catacombs? Fallout shelters? Hidden fortresses? Secret research labs?

Martinez had only recently been promoted to Section Chief of the bureau's critical incident and response group. It had taken years to navigate the layers of law enforcement bureaucracy, and the Metro bombing was his shot to oversee a nationwide terrorism investigation.

And he seemed to be doing it all wrong.

Plane bombings. Train bombings. Mass shootings. Those events he'd trained for. Human hide collecting, crossword puzzle mass murder linked to secret government research programs run out of the basements of abandoned insane asylums? Uncharted territory.

His cell phone rang jolting him from his thoughts.

"Martinez," he said, glancing at the number displayed—the SIOC B Watch Unit Chief, Alice Watson.

"Dix," Watson said, "Watson here. I've good news and a whole lot of bad news."

He stepped into the closest arched corridor. Poured granite concrete sidewalks, columns, and arched ceilings gave the elongated perimeter a private, movie-like setting.

"Don't hold anything back," he said, strolling the path's impressive length.

"There's been another bombing and a collapse of earth."

He gasped, feeling like he'd just been sucker punched in the gut.

The report came rapid fire. St. Elizabeths East. Blocks from the Gate Two. Car bombing. Five dead. One wounded. Military personnel, branch of service unknown at this time.

No immediate correlation tied the bombings or the sinkhole together.

Martinez doubted coincidences. He stopped in front of a tiled mosaic labeled "The Finding in the Temple." The carefully crafted picture depicted a youthful Jesus asking questions of, if not teaching, temple leaders. A woman, also haloed, stood behind the boy. Mary, his mother.

The random stops on a map meant something. But what?

He turned and passed through shadows piercing the breezeway's sides as Watson told him a sabotaged main sewer line failure had flooded the basements of St. Elizabeths south structures. A sink hole had collapsed a portion of Martin Luther King Jr. Ave.

More coincidences. Hardly.

The unit chief moved on to crime scene updates. Three overseas terrorist organizations had claimed responsibility for the WMATA bombing. The Internet and social media were saturated with conspiracy theories. Investigators had scrutinized metro surveillance feeds. Nothing showed anyone accessing the train tunnels before the bombing. Security access logs were cross-matched—no unauthorized access was recorded.

The metro bombing sounded like an inside job—someone inside WMATA.

"As for FR," Watson said of the bureau's facial recognition technology program under its Facial Analysis, Comparison, and Evaluation (FACE) Services Unit, "CCTV came up empty. No cross-matches to watch lists. Whoever planted the bombs managed to get past security measures."

His ears perked up. "Since I don't believe in ghosts, my bet is the terrorist has a security clearance. Direct investigators to search for companies with booked contracts, matched to WMATA and St.

Elizabeths. Screen vehicle logs and license plate numbers and search for correlations."

"One of our leads," Watson said, "is a firm called RMG Global Solutions. They have multiple master service contracts but also past network breaches. We don't know who hacked them. Maybe something will turn up along that front."

He'd never heard of RMG before. Not unusual. Federal agencies employed numerous civilian contractors and consulting firms.

"How about some good news?" he asked.

"Thought you'd never ask," Watson said as she video-conferenced in the National Transportation Safety Boards (NTSB) forensic supervisor, Connie Olson, a woman he'd worked with on a Pennsylvania Norristown High Speed Line derailment investigation. They exchanged greetings.

The NTSB supervisor hammered him with an onslaught of crime scene updates. Not good news or bad. Just facts.

"Five IEDs," Olson said of improvised explosive devices as her camera panned the train tunnel. "The placement and detonation of the explosives were strategic."

Martinez squinted at the tiny video images on his phone. Under temporary work lights, FBI crime scene investigators worked beside NTSB teams as they sifted through the debris and placed yellow markers at potential evidence locations.

He took a breath. "What makes that kind of hole in concrete?"

"We suspect blasting grade explosives," the woman said, "although creating craters was never in this bomber's grand scheme. From what we can detect, v-shaped linear charges were used. Those charges have a unique copper casing and contain a malleable high-explosive called RDX. The compound has more explosive power than TNT. Besides the military, it's popular with demolition crews. They use RDX to slice through steel girders and raze buildings."

He frowned. "Demolition—?"

"See here." The woman clicked on a flashlight to better illuminate the remaining tracks and wiped a white gloved palm against the crisp break in the steel rail. "The tip of the 'v' in the charge is faced away from the steel. This rust-like color is from the copper casing. The high-temp explosion pushes the copper right through the rail. Linear charges cut cleaner than torches."

"So our terrorist is a demolitions expert?"

"It's a theory." The woman panned her camera to offer a wider view: mangled train tracks; Orange line commuter cars were smashed together, staggered, and tipped over; debris was everywhere. "After the rails were severed, kicker charges pushed the rails at an angle to drive the train into the tunnel wall. The separation guide was blown to allow the train to plow ahead without depleting its kinetic energy."

Martinez wrinkled his brow. "This demonstrates precision." He reflected on the sonic communication cannons placed outside the ELIZABETHS LAB—those devices were clearly military grade. Another coincidence. Not anymore. "Wouldn't the terrorist have to know how fast the train was moving in order to time the bombing?"

"Yep," the NTSB supervisor said. With camera in hand, she traversed down the tunnel and away from the mangled and charred train. "It's basic math. If little Scotty rides his bike at a constant speed of x, how far will he travel in one minute?"

He felt patronized. "All right. I yield. How far did little beam-me-up Scotty travel?"

The camera's motion froze and locked onto a thin stainless steel cylinder no bigger than an ink pen, perched atop two thin wire legs. The contraption stood no more than two feet tall.

"Infrared sensors?"

It looked like a miniature silver flamingo—long stilt-like legs holding up a compact body.

The NTBS forensics supervisor swung her light across the track. A reflector affixed to the opposite wall returned the beam. "The circuit activation occurred when the beam was broken."

Martinez sighed. "It's a trigger, a switch."

"Elementary physics. Distance, time, and speed. After the train passes point A, how much time elapses by the time the train gets to point B, assuming the train is traveling at a constant rate of speed?"

He groaned. "I hate math word problems as much as I do crossword puzzles."

She laughed. "For maximum death and destruction, the train was hacked to increase its rate of speed." She took a breath. "Here's how he did it. The bomber picked intervals ahead of the explosives to sync the train's speed. A simple computer chip reconfirms the speed between sensors, which then tells an upstream controller when to detonate the explosives."

Martinez swore loudly, then remembered he was standing near a bunch of friars outside their church. Their eyes shot him a collective reprimand and he ducked his head apologetically.

The NTSB supervisor cleared her throat. "Explosives targeted the tracks. The bomber's end goal was to derail the train, not blow it up. The killer's prescribed devastation matched a desired outcome: mass casualties and maximum horror for those who survived."

Of that he had zero doubt.

He spied Kate still chatting with the friar.

The Orange line had been targeted because she was on it. Martinez understood it: the terrorist wasn't just talking to FBI Agent Katherine Morgan. He—it was almost certainly *he*—wanted to draw her in close, torment her, and validate his dominance over her. He wanted her to experience artwork, shrines, and overarching masterpieces.

The twisted crusade was meant to expose more secret government research.

Another reason he needed inside the damn monastery.

21
THE RETURN OF A LOVER

United Medical Center (UMC), Washington, DC

Phillip Barnes pushed through people crowding the hospital's ER check-in counter.

"The soldier from the explosion," he said as a statement rather than a question. He held up medical credentials matching the fake embossed name on his white doctor's coat: Mark Sloan, M.D. "She was just brought in."

Outside, he had passed patrol cars and turned to notice Washington Special Police officers sipping coffee in the corner of the waiting room. Their attention was glued to a television and the recycled news from the morning's metro bombing.

Coming to the hospital was risky.

Security cameras had undoubtedly captured his appearance by now.

Little could be done about that. He hoped his ginger-brown disguise—a wig and matching ginger mustache, carefully placed mole on his cheek, and the accompanying doctor's coat—was enough to distort staff recollections of his appearance.

His pulse ticked up. This deviation added dangerous variations to his meticulously choreographed plan. Luckily, a replacement waited in a church to deliver what he could not.

That foresight had afforded him this opportunity.

"She's waiting for BERT," the clerk said, barely glancing his way.

Barnes understood the jargon. A behavioral emergency response team (BERT) and a psych consult had been ordered to assess the mental health needs of a combative patient.

The clerk pressed an access control button under her desk. "Exam Five."

He nodded his gratitude and pushed through the ER doors.

Inside the emergency department, hospital staff moved about treating a variety of patients. Barnes passed the nurse's station and lingered in the main corridor. One room appeared to be the center of the staff's attention: Trauma One. A monitor pinged persistently.

Nurses bustled in and out of Trauma One, leaving its door open. A man. Significant burns. Blood was everywhere. The patient was in cardiac arrest.

"Starting compressions," an African-American doctor said, leaning over the patient.

Barnes understood the soldier's injuries without seeing him up close. The doctor's last-ditch efforts would be to no avail. Death was inevitable, even in the most skilled of hands.

East of the Anacostia River, UMC was a financially challenged health provider serving DC's poorest residents. The revenue-strapped hospital offered only core services. A better option for first responders would have been to transport Rachel and her Ranger team to a Level 1 trauma center such as George Washington instead of the closest hospital.

He yearned to linger, but time didn't permit further detours. He scanned the traditional wayfinding signage to track down Exam 5.

The exam room's door was open. Inside, a nurse updated vitals into a computer.

"May I help you?" she asked, not recognizing him as regular UMC staff.

His heart rate accelerated, and his rehearsed response stuck in his throat.

Dressed in a patient gown, Rachel Pratt lay in a hospital bed, her torso at a thirty-degree angle. A pole-mounted IV bag delivered

Ringer's lactate to a catheter in her arm. Velcro restraints secured her wrists.

No wonder a psych consult had been called.

The staff felt threatened by her presence.

A thin smile cracked the edges of his lips. Their concerns were well founded.

U.S. Army Captain Rachel Pratt was a bred and trained killer who had survived death twice.

Even with oxygen tubing looping beneath her nostrils, a recent splash of abrasions and small burns across her mocha-colored face, Rachel looked like an angel. At least to him. Inside, feelings stirred. Her closeness invigorated his senses as he watched her breath rise and fall.

She was alive, her repose vastly different from the last time they had been together.

The ABI program gave weakness no quarter. Failure earned harshness. A forbidden intimacy brought brutal consequences.

Barnes closed his eyes, recalling their last moment together. In an underground cavern, her naked form pressed against his. She gasped and shivered. For the first time since she'd been a child, fear showed on her face. As life drained from her body, their dream of escaping to Shangri-La slipped away.

The program's principal investigator, an Army colonel at the time named James Davidson, had shot Rachel as she tried to shield Barnes.

She had taken a bullet in her chest for him. Her sacrifice had been for love. Or so he thought. And that gunshot wound had proved fatal—in normal human biology.

But Rachel was different.

The difference between life and death: the Advanced Biogenetics Initiative (ABI). The program's focus was Advancing Human Evolution (AHE): perfect people, a new generation of soldiers or astronauts who could endure extended space voyages. A manipulation of test-tube genetics gave Rachel unique traits—beyond strength—a self-healer with advanced cellular regeneration capabilities. Many organs in the human body were discreetly encoded that way. ABI had just pushed those biological limits further than competitive research endeavors.

Rachel's body accelerated homeostasis, regulating its biochemistry to promote rapid angiogenesis and tissue reformation.

While she couldn't directly repair a bullet hole through her own heart, her body had the ability to self-heal provided that heart surgery created the framework to foster tissue regeneration.

ABI had brought back Rachel from the dead. James Davidson and his band of miracle workers had created a resurrection moment.

A sobering thought.

Barnes' hand slipped into his coat pocket and caressed the coldness of a semi-automatic.

Rachel's tranquil façade hid a deep-seated restlessness—a slumbering strength waiting to be awoken—a raw strength that made her a better field soldier than he could ever become.

Where he questioned, she'd proven loyal to a fault.

ELIZABETH'S LAB had been her chance to rediscover feelings and break the cognitive reconditioning that controlled her. But the moment Rachel chose to save her fellow Rangers, she'd revealed her true heart.

Now he harbored no illusions that Rachel would kill him, if given the chance.

The smart move would be to strike first, kill her where she lay. If the roles were reversed, she would, without deliberation.

"Doctor, can I assist you with anything?"

The nurse's question almost startled him. He shrugged off the question, shut the door to Exam 5, and returned bedside.

"I presume she's sedated?" he asked.

"Yes. The patient exhibited severe anxiety upon admittance, an uncontrollable hostility. The attending prescribed a moderate intravenous sedation." The nurse shot him a quizzical look. "What can I assist you with, doctor?"

"Nothing." He produced a Beretta 9mm with a suppressor threaded to its barrel.

Quick movements beat the nurse to a scream. The weapon's muzzle flashed twice as lead punctured her scrubs, sending her flopping to the floor. Two bloodied slugs had penetrated the tiled wall behind her.

The shots had been muffled but in no way silenced.

Unlike the myth perpetuated in Hollywood movies, suppressed gunfire made noise. More than he desired. Unsure whether others had heard the loud snaps, he doubted he'd be able to explain the nurse's murder.

Time was short, but he needed answers only Rachel could provide.

Barnes kissed her, allowing his lips to linger on hers. The nose of his suppressed handgun pressed firm against her temple. Lingering smoke drifted from its barrel.

His nostrils flared at the unpleasant competing fragrance. He had dreamt of this closeness, no matter how brief, and a chance to take in her natural scent, sweat, and oils of her skin. But the embodied stench of sewer water overrode the scent of her breath, accented by the light wisp of oxygen flowing through her nasal cannula.

He withdrew his lips and tightened his finger against the weapon's trigger.

He'd loved her, even with the lies.

Perhaps Rachel, as a soldier, didn't deserve to die helpless, unarmed.

The back of his brain jerked forward, forcing a flood of unwanted memories.

Caressing her neck, her skin felt silky soft, her ebony color contrasting his own skin tone. Yin/yang. Well, it used to be. He let the pistol linger near her head as his other hand drifted lower, traversing the curvature of her body beneath her hospital gown.

The repeated thrum of her heart was strong and vibrant. That was scarred, too.

Untying her gown, he exposed her mocha-colored bodybuilder's physique, interlocking muscles running from rounded shoulders to sculptured abs.

The scar was not where he remembered it.

That was the grand lie, told to him by James Davidson.

He probed his mind for memories. Rachel's form pressed against his. The sticky warmth of blood painting her motionless body. Her death, her murder, had robbed them of time and a chance to share their lives together.

His fingers slid to faint ripples in flesh, a spot once closed by sutures. Through his fingertips, he felt the rhythmic pulses mirroring the beat of her heart. The bullet had penetrated her sternum more in line with her heart, or so he had thought. The scar was higher, straddling the lower left superior lobe of her lung. Vital arteries withstanding combined with the timeliness of skilled medical treatment, Rachel's actual gunshot wound offered a greater chance of survivability, especially for a self-healer.

Barnes recoiled at the revelation. The hand clutching the gun shook and he steadied its aim, placing the weapon's barrel squarely between her eyes.

The lie cloaking Rachel's fateful resurrection grew clearer, its veil of deceit lifted.

Lies had variations. The truth none.

She'd died not to save him, but to drive him away.

Her choice was clever. Without their bonds of love, he was no longer a slave to the program—the trade she'd made. A tarnished truth had set him free.

Believing she was dead, he had abandoned her to save only himself.

Driving the thought from his mind, he took a labored breath before dialing off his weapon's silencer and tucking it in his coat.

He removed Rachel's left restraint to free a hand and slid the gun beneath the small of her back. Her bare skin felt warm. He allowed his hand to linger before repositioning the hospital gown to cover her form.

He yearned for a goodbye kiss, but it troubled him to know that the next time they met, one of them would surely die by the other's hand.

Moving swiftly, he snatched a pen off the dead nurse. He scribbled 51 DOWN MEETS 60 ACROSS on the palm of Rachel's freed hand, closed it, and left Exam Room 5.

The next move was hers.

22
SACRED GROUND

Franciscan Monastery of the Holy Land in America, Washington, DC

A sense of awe overwhelmed Kate.

The monastery's cathedral was a blend of classical European Christian architecture with three-storied arched ceilings. Frescos, paintings, shrines, and gold leaf adorned the walls. High above the cathedral's chancel altar, an oculus cast a beam of sunlight across glossed marbled floors, conveying a serene reverence. The picturesque sanctuary boasted more cross variants than she could count—some encircled like a Cross Barbée, while others were framed inside a Star of David. Their religious significances escaped her comprehension.

She chuckled quietly. The last time she'd been in a church, she almost shot a colonel working for the NSA—one of the good guys. That act would have probably come with its own special damnation.

She turned her attention from the physical setting to its visitors. A friar led the tour group who had gotten off the bus outside. A few more people prayed in pews. A woman holding a wooden box knelt at an altar.

Martinez and one of his officers stepped through an archway marked Nazareth and out of the catacombs, escorted by Brother Padua. As part of the friar's pre-warrant negotiations, firearms including hers stayed outside the sanctuary along with the rest of CIRG's agents.

Still, camo-wearing law enforcement officers seemed out of place in a house of God.

Martinez sighed. "Besides a centuries-old dead child—"

"St. Innocence," the friar corrected, closing the swing gate behind them.

Martinez continued. "And the partial bones of another saint and two unnerving mosaics, a skeletal reaper and a fella raising skeletal zombies from the dead—"

"The latter is Ezekiel in a restoration and unification story for the children of Israel," the friar interjected. "Officer, I told you earlier there's no one but saints down there."

"Yes, sir, you did." Martinez let out an exasperated sigh. "Kate, the catacombs are as advertised. Replicas. Mockups of holy sites."

"This is the place." Kate, flushed with anger, walked toward the chancel and stepped into the sunlight penetrating the oculus above. Glancing up, the penetrating stream blinded her as the sun's infusion refracted into a cross. Its center radiated out four purple beams from a bright white core. She didn't believe in signs from God, but welcomed any divine guidance law enforcement could get.

Martinez put a hand on her shoulder. "Brother Padua has agreed to share CCTV recordings to confirm nothing out of the ordinary is happening here. It's a pretty church, that's all."

She looked away from the light. It took a moment to blink out temporary blindness. Across the sanctuary, Kate spotted a woman holding a lit blue candle, who averted her eyes only after sharing a glance. She'd noticed the woman with a box earlier.

She turned to Martinez. "Give me a few minutes."

"Sure. I'll be reviewing video logs." Before following his friar escort out of the sanctuary, he said, "Morgan, stay in the church. That's an order."

She nodded and hurried into an alcove labeled Mary's Chapel, where stained-glass windows loomed high above an altar. It featured statues of the mother of Jesus, reenactments of the woman in her holiness, and lit blue candles. Two wooden crosses mounted to circular backings, similar to the killer's Cross Barbée, hung from the ceiling.

Below the suspended crosses, the woman Kate had seen knelt on a red pillow and prayed before Mary's altar. Two lit candles perched on a wooden railing, one in front of the woman and the other beside her.

"Are you Katherine Morgan?" the woman asked without glancing at her.

"You know my name?" Kate closed the distance between them, studying the woman in greater detail: a mop of frazzled dark hair mixed with silver streaks, wrinkled clothes as if she had slept in them, a handcrafted rosary wrapped around one wrist. Her other hand still held a wooden box. Kate thought of the woman who had ridden next to her on the Orange line, reading the Book of Revelations.

"8 DOWN," the woman said flatly. "I was told to tell you that."

Her pulse quickened. "8 DOWN? What does it mean?"

"ELISION."

Kate frowned. "An omission?"

The woman shook her head. "No. The process of merging abstract ideas."

Kate pondered the clue. "Who sent you?" she asked.

"A soldier," the woman said, exhaustion etched in her voice. "I was told to repent for my sins and demonstrate my faith, or my daughter would die before midnight."

"A soldier?" Kate's eyes locked onto the small wooden box. Its engravings matched the rosary wrapped around the woman's wrist. "What's your name?"

"Mary Davidson."

"And your daughter?"

The woman gave her a glare that cut straight through her, as if Kate were a specter. Red eyes and pale cheeks in her sixtyish face showed evidence of intense crying.

The words came at Kate like an accusation. "The pictures I saw of Frances no mother should ever see of their child. I'm afraid for my daughter."

Kate knelt beside the woman and touched the flames of the candle with her fingers.

"I asked James to follow our instructions. He insisted on handling the situation. I think his actions have made things worse. Too much is at risk now."

"Who's James?"

The woman passed over the box. "My husband. Army Major General James Davidson. He oversees several applied research initiatives for the Pentagon."

"Research?" Kate took in the news flash and felt the weight of the exquisitely crafted box, tipping it, and inspecting its edges. "Mary, was Frances taken because she was involved in some kind of covert research?"

Mary's expression hardened. "You're asking the wrong question."

Kate swallowed. "What should I be asking?"

"How do you stop this godless bastard and cut out his heart?" A tear streaked down her cheek. "I know he's responsible for bombing the Metro. Army. Former. James missed his chance at St. Elizabeths."

Kate's throat tightened as she listened to a mother give details about her only daughter, Frances Davidson, a consultant to DARPA. She had experience with fringe medical research programs; during her last investigation, Kate had nearly died trying to find a missing senator and exposing illegal human research trials.

"Mary, let's sit," she said, leading the woman out of the alcove, abandoning the burning candles at the altar. They sat facing each other in a vacant pew.

The killer's words pinged in Kate's brain as she caressed the exquisitely hand-crafted box. It had an over-the-top cremation container feel but it was too small to hold human remains. *Each stop earns you a reward. Log the tour. Seek the truth. Save those you can. Lose my tools, people die.* If the killer wanted her dead, he would have obliterated the Orange line train and everyone on it.

Kate studied the mysterious box. Opening it was a risk, no different from walking into an undocumented bomb shelter under a shuttered insane asylum and enduring sonic torture.

Would blowing up a church and everyone in it advance the killer's agenda?

"What's in the box?" she asked.

The woman's voice sounded uncertain. "I was told that if I opened it, Frances would die."

Kate shrugged. "And you weren't tempted?"

Mary Davidson cleared her throat. "I'm still confused how I brought all of this upon us, but all I want is my daughter back safe."

Kate felt her pain. Straightening up, she reflected that this task was too easy. Why follow clues to the monastery and not deliver an earthly destination?

"So, did this murderous soldier say anything about me?"

Mary said nothing.

Kate's fingers rapped against the box's gold latch.

Mary placed a shaky hand on her arm as Kate closed her eyes, wanting to cover her ears to avoid another sonic assault.

Oh, what the hell. Kate flipped up the latch and cracked open the box.

No explosions. No invisible attacks. No skull-crushing headaches.

Inside, a custom black felt pocket held an object.

Kate spun the box around for Mary to see the contents: a rustic skeleton key.

"What were your instructions after you gave me this?" Kate asked.

"Pray."

Really. Kate scrunched up her nose. She and God weren't on that kind of speaking terms.

Mournfully, Mary said, "In my prayers, I'm asking God for forgiveness and to give you the strength to rescue Frances and cover my penance. I've made sacrifices, personally and professionally. Because of those, I've struggled with my faith. Now I'm being called out to take a stand. I don't know if I can do it. Promise me, agent, that you'll kill him and save my daughter. Promise me you'll do that."

"I can't." She shuddered, knowing she was no mercenary of justice.

Studying the skeletal key in the box made something Mary said echo in her mind. *Being called out.* The killer, a former soldier, gave her a message. BE MINDFUL OF ORIGINS. Kate saw a connection. The key might access ORIGINS.

And the ORIGIN of the Franciscan faith was Saint Francis of Assisi.

Snatching up the key, Kate shoved the empty container into Mary's hands. "I know where this goes!"

23
AWAKENING

United Medical Center (UMC), Washington, DC

From a world of blackness, Rachel Pratt heard a woman's scream, then a rumble of chaos, voices all chattering at once. She blinked open eyes that felt pinched shut by clothes pins. Shades and shadows moved about in a bright room. Sterilizing light was everywhere. A hospital room. The vagueness enveloping her was the result of drugs. Doctor and nurses had ordered restraints and sedation to tame her combativeness.

Memory sprang to life: Phillip Barnes. A car bomb. Fire. Five Rangers. Dead.

"Move her to Trauma Two," a doctor said. "Type and crossmatch."

Rachel blinked her eyes and focused. A woman with gauze-covered chest wounds was lifted off the floor and placed on a gurney. A nurse. Blood was everywhere. She'd been shot, an easy deduction to make from the bullet holes in the tiled walls.

Heart shots mere inches apart. Rachel knew this experience intimately, with the scar to prove it. The nurse didn't have Rachel's unique advantage. Death was a condition most surgeons couldn't reverse.

How'd a nurse get shot?

She spotted two Washington Special Police officers in bullet-resistant vests lurking in the corridor, their accusing eyes watching her.

Barnes. The only explanation.

The medical staff pushed the gurney into the corridor and disappeared. In their wake came the cops.

Rachel took a breath and pushed herself up in the hospital bed, feeling something hard and uncomfortable wedged against the small of her back. Whatever the object was, it chafed her skin. Her pulse accelerated as she detected something else odd. One of her wrist restraints had been released, its Velcro band completely off.

In a flash she understood: she'd been set up.

She scanned the room for clothes, anything other than a hospital gown. Nothing.

The cops examined the bloodied wall before turning to her.

"What can you tell us about what happened?" one asked, his gaze sweeping from her head to her feet. The other officer peered beneath her hospital bed.

Rachel smacked her lips together and feigned a croak-like whisper. "My voice," she said faintly, drawing the officer closer. "I saw…"

She waited to capture the second officer's attention. Moving her lips, she pretended to speak, hoping to coax the cops within arms' reach. The ploy worked.

Partially bound as she was, the outcome was close.

She struck like a snake, thrusting an open palm against nose cartilage. The follow-up was a roundhouse back fist against the bridge of the second's man's nose. She grabbed his vest and jerked him closer. Her single-armed attack was fast and focused, striking and restriking without pause.

The first man, now lying on top of her, tried to spin away. A hand behind his head and a crunching knee to the face stopped him with a howl. Swinging her bare leg up and over him, Rachel interlocked her ankles and executed a choke hold between her thighs, pinning him to the bed. The first officer's sidearm was in reach. She snatched it out of his holster and struck the temple of the second officer, who collapsed to the floor. The man pinned between her legs squirmed and punched at her exposed legs and midsection. She grimaced at the pain, but it was nothing she hadn't experienced before. A final strike to the back of his head with his own sidearm, and he was limp.

Rachel fell back and caught her breath, thinking of her endless hours of close quarter hand-to-hand combat drills. Nothing had prepared her for being confined to a hospital bed, with only one arm and two legs to defend herself.

Reaching beneath her, she located the source of her back pain. A Beretta 9mm.

The weapon used to kill the nurse? A gift from Barnes?

His visit perplexed her. He wanted something from her.

She looked across the room at the bloodied spots in the tiled wall.

Barnes wanted her heart, or least what was left of it.

Using her feet, she shoved the first cop off the bed. His body dropped to the floor with a thud. A breeze tingled her skin and she noticed that her gown was askew, exposing her midsection and legs. No matter; the U.S. Army and Ranger training had drilled out any modesty long ago.

Rachel removed the remaining restraint and IV tube, freeing herself.

Stepping over the second cop, she saw his frame and shoe size weren't far off from her own. His clothes solved a need. After hand-cuffing the first cop to the bottom of the hospital bed, she stripped the second cop and used his cuffs to secure him similarly. His uniform fit on the baggy side, but did the trick.

She retrieved her own belongings—what had survived the explosion and didn't smell like sewage—from a clear plastic bag stashed beneath the bed. The cops' sidearms went into a soiled linen container—no need for their weapons with a gifted Beretta that undoubtedly linked her to a murder of a nurse.

The costume change gave her a fifty-fifty chance to make an escape. From the ER corridor, Pratt followed signs to the building's closest exit.

Outside, cool air flushed her cheeks and helped revive her senses.

A cop car was parked at the curb. She was glad to find car keys in the acquired pants' pocket, and took the vehicle out onto Southern Ave. SE.

Her mission had always borderlined on personal.

Killing her fellow Rangers had made it more personal.

Phillip Barnes would soon regret ever knowing her.

24
THE ORIGINS OF A CHURCH

Franciscan Monastery of the Holy Land in America, Washington, DC

Kate's lungs fought for oxygen as she sprinted out of the cathedral, lunging past tourists and exploding into the monastery's courtyard and gardens. From the corner of her eye, she caught sight of an idle K9 agent, his dog, and armed CIRG agents lingering by vehicles.

Winded, she stopped short of the Portiuncula Chapel, a stand-alone one-room stone church dwarfed by the monastery's cathedral. Another replica. But it was a structure that at least in appearance had doors mated to the black skeleton key she clutched in her hand.

On the ride over, she had read about Giovanni di Pietro di Bernardone, the man who became St. Francis of Assisi. His ministry focused on the poor. One day a vision came to him: "Francis, Francis, go and repair My house which, as you can see, is falling into ruins." Francis took this decree literally and returned home to a derelict little church in the woods: St. Mary of the Angels stone church. It was there that a movement germinated and became greater than the man himself.

The Portiuncula was where the Franciscan order started.

Two years before he died, during an apparition of Seraphic angels ceremony, Francis requested the Five Wounds of our Lord.

Those marks of heavenly favor, the brandings, he bore for the rest of his life.

The clue for 69 ACROSS was a BRAND OF DISGRACE.

STIGMA. The secular shadow of stigmata.

St. Francis had taken on the sacred wounds as a rite of passage. His expression was a declaration of faith and servanthood. In contrast, a mass murderer removed the skin of his victims to demonstrate his mastery and brand them for a twisted cause.

The CIRG agents finally caught up to her. Without a word, she motioned for them to surround the one-room chapel.

An officer returned her Glock.

Kate felt the weapon's weight and allowed her fingers to tighten around its plastic grip. With no idea what awaited them, she decided against holstering the semi-automatic.

Gun and key in hand, she circled the building and slowed her breathing. The chapel's stonework and bell tower were unpretentious. The ascetic structure contrasted the alignment of elaborate emblems and crucifixion systems heading columns on a nearby breezeway. The chapel had three doors—two with protective gates and modern hardware—and an old door at the head of the chapel required a skeleton key.

Sliding it into the lock, Kate turned the key. The lock disengaged.

The K9 handler and his Belgian Malinois nudged beside her.

From across the courtyard, a voice yelled, "Morgan, stand down—"

Ignoring Martinez, Kate wrenched open the door and targeted the enclosed space with her weapon. Cool air greeted them as daylight vanquished darkness and washed away the slit of light piercing through the embrasure, a narrow window in the stonework. After a command, the dog launched itself inside, its handler lingering at the doorway. A second later, a bark communicated something had been located.

The entrance into the tiny chapel didn't allow for a large breach by law enforcement, so Kate followed the dog's handler inside.

She saw the back of a crucifix looming over a small stone altar. Wrought iron fencing and swing gates fronted a raised concrete worship platform. Clearing steps, Kate saw flowers planted in dirt mounds around a woman's body, her bare feet poking out of a white silk robe. The semi-see-through, angelic-style robe was purposely arranged to reveal lots of skin beneath reverently crossed arms. One hand clutched a dark-colored scroll.

The Belgian Malinois sat dutifully beside the tranquil woman.

Kate thrust her fingertips against the woman's neck. A carotid artery pulsed slowly, but rhythmically. Without touching the scroll, Kate slid the woman's arms aside and studied her torso. A blank skin graft covered her left breast. The replacement patch had been fused into her skin like the victim at St. Elizabeths. Kate jabbed the artificial cover with her finger to test skin tone: pink at first, before returning to a natural peach color. Kate performed a sternum rub, grinding her knuckles against the woman's chest.

The comatose victim showed no response to painful stimulus.

Was this victim linked to secret research programs?

"Morgan," Martinez said, leaning past the altar, "what the hell are you doing?"

Ignoring him, Kate slid back the woman's eyelids and splashed vacant eyes with a flashlight beam. Sluggish pupil response was consistent with the man they'd found earlier.

"You're here to help now?" she said to Martinez.

Kate stepped back to stage the scene in her mind. She and the dog had made a mess of the flowers encircling the victim, scattering dirt and blossoms everywhere. The handler had withdrawn the dog to give Kate room to work.

"I told you to stay inside the church."

She shrugged. "This is *the* church. St. Francis' Church."

"I can't protect you if you're going to be reckless." Martinez crossed his arms.

"I never asked for your protection. So stop being chauvinistic."

"You know who you report to, don't you?"

She rolled her eyes. "Let me guess. Someone who's not sleeping beauty."

He frowned. "Morgan, follow orders whether you like them or not." He took a breath and surveyed the small stone church. "Okay, smartass, who's your victim?"

"Ask the mother in Mary's Chapel to come and identify her daughter," Kate said. "Then arrest her husband for obstruction of justice."

"You going to fill me in on what we're talking about?"

She crouched and studied the woman dressed in a Halloween costume—a sleeping angel—an illusion, much like the other replicas on the monastery's grounds.

"Any day now, boss," she said. "The woman's name is Mary Davidson."

Martinez radioed for agents to escort Mary Davidson from the church, while Kate continued to scrutinize the scene.

Seven red begonias had been placed at even intervals around the victim. Kate knew enough about the flowers not to send them in floral arrangements—they meant something like a warning of future misfortunes. The color red conveyed varied social meanings, anything from romance and love to danger or death.

Danger and Death. Quite the message.

The real message, after getting past the trampled floral décor, was on the brown parchment rolled up in the woman's hands.

The next set of clues, Kate thought with a mixture of hope and dread.

25
THE DISCLOSURE OF THEME

**Strategic Information & Operations Center (SIOC), FBI
Headquarters, Washington, DC**

Will Shortz absorbed the organized frenzy.

The SIOC was a foreign world, a long way from his New York
home. The big board in the front blazed with graphical maps and
satellite images, streaming data and cable news feeds, and camera
shots of the Foggy Bottom—GWU Station. On his left and right, a
mix of suits and uniforms sat in long rows of workstations, intense
people solving problems.

Card stock labels embossed with the FBI's emblem dotted shallow walls and labeled computer terminals. His name reserved a seat
in the back row. Downstairs, security had processed him, presented
a strict list of dos and don'ts, required a signed non-disclosure
agreement (NDA), and the surrender of his cell phone. The personal
identity verification (PIV) smart card hanging about his neck was
the outcome of his in-briefing.

A woman in a suit approached. "Mr. Shortz," she said, "thank
you for coming."

He nodded politely. He hadn't thought he had a choice.

"Alice Watson, one of the SIOC unit chiefs," she said, extending
a hand. "Your unique skillset is an asset to law enforcement. What

can you tell us about these clues? What kind of puzzle are we looking at?"

He had given the response some thought. "I'm out of my comfort zone. This is just instinct, but your bomber is attempting to demonstrate clever wordplay. Seed clues and answers produce a theme, the relevance of his story. If there are filler words, they may or may not have value in the final puzzle solution. We have already learned the puzzle includes abbreviations."

Watson nodded for him to continue.

"Even without a grid, I'm suspecting clues and answers won't follow traditional conventions, like that of an American crossword format. That's not a priority for your bomber. But as an editor, I reject two-letter words, uncommon symmetry, extreme jargon or vernacular."

What Shortz had seen troubled him deeply: human skin and 13 ACROSS. If he could solve the clues and fill in the grid, that would give authorities a distinct advantage the bomber might not expect.

"He's made this into a game," Watson said.

"Think of it as a challenge," he said. "A test. Puzzles translate the unknown to known. Holistically, they're a way for us to put the world in order. Puzzles deliver revelations. I work cryptic messages in every shape and size imaginable, and sometimes clues have multiple translations. That's the case here."

They walked to his dedicated computer terminal.

Shortz's mouth ran dry as he looked at a large screen at the front of the room that displayed clues and answers. "Can I ask a question?"

Watson pinched her brow. "What's that?"

"On the flight down, I couldn't help thinking that constructing crosswords and demonstrating a prowess with wordplay is one thing. But why go to the trouble of tattooing people?"

The agent's face hardened. "Based on statistics, data, and patterns of behavior, our profilers have made several assumptions. This mass murderer, a domestic terrorist, is male. Caucasian. College educated. Former military. He knows how law enforcement responds to situations. The premeditated bombing is either the work of a single individual or a tight-knit group of bad actors. Branding people with crossword clues gives him bragging rights. People choose to get inked for a variety of reasons. And those who scar others do it to demonstrate dominance, dictate ownership, or mark property. Summing up the actions of a sociopath is not an exact science, but abducting and tattooing victims are a manifestation of his personal connection to them and allows him to proclaim an overarching ideology."

Shortz considered the character profile. A lunatic's challenge delivered an inevitable terminus. Each stop on the journey highlighted theme entries, valuable clues that infused a cinematic performance with a deeper meaning.

"Do we know anything about the victims?" he asked.

"The first is a scientist. We're running missing persons reports to see if there's a link."

"What did we learn from the first clues?" he asked.

Watson pointed to screens displaying patches of tattooed skin. "He's demonstrated an obsession with one of our own."

"Katherine Morgan. I talked with her on the phone." Shortz gestured back to the screens. "Your terrorist wants her to survive a trial by fire. Personalized clues will prove interrelated. It started with Agent Morgan. My hunch is that it ends with her."

"Ends with her?"

Shortz took a sharp breath. "KNOW THAT THE PUZZLE IS GREATER THAN RIDDLES AND PAIN. Each threshold, a stop on the map as it were, requires payment. Victims. Maybe something else. A sequence of clues charts to a final destination. Clues inside clues deliver an end game. Think of it like a big reveal. A QUEST FOR THE TRUTH IS NOT FOR THE FAINT AT HEART. The emphasis on TRUTH represents undisputed knowledge. And that knowledge must be earned. Katherine Morgan is expected to earn her way through the clues."

Watson frowned. "Solve this puzzle and help us find the madman behind the curtain before more people get hurt. Let me know what you need."

Need? Tough to know what was needed when you were still figuring out the rules and have no idea of what to expect at the end. The design of the piecemeal wordplay was meant to stretch to 55 DOWN, SHORT MON'S FOLLOWER.

The stroke of midnight.

Shortz cleared his throat. "Keep the clues coming."

26
FINAL PREPARATIONS

Washington, DC

Barnes thought of Rachel Pratt during the entire drive. His autonomous black transit van he rode in turned onto Water Street SE and passed through a secured gate on the north bank of the Anacostia River, between the District Yacht Club and I-695. Subleased from the U.S. Navy, the waterfront industrial property served as his base of operations. From the street, fencing obscured the largest assets of a secretive enterprise: a fleet of autonomous self-driving vehicles, a composite building that sheltered a bank of satellite dishes, and a control building.

The van rolled to a stop inside the compound.

He hadn't expected his feelings for her to be so strong. Doubt wormed into his mindset and undermined his resolve. The logical action: he should have executed her and closed that chapter on both of their lives. Permitting any unnecessary clutter to linger only diffused clarity and purpose. His actions had delayed the inevitable.

Rachel Pratt, a cousin of sorts, a former lover, would die before the stroke of midnight. Only one of them would see morning's light.

Barnes got out of the vehicle and badged into the metal structure. He strolled concrete floors past white modular labs and a fenced pen area.

Backpedaling, he took in a seven-cot cage, its door wide open and unlocked.

Two comatose figures lay exactly where he had left them. No sense relinquishing his final signposts, a man and a woman, before it was absolutely necessary. Seven had been branded as conspirators. Marked, their lifeless existences served a grander purpose and would ultimately bring down the Executive Branch of the United States.

Specifically, the White House and the Vice President.

The authorities had logged only two stops, leaving five in play. Each of his seven pawns matched a number he'd assigned to the quest. Once, he too had only a number and no name.

But that had been a long time ago.

By now, even slow-on-the-uptake law enforcement would finally start mining missing persons' reports and riddling out identities. No matter, though. Matching names to victims was hardly rocket science.

Barnes took satisfaction in knowing that dangerous events matched the falling sand inside an hourglass.

Midnight.

By then, secrets would emerge so severe that not even the White House or the Defense Department could cover them up.

He grinned at the thought. *When exposing a crime is treated as committing a crime, you are being ruled by criminals.* The criminals would finally find their judgment by the light.

Reaching his right-sized command center, Barnes grabbed a seat and faced a group of monitors. On screen, a dated notification popup required his immediate attention.

It raised more interest than concern. Surveillance images from Reagan National Airport flagged a corporate jet parked outside a private terminal. A scan of aircraft registration linked it to the Federal Bureau of Investigation.

Marked white SUVs awaited passengers. Two men deplaned. Facial recognition identified both: one was FBI, the other a civilian, Will Shortz.

The *New York Times* crossword puzzle editor's recruitment was a logical move. They'd brought a puzzle master in to help solve answers in advance without the need for staggered clues.

Barnes chewed on his knuckles. The ringer's presence required tighter timetables, perhaps even accelerated ones.

His quandary: the seven puzzle segments had been cemented. He could not change his plan without creating new clues.

His resolve deepened. Their course had been charted.

Seven numbers. Seven destinations. One outcome.

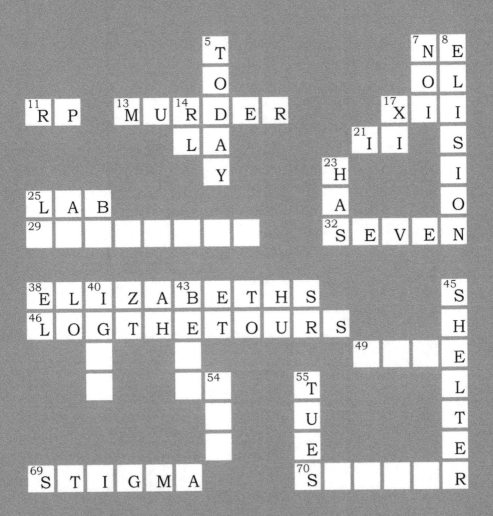

27
THE PATH OF FOOTSTEPS

Portiuncula Chapel, Franciscan Monastery of the Holy Land in America, Washington, DC

Kate liberated the scroll from the comatose victim and spread out the patch of dark skin on the altar. Her gloved fingers traced the parchment's edges. Melanin pigments suggested an African American ancestry, and she knew a first year's forensics assessment would confirm that with DNA testing. On a darker foundation, the effect of the tattooed lettering and symbols seemed muted.

The prior two stops had each been different, as had each patch of skin. Something connected the victims, messages, and locations together—elements beyond her comprehension—elements that led to a killer.

"I'll get this to ops," Martinez said, quickly documenting the scene: the puzzle, the victim, the altar. Everything was forwarded to SIOC.

Her mind struggeld to process questions. How were the victims selected? What made them special? What kind of hell did they go through... tattooed, tortured, maimed?

Kate avoided studying the actual wording until the surge inside her was unbrearable and pushed her toward the inevitable. Her eyes turned to the message.

KATHERINE MORGAN, TREAD THE PATH OF FOOTSTEPS IN THE GRASS LEST YOU MISSTEP. VITAE SUMMA BREVIS SPEM NOS VETAT INCOHARE LONGAM.

ACROSS	DOWN
29 METHOD TO IMPROVE HUMANS	40 RELATED TO ING
49 SCARLETT'S TARA	43 TESTED VERSION
70 SMARTER THAN FOOD FOR POWDER	54 PROFILE

Another personalized message. FOOTSTEPS IN THE GRASS? MISSTEPS? An ominous command. The second phrase was Latin. She challenged her recall of the language, an undergrad subject that had come in useful when she got to medical school. LIFE SUM BRIEF HOPE US FORBIDS BEGINNING LONG. The dead language sentiment made no sense. She reordered the words in her mind. A SHORT LIFE FORBIDS US LONG HOPE.

Words of warning like a prophecy.

SHORT LIFE?

A terrorist's way of announcing her death? A lovely sentiment.

And what on Earth did an up arrow represent? Heaven?

Martinez peered over her shoulder. "Medical transport is en route and command has photos. On a positive note, your puzzle expert arrived and has provided a few interpretations."

Kate finally broke a thin smile, relieved. "Tell him 8 DOWN is ELISION. Translate its meaning as the process of merging abstract ideas."

She saw Martinez stare out across the tiny church, beyond the unconscious woman toward vacant two-seated pews.

"Jack," he said after taking a breath, "wanted me to protect you. Keep you safe. Out of harm's way. Yeah, that sounds chauvinistic. I'm old fashioned."

She hadn't thought about Jack Wright or Thomas Parker in hours and missed both of them. Jack had reappeared in her life a little more than a month ago, years after she left him for his infidelity. A senator's missing persons investigation led her straight to Thomas; where Princeton had proven to be a crucible of fire and a place where Jack had died. Supposedly. Time in the tropics with Thomas had given her an opportunity to heal.

A woman's wailing jolted Kate from self-pity.

"Where is my daughter?" Mary Davidson screamed. "Where is Frances?"

It took a stunned moment for Kate to process the questions. She had jumped to the conclusion that the woman in the chapel would be her daughter, a namesake of St. Francis of Assisi.

Mary dropped the handcrafted box. It fell hard against the concrete altar floor.

Kate's eyes followed the box, and she noticed a piece of wood had dislodged from its decorative shell.

The woman's accusing words fired at her like daggers. "You were supposed to rescue my daughter."

28
FOUNDATIONS OF A KILLER

Strategic Information & Operations Center (SIOC), FBI Headquarters, Washington, DC

Will Shortz knew he'd once said, "I'll turn anything into a game."

This was different. He hadn't been talking about murder, torture, or disfigurement.

Instincts told him the terrorist's grid felt similar to the *Times'* Monday through Saturday fifteen-by-fifteen crosswords, rather than the twenty-one-by-twenty-one grid used in Sunday editions. A fifteen-block puzzle typically included between sixty and eighty words or phrases. The two rationed releases had revealed seventeen clues. Limited wordplay.

Key answers remained elusive. Deliberate, of course. It kept control and pace squarely in the terrorist's hands.

An aptitude for solving Sudoku and KenKen had helped honed pattern recognition skills. But establishing a grid without word placements and without a point of reference was a particular challenge.

As an editor, Shortz worked predefined templates with minimal freeform. Even though he had invented hundreds of puzzles, his favorite had always been American-style crosswords. In this fragmented challenge, the cornerstone word had yet to be laid: 1 ACROSS and 1 DOWN. Also missing were fifteeners, grid-spanners, and bridge words that anchored the grid and forged boundaries.

Absent the lead word or phrase, the lowest known answers were DOWN: 5, 7 and 8; TODAY, NOI, ELISION. The Ds in TODAY and MURDER probably crossed.

A growing commotion caused him to rise from his workstation and peer across the room, abandoning his efforts to construct a grid. Agents and investigators had gathered around one of the sub-screens, in what he learned the bureau called their big board.

Alice Watson snapped her fingers and issued updated assignments.

His gaze locked onto a series of new photographs on display.

A fragment of brown skin had been cut from a human chest.

Horrifying.

The third batch of clues hit him fast, sending his mind racing on a course of its own.

The arrival of 70 ACROSS meant there were at least 70 answers in this enigma.

A new symbol. Six clues.

Another prologue addressed to FBI Agent Katherine Morgan. FOOTSTEPS. MISSTEPS. Warnings. The second sentence in Latin had been translated.

"A SHORT LIFE FORBIDS US LONG HOPE," an agent said two rows up from his. "What does that mean?"

Shortz wanted to say something pithy, but held his tongue.

Love and hope won't save us from death.

Shortz's gaze tracked to the clues as he absorbed them at random, focusing on the easiest to solve first. Low-hanging fruit: 43 DOWN's TESTED VERSION. BETA.

49 ACROSS and SCARLETT'S TARA was HOME or PLANTATION. The importance of land was a theme in Margaret Mitchell's *Gone with the Wind*. SCARLETT prized her HOME over failed love. TARA had survived long after the American Civil War had faded and the men in Scarlett's life were gone.

He skipped PROFILE and 54 DOWN. A purposefully vague clue. The final answer would be along the lines of a biography, rap sheet, outline, or silhouette of a person.

40 DOWN had meat to it, more than memorized meanings or ambiguous wording.

RELATED TO ING? Shortz didn't need a computer to eliminate financial advising and investments. This clue had a personified answer. His eclectic mind ran wild as he typed at a terminal. A web search confirmed ING belonged to Norse mythology: the Norse god Freyr. The Anglo-Saxon pre-Germanic name ING was an earlier version of Ingunar Freyr. He paused when he stumbled on translations for ING. Not holistic relations but the same godlike being. The time spent down this rabbit hole didn't end with Frankenstein's lab assistant, but rather the translation of Ingvar from Danish, Norwegian, and Swedish to Slavic languages.

ING was IGOR.

Watson approached. "You seeing this?" she asked, noticing his attention was directed to his computer rather than the newly branded patch of skin.

He raised a palm without looking up. "Minute, please."

"Oh, of course. I'll wait," she said, resting her hands on the wall of his workstation.

His eyes scanned the listed search results for FOOD FOR POWDER. It was Shakespeare's cynical reference to the cavalier regard those who waged war had for the men who fought their war. In Henry IV, Falstaff called common foot soldiers nothing more than cannon fodder, food to be consumed by battle. The clue's preceding tag of SMARTER THAN modified the wordplay emphasis. Synonyms for smart soldiers linked to the terms combat engineer, military specialist. SAPPER. The French label derived from sapping. Digging and trench warfare. SAPPERS demolished enemy obstacles and bypassed fortifications.

Shortz got up and walked to one of the side monitors. "Bring up the photos from the Metro bombing and the NTSB's preliminary assessment."

A technician brought up a new screen.

"Enlarge," he said, squinting at the document's fine print.

Words jumped out at him. High explosives used in demolition work.

Shortz spun on his heels.

Anxiety rose in his voice. "ORIGINS. This theme comes from where you found the clues as much as what the answers say themselves." He hustled over to a whiteboard and jotted down five of the six answers: BETA, HOME, IGOR, SAPPER. He ran with BIOGRAPHY as 54 DOWN. It was a close enough placeholder. He drew a circle and placed an arrow inside it. A detached foot went below the arrow. "I'm not a symbologist, so I'll leave that expertise to others. Each symbol thus far represents a destination. This is no arrow. It's a building. An outline. A silhouette. A house with a basement or porch. The next destination is a HOME for SOLDIER."

The SIOC fell silent.

Shortz grinned sheepishly as every eye in the command center landed on him.

"SOLDIERS' HOME," another technician announced. "Fort Totten."

Watson faced her team. "Okay. Cross-reference locations to known fallout shelters." She turned to him with a wry smile. "From here on out, I'm calling you professor."

He downplayed the compliment with an awkward shrug. "It's what I do for a living."

"And I thought you just worked for a newspaper."

He chuckled. "Professor, eh? You have a favorite? Hinkley or X?"

Watson's expression turned serious. "Moriarty."

"Oh, that hurts."

"Well, you did only give us five out of six."

"Yeah, about that." He took a nervous breath. "METHOD TO IMPROVE HUMANS. 29 ACROSS. It'll be tied to his ORIGIN. An ORIGIN of a SOLDIER. Now obviously I'm not privy to the deeper meanings in play, but I suspect authorities won't like that answer when I figure it out."

29
THOUGHTS OF REVELATION

Franciscan Monastery of the Holy Land in America, Washington, DC

A driverless black Transit van slowly moved past emergency vehicles blocking the main entrance of the monastery and turned into the tree-lined north service drive, stopping parallel to the tiny church that lay just inside the courtyard's gardens.

In his Navy Yard command center, Phillip Barnes listened to first responder cellular, radio, and voice communications, his surveillance platform capable of intercepting and decrypting commercial and law enforcement transmissions. His sophisticated intelligence platform was a variant of the one Israel's Mossad had used to tap U.S. Secretary of State John Kerry's phone during peace talks. The vehicle's roof-mounted cameras were limited in visibility behind a rise of a hill, mature trees, and a breezeway, and required supplementing with satellite images.

Surveillance feeds captured drones. Their arrival in law enforcement activities had grown common. Three shoebox-sized radio-controlled aircraft flew above the church and documented the scene.

Barnes brought up the vehicle's defense console and was about to fire its intercept laser to pick off the drones when something on audio caught his attention.

"Martinez," a female voice said as a display registered the cellular communications. "We have the next location. Soldiers' Home. Nine minutes west of you."

A man's voice replied, "That's record time, Watson."

Voice recognition identified the man as FBI CIRG Section Chief Dix Martinez.

"We had help on the solutions."

Barnes frowned. The government's imported ringer, the puzzle master from New York was unraveling clues faster than desired.

And Shortz's presence changed the pace of the challenge, which translated into less time for Katherine Morgan to progress through her trials and tribulations. The man was altering a precise sequence of events. Somehow his intrusion had to be addressed.

"Just a heads-up. We haven't located the exact building at Soldiers' Home yet, but we're closing in on a location."

Barnes chuckled to himself.

"MPDC will establish a perimeter," Watson said.

"We mobile in five," Martinez said.

"Roger that."

"Watson, what's the latest on that Army general?"

Barnes smirked. Good luck on that front.

There was a pause. "Davidson remains unavailable, holed up at the Pentagon. The jackass is refusing to cooperate. On our end, we've named him as a person of interest. A judge has conceded our case and we'll be issuing warrants for his financials, personal communications, and a search of his home in Arlington. The bureau's General Counsel has petitioned the Secretary of Defense's office, but DoD is restricting our access to him based on matters of national security."

"You think the White House is stonewalling?" Martinez asked.

"Hard to tell."

"What about the general's daughter, Frances Davidson, the DARPA researcher? She appears to be a victim."

"Perceived victim, since you don't have a body," Watson said. "DARPA has no comment on her or her involvement in any ongoing research." She paused. "Find a patch of skin that matches her DNA and then we can put a full court press on DoD."

"Maybe we'll get lucky and she'll be at Soldiers' Home."

"Let's hope so."

Barnes sighed. Law enforcement's step-by-step myopic approach was preventing them from seeing the larger picture.

The free-of-charge 8 DOWN: ELISION had been put to poor use.

Revelation can be more perilous than revolution.

Katherine Morgan would learn that lesson.

30
REFLECTIONS OF MEMORY

The Pentagon, U.S. Department of Defense, Virginia

Rachel Pratt knew a Pentagon duty assignment was like none other: 26,000 people, a mix of service members, civilians, and federal administrators. For armed forces personnel, time served at "The Building" came with blessings, curses, arcane policies, and bureaucracy. Endless bureaucracy. Civilians were the continuity between the cycling waves of uniformed appointments. And the regimented layers of bureaucracy always outlasted the lifespan of those working inside the ringed wedges.

In the Pentagon Athletic Center, Pratt stepped behind a curtain in a long line of shower stalls. The rhythmic pulse of hot water flushed her bare skin. Closing her eyes, she soaked in the moment. Her fingers felt the faint ripples in skin where a bullet had once pierced her chest. She thought of the dead nurse.

Her assault on Washington police would make her the prime suspect in the nurse's murder.

In a matter of hours, her life and career had been derailed. Barnes had sowed the seeds to destroy her, if not send her to prison.

Lathering and rinsing, she wanted nothing more than to wash away the lingering stench of sewage and feces. Chalk that up as another reason to kill a former lover, along with getting a measure of vengeance for Rangers murdered at St. Elizabeths.

The only way to make things right and clear her name was to finish the mission.

And that result ended with the death of Phillip Barnes.

Which was why she needed to see a general.

But Major General James Davidson's abrupt reassignment to the Joint Rapid Cell team reporting to the Office of the Under Secretary of Defense for Research and Engineering (USD R&E) added complications. The general had inside information on Barnes, so meeting him face to face was a risk worth taking.

That was if she didn't get arrested by the Pentagon's Force Protection Agency, the police force everyone referred to as the "cops."

She dressed in clean fatigues and boots.

Cutting through corridor spokes, she reached the Pentagon's iconic courtyard, where she spotted the general sitting on a bench, with an ARMY magazine in his hands.

Pratt hesitated, making sure the coast was clear before sitting beside him.

The magazine was open to an article entitled "Meet Your New Battle Buddy: Soldiers Will Pair with Smart Machines to Fight Future Battles."

"Machines and weapons are useless without great soldiers." Davidson set the magazine aside and stared down at his dress shoes. "This conversation never happened. Understood, Captain?"

"Yes, sir."

"Those were fine soldiers," he said, his weathered features looking rougher than anytime before, and his steel blue eyes carried an emotionless distance. "They accepted the risks without question. Death can be a dark reality. Soldiers wage war. War has casualties. Regrettable but true."

Pratt cleared her throat. "Their deaths are on me, sir."

"Spoken like an officer." Davidson studied the fading scars and cuts on her face. "You've healed better than the Program would have expected."

She looked away. "Sir, who was on the phone when I called earlier?"

Davidson sighed. "The Vice President." From the magazine, he extracted an envelope and passed it to her. "As fathers, we have more in common than I realized."

Pratt squared up to him. "Meaning, his son and your daughter are two of seven?"

"Yes. They worked on tangential applications of your program. Their public disclosure and involvement will expose a great deal of research. Sensitive research."

She shook her head. "Which part? Perfect people? Self-healing soldiers? Advancing Human Evolution? The Advanced Biogenetics Initiative?"

"Does it matter?"

She supposed not.

"Captain, you'll know what I mean when I say I have no capacity to support a fugitive from the law. Washington police want to question you about the murder of a nurse at a hospital." He stood, leaving the magazine on the bench. "Locate a tan SUV in the Boundary Channel Drive Lot in the official vehicle area. Change the plates when you get to DC."

Pratt opened the envelope and found photographs, a new CAC card with her picture and a different name on it, and a set of car keys.

"How do I find Barnes?"

"Your window of opportunity is narrow." He gestured to the magazine. "The book reviews are enlightening."

She turned the pages and found an address. A safe house. A place she'd visited before. Dupont Circle.

"Rest up. Your time will come, Captain."

"Barnes will put up a fight. It could get messy."

He nodded. "I'd expect no less from him. He's a bred soldier, as are you. It's easier to grow wiser after the event. I should've killed him instead of you. His intellect over your brawn was supposed to be our future."

His emotionless eyes changed briefly, suggesting remorse—not for saving or not saving Barnes, but for missing an opportunity to keep the original test tube children together.

A familiar pain pricked Pratt's chest. One that she'd felt before. A memory that cognitive recalibration could not erase.

Davidson had shot her to prove a point.

No amount of cognitive whitewashing could blot out her entire past. Resilient memories had a way of returning as reflections. Unwanted moments in their lives Barnes felt compelled to revive.

Perhaps it wasn't so much a bullet to the heart she felt as much as a broken heart.

She knew the rules. They knew the rules. Rules had been broken. Consequences followed.

And it came down to a rather simple choice.

She wanted Phillip to save himself.

The pain in her chest returned. Barnes' touch, their fleeting skin-on-skin warmth faded.

Pratt shuttered away a splash of emerging coldness.

Death was the solution to her problem.

31
A SHALLOW GRAVE

Portiuncula Chapel, Franciscan Monastery of the Holy Land in America, Washington, DC

Under the faint glow of chapel lighting, Kate knelt beside the altar, next to Mary Davidson who sat on concrete steps and sobbed. Normally, law enforcement separated a potential witness from a victim and a crime scene. But this was an exception. And these were no ordinary crimes.

The bureau needed answers.

And the God-fearing wife of an U.S. Army general needed her cage rattled a bit more.

Before them, past an altar and wrought iron gates, red begonias and mounds of dirt surrounded Sleeping Beauty, the third victim, who lay unaware of her angelic placement inside a cramped one-room chapel.

Crime scene agents started their preparations, but Kate had requested a moment with her witness.

Mary fought through her tears. "My daughter doesn't deserve to die in a shallow grave. You were supposed to save her."

Kate asked, "What kind of grave did you see? Where is your daughter?"

Mary's gaze was bound to the unresponsive woman. "No one deserves to die like this."

"Their conditions resemble that of comas. They're not dead. Not yet, anyway." Kate took a breath. "Where's Frances? What did you see in the photo shown to you?"

"Something's wrong with her chest," Mary stammered.

Kate decided a lie was easier to explain than the truth. "Don't worry about that. Think of it like a patch, something to protect her."

Mary's voice fell distant. "Rocks. Carved stones form her casket. White like tombstones. She's alone. Nothing covers her. Dirt waits beside her grave..."

"Carved stones?"

"Piled together like firewood."

"Piles of stone. Like a shrine?" Kate craned her neck to study the suspended candelabra with its ringed spokes above them. The Portiuncula Chapel represented an ORIGIN of the Franciscan Order. It too was a shrine.

Getting up, Kate lay on the concrete floor parallel to the victim, careful not to interfere with the piles of dirt or flowers. The candle-spoked light created a halo around them, but the different perspective offered little more value.

"Morgan, what are you doing?" Martinez asked.

"ORIGINS," she said, searching her memory. "St. Mary of the Angels was the first church of St. Francis. Mary, your role is important here. Why?"

"My husband?" the woman asked meekly.

"You're here to show us *The Way*." Standing, Kate gestured for agents to take Mary Davidson away so the crime scene techs could get to work.

Moving to the altar, Kate slid on plastic gloves, and examined the box Mary had carried into the chapel, the one that contained the skeleton key.

"What are you looking for?" Martinez asked, splashing the altar with illumination from his flashlight.

She studied the box and felt its weight. "He told me not to lose his tools."

The mass murderer had planned all of the details, from Mary Davidson to her instructions to the box. The skeleton key had led them to a brown-skinned parchment and the next victim.

The key unlocked ORIGINS.

Her fingers probed the ornate, hand-crafted edges of dark wood until a pair of elements shifted and unlocked the bottom of the delicate box, revealing a cavity that held a long, thin shaft.

Martinez leaned closer. "You're just full of surprises."

"It's a puzzle box."

She studied the shaft. It had a button at one end and a pinhole in the other.

Kate clicked the button and the device came alive.

"Turn off your flashlight," Kate said.

"Yeah, yeah," Martinez said, turning off his light.

The altar sparkled with a luminous watermarking.

Kate swished the magic light across the church.

"Ultraviolet," she said. "My father worked as an electrician in downtown Chicago. When I got good grades, we'd take father-daughter excursions in the tunnels below the buildings. One year, he gave me a UV reader to search for clues, while he told stories of how George Washington's Army wrote hidden messages in invisible ink to thwart the British. My interest in puzzles comes from my father. He taught me more than I wanted to know about electricity and chemistry. In Princeton," she said cracking a smile, "science came in handy."

"I bet," Martinez said.

"This looks like a Greek acropolis," she said, returning the glow of the magic pen to the altar. The detailed image followed classic Greek architecture. A letter marked each of four columns of a monument: G J W S. The columns supported a top beam. Below its Frieze in the Architrave was marked with an inscription: HIRAM.

Images flashed through Kate's mind: tunnels, SUBLEVEL markings, a neon stencil locating the ABI LAB.

She turned to Martinez. "Do we have confirmation on which government entity ran that lab at St. Elizabeths?"

He shook his head. "Not yet. SIOC is still working on it."

32
THE PURITY OF MAN

Strategic Information & Operations Center (SIOC), FBI Headquarters, Washington, DC

Will Shortz felt adrenaline course through his system as he arranged the wordplay in a fifteen-by-fifteen grid, while simultaneously putting Google search through its paces to find a METHOD TO IMPROVE HUMANS. Most listings linked to self-help solutions, mind, body, spirit, and relationships. Not helpful.

An article in Scientific American discussed *gene-editing;* was it "medicine or meddling?"

Something familiar about that question spurred a train of thought.

He almost clicked the browser's back button when he spotted an article on the ethics of gene manipulation. A troubling tangent. Opening parallel web-searches, he queried "human enhancement" and cross-referenced it with genetics.

Instinct told him to drill down on eugenics, the pseudoscience of improving human population by controlled breeding. Not a novel concept; a historically old mindset, in fact.

The practice of singular- or cross-breeding created hardier and sometimes superior stock. Selective breeding practices had influenced agriculture, animal husbandry, and human existence. Darwin had espoused selective breeding in his *On the Origin of Species* in an effort to support his theory of natural selection. The Greeks and the Spartans had practiced forms of racial purity and population control. Plato and Aristotle both spoke on the ways to supply the guardian classes with the finest possible progeny, the raw material needed to sustain a great nation. Sparta took artificial selection further to impose infanticide, discarding infants with less than desirable traits or deformities.

Eugenics, the darker and modernized view of selective breeding of humans, was a label coined by an Englishman named Francis Galton.

The term resonated in Shortz's thoughts.

Deconstruction of the human genome and advanced genetic refinement had evolved well past the old-fashioned, hand-picked notion of physical selections between mates.

A Chinese researcher had recently made headlines by manipulating human genes. His work portended an alarming future in which laboratories now offered designer baby options, if not forecasting where street corner labs could evolve to provide a new pick a baby marketplace.

Shortz scoured his memory for what he knew of the eugenics movement. Being the *New York Times* crossword puzzle editor required a broad exposure to aspects of popular culture and world history, even the darker sides of human existence.

On a roll, he tracked down references to the eugenics movement in America. In the early 1900s, state and national officials had sanctioned social regulation and enacted laws similar to Plato's views of his grand Republic. Compulsory sterilization and localized euthanasia efforts served as physical population controls among the poor, disabled, and immoral. Miscegenation laws created racial segregation and criminalized interracial marriage. Prominent business titans of the era, the likes of Carnegie, Rockefeller, Harriman, and Kellogg, financially supported a social elite class and the population purification movement.

Influenced by the writings of an American, Hitler supported a nationalized model of eugenics. At the seventh annual Nuremberg

Rally, the announcement of the "law for the protection of German blood" enforced racial hygiene and social reforms. A linked reference connected America and the Rockefeller Foundation again to Germany's early eugenics initiatives. The Lebensborn state-supported association was formed shortly thereafter, and Nazi Germany's Aryan National programs focused on strengthening a "purer" Nordic race.

He read a quote from Hitler: "Sparta must be regarded as the first Völkisch State."

And Nazi Germany was the second.

Shortz swallowed hard and slumped in his seat.

It made disturbing sense.

No handwritten side notes were needed for 29 ACROSS.

EUGENICS.

The third patch of skin served as a biography, a diary of sorts.

If his deductions were correct, the mass murdering sociopath was a genetically engineered, first generation, high IQ trained killer with Scandinavian ancestry.

A designer child from hell.

Shortz pushed back from his workstation and rushed over to Alice Watson, who was huddled around a team studying the graphical luminescence of a Greek monument. Four columns were marked with G J W S. The painting's title was HIRAM.

A technician typed a query on HIRAM.

A common puzzle clue for history buffs.

Shortz managed a tense grin. "The most famous American Hiram is Ulysses S. Grant. Civil War General. Our eighteenth President. A mistake on his academy application was the reason his name changed from Hiram Ulysses Grant." His fingers tapped each pillar. "G-J-W-S. Probably war generals. Grant. Jackson. Washington. And I think Scott."

"Soldiers' Home?" Watson directed the team to track down site locations correlating to Grant, then turned back to Shortz. "You're making it damn tough to stump the professor."

"You ought to see me with Jeopardy." He gestured to a breakout room overlooking the command center. "Let's talk about 29 ACROSS someplace private?"

33
HOME

Kate checked her watch. The bureau's speeding caravan cleared MPDC's barricades and bands of cop cars. Cemeteries marked with tombstones lined both sides of Rock Creek Church Road NW. The one on the south went by the name of Soldiers' Home, a U.S. National Cemetery. Through the front windshield, Kate spotted a three-story, Beaux-Arts, Renaissance Revival, tooled marble structure drawing closer.

"X" marked the spot.

Soldiers' Home was a massive piece of property that even included a golf course. NO TRESPASSING signs secured to fencing and a stonework boundary announced their latest stop on some sick and twisted yellow brick road.

Kate had never visited the site and knew of it only because of Lincoln's cottage, a presidential summer retreat, where Lincoln had written his preliminary draft of the Emancipation Proclamation.

What Kate saw was the Grant Building, a large structure taking up an angular intersection on the north end of the Armed Forces Retirement Home property. The SIOC team had forwarded historic preservation maps from the Library of Congress archives. Originally constructed as a dormitory and mess hall, the early 20th century relic had been shuttered by fiscal constraints and site consolidations.

Its exterior was impressive. Parts of the first story vaulted two stories high, while the roof looked like a castle with an embrasure-style parapet.

In castles, the roofline crenellation offered soldiers essential high-ground protection so they could defend the fortress from invasion.

Not a welcoming feature if you were the one doing the invading.

A mass murderer had drawn in law enforcement, knowing the government would be arriving in force.

Kate took a solemn, fearful breath.

District Fallout's posted Community Shelter Plan listed the eleven buildings at Soldiers' Home with fallout shelters. There were likely more than that. Scans of hand-drawn plans showed an enormous basement under the Grant Building—a reinforced fallout shelter capable of housing five hundred people. Additional maps revealed service tunnels spreading south underground to the Sherman Building and Stanley Hall Chapel.

The parade of SUVs ground to a halt at the Harewood Road intersection. CIRG agents bolted out of the vehicles and established a perimeter.

Kate fretted about this stop. The clues were too damn easy. Perhaps that, too, was part of the killer's plan.

"Close the charter school and the retirement home," Martinez said. "Dismiss non-essential personnel. Stage teams at the north and south entrances. We'll enter on my call." He turned to Kate. "Morgan, you're grounded. I'm not running after you this time."

She gave him a glare of objection.

"You're an observer. That's your role." His radio crackled, and the message came through Kate's earpiece. "Exterior is secured. UAVs are ready."

The UAVs—unmanned aerial vehicles—were the responsibility of a team of technicians from the bureau's Aviation Division, who were dressed in blue shirts and khakis and worked from portable consoles. A swarm of drones, each about the size of a dish plate, buzzed into the air.

Martinez had discussed the shift in operational strategy on the drive from the monastery. For better situational and tactical awareness, operations and upper management wanted UAVs as the advanced unit leading the breaches. Throw bots would follow. Then live assets: K9 teams and CIRG agents would trail the technology inside only after an "all clear" signal.

"Get us a bird's eye view," Martinez said.

Kate counted ten drones breaking out of a cluster. Four targeted the roof, four scanned through second and third floor windows, and two took up positions at the two entrances that were about to be breached.

"Roofline is clear," a female tech said over the radio.

"You guys just run with that thought," Kate said under her breath.

Martinez glanced at her. "You have something to add?"

Kate said nothing, thinking she deserved grounding after the monastery. The little stone church could have been a trap, and she would've marched everyone straight into it.

Bomb squad agents unpacked a series of backpack-sized robots, nicknamed "throw bots." Under the control of their operators, the bots darted across sidewalks and climbed the building's entry steps.

Jumping back on his radio, Martinez took up a position in front of the massive structure. "Secure your positions and get ready to advance inside."

Uneasy, Kate shuffled her feet. She pivoted to face the fenced-in U.S. National Cemetery. Rows of tombstones spread across a landscape of trees and grass, behind a Greek-style gateway. Chiseled into its street-side columns were the names of Grant, Jackson, Washington, and Scott. The corner entrance exactly matched the graphic painted on the altar in the chapel.

Stay alert, she told herself.

More CIRG agents carrying submachine guns jogged around the Grant Building to take up their station at a north entrance.

As Kate's anxiety mounted, she forced herself to turn away and stroll down the Harewood Road, where her gaze caught the names on the near endless spread of grave markers. One tombstone marked with a cross read UNKNOWN U.S. SOLDIER.

Mary Davidson had said that her daughter's shallow grave was surrounded by discarded stonework—a location vastly different than that of Soldiers' Home.

That mental picture triggered a thought. She snatched her cell phone and reluctantly typed in a number.

The call connected and a man answered. "Colonel Randall Wang."

"I should have shot you in the church when I had the chance." On her last case, she'd been coerced into supporting the U.S. Army spy colonel, a liaison to U.S. Strategic Command and CYBERCON, the U.S. Cyber Command component and Central Security Service (CSS) officer assigned to the National Security Agency (NSA).

"FBI Special Agent Morgan," Wang said. "How was your vacation? How's Thomas?"

She ignored his questions. "Saw Jack Wright this morning. In flesh and blood, no less. How'd the NSA manage Jack's resurrection?"

"My apologies, Morgan. Any life-altering circumstances he has are classified."

"By whose orders?"

There was a pause. "What kind of phone are you calling from?"

"Colonel, stop being paranoid. I deserve to know."

She heard him sigh. "Your Director. Now five of us in the world know."

"Including Dix Martinez?"

"Is that what you called about?"

"No," she snapped. "In Princeton, I did you a favor. Got suspended for it. Nearly killed. So by my math, you owe me. And I don't care what laws you have to circumvent to pay this debt. The NSA thrives in the shades of gray, so make it a priority, Colonel."

"I can't continue this conversation, Agent."

She got to the point. "I need three things, immediate and without question. One: who is RMG Global Solutions? Who are they and what details can you dig up on them? And what government contracts do they manage?"

On the drive over, she recalled Martinez mentioning RMG during a verbal brief. RMG was the only company linked to both WMATA and GSA St. Elizabeths West Campus on-call service contracts. Maybe the killer had used their contract process to gain access to both properties.

Wang cleared his throat. "Why?"

She spelled out what the bureau knew about the Metro bombing, and their theory about the mass murderer being a soldier: his stealth-like ability to move in and out of sites without detection, and the possible connection to more covert research programs.

"Okay. Your other demands?"

"What is or who is A-B-I? Who runs it, and what's it about?"

"I'll see what I can disclose."

"Lastly, you know an Army General named James Davidson?"

"Never heard of him. The Army has nearly half a million service members, not counting civilians. Three hundred of them are generals. And I don't know most of them."

Her face flushed with anger. "You're Army. He's Army. He's at the Pentagon. When you're not at Fort Meade, you're there. Find Davidson and escort him out of the building. I want to interrogate him."

"I'm not kidnapping a general for you."

East of the Washington Navy Yard, Washington, DC

Behind a string of consoles, Barnes directed an autonomous surveillance van to turn into the residential neighborhoods west of Soldiers' Home. Real-time satellite images showed MPDC's blockade had restricted access to the U.S. National Cemetery and the Armed Forces Retirement Home.

Crowds had assembled along Rock Creek Church Road to watch.

Video footage from a telescopic lens showed FBI agents mustering at the Grant Building's south main entrance. Bomb squad and drone teams had brought some toys.

Barnes grinned broadly. It was about time someone else brought technology to the festivities.

Intercepted communications came in through speakers at his console.

Beyond the official radio chatter, a cell phone call had been intercepted. Barnes heard a woman's voice in mid-conversation. "You're Army," she said. "He's Army. He's at the Pentagon. When you're not at Fort Meade you're there. Find the general and escort him out of the building. I want to interrogate him."

Katherine Morgan was assertive, demanding. Exactly how he wanted her.

"I'm not kidnapping a general for you," a man's voice said.

The call went dead.

Interesting. Major General Davidson was about to be rooted out of his bunker.

It was about damn time someone rousted his fat ass out of a chair.

The mention of Fort George G. Meade worried him. To anyone familiar with the national security apparatus, Fort Meade meant one thing: the National Security Agency. While the Army base served other functions including military intelligence, warfare operations and training, and cyber command, those initiatives were publically overshadowed by the NSA and its Puzzle Palace. If the NSA had joined the cast of characters, that represented a problem.

34
RETURN TO EDEN

St. Elizabeths, West Campus, Washington, DC

Rachel Pratt wasn't disobeying orders when she followed I-695 signs east and took the highway south across the Anacostia River. Vague orders hadn't explicitly directed her to avoid detours on the way to Dupont Circle.

And she needed the government van and its plates to return to St. Elizabeths.

Her gaze spotted an electronic bulletin board that read THREATCON CHARLIE. She took a long breath. If force protection rose to DELTA, she stood zero chance at getting on base.

At the Gate 4 visitors' center, she flashed her newly acquired military CAC ID. Coast Guardsmen swept her borrowed van before allowing her to drive onto the U.S. Coast Guard (USCG) Headquarters base. She parked in the parking garage and exited to the east.

Her first sight was the twin stacks of the old power plant—landmarks for an underground bomb shelter and secret labs. During her initiation into ABI's program, her band of lab rats had called the two spires "the goal posts."

Uneasiness washed through her. Her memories of St. Elizabeths, the ones she had managed to accept, were sterile, lifeless moments.

The loss of her Ranger comrades on the other campus made her return home feel even more hollow.

Pratt looked across to the vehicles and flashing lights on the horizon. At the Birch Street SE guard shack, she badged off the Coast Guard base and onto St. Elizabeths West Campus.

For a split second, Pratt felt time retract. A moment of déjà vu unlocked something deep inside her mind and an invading wave that she could not stop. She had returned to St. Elizabeths, back to ABI's second phase of programming. Those were days without bombings, Charlie alerts, or lockdowns. The campus' derelict buildings were the perfect disguise for what existed below. Nameless scientists and doctors controlled the west campus, a place where lab coats ruled. An endless series of testing and experiments had put an original band of twelve through their paces. Only six had survived the initial trials to progress on to Soldiers' Home and ABI's field implementation stage.

Regardless of how she once saw St. Elizabeths, back then it was Eden compared to the hell that Soldiers' Home became.

Shrugging off the memories, Pratt focused on FBI agents approaching the barricade. Stepping behind them, she held up her CAC card to security working the perimeter. Hanging close, as if she was one of them, she followed law enforcement into abandoned structures.

LED lighting lit the passages, and stairs led below. One of the agents updated the others.

"The researcher we found here," the agent said, "was put into some sort of metabolic stasis. We're not sure how he got that way. He's completely unresponsive."

"What was he doing for the Pentagon?" another man asked.

The first man chuckled. "We have no idea. It's got to be something pretty nasty for Defense to clam up like they did."

Pratt broke a faint smile. *You have no idea.*

The bottom of the stairs opened into a larger passageway.

A neon splash caught her eye. The paint markings were similar to the ones she'd seen in the tunnels leading to St. Elizabeths' east bomb shelter. Instead of her image, though, Barnes had painted ABI.

His version of bread crumbs.

Vault-like doors led to an enormous barreled-ceiling bunker.

She recognized the vast underground chamber and its labyrinth of modular labs. This was ABI's secret lab.

Memories trickled into her consciousness. Faces from the past lit up her vision. Eleven others. All soldiers. Men. Women. Different ethnic backgrounds. Different skill sets. Barnes was there, too. Their twelve-person tribe was nicknamed the Bennu, a name borrowed from the ancient Egyptian deity Bennu, a self-created being that played a role in the formation of Earth and its inhabitants.

The Bennu were to become a new generation of Perfect People, Perfect Soldiers.

Pratt forced her mind back to the present. She studied the cavernous void, now lit up as bright as heaven from work lights mounted on portable stands. Crime scene investigators had dotted the internal landscape with evidence tags. The room buzzed with uniformed personnel and people in suits.

She tracked down an unattended, open laptop computer. Its screen displayed a photo of a half-covered unconscious man. She recognized him from the blur of lab coats during ABI's research trials. In the photo, the skin covering his left breast appeared wiped blank.

She placed a hand over her own heart. Beneath her uniform and undershirt, she could feel the scar of the bullet hole.

Barnes had disfigured and mutilated his victims as a way to disclose the half-truths of the human heart.

Pratt took a breath. The victims were maimed and tortured because of her.

Moving on from the reflection, she perused cloud-based evidence logs that were filled with photos. Lots of pictures. Another human hide had been discovered providing more clues. Law enforcement had progressed to a monastery and now a cemetery.

Pratt backed away from the laptop, unable to break her gaze from the screen.

Soldiers' Home was more than a stop in the madness—it was hell on Earth.

35
THE DISCLOSURE OF SECRETS

National Security Agency (NSA) Headquarters, Fort George G. Meade, Maryland

U.S. Army Colonel Randall Wang connected the dots.

And that was not good.

Maintaining plausible deniability, the Department of Defense had distanced itself from out-of-control illegal human research programs.

Prior efforts had kept the Department of Justice and related agencies none the wiser.

Wang had made a mistake, one that put everything at risk. Taking an unsecured call from a suspended FBI Agent in the dead center of a media firestorm was a killer mistake.

In NSA headquarters, west of the CYBERCOM, he inputted his biometrics and badged into a sensitive compartmented information facility (SCIF) room and sat at a JWICS network terminal. Since the events in Princeton, the NSA had ceased its full-court press neuro-intelligence initiative, Synaptic Touch, and archived all records to an off-site, undisclosed facility.

The SCIF terminal in which he sat was required to access the intelligence he'd collected on a company called RMG Global Solutions: its financials, billing statements, operational contracts, and proprietary data.

The means by which he'd originally obtained RMG's files were illegal. Highly illegal.

But worth the risk, since his tactics yielded results that had not only benefited the NSA, but also saved his daughter's life. Without question, he'd do it all over again.

Simply put, RMG Global Solutions was an expendable pawn in a vast conspiracy.

A month ago, after Wang's deep dive into the RMG corporate networks, the company experienced an epic information technology anomaly. The catastrophic meltdown lasted days. By the time networks had been restored, his infiltration and corporate sabotage were undetectable.

Wang owed Morgan more than he could repay. Her sacrifice had won his daughter's life.

On the JWICS network, he queried master services agreement (MSA) contracts. RMG was an open book to the agency that had bootlegged copies of its corporate records.

Specific records weren't hard to track down for WMATA and St. Elizabeths Hospital. Contracts listed a third-party security and technology consultant: EyePoint Applications.

The tech company's logo mimicked the Eye of Providence, without the pyramid—the all-knowing, all-seeing eye on the back of the one-dollar bill.

That was interesting.

Wang checked EyePoint against the Pentagon and a general named Davidson. Nothing. The dead end led him to drill down on the two-star himself. Most personnel files were classified, under sensitive compartmented information (SCI) and out of reach. The career soldier's duty station was the Pentagon, where he oversaw top secret (TS) initiatives. A prior appointment listed him overseas in Pakistan, his theatre appointment under United States Central Command (USCENTCOM) counterintelligence operations.

Davidson appeared to be an "olive spy," a nickname given to spymasters within the ranks of the armed forces.

Wang sighed. He too fit that tag, but suspected their intelligence directives pursued different mission statements.

He backtracked, investigating associations between Davidson and research projects. While Wang's own security clearance had limits, he assembled enough tangential pieces. As a principal investigator, Davidson had transitioned from intelligence to research. A photo taken during a fundraising banquet showed him with his wife, Mary, an extremely accomplished medical researcher in her own right, and his daughter, Frances, who had followed her mother's career path.

Davidson oversaw work called the Advanced Biogenetics Initiative (ABI), a tentpole with governance over several subordinate programs. Its secretive research dated back to the 1940s and once carried the name of *The Perfect People Initiative* until it was restructured to ABI, with a core focus on advancing human evolution (AHE).

A series of snapshots put ABI into clearer focus and gave it a home base. A memo authorized user agreements for mothballed portions of the insane asylum and permitted ABI to set up a base of operations at the semi-dormant facility.

Wang was not easily shocked, but this shocked him. The Pentagon had sought to create genetic improvements and human replication through DNA modifications.

ABI was in the business of building Captain Rogers-like super soldiers.

That meant Army Major General James Davidson was a very dangerous man.

Troubled, Wang shook his head. He needed to visit St. Elizabeths.

36
SLUMBERING HEARTS

The Grant Building, Soldiers Home, Washington, DC

Dix Martinez watched drone masters and whiz kids do their thing. The Aviation Section's cadre of modern-era tech junkies scared the hell out of him with what they could do with children's toys.

Behind a barricade of mobile monitors and control stations on a treed lawn, the techs worked their magic. Video feeds relayed images from the small fleet of aerial drones entering the structure: two each on the south and north fronts, one low and one high. Third-story windows had been taken out in the maneuver called a strafing run. As an arsenal, drone breaches and intelligent forward observation activities required constant communication signals. In a monolith like the Grant Building, keeping signal communication linked was a challenge. That was where the bomb squad's small footprint throw bots came in handy. The bread loaf-sized robots served as "boots on the ground" foot soldiers equipped with antenna repeaters, allowing all of the bureau's gizmos and gadgets to communicate inside the dense structure.

Martinez scanned the monitors. Three birds called "eagle eyes" hung back, one on each south and north face and one hovering directly over the boxed-in courtyard. The exterior drones captured the gothic and classical revival arcades, parapets, and high-relief eagle decorations. Interior building spaces flashed across the monitors as if this surveillance was an everyday occurrence.

The drone operators ran with their own lingo, their voices taking turns on the comms.

"Infrared is blue," one of the techs said, pointing at a screen. "Heat signatures non-existent. Hey guys, we have some Jell-O on drone five. Clean up that video."

"Roger that."

"On lower levels, the dense structure is interfering with signal acuity."

"Air samples register no definable contaminants."

"Increase altitude on ten and pan out. Four, maneuver to the room on the right."

Martinez keyed his radio and said, "K-9s move ahead and hold at the entries."

He noticed that Morgan stepped beside him.

"Where'd you go?" he asked, without glancing her way.

"I had to make a call."

"Not to that professor, I hope."

She shook her head.

"Ops, what's your call? We're picking up nothing here."

"Standby, over," a voice said over comms. After a long pause the announcement came as expected. "CIRG is cleared to engage. Proceed with caution. Over."

Martinez clicked his comms. "K-9s and forward teams, advance. Any sign of danger, retrieve your dogs and get the hell out. Be sharp people."

The drones captured handlers releasing their dogs, and the first wave of armed agents stormed the building.

"You're an observer." Martinez tapped the patch on front of Morgan's bullet-resistant vest and tugged on her helmet. "Not an inch closer."

If she was disappointed by his directions, he couldn't tell. He pivoted back to displays that showed tall open rooms, void of furnishings. Infrared scans still showed panoramic realms of blue and green, and the swift movement of orange-yellow shapes into the structure. Original building plans and photographs had indicated an open first floor layout as a mash of dining and interior sports spaces. A vast basement functioned as storage. Upper floors were relegated to dormitory-style rooms.

Snatching up his H&K MP5 submachine gun, Martinez fell in behind CIRG's advance team, bounding up front steps and into the Grant Building's main entry.

Inside, the views were exactly as they appeared on the drones' cameras.

Radio chatter marked the progressions of CIRG agents progressing into deeper areas of the massive building. Below, a forward team had worked its way into basement levels.

"Ops?" a voice from one of the CIRG agents said. "You seeing this recent construction? It looks like new vent piping and tubular ductwork. These upgrades never appeared on the drawings. Over."

Martinez stopped in his tracks when he spotted stenciled signage on the walls.

The neon welcome sign glowed: ABI.

The same signature as the one found in the bunker at St. Elizabeths.

Mind-sight antennas crackled with concern.

"K9," he asked, "anything to report? Over." No human or electro-mechanical sensor mounted to any drone could match what dogs did for law enforcement. Bomb-trained canines had indispensable senses and the capacity to detect 19,000 explosive combinations.

"Nothing so far."

Kate stood beside the drone operators and pointed to a screen.

"Where's that one?" she asked. "Can you back up on that image?"

"Seven," he said, "fall back a bit." He pinpointed its location on a three-dimensional map of the building. "Upper floor. West quadrant."

She circled her finger to the right. "No. No. Go that way."

The fresh-out-of-college operator cringed. "Really?"

"Yeah. Make it go into that hallway."

"Seven. Redirect. Head down the north-south corridor."

Kate pursed her lips and nodded.

Fourth floor room numbers panned by the lens of the drone. The number 1236 marked an open doorway.

"Stop!" She jutted a finger at the screen. "There. Take it in that room."

Her face flushed. Not a number she'd soon forget. She turned over her wrist to expose the faded sequence on her skin. 1236. The number she'd been assigned after the Metro bombing, the combination to a briefcase that she'd never owned.

"Lead, I'm registering a heat signature," a voice said over the comms.

"Confirmed," said the drone manager. He brought up an infrared map that identified a long, rectangular orange and yellow shape on the floor placed up against a side wall, out of sight of the doorway. "Proceed into the room."

The image on the screen squeezed through a doorway and swung to its left.

On the floor, a man lay naked, face up, with his hands at his sides.

Kate took a ragged breath as the drone's camera zoomed in to relay the obvious.

In its usual spot, skin had been replaced.

Scrawled on his right breast were the words THE BATTLELINE BETWEEN GOOD AND EVIL RUNS THROUGH THE HEART OF EVERY MAN. AND THIS SLUMBERING HEART CANNOT BE REDEEMED.

"Martinez," the drone lead announced, "one male has been located on the upper floor in a room off the north-south corridor. He may be the next victim. Over."

Martinez cupped his earpiece, making sure what he was hearing from other agents was correct.

The barrage of simultaneous conversations started to come across comms all at the same time. Something about a victim? Mechanical systems? Pumps?

"Mechanical?" he said into his comms. "Repeat what you just said. Over?"

Across the comms, a CIRG agent in the basement advanced team said, "A series of pumps have come online and there's some pressure gauges that are spiking. Some sort of fuel system is being charged."

Martinez shouted into his comms. "Fall back! Everyone out! Now! Fall back!"

37
PREEMPTIVE STRIKES

East of Washington Navy Yard, Washington, DC

Frantically, Barnes worked consoles communicating with his autonomous van parked west of the Grant Building at Soldiers' Home. Real-time satellite images forwarded what he couldn't see from long distance surveillance cameras mounted on the van. Interactive overhead imaging had the capability to tag and track specific individuals. Katherine Morgan's location was referenced as she stood behind mobile stands that operators used to control the bureau's drone fleet and robots.

Two-way law enforcement radio chatter played across speakers and provided additional audio cues.

The FBI had deployed drones, robots, canine, and first and second wave advanced teams into the dormant structure.

Law enforcement seemed to be all in. Now it was his turn.

On a screen, a progress bar stretched to 100%. Systems were fully charged and exactly what he needed.

On other screens he initialized offensive measures.

Tracking systems targeted the drones first.

Barnes tapped a red button. The displays before him relayed what he knew was coming next.

Concealed inside the roof of his autonomous van, an EMP cannon released a single blast.

Screens displaying satellite mapping fuzzed over before recrystallizing back into view.

Static overtook audio communications.

The three drones that buzzed above the Grant Building dropped from the sky like dead flies.

Outside the building, peripheral agents seemed paralyzed, their momentary inaction a symptom of lost electronics and communications.

A figure who had huddled near the drone operators broke into a sprint.

Katherine Morgan was joining the fray.

Barnes typed in a line of executable code at a command prompt and clicked ENTER.

On screen, the square-ringed building flashed orange as concussive blasts radiated beyond its walls. Cascading waves pulsed rings of fire. Vents along the roofline erupted like volcanoes.

Bodies fled the Grant Building, some collapsing on the sidewalks outside.

The FBI agent at the center of his grand plan lay immobile, hurled backward by the very force that she had sought to enter.

Barnes rose from his seat and took a sharp breath.

Katherine Morgan had died before the strike of midnight. Her fate had been predestined, inevitable, whether it occurred early or on the last stop.

38
LOST COMMUNICATIONS

Strategical Information & Operations Center (SIOC), FBI Headquarters, Washington, DC

Death. Destruction. The raid seemed to have been doomed from the start.

"Agents are down!" shouted a technician.

Will Shortz took a shocked breath. The images were horrific. The moment surreal. On the screens, agents had entered the building. Then a dark neon consumed the screens. When images rematerialized, churning rings of fire billowed smoke upward. Debris was everywhere. Bodies were scattered like dominoes. The air grew black as smoke restricted satellite visibility.

The SIOC Unit Chief Alice Watson took over and directed traffic. "Dispatch first responders and fire departments. Establish a direct line with MPDC command. We'll need everyone they can free up. Alert Providence and Howard University hospitals. They'll have incoming. Come on, work the scene. Take care of our people."

"Active scene communications on site are down," someone else called out.

Shortz studied Watson's demeanor: resolute, confident. It was as if she'd rehearsed this kind of catastrophe before, as if any amount of training could prepare her for a disaster of this magnitude.

Conversations hummed across the room. A constant, rapid fervor grew as SIOC personnel took their cues and went to work.

A mass murderer had set his sights firmly on anyone who got in his way.

Shortz reflected on what he knew from the clues and what he'd been told from initial FBI profile assessments: a single killer or small, tight-knit group of killers; while males, ex-military, over the age of twenty-five, consumed with resentment, anger. Associations with EUGENICS. Throw in explosives training, and they were a national threat.

Shortz knew what he needed to do: work his version of the situation before this murderous lunatic hurt more people.

Unable to add value to the disaster response, Shortz uncabled his bureau-issued laptop, snatched up a writing tablet, and found solace in the conference room adjoining the SIOC.

He took a seat at a conference room table and tried a different tack on laying out answers and constructing a puzzle. A fifteen-by-fifteen grid with random word assignments felt more like Scrabble than actually solving a crossword—form-fitting letters and intersections based on gut instinct.

Each destination in the mass murder's pick-a-stop tourist map offered unique clues and another victim.

At least until Soldiers' Home, when everything went up in flames.

39
FIELD RESEARCH

St. Elizabeths, West Campus, Washington, DC

Wearing his class B Army service uniform, NSA Colonel Randall Wang cleared security, even though threat conditions had risen to THREATCON DELTA. The attack at Soldiers' Home put all federal sites on the east coast on lockdown.

No personnel were permitted to enter or leave the premise. Exceptions to that policy were rare. Luckily, Wang was one of those rare exceptions, after a call from the Deputy Chief's Central Security Service office.

Site security escorted Wang to the underground bunker. Stenciled markings on corridor walls announced their arrival. ABI's use of the massive underground bomb shelter was impressive as modular labs dotted its vast floor space.

In typical Department of Defense fashion, the Pentagon released boilerplate narratives and stonewalled all inquiries, citing national security concerns. An eleventh-hour staff shuffle made General Davidson disappear into thin air.

The Pentagon's business was now in public view as the nation's capital lay under siege by one of its own. An ex-soldier. Likely one of their lab rats. On the drive over, Wang had listened to radio news updates on the morning's Metro bombing; a bombing on St. Elizabeths East that killed five soldiers and injured one, the sole survivor of that bombing now a person of interest in a murder investigation of a nurse at a hospital; and the bombing at Soldiers' Home.

A malcontent with a vendetta was picking apart Washington, DC, one piece at a time.

"Colonel Wang," the bureau's crime scene manager said. "Glad to have the NSA's assistance on this. We need all the help we can get."

"Sorry to hear about your agents at Soldiers' Home," Wang said as they shook hands.

The man nodded solemnly.

Wang looked around the domed bunker and took in the array of white lab-in-a-box popups. The manager provided an abbreviated brief tour. Evidence tags marked equipment and labeled rooms.

"What was the function of these labs?" Wang asked, not wanting to reveal information he already had gathered.

"We're still collecting that information."

Wang grabbed the man's arm. "That's not an answer. What's your hunch? What did the last users do here?"

The man hesitated before answering. "It's only a rumor, but it's connected to genetic, cognitive, and human performance testing. On soldiers."

Wang withdrew his hand, content to play along. "Well, that's news."

What had Morgan gotten herself mixed up in?

The manager fired up a laptop. Images came quickly. Two victims. A man. A woman. Naked. The skin on their chests looked odd.

"Are they dead?" Wang asked.

"No. They're in some sort of induced coma."

The statement rocked him and he forced himself to catch his breath. In Princeton, victims had been placed into chemically induced comas so experiments could be performed on them. His daughter had been one of those victims.

"What do we know about the man, the woman?" he asked.

"They're researchers." The agent rattled off additional facts: what was known about the victims; their ties to DoD research; that each had gone missing more than a week ago.

Wang absorbed the information. Beyond his authorized divergences into international and domestic espionage, his core skillset included encryption, cryptography, and computer systems analytics. And to some degree offensive hacking. He and his band of NSA cyber-freaks faced countless, anonymous combatants and foreign state-sponsored actors. In the daily grind of their cyber-worlds, the shadowy games employed by those attacking the United States and its allies were numerous. He had learned to understand the tactics of adversaries.

Being an intelligence operative was a lot like being an assassin.

That was the case here.

Clever, really. One of the best offensive strategies was to lead your prey to the killing field rather than perform your business in public view.

This domestic terrorist, a modern merchant of death, had devised his murderous game not for simple amusement, but for revenge. The casualties of his actions would be circumstantial, but necessary.

The scheme was meant to tear down and expose secrets.

Wang took a breath. It seemed he needed to see a man about a girl.

40
ARTIFACTS OF THOUGHT

The Grant Building, Soldiers Home, Washington, DC

Kate awoke to something burning in her lungs. She coughed, expelling air saturated with petroleum fumes. Her entire body ached. The ringing in her ears was relentless. Her dulled mind could not process time any faster. It took several attempts to roll onto her back. Her face and hands tingled and felt hot. Drained of strength, sitting up seemed impossible. Dark, churning clouds hung above her like a wraith hovering over a battlefield. Death had come to claim the fallen.

A heavy sky had turned orange, almost bloodlike in spots. Fire licked at building openings, places where doors and windows had been. Another bombing. No one inside could have survived the explosion.

Kate closed her eyes and did the only thing she could, cough.

Her mind felt heavy, tired.

This was her morning commute all over again. The tally of innocent people dying for her perceived sins had increased again.

Muffled shouts mixed with screams rumbled in the distance.

She managed to crane her head up just enough to take in the pandemonium. Around her, patches of grass were on fire as low-burning flames fed their own plumes of smoke. Bodies of agents and police officers lay on the ground. From the neighborhoods to the west, civilians sprinted toward them and climbed over the perimeter fencing.

Kate closed her eyes again as heaviness overtook her. She needed to rest a bit.

Dropping her head back, she heard the muted thump of her helmet against the concrete sidewalk. Inside her battered thoughts, she saw U.S. Army Captain Pratt staring down at her from the blown-out windows of an overturned train. Smoke and fire filled that world too. The story of Pratt coming to the rescue and saving survivors was a lie. The Army captain was there because an anonymous message had told Pratt to find her at the Metro and hinted at 13 ACROSS.

Something about Pratt didn't add up.

Kate wanted to be angry at her, but sensed they had a vague kinship. Some distorted interaction with a terrorist? What sins did Pratt have to pay for?

Her mind slipped deeper toward sleep, eyelids already locked closed. An emerging dream drowned out the distant noises and voices and the ringing in her ears.

Memories percolated in her dream. Pratt directed her to turn over her wrist. 1236 marked her flesh. It was a random number assigned by a WMATA worker in the Metro.

1236. The magic trick number worked like a key or landmark. The four digits matched a briefcase containing the first clues. At St. Elizabeths it led to a room designated as CYTOGENTICS. The Grant Building offered a third victim, a man, lying on the floor. His body was muscular, as if he were a Greek god cut from stone. Fire swept into the room, causing the man to bolt awake and scream in terror. His eyes glowed red. The proclamation on his chest became clearer: AND THIS SLUMBERING HEART CANNOT BE REDEEMED.

The victim had been sacrificed in the inferno.

Why was that man different than the others, who were meant to be found and paired with clues? In her dream, Kate returned to Portiuncula Chapel, St. Mary of the Angels Church, at the Franciscan Monastery of the Holy Land. She knelt on a hard concrete floor. Between her and a stone altar was a sleeping woman dressed in white silk like a Renaissance angel. Mounds of dirt and red begonias encircled her.

It was a place where 1236 was relevant but not welcomed.

Its presence or lack thereof was significant.

And how did Pratt even know about the digits on her wrist?

Elements of that mystery remained out of reach.

Outward pressure compressed her body, driving hot tingling sensations across the surface of her skin. Her dreams wrinkled in and out. She found herself standing inside the Grant Building beside Martinez and the other CIRG agents. She screamed, but no sounds left her mouth. Their eyes widened in horror. Bright flashes consumed them and she was violently thrown back. Throbbing pains preceded motions of pitching and rolling. She felt as if she lay in the bottom of a boat as it drifted on a torrent of water at the top of a geyser.

Her world was about to erupt.

Her booted feet tugged at her torso. Something was happening.

Somewhere distant, sirens sounded.

Kate commanded her eyes to blink open.

Heat splashed her face and tired eyes locked onto the raging fireball devouring the Grant Building. Above, smoke blotted out sunlight as an orange colored day turned to night.

Treetops smoldered and dripped chunks of ash to the ground.

Arms took hold of her. People were dragging her to safety.

"Stop," she said.

A building that she vaguely recalled as Stanley Hall Chapel came into view.

A group of civilians set down her down at a stretch of curb, far away from the glowing carcass of the Grant Building.

Others had been placed around her. Some of them were corpses.

"Are you injured?" asked a woman. The name badge on her scrubs identified her as from the Armed Forces Retirement Home. "Do you need medical attention?"

Not the first time she'd been asked that questions since the day began.

Kate shook her head. She was alive enough. Nothing felt broken or dislocated. She performed her own quick assessment: wheezing meant a constricted airway brought on by fumes; the ringing in her ears was a result of the concussive blast; a heavy head with slowed thoughts and the moment she blacked out meant she'd probably sustained a concussion. Other than that, she was alive enough.

"How many made it out?" she finally asked through a half-cough.

The nurse's expression flattened. "Not many."

"I'm fine," Kate said, allowing her voice to trail off. "Go tend to others."

The woman nodded. "Speak up if you need anything."

Kate unbuckled the chin strap to her helmet and tossed it aside. Agony seized her spine as she rolled to all fours and forced herself to stand. Her gaze seemed like a compass needle drawn to magnetic north as it locked onto the bank of fire enveloping the distant structure.

Staggering to a tree trunk, she steadied herself and prayed that by some miracle Martinez and his CIRG agents had made it out.

41
SCRABBLE

An empty stomach drove Will Shortz to the cafeteria. A fan of sorts intercepted him as he mulled over deli choices. Special Agent Betsy Carrick had recognized him from several TV appearances and a documentary called *Wordplay*.

"I love hearing you on NPR," she said.

Shortz took the praise in stride, grateful for any relief from the grimness that had engulfed the bureau—the dead, the injured, the missing. He assumed she had drawn her conclusions about why he might be assisting the FBI. They continued chitchat through the cashier station.

He paid for a tortilla chicken wrap and root beer to go.

"Mr. Shortz, you need anything?" Agent Carrick asked as he started to leave. "Is there anything I can get for you?"

The question caught him off guard. His response came out clumsy. "Scrabble."

Agent Carrick cocked her head. "I'll see what I can do about that."

Ten minutes later, two vintage board games showed up in the SIOC. Brittle and yellow tape held together well-used game boxes.

Scrabble.

Intruigued with his new layout flexibility, Shortz dumped the game tiles into a pile on the SIOC's conference room table. His fingertips slid wooden squares into place. Sticky notes marked the boundary of a fifteen-by-fifteen frame. Instinct ran ahead of his brain as he shuffled etched letters. Concentrating on the knowns, he let his movements settle into a rhythm. This insane terrorism was rule-based, even if the scheme deviated from traditional crossword puzzle standards.

Here abbreviations and asymmetry were allowed.

8 DOWN, ELISION, became the top right boundary.

With the marquee theme in play, 13 ACROSS—MURDER—went three lines down and centered. 5 DOWN, TODAY, intersected with the D in MURDER.

In the bottom right, 70 ACROSS—SAPPER—and its ending R completed 45 DOWN, SHELTER.

The remaining knowns took shape and a landscape started to emerge.

Alice Watson entered the conference room and punched a button on a speaker phone in the center of the table.

She raised a skeptical eyebrow. "You're playing a board game?"

Shortz cracked a grin. "Oxyphenbutazone racks up 1778 points."

Watson rolled her eyes. "I just thought you played ping pong when you weren't making up puzzles."

He chuckled. "I edit—clues, mostly. And it's table tennis."

"Go ahead, Morgan," she said into the phone. "You asked about a number?"

He hadn't heard she'd been confirmed among the survivors.

Over the phone, Morgan coughed. Her voice sounded raspy, strained. "Twelve-thirty-six. Repeat. One-two-three-six. What's its significance? Why didn't we see the number at the monastery?"

42
THE WINDOWS HAVE EYES

Stanley Hall Chapel, Soldiers Home, Washington, DC

Kate returned a borrowed cell phone to a paramedic. Hers, and everyone's who was on the scene at the time of the explosion, had mysteriously stopped working. Not a coincidence.

Staggering toward the building's burning carcass, she left first responders and the retirement home's doctors and nurses to perform triage. The thick, tainted air made breathing difficult as she continued to wheeze. The ringing in her ears evoked her earlier participation in a sonic attack.

She walked like a zombie, thinking of the words inscribed for her at the monastery. TREAD THE PATH OF FOOTSTEPS IN THE GRASS LEST YOU MISSTEP. The translation of the companion sentence drove home the terrorist's real message: A SHORT LIFE FORBIDS US LONG HOPE. The goal was not only terror, but despair.

This stop was meant to tear her down further and shake up law enforcement even more.

Kate stepped off the sidewalk and into the grass. Charred spots looked like a giant's game of hopscotch.

Fire trucks had arrived and fire fighters disembarked to combat a diminishing fire, which seemed to have lost its source of fuel. By nightfall, only blackened stonework would remain.

Falling to her knees, Kate let emotions and exhaustion overtake her. Her eyes stung as tears mixed with smoke and ash. Tears flowed easily, not because of physical pain but because a madman's vendetta had callously claimed so many lives—husbands and wives, sons and daughters, brethren and sisters in law enforcement. People she'd spent the day with. The disregard for human life, beginning with the deaths on the Metro, was staggering. Tiny daggers, one for each death, pierced her heart. She clutched her chest, where the patches of skin had been stripped away from each victim. She thought of Frances Davidson in a shallow, unmarked grave waiting to be found.

More stops had been promised, and somehow the killer's treacherous game needed to end.

Kate took a ragged breath and dried her eyes. Fighting through sniffles she concentrated on the victim who'd yet to be found—the DARPA medical researcher, Frances Davidson. A general's daughter. Kate let Mary Davidson's description of the photo cycle through her mind, a mother's words. Old stones surrounded an open hole. Dirt waited to be dispersed over the body. Dirt mounds had circled the victim in the monastery chapel as well. The scenes mirrored each other.

Old church. Old stones.

She cocked her head to take in Stanley Hall towering beside her. Another chapel.

And a place for her to atone for her sins. For the murder of a madman's family.

Staggering to her feet, she gazed up at the marbled structure, its exterior washed in orange hues, its windows reflecting the Grant Building's fire.

High above, at the center of an attic's tight grouping of three arched windows, she spotted a figure dressed in white. The figure was back-lit, ghost-like.

Kate thought of the victim in the Portiuncula Chapel.

An angel in Mary's chapel.

The ringing in her ears disappeared as clarity hit her.

The terrorist had told her at St. Elizabeths, "Log the tour. Seek the truth. Earn my rewards. Save those you can. Lose my tools and people die."

Shoving a hand into a pocket, she retrieved the ultraviolet flashlight that had been in the keepsake box at the monastery, then trudged up the marble steps leading to the chapel.

She panned the killer's decoder light across the chapel's heavy doors, revealing—again—the number 1236.

One hand dropped to her sidearm while the other grasped the door's ornate handle. Its knob squeaked as it turned. She withdrew her semi-automatic. The heavy door required extra force to open, so she gave it a hard bump with her shoulder. Iron hinges moaned as the door swung open and faint lighting greeted her.

Through the interior doors of an entry vestibule, she saw past the nave to the chancel area at the far end of the church.

Kate took a calming breath. Entering an old church with ghosts lurking in its attic right after a terrorist had set off an inferno was the definition of stupidity. Doubling down on stupidity was going in alone—without backup.

Ripping off her OBSERVER patch, she discarded it on the steps of the church.

Only one thing was waiting inside, and she was determined not to keep trouble waiting.

"FBI!" she yelled. "Anyone in here?"

Her words echoed, but produced no response.

"FBI! If anyone's in here, time to speak up!"

She was surprised to see the chapel deserted. It could have been used for triage, or at least a place to lay corpses.

After swapping out the black light for a conventional flashlight, Kate set one boot in front of the other and pressed forward behind the notch and knob sights of her Glock. The first time she'd ever drawn her weapon in the field was in a church.

Her vision swept across the Protestant chapel. Casting the flashlight's beam toward the ceiling, she scanned for sonic devices or anything else that could render her paralyzed and helpless. It wasn't an experience she needed to repeat.

The bombing's heavy smoke had turned the outside day to night, restricting sunlight into the chapel. Thick haze collected near the ceiling. An orange cast penetrated west windows, turning the chapel's interior to a muted tawny color.

Planked flooring creaked beneath her as she moved past pews. Keeping her weapon moving, she cleared hiding spots, seeking to avoid another ambush.

Light shone through stained glass motifs and onto a communion table. An artist's renderings retold Old and New Testament stories, except for the panel that featured a saint-like, battle-dressed George Washington knelt in reverent prayer. A wooden cross hung on the chancel's back wall.

Kate tensed as she approached the illuminated communion table. Unlike the Portiuncula Chapel's altar, this centerpiece was constructed of wood. In the chancel area, twin wall-mounted lights fulfilled a dual purpose. The first lit the table. The second beamed diagonally across the church, like Gotham's bat signal. Batman would be a welcome addition to the team, she thought.

What she had seen from the outside was neither a person nor a ghost. It was backlight.

Stupidity and vanity had led her into a terrorist's murderous sights. Again.

Where the hell was Batman when she needed him?

Kate was about to retreat when she noticed objects on the communion table.

Bait.

43
BREAKS IN THE CASE

Strategic Information & Operations Center (SIOC), FBI Headquarters, Washington, DC

With his heart pounding, Will Short tracked down Alice Watson.

She was entrenched in heated discussions with several technicians. They stood in front of active satellite maps that radiated off the big board. One screen showed a haze-filled landscape. The other offered a crystal clear view of Soldiers' Home.

He sensed presenting a year in history needed to wait.

"Don't tell me what you think you know," she said, pointing at the screens. "Tell me what you do know."

A technician cleared his throat. "It's a two-pronged assault. The first wave hit before the explosions."

The technician typed at a computer terminal and moved one of the satellite images forward in time, progressing through bird's eye fractional moments. A digital clock reported the time. Seen from above, agents stormed the Grant Building. A clear distance back, a semi-circle of agents worked behind mobile stations. Three drones hovered: north, south, and center. A splash washed across the screen like a dark spectrum of neon paint, sweeping from left to right. Before the incremental energy wave crested, each drone dropped from the sky. The entire screen flared up and finally went black.

"I'm telling you, it's electromagnetic," the technician said.

"You're positive?" Watson asked.

Shortz knew this had something to do with EMP: an electromagnetic pulse.

"That explains how the blast took out our electronics and communications," said another technician, this one stockier than the first.

A mathematical waveform with green lines and degree vectors was overlaid onto the satellite map. The sky high view was replayed. The dark neon spread across the modeled representation.

Alice Watson processed the information. "But it wasn't nuclear?"

"It's not." The technician cupped his hands before moving them apart as if he was tugging on invisible strands of string. "I know you're linking events to fallout shelters, but a fission blast behaves differently. And, hey, we're missing the whole mushroom cloud, end-of-the-world thermonuclear part of that equation."

A man in a khaki uniform squeezed into the conversation. "It was a tactical, close-range weapon. The Chinese, Russians, Brits are working on similar tech. DARPA and the Air Force Research Labs developed the precision strike EMP cannon years ago. The Air Force tested its multi-domain technology for use in game-changing, hypersonic intercept vehicles. The fuel-to-weight ratio proved challenging, so we repurposed the asset to platform solutions, ship- and ground-based countermeasures."

Shortz noticed the officer's silver eagle and shield insignia pin on his collared shirt. For Navy, he was a long way from a naval port or ship. Most likely on loan from the Pentagon, he thought.

Watson turned to the screens. "So we're dealing with military tech?"

The naval officer handed her a tubular device. "Your terrorist has access to a great number of toys. Compliments of the Defense Intelligence Agency."

"What's that?" asked one of the technicians, beating Watson to the question.

The naval officer said, "A hundred thousand dollar dog whistle. A device that is so sophisticated it can debilitate one person standing in a crowd. It's nearly lethal. The intelligence community calls it configurable sonic deployment."

Frustration painted Watson's expression as she passed over the spy tech to others for their study.

"This was what was used in the Cuba embassy attack?" the first technician asked.

The Navy officer offered a non-committal shrug.

"Don't forget China." The stocky technician chuckled. "Oh, you Navy folk just love your whistles." The man's forearms displayed U.S. Marine tattoos. Obviously there was an ongoing joke between the two concerning the Navy's use of Bosun's calls.

"You're not the first to imply the terrorist or terrorists are ex-military," Watson said as a statement, not a question. She tossed a hard glare at Shortz, her gaze telling him not to add to the conversation. "You have any names for us, or is that wishful thinking?"

The Navy man shook his head.

Watson never took her eyes off Shortz as he reflected on 29 ACROSS—EUGENICS—METHOD TO IMPROVE HUMANS.

He kept that solution to himself.

"How'd bad actors get access to military tech?" Watson asked. "There's got to be a breach in security."

"We're investigating leads just like you are."

Watson frowned. "I bet you guys are doing a stellar job at it."

The flashlight-sized device made its way around the circle and ended up in Shortz's hands. He felt its weight and studied its configuration. A fish-eye lens capped the end of a long black tube. It looked and felt like precision machinery.

The ex-Marine technician redirected the conversation to the satellite screens, dialing back to seconds before the blast. "The blast originated here. Can a vehicle of this size deploy an EMP cannon?"

The neighborhood scene was expanded to zoom in on a black van.

The Naval officer gave a half-committed shrug. "It's possible."

Watson sighed. "Track down that van. Make it a priority, people."

44
THE INQUISITION

Shortz closed the conference room door behind Alice Watson. She clicked a button on the wall and the glass windows overlooking the SIOC hazed over, keeping their conversation out of view from the ops center.

"Tell me about 1236," she said.

He cleared his throat. "If the number represents a year, it ties back to the Franciscans."

Watson nodded for him to continue.

"The 13th century. The High Middle Ages. Europe. The year gave us the typical monarchial marriages, deaths and births, one nation invading another. The Catholic Church and its papal power dominated and fueled the campaigns of the crusades. 1236 is ten years after the death of Giovanni di Pietro di Bernardone, Saint Francis of Assisi. In 1209, Francis met with Pope Innocent III and asked permission to form the Friars Minor. The caps of their heads were shaved, tonsured, to demonstrate obedience to the church. Innocent III was no different from other papal autocrats. The church, by its ordination from God, ruled over all earthly kingdoms. Dissidence and heresy, anything that challenged the church's authority, couldn't be tolerated. Outlier sects who did not kneel before papal rule were crushed. Inquisitions and mob lynchings became tools of the emboldened."

"And this is relevant how?" Watson asked.

"I'm getting there," Shortz said. "Two Popes later, Gregory IX established a semi-legal process to address heresy. Under Gregory, the sovereign church ordained the Franciscan and Dominican Orders as inquisitors. From their power structures rose the real inquisitors of the Catholic Church."

Shortz pointed to his SCRABBLE outlay on the table.

Watson's eyes tracked his fingers to the corner Post-it note tagged 69 ACROSS.

"STIGMA," she said, her expression etched with concern.

"1236 was the year when the Franciscans became inquisitors. Probably not what a man who'd taken on the wounds of his Lord and Savior would have ever wanted."

Her eyebrows narrowed. "Your conclusion?"

Shortz took a seat and glanced crosswise over the SCRABBLE tiles.

Beside him, Watson leaned against the table and exhaled tension.

A hundred questions filled Shortz's head. "Sorry about your agents," he finally said, without answering her question.

Her voice fell reminiscent. "I spent time with our CIRG field units before moving to SIOC as a unit chief. Knew some of them. They were good people. They'll be missed."

Shortz dragged a breath between his teeth. He plucked an A and an E from a pile of wooden tiles and placed them beside 43 DOWN—BETA—and intersecting the H in LOG THE TOURS.

AHE. They'd seen the declaration at St. Elizabeths.

He squirmed in his seat. "A total guess in my part. Advancing human evolution."

She fixed her gaze on him. "Our perpetrators are a new race of super soldiers with security clearances and vendettas against the church?"

He shook his head. "Not against the church. Against those who made them. It's a statement about the hypocrisy of those who create BETA subjects."

"ELISION?" Watson asked.

He nodded. "The merging of abstract ideas."

She logged into a computer terminal and loaded video on a large wall monitor. "This was recorded right before the EMP blast."

Flight log info accompanied the video, information he didn't comprehend. Among the techno-gibberish, he figured out DRONE 7, time stamps, and GPS coordinates.

The drone buzzed through the upper hallways of the Grant Building. 1236 identified a doorway. A heat signature overlaid a corner of the video. The drone floated into the room and panned around. On the floor, in a corner, was an unconscious man. Scrawled across his right breast was a message. His left was virgin canvas. A tattoo marked his arm.

Watson zoomed in on the video. She froze the message and rotated it, making it easier to read.

THE BATTLE LINE BETWEEN GOOD AND EVIL RUNS THROUGH THE HEART OF EVERY MAN. AND THIS SLUMBERING HEART CANNOT BE REDEEMED.

The quote sounded familiar. Using his laptop, Shortz tracked it down.

He frowned. "Solzhenitsyn. A Russian writer."

"And its meaning?"

"There could be a couple of tangents," Shortz said. "Aleksandr Solzhenitsyn was imprisoned for writing anti-Soviet propaganda. He was critical of Stalin's Soviet Union. *The Gulag Archipelago* won him a Nobel Prize. Perhaps your genetically enhanced rogue soldier wants to expose the evil that he himself endured and separate the wheat from the chaff."

Shortz pointed to the man with a message on his chest. "Law enforcement was never supposed to reach this guy. Check out his arm. A Marine."

"Another soldier." Watson leaned in closer. "What if this fella was one of them? Family of sorts? An enhanced super soldier?"

Shortz shrugged. "Maybe that's why he was out-of-bounds to us."

45
EXPOSURE

East of the Washington Navy Yard, Washington, DC

Phillip Barnes took a moment to collect his thoughts, scarcely believing events materialized so close to his charted course. The bombing of the Grant Building had gone over the top, and weakened his cloak of invisibility. Up to this point he had had the opportunity to slip into the darkness, drop off the grid, and disappear. It was too late for that now. He had cemented his path. He could not turn back. He could not escape. He felt even more driven to finish what he'd started, even if that meant every DC cop and surveillance satellite would be looking for his autonomous vehicles.

Discovering the van would ultimately lead authorities to the Washington Navy Yard. At least his actions had set back law enforcement and stymied their efforts.

The satisfaction of his contest had diminished slightly, though. It wouldn't be the same without FBI Special Agent Katherine Morgan. Her proximity to the blast made survival unlikely.

Unleashing the combustibles a fraction earlier could have saved her life. Because of that error, Katherine Morgan had received her sentence early—the consequence for killing his family.

Barnes searched his memories for the time he had first met her. Elk Pass, West Virginia. He was only a boy when he entered the crowded clinic with his mother. Outside, the town burned from a coal mine explosion and a railyard tanker fire. Wounded and dead littered a small ER. A few nurses and one female doctor moved frantically from one patient to the next.

Fear. Screams. Pain. Families. Blood. Death. Loss. It was all there in the clinic.

He found his father streaked with blood and motionless on a stretcher. The paleness of death had bleached skin in places the coal dust did not cover. His father's eyes were fixed, dark like glass marbles. He peered into his father's eyes, but saw nothing in return.

Moans lured his attention away and he spotted his uncle and brother on gurneys, their skin burnt and charred from fire. His uncle had already passed. His brother, Henry, didn't seem to be faring much better. Henry's hand twitched as if he were trying to pat their dog, Sparky. Henry's breathing shallowed, slowed, and then stopped.

He reached out to take Henry's hand, but froze. He wanted to shed tears for his father, brother, and uncle, but couldn't. He never had shed a tear before and wasn't starting then.

People brushed past him: Rachel Pratt and her family. The women in her family were crying and weeping, everyone except Rachel. She wore a somber mask similar to his and kept her emotions in check. He knew her father and two brothers were being treated by the same female doctor. Their conditions were grave, and things weren't going well.

Rachel, lingering in her mother's wake, turned back to him. Their gazes met, conveying mutual emptiness that each felt. No tears filled her eyes. No expression of warmth or even sorrow was visible.

He watched Rachel as she drifted down the corridor and finally out of sight behind a bed curtain. He had no way of knowing that was the last time he'd see her until they were reunited in the Perfect People Initiative.

Elk Pass had lost so many lives that night, with so many families torn apart.

And only one person could have made a difference.

Katherine Morgan, MD, had killed fathers and brothers and uncles. Her lack of training and failures as a doctor sealed the fates of the injured. That incompetence was unforgivable, no different than malice and murder. Her sins required atonement.

Barnes blinked his memories away, and turned his attention to satellite images.

The Grant Building churned dense pillars of smoke into the air as orange-gray clouds cascaded across northeast Washington, DC. His multi-billion-dollar, real-time video coverage was mostly useless.

But shifting wind patterns offered hope.

The moment was now for him to address his at-risk asset.

Returning the black van with its stolen EMP cannon to his base in the Navy Yard was risky. Too risky. The vehicle had too much urban landscape to traverse. DC surveillance and traffic cameras would capture the van even if surveillance satellites overhead did not. Plan B—ditching the vehicle west of Soldiers' Home—came with similar risks. It might be able to reach a lake or the Anacostia River, but that effort was too exposed for his liking.

Barnes took a breath. It was Plan C or bust: a narrow window of opportunity with better odds to abandon the vehicle someplace inconspicuous close to Fort Totten, even if only temporarily.

Programming his autonomous van to drive northwest, he kept it under cloud cover and moved it around Rock Creek Cemetery via New Hampshire Ave NW. Catching side streets east, the vehicle broke through the smoke and connected with Brookland Ave NE. The dedicated road sliced through a portion of Fort Totten Park that served an aggregate processor.

A gravel turnaround for cement mixers allowed his van to sneak beneath a treed canopy, sheltered from prying eyes. It would take law enforcement weeks or even months to find it.

By then he'd either be dead or someplace remote, far off the grid.

46
RELEVANCE

Strategic Information & Operations Center (SIOC), FBI Headquarters, Washington, DC

Alice Watson fumed, not from her meeting with the puzzle master but from the extended ass-chewing she'd just received in the FBI's executive situation room.

Senior leadership had chosen to suppress the terrorist's string of puzzle clues with other law enforcement agencies and non-agency personnel. Release and disclosure of sensitive evidence was unacceptable, punishable by termination and jail time. Above her, the Director, the Acting Deputy Director and Section Chief reinforced protocols and established new political edicts. Watson understood her wings were being clipped and her duties restricted as other Unit Chiefs and Watch Commanders were brought into the fold. Additional to this, the Special Agent in Charge (SAC), the Assistant Special Agent in Charge (ASAC), and Case Agent reassignments had been implemented. After Soldiers' Home the entire bureau deck was being reshuffled.

The clues and puzzles were to be turned over to the crime lab for analysis. Moving forward, exchanges of information would be approved by the new SAC, no exceptions.

Both the Director and Deputy Director expressed dissatisfaction over the lack of focus on the Metro bombing case, as well as the botched operation at Soldiers' Home that had cost agents their lives. Their deaths were unacceptable. While neither situation was her fault, she was the natural target of their ire, since the bureau had received the lion's share of criticism. Results mattered in the age of 24/7 media coverage and streaming public opinion.

The not-so-subtle threads of Beltway politics and preemptive scapegoating circled back to her as the SIOC's B-shift Unit Chief.

Turning a corner outside the executive situation room, Watson paused to purge pent-up frustrations. The lieutenants of the Director and Deputy Director had cut her off when she brought up genetically enhanced super soldiers and covert research programs under other branches of government. That was secondary to catching the domestic terrorists at large, they said, and none of Special Agent Alice Watson's concern.

Her request to interview Major General James Davidson was deferred and forwarded onto the new SAC for consideration. That deferral meant "no"—go pound sand, and keep your mouth shut.

A technician carrying a tablet approached. "Ma'am, we have a hit on individuals linked to government-sponsored employers, cross-referenced with missing persons in the tristate area. Five names made the list. All five disappeared in the past three weeks."

Watson's eyes flashed wide.

The last name on the list was the son of the Vice President of the United States.

"According to the IRS records, everyone on this list works for DoD research labs that specialize in genetics or human physiology. All are prominent PhDs or MDs. The first victim is Frederick Lock, a genetic engineer specializing in the advancement of DNA constructs."

"Now we're getting somewhere," Watson said under her breath.

"The second, Nellie Groves, was NIH's"—the National Institute of Health's—"deputy principal investigator supporting a subsector of medical applications in the Human Genome Project. Dr. Groves released a white paper entitled 'Human Evolution and the Necessity of Creating Designer Babies,'" the technician said.

"That's two for two."

"And you're going to like this," the technician added. "Since we believe Dr. Frances Davidson is among the victims, we checked her background. She worked for Google's Baseline and Calico projects before taking a lucrative position at a DARPA-funded think tank. Her contribution to this trio is an Advanced Biogenetics Initiative with a secondary emphasis in Human Immortality—HI for short."

Watson winced. No wonder the Pentagon had stonewalled access to General Davidson. The involvement of the general's daughter's and the Vice President's son's was a "look here" moment and a major threat to the Department of Defense and the White House. Combine that with recent public relations fiascos on other human research concerns, and it was no wonder no one wanted to discuss the construction of genetically enhanced super soldiers. FBI executive leadership had similar concerns.

Will Shortz had nailed his assessment. Its accuracy almost frightened her.

Watson took a somber breath. "Any update on the dead and unaccounted for?"

The technician shook her head.

Watson reflected on the puzzle solutions so far.

The terrorist, mass murderer, perpetrator at large had punched holes in Big Brother's dam. The killer was determined at all costs to tell a story, regardless of human collateral or the government's position. Trying to keep a lid on questionable programs to advance human evolution would be like plugging holes in a fragile dam. Plug one gusher and another was bound to spring up.

"What about Katherine Morgan?" she asked.

"No word from her," the technician said, checking a status log.

47
DISCOVERY

Stanley Hall Chapel, Soldiers Home, Washington, DC

With adrenaline racing through her veins, Kate heard the thumping of her heartbeat overtake the ringing in her ears. Breathing had ticked up too, and she fought to smooth it out. Forcing her gaze to sweep high and low, she studied the chapel and let her semi-automatic lead the way.

Bringing up her flashlight, she pressed it tight against the pistol's trigger, taking a two-handed grip to brighten and sight her field of fire.

The chapel's communion table glowed. Objects were on display.

Red begonias bookmarked pages in a thick book. Beside what appeared to a Bible, a Fido jar was half-filled with a black, granular substance.

Kate panned her flashlight and semi-automatic across the chancel area.

Just another church. Two doors, one on each side, needed to be cleared. Her raging heartbeat was almost too much to bear as she approached the first threat. Pivoting her body to the door's hinge side, she swung it open and darted inside behind the light and muzzle of her weapon. She took a frantic breath.

Tables. Chairs. Lamp holders. The vestry had been converted into a storage room. Using the same technique, she tackled the second door and encountered the same result.

Lowering her weapon, Kate flushed her lungs with several forceful breaths. Her heartbeat slowed.

Returning to the welcome gifts, she pocketed the flashlight and plucked out the black light. The wall-mounted spotlight to the side and above neutralized the ultraviolet light's effectiveness, so she stood between the source of the white light and the table.

Jackpot. Once hidden, phosphorescence emerged in an ultraviolet glow.

The jar's surface refracted the light. Inside, a bright purple object glowed. A cascade of images popped out on the table surface. A hieroglyphic-like sketch resembling the Eye of Ra centered the jar. Beside it, a caption read: ALL TRUTHS ARE EASY TO UNDERSTAND ONCE THEY ARE DISCOVERED. THE POINT IS TO DISCOVER THEM.

Kate swore as she processed the words, which seemed like a quote but she didn't recognize it. She took one final look around before holstering her weapon.

Flipping to the section of the Bible marked by the wretched flowers, she discovered a highlighted passage and a dog tag on a chain. Proverbs 14:12. *There is a way which seemeth right unto a man, but the end thereof are the ways of death.*

The deranged sentiment was beyond ominous.

At St. Elizabeths, the terrorist had claimed he was "a purebred soldier."

The killer had set himself as judge, jury, and executioner—eliminating threats: competitions, soldiers. Innocent lives lost? Didn't matter.

She cupped the dog tag in her hand and examined it in the handy radiance of the table's spotlight: CARPENTER MARTIN J A POS; a social security number was followed by USN. U.S. Navy. A tiny slogan was crammed onto the bottom of the tag: THE ONLY EASY DAY WAS YESTERDAY!

The slogan stumped her, but she suspected it belonged to the man seen through the Drone's camera. He'd been sacrificed. Murdered. Without hesitation she pocketed the tag and closed the Bible, leaving the kiss-me-when-I'm-dead flowers in its crease.

Turning her attention to the jar, Kate scrutinized its contents without touching it. The glass held an ivory-colored, rectangular object perched on what looked like dark dirt. She shuffled sideways to block out the holy splash of illumination and swept her black light back across the table again. On the altar, a painted eye stared straight into the bottom of the jar as if watching its valued contents.

The rectangular object, a tool or an object of desire or a treasure for the heart, was being watched.

Biting her lip, Kate pondered the revelation and looked around the church for hidden cameras. Seeing none, slowly—excruciatingly slowly—she lifted the jar off the table.

Her feet felt movement first, before her brain realized what was happening.

Beneath her, the wood floor buckled.

"Don't!" shouted a voice from across the chapel.

Frantically, Kate jerked her head up as gravity seized her body. She was dropping, falling, rapidly.

Army Captain Rachel Pratt sprinted toward her, her face desperate.

Kate lost sight of everything—the tawny colored chapel, the present-laden table, the All-Seeing Eye, and the advancing soldier. Her breath stalled in her chest as a dark void swallowed her whole.

48
A GENERAL SEARCH

The Pentagon, U.S. Department of Defense, Virginia

NSA Colonel Randy Wang knew hunting down a two-star in a massive five-story complex filled with generals was near impossible. Even after trimming ranks and a congressionally mandated twenty-five percent staff reduction, the star creep of officers migrating from one to four stars was at its greatest since the early 2000s. Lucky for Wang, his intelligence background built gambler-like instincts on how to track down strangers who didn't want to be found.

Like Army Major General James Davidson.

Archaic structures and bureaucratic protocols benefited his search, limiting how much deck chair shuffling could be executed within military ranks. It was far easier to conceal a captain under the proverbial rug than a general. Except in the rarest circumstances, no general would ever be found reporting up to a colonel. Standard, non-wartime duty assignments required that supervising officers were at least equal in rank to the officers who worked for them. Davidson was an Army two-star. And Army guys generally didn't work inside Air Force or Navy commands.

That left Davidson tied to either Army or Pentagon directorates. A few careful phone calls led Wang to a Joint Rapid Cell team that reported to the Office of the Under Secretary of Defense for Research and Engineering (USD R&E). U.S. Pentagon Police (USPPD) confirmed Davidson's latest building access matched the reassignment. The reset put Davidson in a position to continue peripheral oversight on aspects of the Defense Advanced Research Projects Agency (DARPA) and Research & Defense Innovation Unit Experimental (DIUx) programs.

Wang navigated the inner E Ring corridor and took a spoke to an NSA-operated SCIF. After badging into the secured area, he deposited his cell phone in a cubby and grabbed a terminal. Outside of approved tablets, laptops, and limited fat client computers, most DoD user computer terminals were thin client stations; the device worked off a larger network, a server-based infrastructure. That meant the general's network footprint was trackable to the right person. Handy for Wang, he was a Pentagon liaison to the Deputy Director of CYBERCOM on cybersecurity and advanced initiatives, with broad SCI/TS clearances.

Hacking and cyber-stalking were just a few of his numerous talents.

And Davidson's digital shadow matched his fat bureaucratic ass.

The general's network history linked to DARPA and DIUx classified projects. While his own clearance restricted him from reading program reports, Wang sorted out that the general oversaw a multiyear, fifty million-dollar program called the Advanced Biogenetics Initiative (ABI). ABI had two missions: advancing human evolution (AHE) and human genetics & operations applications (HGOA). Davidson became the principal investigator (PI) for peripheral sub-initiatives after its prior PI was forced out of research efforts. The prior PI's name had been redacted and scrubbed from reports. An archived footnote linked closed records from an interagency enterprise called the Perfect People Initiative (PPI).

Wang took his time in considering the interrelationships.

Davidson was creating designer soldiers. Likely another out-of-control research program gone awry.

Wang did a double take when he noticed cooperative research exchanges with a company called the Phoenix Consortium. The same outfit had provided oversight management at the Advanced

Neurological and Cybernetic Research Institute (ANCRI) near Princeton. Davidson's research network had been compromised by a series of shadowy actors, ranging from the Phoenix Consortium to RMG Global Solutions to EyePoint Applications.

The coincidences were striking.

FBI Special Agent Kate Morgan's call made sense. Bureau investigations were just following the bread crumbs that led straight to the Pentagon's doorstep.

Perhaps he did owe her a deeper dive on ABI and Davidson. And in the long run, no amount of Potomac self-preservation could protect a general with a bullseye painted on his chest.

Davidson had become a man with limited options, desperate to survive another day. Whether the general knew it or not, he'd eventually be sacrificed for the common good. The Pentagon and its bureaucracy survived those who transitioned through its rings.

When called upon, all dutiful soldiers fell on their swords.

49
DARKNESS

Stanley Hall Chapel, Soldiers Home, Washington, DC

Falling. Kate groped air, her limbs trying in vain to make contact with anything and slow her descent. The portal from which she'd entered evaporated, taking with it the presence of light. Her dream-like drop through darkness offered no spatial perspective.

Just falling.

The eventual strike came hard, impossible to prepare for.

Air ruptured from her lungs as she tumbled head over heels, ricocheting off immovable objects. The tumultuous drop continued until she came to rest face-first in liquid.

Gasping for breath, she inhaled the cold liquid into lungs need-ing air. Hacking and coughing, she wrenched her head back. Stars winked in and out of blackness. Her arms pressed against cold, submerged flooring. Her long wet hair painted her face. She tasted something musty and gritty. Water. Dirt. She coughed out moisture until something close to heavy breathing returned. Her throbbing mind registered water lapping at her arms: a shallow pool around her.

Waves of pain followed. Every part of her body hurt and wanted attention.

Groggy and flailing in the dark for a handhold, she finally latched onto the tempered surface's hard rock.

Something warm dripped into her eyes. She patted her face with her hands to feel the difference in wetness. Smelling her fingertips, she recognized the scent of blood. Her blood. No need to be a forensic specialist to figure out that. Her head must have struck something during her fall.

She had fallen. Where? Below the chapel? Into a fallout shelter?

The darkness was bone-chilling. As stars pinged at her beyond situational blindness, she felt a force tugging at her. Drained of energy, she didn't want to resist.

Sleep. Just lay down. Fall asleep in the water. It'll be okay.

Don't do it, said another voice inside her head. *You'll drown. Stay awake.*

Kate shook her head to drive out an embedded lightheadedness.

Stay moving. Don't stop. Don't rest.

After fumbling in a pocket for her flashlight, she clicked it and discovered she had been cast into a deep granite dungeon. Chiseled, shaft-like walls towered up and met ledges beyond her reach.

Kate slumped against the cold rock and brushed her palm across its smooth vertical features. Her entrapment came with no handholds for climbing out. If she even possessed the strength to attempt a climb.

Glancing around her keep, she couldn't locate the mystery jar she'd held.

Tired, her mind drifted. Wisps of memories sparkled, driving away the stars sprinkled over her muted sight.

As she sat in waist-high water, cold crept through her fatigues and into her skin, making her shiver. The cold reminded her of death—inescapable, inevitable, forever.

This was no wishing well—the opposite of a penitence-paid plea to manifest earthly desires—it was a frigid water hole beneath a graveyard's church.

She patted the surrounding stone. Marble? Polished marble. Broken tombstones scattered around open graves. Frances Davidson waited to be found, a victim dropped into a cold hole in the earth.

Vivid images flashed through her mind, out of sync. The Portiuncula chapel and its stone altar—Saint Mary of the Angels. People. Faces. Friars dressed in brown robes. A mother afraid for her daughter. People on a morning commute. Jack Wright. She missed Jack. How'd he survive death? Randall Wang made his resurrection possible. Dix Martinez. Rachel Pratt. The drone flyers. She smiled when Thomas Parker appeared. She missed Thomas more than Jack, missed their recent closeness in the Caribbean.

The flashlight slipped from her grasp, splashing into the water. Lit from below, ripples pulsed across the water's surface. Angelic halos, shimmering and gold, throbbed away from a source of light. The hypnotic moment fed a deep-seated weariness.

Move. Do something. Don't rest, not even for the angels.

Fighting her stupor, the result of another head wound, she snatched the flashlight out of the water and passed its beam across her cylindrical confines. Was there a way out? She'd have to search for one, as her light brightened only solid rock. No alcoves, no splintering-off chutes, no ladders, for crying out loud.

In the tiny spray of illumination, her reflection materialized where the halos once resided.

"You look like hell," Kate said, surprised to hear that her voice had become raspy, mournful.

Words haunted her and a terrorist's ghost-like condemnation chilled the water further.

THE QUEST FOR THE TRUTH IS NOT FOR THE FAINT AT HEART.

Truth? Hearts?

She was tired of the taunting.

Beyond her participation, authorities had never received any demands. No ultimatums. No opportunities to barter or negotiate.

This retribution was judgment on her. The condemning messages alluded to death: hers, his, CIRG agents, those sacrificed in the Grant Building.

Before Soldiers' Home, the conversational focus had been on her.

No revelations in the stupid puzzle hinted at agents being murdered or her being dumped at an altar and thrown into a dungeon.

And where was the promised strike of midnight? The emergence of Tuesday? The remaining victims?

Still sitting, water continued to lap at her midsection. She'd been cast here for a reason. For another lesson? Why?

Under the glow of the flashlight, she glared at her reflection and pulled wet hair out of her face.

The mask staring back at her was that of a different person. A victim. She looked like a victim.

It wasn't true. She was no killer, and certainly no damn victim.

A nascent desire to heal people had led her to medical school. After a horrible community outreach experience, she focused on getting her medical license and becoming a forensic pathologist. And she'd learned that dead people needed an advocate as much as the living.

The killer's words came back to her. "I'm a patriot. A purebred soldier."

This episodic manifestation was all the result of a psychopath's atonement for his own sins. A grander wishing well moment. By disclosing his secrets, he sought to buy favors and good fortune in a distorted quest to expose sins that were greater than his own.

The use of water was commonplace in ritual purification. In certain settings, it was believed to have healing properties.

This was her cleansing and purification moment.

Kate wondered if the terrorist saw himself as some kind of patron saint.

She cycled between disjointed thoughts and patches of text, searching for something innocuous, innocent at first glance. Deeper meanings. 14 DOWN, an abbreviation, came with a first-pass translation of RL, REAL LIFE. RL was no filler set of letters, but implied an association. It linked to something important. 11 ACROSS. That was it. An abbreviation for a SYMBOL PORTRAYAL was RP.

RP wasn't ROLE PLAY. It was a ROLE PLAYER in REAL LIFE.

Kate fought with all her might to stand and soak in the moment.

A better translation for RP was RACHEL PRATT.

Damn! The killer knew the U.S. Army Ranger Captain, a ROLE PLAYER in REAL LIFE.

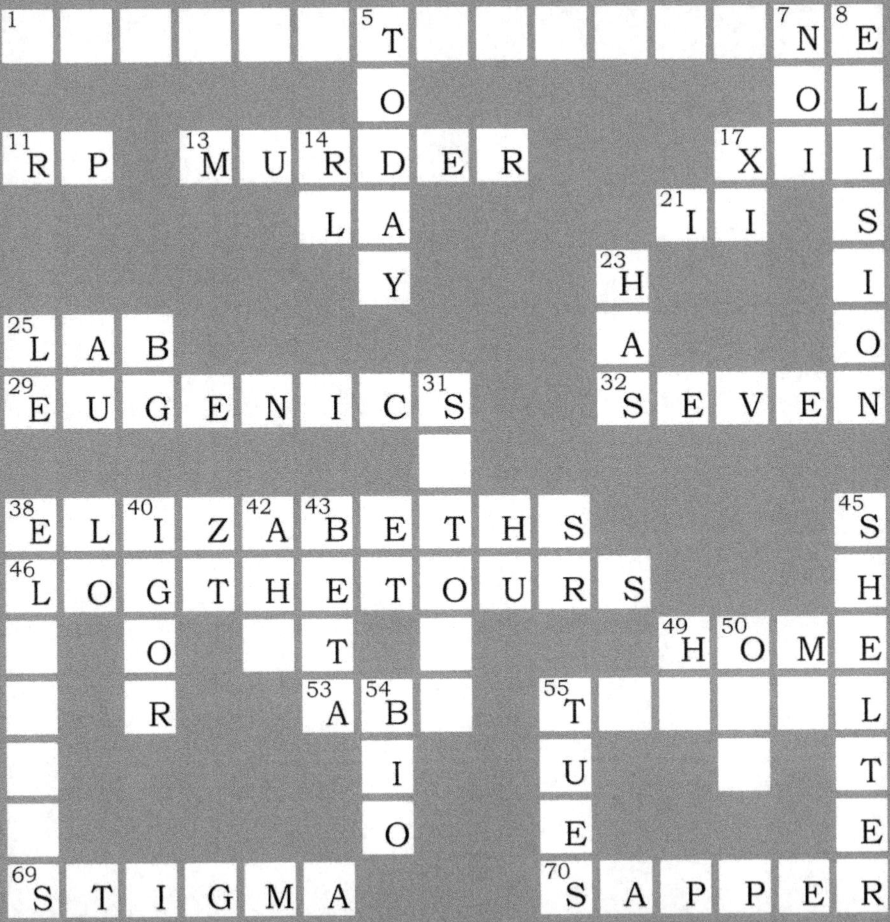

1 5 T 7 N 8 E
O O L
11 R P 13 M U 14 R D E R 17 X I I
L A 21 I I S
Y 23 H I
25 L A B A O
29 E U G E N I C 31 S 32 S E V E N
38 E L 40 I Z 42 A 43 B E T H S 45 S
46 L O G T H E T O U R S H
O T 49 H 50 O M E
R 53 A 54 B 55 T L
I U T
O E E
69 S T I G M A 70 S A P P E R

50
THE PIT OF MISERY

Below Stanley Hall Chapel, Soldiers Home, Washington, DC

Kate staggered around the perimeter of the dungeon, which lay an indeterminable distance below the chapel. Taking solemn breaths, she tried to clear her mind. Water licked her pants legs halfway up her calves. Her flashlight brightened the circular chamber. Running hands across cold stone, she searched for hidden gaps or ridges—elements or defects that might function as handholds. The rock was not as smooth as she'd initially thought. The chasm's diameter equaled two small cars parked end to end. Above, a rimmed ledge offered no immediate benefits—impossible to reach without a ladder or help from above. Climbing tools would be handy.

Tools. She swept the flashlight across the surface of the water.

The Fido jar from the altar was lost on the way down.

Kate thought of Rachel Pratt sprinting into the church, the soldier's entrance timed eerily late. It had probably shocked the hell out of the soldier when Kate dropped out of sight.

"Can anyone hear me?" she yelled, her voice echoing. She thought of the Bud Light commercial in which the king sentences a subject to a private tour of the Pit of Misery for daring to bring mead instead of the king's favorite light lager. "Hello?" she called. "I'll take that Bud Light now . . . dilly, dilly!"

It was worth a try.

She looked upward, hoping to see Pratt. A sloped chute merged into the ledge. The subterranean channel delivering her to the keep had slowed her momentum just enough, allowing her to survive a premeditated fall. At least that explained why she hadn't died.

The tunnels below St. Elizabeths had once served as pathways for winter laundry and meal delivery, and raceways for power, water, and sewage. Its fallout and bomb shelters were areas of refuge. Somewhere above her, Soldiers' Home likely had similar passages and hidden chambers.

All she had to do was find a way up.

Foreboding words returned. *Lose my tools, people die.*

Did the Fido jar count?

She took a breath and pressed her mind to search for options: the ultraviolet light.

Besides playing with blacklights as a child, she knew of Wood's Lamp applications in medicine and forensics. TV crime shows depicted it all wrong when detectives or crime scene technicians searched for physical evidence, such as blood, using blacklights. Blood had no fluorescence under UV or visible blue light; the technique was useful only for seminal fluids, saliva in certain conditions, and urine. Applying select chemicals to blood caused it to luminesce, which made the whole blue light technique unnecessary. In medicine and forensics, Wood's Lamp UV light and filter techniques helped in dermatology evaluations, diagnosing fungal or bacterial infections, and ethylene glycol poisoning.

Kate swapped out the lights again and clicked the UV light on. The bottom of the well radiated a brilliant violet fluorescence.

Stars and constellations painted the floor of the well.

It took a few moments to wrap her head around what she was seeing. The black light revealed what normal light could not.

A scarf-shaped movement drifted in the water, like a long eel swimming out of a submerged den. A gleaming message encircled an eye, dead center in the well's floor.

A HUMAN BEING IS ONLY BREATH AND SHADOW.

The eye blinked as she drew closer, and the scarf floated away from the eye like a teardrop.

Ebbing in the movement of water, she realized that the eye was detached from the bottom of the well.

The canning jar encounter above caused her to pause. The chapel's communion table had seemed innocuous enough—before a trap door swallowed her up and a rough-and-tumble fall dumped her to a secret chamber, a place that a killer wanted her to experience firsthand.

What made the well so important?

She took a steadying breath, fearful that if she messed up this time around, she just might end up being flushed all the way to hell itself.

Pivoting on her heels, she studied the scattered stars below her submerged in water. She recognized Ursa Major and the Big Dipper, Orion, Taurus, Gemini, Scorpius, Pegasus, Phoenix, and Cassiopeia. From high school astronomy, she recognized that the stars weren't laid out in the correct order.

It was obvious that the order of stars would be a clue of some sort, important, but her mind struggled to solve a grander pattern.

Returning her attention to the eye, she concentrated on the focal point of her keep. The declaration on the altar popped into her mind: ALL TRUTHS ARE EASY TO UNDERSTAND ONCE THEY ARE DISCOVERED. THE POINT IS TO DISCOVER THEM.

Casting apprehension aside, Kate plunged her hands into the cold water and snatched up a weighted tarp bearing the symbol of an eye. The thick, wet fabric was larger, heavier than the patches of skin. The blacklight revealed no other markings on the tapestry. Glancing down, she saw that it covered a bowl-like depression. Her skin prickled with foreboding.

Inside a concave recess floated a flat, waterproof plastic bag. Inside the see-through envelope, clues were etched into another patch of human skin—the next stop.

Kate lifted out the protected parchment. Nothing glowed on it except tiny etchings striping the sides of the skin. She lit it up with her flashlight.

KATHERINE, NEW TRUTHS BEGIN AS HERESIES. HEED THE LESSONS AND THE SACRIFICE AT THE ALTAR OF KNOWLEDGE. TRUE SCIENCE AND TRUE RELIGION ARE BUT TWIN SISTERS, AND THE SEPARATION OF EITHER FROM THE OTHER IS SURE TO PROVE THE DEATH OF BOTH.

ACROSS

1   RUDIMENTARY ADAMANT

53   ABBR: CREATORS OF 40 DOWN

55   SERVANT OR SLAVE

DOWN

31   SUDDEN ENLIGHTENMENT

38   PLACE OF YOUR CRIMES

42   ABBR: 53 ACROSS MISSION STATEMENT

50   SLEEPS IN SEED

51
BREATH AND SHADOW

HEED THE LESSONS? Kate thought of the chapel's communion table. The all-seeing eye had been sketched there too. Removing the jar from the table was like bringing mead to king's banquet. The penalty was a personal tour of the Pit of Misery.

Her eyes scanned the clues, stopping at 38 DOWN, the PLACE OF YOUR CRIMES.

She sighed, unable to translate the PLACE OF *HER* CRIMES.

In the flashlight's glow, Kate inspected the patch of flesh. The skin's genetic pigment was cream in color. It could belong to a man or woman. Impossible to determine without forensics and DNA testing. The tattooed circle filled in with blocks looked like stones from a child's Minecraft game, or a robotic happy face.

Her quest and trials weren't over. The stroke of midnight still remained. She was meant to escape this keep, and not be condemned to die in an earthen dungeon.

Hope gave her strength. She was getting out.

Switching between the blacklight and flashlight, she reassessed the water-covered floor beneath her feet.

A HUMAN BEING IS ONLY BREATH AND SHADOW.

An idea formed in her head. The declaration encircled the indentation in the floor. Water filled the well from an underwater bubbler, yet the water level in her holding cell never rose.

Her vision tracked the eel-like scarf, a tear leaving the eye. It started in the depression, then waved and flowed outward like a vector. Tracing the continuous luminescent trail, Kate discovered that it disappeared through a shadow at the edge of her confines.

Dropping to her knees, pressing her face below the water, she reached into a void. The trough-like niche was hewn into solid stone, at a spot where floor met wall. Her hands measured the coffin-sized cavity. Its height and width were enough to squeeze her body into, barely.

Clicking on her flashlight, she scanned the horizontal shaft. The scarf followed the flow of water and seemed to run forever, and her flashlight beam never reached the end of the shaft.

Ripping her head out of the water, she sucked in several deep breaths.

BREATH AND SHADOW. Not particularly a helpful sentiment.

The space wasn't overly large. She could get wedged inside and drown—a horrifying thought, since she'd been claustrophobic for as long as she could remember. As a child, spelunking and treasure hunting in the tunnels beneath Chicago skyscrapers with her father helped overcome her fears. But never were those spaces hip-tight.

Kate took a breath and realized her escape route was merely a challenge—one she'd trained for, though not deliberately.

Her month of water, sun, and sailing in the Cayman Islands with Thomas Parker had included PADI certification, since Thomas—to her surprise—was an accomplished sailor and diver. The test had required her to hold her breath for over a minute without panicking. She had held hers for more than two minutes. She remembered visiting Amphitrite, the submerged Siren of Sunset Reef as the goddess peered hopeful to the surface of the water. She could do it.

All she had to do was be smart and think through her escape.

Seeing her boots beneath the surface of the water, she realized she couldn't swim with anchors. Taking forceful breaths to oxygenate her blood, she removed her boots and used them to stash her contraband: the tapestry of skin and eye-marked cover. She took more breaths to oxygenate her blood, then tied the bootlaces together and slung the boots around her neck.

Sizing up the chase one last time, she understood her bullet-resistant vest would have to go, too.

Kate took a final breath before sliding into the water.

Placing her hands and flashlight out in front, she glided into the duct-like tube. Keeping her heartrate down, she kicked in rhythmic strokes. Once inside, she noticed that no sound penetrated the tight confines as it sloped downward. Something tugged at her, and she felt the water's gentle current take hold.

Looking straight ahead, she waited for a sign of hope. Beyond her flashlight, no outside light pierced the channel of darkness.

Relax. Conserve your energy.

She wanted to count passing seconds, but she told her mind to be silent, patient.

Her kicks started to slow. The tunnel showed no sign of ending.

It'll be there.

She was tiring and wanted to take a breath. Her heartrate ticked up.

Ahead, the lid of the horizontal shaft disappeared in a broadening blackness.

Slithering through a trap-like transition, she broke out into a larger expanse of water. The extra exertion caused her lungs to ache in a desperate need for air.

As she pivoted in the water, the flashlight's beam failed to reach other walls. Whatever she was in was vast and deep, larger than her baptismal font.

Fearful of being disoriented, without bearings, Kate kicked and pulled her arms against the water in an effort to rocket her body upward. Seconds later, she broke the water's surface.

Wrenching her head back, she gasped for breaths. She twirled in a circle and cast the flashlight's beam around to illuminate her new surroundings. The granite encasement looked like an ancient, hand-excavated water vault. Swimming to a rock ledge, Kate latched onto its firmness and hauled herself out of the water.

Collapsing onto her back, she rested to catch her breath.

As her breathing settled, she felt hard stone beneath and the coolness of air on her skin through wet fatigues.

Above her, the flashlight's spray caught a rusted old ladder.

A way out.

Leaning up, she extracted the materials from the hollows of her boots and stuffed inside her wet shirt. She laced up her soggy boots and put herself in motion. Instincts and reflex propelled her as her mind searched for options.

Kate had no idea where she was going, only that it was up. Latching onto the ladder, she started climbing, challenging tired and quivering muscles.

The flashlight she held clinked against aged steel. Old, fatigued metal groaned in protest. Rungs came and went as she ascended. She noticed a wooden pulley system rising vertical beside her, a method of drawing water from the reservoir below.

The ladder ended at a wooden platform and a vaulted door.

Kate clambered onto the platform and grabbed the door's iron handle. She tugged and pushed against thick wood. She put her shoulder into the door. It barely budged. The inside had no lever mechanism. It was locked from the outside. She swore, then drew her semi-automatic. Targeting what she guessed was the latch area, she fired consecutive shots no more than a foot away. The weapon's discharge was deafening. She fired again. The door shuddered and a gap appeared in the door jamb. A heel of her boot sent the door swinging open.

The world beyond was dark, unlit.

Footsteps approached.

Kate stepped through the doorway and saw dark pupils in intense eyes surrounded by brilliant white conjunctivas. The radiance of her flashlight showed a brown face around the eyes.

A movement came unexpectedly, fast. A blur of dark muscle accelerated and led with knuckles. Kate tried to block the oncoming strike with her flashlight, but her counter move was slow. The blow landed right between her eyes.

Kate's body careened backwards, feet lifting off the ground. She was unconscious when her body thumped to the stone floor.

52
BETAS AND SMALL LEADS

Strategic Information & Operations Center (SIOC), FBI Headquarters, Washington, DC

An hour before sunset. Alice Watson's forehead beaded with perspiration.

The arrival of darkness complicated urban landscapes and made their job more difficult.

Taking a long breath, she reviewed the tsunami of field reports. The SIOC's big board sectionalized each active scene: St. Elizabeths times two, the monastery, Soldiers' Home. The Grant Building fire had been contained. In the explosion's wake, the counts finally came in: twenty dead, another thirty injured. ATF's strategic, explosive & arson (SEAR) task force agents and investigators assisted FBI boots on the ground to determine the cause of the explosion.

Watson exhaled slowly, knowing how critical the first twenty-four hours were to a terrorist investigation's success. But no set of planned protocols, rehearsed scenarios, or preparedness drills would've made a difference this time out. Law enforcement faced politically motivated BETAs, the informal nickname investigators had given the deadly perpetrator or tightknit group of perpetrators.

Military-designed EMP weapons were a terrifying addition to the threat of more bombings, to say nothing of rogue super soldiers and their origin. Even superheroes turned on their alliances, as an

SIOC tech and comic book junkie had noted: in alternate universes, Captain Steve Rogers, America's recipient of Super-Soldier serum, had a checkered past—one in which the character railed against his core values. The heroic figure became a dreaded Hydra sleeper agent, siding with Hitler and the Red Skull.

"He even killed Black Widow," the tech had said, stating the rogue action was Cap's biggest crime.

BETAs: puzzle-wielding, disenfranchised super soldiers possessing high-tech weapons.

Law enforcement had no plan for that.

And passive-aggressive pushback and doublespeak from the Defense Department and the White House didn't help. It seemed as if one of their own monsters, or perhaps a small village of them, had come unhinged and waged war on DC.

Watson studied the missing's persons file on the Vice President's son: Andrew Mears. A former Navy doctor, the VP's son was a subject matter expert working for the Pentagon's Defense Research and Engineering for Advanced Capabilities (DREAC) directorate. All of Mears's research was classified, but he was a central figure in military sponsored research efforts. And Mears was a known associate of Frances Davidson, the general's daughter.

This incestuous group of soldiers and lab coats was starting to annoy her.

A technician knelt beside her and pointed to a desk monitor. "ATF and NTSB updates arrived."

Watson brought up the files.

"The crime lab," the tech said, "IDd the explosives used in the car bombing near St. Elizabeths. Those matched the Metro. Spectral analysis confirmed RDX. Trace compounds originate from a munitions supplier in Pennsylvania. A search warrant is being executed for manufacturing and accounting records and shipping orders. We'll have those records in a couple of hours. Then we can match those records to security contracts, weapons contracts, and vehicle purchases and leases."

Watson scrunched up her nose. "Leading to our mysterious—"

"Black van," the technician said. "Yes. Time lapse footage from satellite scans and traffic cams indicate it was abandoned or hidden within a five-mile radius of Soldiers' Home. Other agencies are helping to search adjacent neighborhoods. We'll find it."

Watson folded her arms as her eyes shot a skeptical stare at the technician. "We better. That van has an EMP cannon capable of wiping out a football stadium full of electronics. It's game-changing weaponry in the wrong hands. Who knows what damage it can do?"

"Give it some time."

She snatched the technician's arm as he was about to leave. "Contact the FAA and close Reagan National. Redirect air traffic to Dulles and BWI. And put those airports on alert. It'd be nice to avoid a scenario where planes start falling from the sky."

"Consider it done."

Watson still felt uneasy. She cleared the dryness in her throat with a cold swig of coffee. "Has anyone tracked down Agent Morgan yet?"

53
SCALE OF MA'AT

Northeast of Dupont Circle, Washington, DC

Kate Morgan blinked her eyes into focus. Drawn shades blocked outside light from the room. Her sense of time and place had been disrupted. Taking a breath, she looked around and realized she wasn't alone. In the corner, the standing silhouette was hard to miss.

Kate's attention returned to her situation. A bed. Her field uniform had been removed, leaving her in a t-shirt and underwear. Raising her left wrist, she discovered it was handcuffed to a headboard, while the right was free.

"Where are my clothes?" Kate asked over a dry knot in her throat.

"They were wet," said the voice from the corner.

Kate recognized the unfriendly voice of Army Captain Rachel Pratt. It had been Pratt's face Kate had seen in the tunnels at Soldiers' Home.

"You punched me." She brushed her forehead with her fingers. Surprisingly, she felt only swelling, not the massive knot she'd expected.

The response was matter-of-fact. "No. You hit your head on the rock walls."

Kate yanked on her cuffed wrist. "You kidnapped me, Pratt."

"I rescued you. You were disoriented. Confused. Lost."

"Yeah, in the Pit of Misery," she said, the pieces coming together. Soldiers' Home. Agents. Death. Explosions and fire. The chapel. An altar. A trap door. The bottom of some sort of well. More clues on human skin. And somehow the Army Captain knew all about it.

She took a long breath. "Where are the clues? A woman is waiting for us to find her." She waited for a response that didn't come. "Her name is Frances Davidson."

Across the room, Pratt switched on a standing lamp, its illumination accenting the brown of her face. The soldier's laser-sighted focus bore down on Kate, as if Pratt was searching for some semblance of the truth. The name seemed to trigger something in the soldier's psyche.

"You know her," Kate said. Her gaze scanned the room. It was decorated in antiques. Chairs, rugs, wall coverings. Even the walnut bed matched the side tables. "You know Frances Davidson, don't you?"

Pratt seemed unsure.

"Then her father. James Davidson. Army like you." Kate raised her cuffed hand as high as possible. "Help me save his daughter."

"That's not in my mission parameters, Morgan."

Kate leaned forward in the bed. "Your mission? Did the general order you to abduct me?" Silence hung in the air and she took a flyer and asked, "You're one of them, aren't you?"

Pratt didn't hesitate. "You can say that."

Kate arched an eyebrow. "A lab rat? That explains a lot."

Pratt tossed her a dog tag on a chain.

Kate caught it in her free hand. "Proverbs," she said recalling the man's tag, left for her in the chapel in the pages of a Bible. "A passage that mentions death."

Pratt's face went rigid. "*There is a way which seemeth right unto a man, but the end thereof are the ways of death.*" She paused in thought. "Martin Carpenter. Navy Seal. Lieutenant. A hero who didn't deserve his fate."

"He's Navy? I thought you'd all be Army." Kate tugged at her wrist. "How about unlocking these and fetching my clothes?"

The pause hanging in the air became awkward.

"Come on," Kate said. "We really need to talk."

Pratt stood at her bedside to accentuate their height difference. "We are talking."

"No. You're holding me hostage," Kate said.

Her captor grunted and left the room.

"Hey, how about my clothes?" Kate snapped, listening to boots disappear on wood floors.

Torqueing herself, she spun face down and twisted the hand-cuff's chain links so she could reach the top drawers of each bedside table. Rifling through the drawers, she searched for anything to use to pick the handcuffs, which dug into her wrist. Nothing out of the usual: pens, writing tablets, bookmarks. Hearing footsteps return, she snatched up a pair of champagne-colored writing pens and lay back on the bed, tucking her contraband beneath her.

Pratt returned carrying a pair of pants, a shirt, and a jacket, which got tossed on the bed. The black set of clothes weren't hers but looked close enough in size. And none of it was FBI sanctioned tans and blues. But at least everything was dry.

Kate swooped up the clothes. "How long was I out?"

"Long enough."

"You hit me that hard?"

"No. I gave you a sedative." Pratt broke a thin smile and tapped her neck. Leaning across the bed, she unlocked the handcuffs. "I needed to slow down time. Slow you down before more people got killed. I'm not smart like Barnes, but I realized you're the timekeeper."

"You drugged me?" Kate touched her neck with her fingertips and noticed a tender spot. An injection mark. "Time... what?"

Pratt held up the patch of skin found in the well. "Phillip Barnes must believe you're dead. That he killed you. That creates flexibility and buys us time."

"Barnes?" The name didn't register. "He's the terrorist?"

"Meet me downstairs," Pratt said, leaving with the clues.

"Ah, Pratt—you should know you just contaminated evidence." Kate grimaced, then hustled out of bed to clumsily slide into the provided pants. Every muscle in her body ached. Bruises littered both arms like inkblots on a Rorschach test.

Startling her, Pratt reappeared in the doorway.

"You got boundaries?" Kate asked.

The soldier's gaze pierced hers. "Barnes is intelligent. He won't leave behind traceable evidence. He's clever. They bred him to be everything the rest of us weren't. We were brawn, no better than second place." Her expression softened. "That's why I once thought I loved him. And why you're going to help me hunt him down and kill him."

Kate's jaw dropped as she pulled on the shirt. "Kill him?"

Mechanically, without a hint of modesty, Pratt unbuttoned her uniform and lifted her t-shirt to reveal her chest. "We broke the rules and paid the price."

Pratt's warrior physique was sculpted like a bodybuilder's, defined by endless hours of gym work. From abs to pecs, muscle fibers rippled below skin.

A soul-touching cold reached deep into Kate's own chest at the sight of the wrinkled dimple of an old wound. Over the left lung. Inches above Pratt's heart. Pratt had survived a high-mortality gunshot wound. It suggested a reason for the terrorist, Phillip Barnes, to choose the skin from the victims' left breasts as his diary material.

For where one's treasure is, there will your heart be also. The friar's recital of the New Testament scripture echoed in Kate's mind, which led to a memory of the Ra-like eye on the altar in the chapel at Soldiers' Home.

Searching her consciousness for scant thoughts, she recalled a snippet of Egyptian folklore—the Judgment of the Dead—where the deceased passed through the trials of Osiris, Lord of the Underworld and Judge of the Dead. In the ritual, Anubis, the god of embalming and watcher of the dead, performed the judgment weighing with the Scale of Ma'at. A person's heart was placed on the left scale, the Feather of the Truth on the right. If the heart was heavier than the feather, the person was judged unworthy. The worthless organ was then fed to Ammit, the crocodile-faced goddess in charge of divine retribution. Once Ammit ate the person's heart, their soul ceased to exist.

The implication was ominous.

Pratt's eyes seemed to turn a shade darker as she pulled her shirt down. "We had a relationship. A forbidden one. The tie that bound us together during our youth at the PLACE OF *YOUR* CRIMES."

Kate dropped her gaze and backed away, her legs weak and wobbly.

The Feather of Truth had judged her.

38 DOWN.

ELK PASS, West Virginia.

The place where she'd murdered a killer's family.

54
YESTERDAY'S TROUBLES

Kate loved antique homes she couldn't afford. She took her time strolling down the broad staircase, fingers gliding across polished hardwood rails. Early twentieth century wood trim framed exterior windows. A crystal chandelier hung above the entry hall. Rich throw rugs covered hardwood floors. The decorations were colonial vintage. A few oil-based paintings with brass name plaques adorned the walls. A grandfather clock ticked off time with its brass pendulum.

It was as if she'd stepped back in history, oblivious to her plight and the attacks on the nation's capital.

That feeling evaporated when she found Pratt standing at a long walnut dining room table, sorting weapons and gear bags. Lowering her hand, Kate tapped her hip where a holster and semi-automatic were missing. Pratt had taken her sidearm.

"So, who shot you?" Kate asked, eyeing the small arsenal: compact pistols, semi-automatic handguns, submachine guns, a sniper's long rifle, and a shotgun. Laser sighting was prevalent on several weapons. Suppressors waited to be threaded on. Tear gas canisters and shock grenades lay beside a stack of magazines. There were enough weapons to execute a small assault. "A murderous ex-boyfriend, perhaps?"

The response was calculated, cold. "Davidson."

"Really?" Interesting revelation. Kate's gaze found the patch of skin at the center of the cache of the table's destructive place settings. Beneath the branded clues was the weighted cover that had held it down in the water. Next to it was the OBSERVER patch she'd ripped off her vest before entering the chapel. The blacklight and Fido jar were there too. The canning jar still contained its dirt and the bone-like rectangle inside. "This all needs to get to the crime lab."

Pratt checked a watch on her wrist. "Not until you agree to help me."

Kate shrugged. "Trade you my Glock and a cell phone." Pressing her fingers into the human tapestry, she spun it around to read its clues again. PLACE OF YOUR CRIMES—obvious now, ELK PASS. SUDDEN ENLIGHTENMENT, RUDIMENTARY ADAMANT, SERVANT OR SLAVE, CREATORS OF 40 DOWN—those solutions needed a *Times* crossword puzzle expert's attention. HEED THE LESSONS AND SACRIFICE AT THE ALTAR OF KNOWLEDGE. Easy to reflect on that after being dropped through the floor of a church and into a dungeon.

Kate glared at Pratt. "NEW TRUTHS BEGIN AS HERESIES. Barnes' message to the world? Besides a political statement, what does he really want? What's his end game?"

"Retribution," Pratt said, an incredulous look chiseled into her features. From a gear bag, she retrieved Kate's semi-automatic and aimed its muzzle across the table. The soldier's hand was steady, without a flicker of nervousness, targeting Kate's heart.

Kate realized the soldier was right.

"I remember you," Pratt said. She sounded detached, as if under a spell. "Must have been ten when it happened. The program suppressed those memories, making it hard for me to recall details. A blotted-out childhood thanks to advancements in cognitive neuroscience. It was my choice. I wanted a clean slate. Sentiment, attachments to the past and family, fosters weakness. And there's no room in a warrior's heart for that kind of vulnerability."

"Or love?" Kate pivoted, turning her chest away from Pratt, blocking a direct shot at her heart. She flipped up the lid to the Fido and sniffed at the black granular substance inside. Coal dust. Reaching inside, she plucked out the white object.

Pratt took the jab in stride. "I remember a pretty woman doctor from the big city. I saw fear in your eyes that night. You were scared. My father and two older brothers were working the second shift at the mine when methane gas caused the explosion."

Kate felt the pangs of truth and tragedy. Children orphaned by heartbreak and misfortune.

"I couldn't save them. I'm sorry." Kate tried to remember the faces of those who had died. Elk Pass. A night from hell. As a family medicine resident, she had little experience in trauma situations; the true genesis for creating resentment, anger, retribution. Although post-case university assessments and medical boards had cleared her of wrongdoing, those affirmations didn't absolve her from failure. Sins required atonement, at least in the eyes of a mass murderer. "Who did Barnes lose?"

"Father, uncle, brother," Pratt said, her face expressionless.

"It rained for two days straight before the mountain blew." Kate wiped the coal dust off the rectangular bone-like object, noticing it had slots and grooves like the shaft of a key. "Doc Mandel, the clinic's physician, died first. I wanted to save him. I tried. But his burns were severe. Yes. Eighteen men died, and I can't change that. I used to think about them. A lot. They haunted my dreams. Afterwards, I couldn't eat, sleep, function as a doctor. I know the loss is hard. Eighteen caskets. And a one-room church where families said goodbye to their loved ones. When my rotation was up, I fled family medicine and sought refuge in forensics and pathology."

Pratt blinked, breaking her gaze and flipped the Glock around, making its butt available to grasp. "I wanted to pull the trigger, for all of us who died that night."

"I know." Kate swallowed hard. She offered an understanding nod, the kind of detached, superficial nod that doctors gave family members when presenting a death notice or a terminal diagnosis. She grasped the weapon, concerned the soldier might take it back.

"A round is chambered." Pratt lowered her head, trying to focus. "I restocked the magazine."

Kate tapped the human parchment with the weapon's muzzle, indicating the black circle with white blocks inside it. "You know what this means?"

"Never seen it before."

Kate studied Pratt from across the table. "I need that phone now."

The soldier retrieved a sat phone and handed it to her.

After getting the passcode, Kate clicked on the device and snapped pictures of the evidence. She closed her eyes. "I can't let you outright murder Phillip Barnes. If there's a chance, he has to be taken alive."

Pratt shook her head. "You won't get that choice. It's him or you."

Kate shrugged off the proclamation and typed a number into the device to initiate a call. She pressed her ear to the phone and turned away from Pratt.

"Federal Bureau of Investigation," an operator said.

Just as Kate was about to state her name and badge number, she pulled back from the phone. Dueling thoughts troubled her as her mind cycled through the moments before the bombing at Soldiers' Home. Shadows, like wisps of smoke in a dream, solidified into a vivid image. Against orders, she had sprinted toward the Grant Building to rescue a man with words written on his chest: THE BATTLE LINE BETWEEN GOOD AND EVIL RUNS THROUGH THE HEART OF EVERY MAN. AND THIS SLUMBERING HEART CANNOT BE REDEEMED.

Somehow, someway, law enforcement had been compromised. Phillip Barnes had known she was coming for the victim.

Deepening her voice to sound like a man, she said, "This is Special Agent in Charge Jack Wright. Connect me with Will Shortz. He's a civilian assisting HQ on the bombings. You'll find him in the SIOC. A new lead requires his immediate attention."

"One moment, Agent Wright."

Pratt cocked her head, eyeing her askew.

"What happened at Soldiers' Home?" Kate asked, waiting for the call to connect.

"How would I know? I wasn't there."

"You're lying, Rachel. And I wasn't asking about the bombing." Kate set aside the bone carving to rummage through the gear bag until she located her holster. Putting the phone on speaker mode, she buckled her holster. Her Glock slid into place. "You'd been there before. Barnes was there. This Navy guy with the dog tags was there. General Davidson ran the show, didn't he? Your secret squad of super soldiers trained there, didn't it?"

Pratt took a tense breath, her rich brown eyes displaying uneasiness about the line of questioning. She swept a hand across the back of her neck to gently massage the base of her skull. They were the first feminine gestures she had exhibited the entire day.

Kate rounded the table. "How did you know to find me in the church tunnels? What happened in its fallout shelter?"

Fear pierced Pratt's confident demeanor, her eyes showing shame and disappointment. "I loved him. Well, I thought I did. Maybe I did. It's hard to tell now. ABI used the tunnels for drills and close quarter combat training. The well spring was a shock therapy pool used for water treading tests. It was rigorous, but all of us fought through everything ABI threw at us—until Phillip started to question their training methods. He questioned our very existence, our future as puppets and pawns. Our relationship went on about a month before handlers got wise to us. Phillip and I knew we couldn't stay."

"And Davidson wouldn't let you leave."

Pratt brought her hands up to her face. "We almost—"

"Who's on the line?" a woman's voice demanded over the phone's speaker.

"I can't multitask these conversations." Kate reached across the table and snatched up the phone. "Hold for one minute," she said, putting the device on mute.

"Rachel," she asked, trying to make eye contact, "what did they do to you?"

"After my father and brothers died, my mother and I moved to Georgia, close to Fort Benning. Mom became depressed and started taking drugs to cope. Died of a heroin overdose on the anniversary of their deaths. A day later I was orphaned. What I didn't realize was that I never really had biological family in Elk Pass. It was an illusion. A foster family. They were raising me until I was ready to leave them behind. The Army controlled our lives the entire time."

Kate ducked her head to catch Pratt's gaze. "You're avoiding what happened in the tunnels."

Pratt nodded. "Davidson ordered us separated, stripped naked, and beaten. Handlers tortured us, trying to break our wills: sleep deprivation, auditory and sensory overloads, no food, little water. The tunnels served as solitary confinement. It went on for days. Somehow Phillip managed to escape his handlers. Rather than save himself, he came back for me. It's a still a fog in my mind, but I remember him killing the guards who stood watch over me. His rage was primal, violent. There was almost no controlling him."

Kate took a flyer with her next question. "Davidson shot you when you were trying to escape?"

"The bullet was meant for Phillip, or so I thought." She sniffed in a breath and closed her eyes. "I took the bullet because I wanted him to live. I barely felt the pain. I remember feeling cold, like my skin had been frosted with a layer of ice. Phillip's warmth, his body against mine had been the only warmth I had felt for days."

Silence swelled between them as Kate pictured the scene in her mind. It wasn't hard, with her firsthand experience of the cold, dark tunnels.

LOG THE TOURS.

The divulging of that moment prompted a stream of neurons to fire in her own consciousness. The chapel. The tunnels. The water. It all made sense. Barnes wanted her own TRIALS to traverse their imprisonment, pass through the depths of their hell at Soldiers' Home.

Kate felt guilty for pressing so hard.

Pratt had just bared her soul. Her dark muscular features softened, as if she was relieved to have told her story to someone not in Army green.

Kate's eyes smiled before her mouth did. It was a thin smile, but a smile nonetheless. Reaching out, she placed the palm of her hand over Pratt's heart. "Let's go get the general's daughter."

55
TAKING THE CALL

Strategic Information & Operations Center (SIOC), FBI Headquarters, Washington, DC

Alice Watson hovered over the speaker phone on the conference table and tried to relax her muscles. Beside her sat an inquisitive Will Shortz.

Per protocol, a trace had been initiated on the incoming call.

An SIOC tech popped his head into the room. Watson waved for him to speak.

"It's not cellular. It's sat. That takes longer to locate an origin because we cannot triangulate between cell towers."

She frowned. Every technological advancement available, with the best law enforcement staff in the world, was sometimes no help at all. "Keep on it."

"Special Agent Alice Watson," a husky voice on the phone asked, "is Will Shortz there?"

"Yes. Who are we speaking to?"

"Jack Wright," the husky voice continued.

Watson sighed. "That's a tough one to pull off, because Special Agent Jack Wright died in the line of duty last month."

The line fell silent.

When the voice returned, its tone was unwavering. "We can play games, but the clock's ticking and I'm on a midnight deadline. We have 38 DOWN, if and only if we can talk on a secured line without a trace or the conversation being recorded. You have three seconds to make a decision."

Watson shot a nervous glance to Shortz, who gave her a "why are you looking at me?" expression.

He mouthed "that's not an answer we have" and pointed to the heavily gapped SCRABBLE puzzle on the table.

"Deal," Watson said. She snatched up a pen and a paper. "What number can we call you back at?"

"We'll call you. Two minutes. No traces. No recordings. Understood?"

"Perfectly." Watson gave the direct line and extension to the phone on the conference room table.

The line went dead.

"Did we get a trace on that?" she yelled.

In the distance, someone shouted back, "No."

Watson closed the conference room door and sat beside Shortz.

"So, Will," she asked, as her gaze darted to a red LED clock mounted on the wall, "how you like working for the bureau?"

He made a noise that was not quite a chuckle. "To tell you the truth, this is nothing like my day at the office. I work from home, mostly. A luxury. Books fill my house. And the best thing is I don't have to pass through metal detectors, carry a name badge, or keep secrets."

Watson gave a bark of laughter. "Just so you know, most of our work is routine. Yeah, we have events, situations, disasters, and some very unpleasant days. But we make a difference. Our jobs really are based on old-fashioned detective work. A lot like solving puzzles, I presume."

He smiled. "I love what I do. Edit and review puzzles. Brainstorm with a few colleagues. Travel to the city, but don't have to live there. Record segments for NPR. Fit in a few TV appearances. Play lots of table tennis. I have a streak of consecutive days played going."

She flashed him a wry grin. "A record of sorts. So I've heard."

He took a breath. "Besides claiming to know 38 DOWN, the caller knows about midnight."

She nodded in agreement. "Agent Morgan is a terrible impersonator of Jack Wright. Who's alive and well, by the way. I probably should've have told you that. Don't tell anyone Wright's alive."

Shortz looked unsettled. "I'm not following."

Watson put her elbows on the table and leaned closer to the phone. "Morgan mentioned 'we.' That's deliberate. A flag. A tip. She's either in trouble or she's teaming up with non-FBI personnel. Attempting to disguise her voice demonstrates she doesn't want anyone to know her identity or that she's alive."

Shortz nodded. "I read about her involvement in research trials last month. It was all over the newspapers."

"That's not the kind of news the FBI wants to promote."

They were both looking at the wall clock when the phone rang.

Watson clicked the speaker button. "Alice Watson and Will Shortz, puzzle master extraordinaire. You can speak freely now. You said you had 38 DOWN."

Shortz readied a pencil.

"ELK PASS," a woman's voice said. "West Virginia. It's known for coal mining."

"Good to hear your voice, Special Agent Morgan. What's your status? Are you okay?"

"That's… relative."

Shortz wrote down the answer and brought together wood tiles to form the word.

A pause lingered and Watson sensed a particular question was coming.

"How many?"

Watson shuddered. "Let's leave it as we took a beating today."

"Martinez?"

"No."

Morgan cleared her throat. "We have the terrorist's name. The main perpetrator. Phillip Logan Barnes. Ex-Army. Consider him armed, dangerous. Extremely intelligent."

A SAPPER. That made sense.

Watson's eyes never left the piece of paper that Shortz took notes on.

"I'm required to inform you that you're to stand down and report back to WFO," she said of the Washington Field Office. She waved for Shortz to pass over his tablet.

He did, with a look of foreboding.

Watson tore off the top sheet, took it to the conference room door and called over the closest SIOC agent, who sped off with the paper in hand.

"We suspect law enforcement electronic resources are compromised," Morgan said. "For that reason, you need to put out a bulletin stating I was killed in the line of duty, along with U.S. Army Captain Rachel Pratt. Both of us died from injuries sustained at Soldiers' Home."

Watson returned to the phone. "Captain Pratt is wanted by MPDC in connection with a fatal shooting of a nurse."

"Well, that's a curve ball." A muffled argument was audible across the line. "She'll turn herself in after zero hundred hours. Until then, both of us are deceased."

Watson spoke sternly. "Rachael Pratt is a fugitive from the law. You are in no position to protect or shelter her, which would make you an accessory to a crime."

"Understood."

Watson shrugged. "Any idea on where we can find this Barnes guy?"

"We're going to chat with someone who can help in that department." She rattled off a phone number and mentioned photos had been sent by email. "Don't post any clues on the network until after Frances Davidson is located. Not even JWICS. That's paramount. Evidence can be picked up as time permits. Mr. Shortz, call when you solve the clues."

The line went dead again.

Spinning around in her chair, Watson brought up an email and downloaded a series of photos onto the screen.

Shortz had his pencil moving, ignoring the puzzle's prelude and jumping to the remaining six clues. Watson saw his eyes brighten, energized by the challenge before him.

He pointed to the screen. "1 ACROSS. RUDIMENTARY ADAMANT. That functions as a cornerstone word. It frames the puzzle. Provides structure." He grinned as his mind ran through potential solutions, his lips ticking off hints of the words themselves.

He tapped the screen, finger targeting the black circle with three rectangles in it.

"Those symbols have always worked like sign posts."

Watson leaned over his shoulder. "Maybe it represents stacked objects, like the pillars at Soldiers' Home."

Shortz took an anxious breath. "It could point back to 1 ACROSS. Something to do with stones or building blocks."

56
WEDGE 5

The Pentagon, U.S. Department of Defense, Virginia

Randy Wang was heading to Wedge 5 and the Army OUSD section when his cell phone rang. Not recognizing the number, he slowed to linger in the C Ring and Corridor 5 intersection while he took the call.

"You find that general?" a woman's voice asked.

"You on a secure phone this time?"

"Yes."

Wang nodded. "I'm taking care of that favor. And I can report I'm pretty much standing on his doorstep." He thought for a moment. "Morgan, you know what you're doing?"

The response was sharp, almost terse. "Took lessons from a master spy once."

He chuckled. "How'd that turn out?"

"Nearly got myself killed, did get suspended, and subpoenaed before Congress." A heavy sigh came across the line. "I think I'm still paying for my sins."

"Thank you for what you did." Making sure his wording was clear, he said, "Look, Morgan, I can't kidnap a general, no matter how much you want him. And I cannot force him to leave the Pentagon against his will."

"When you meet him," she said, "tell Davidson that I have a message about his daughter, Frances. She's alive. And if he works with me—just me—he gets his wife and daughter back. Call me on this number and I'll provide the details to him. After that, he can make his own decision."

He shrugged. "Fair enough."

"Colonel, one more thing," Morgan added. "You ever run across an Eye of Ra linked to RMG Global Solutions?"

Two heavily armed U.S. Pentagon Police (USPPD) officers approached, making their systematic rounds of semi-public spaces. Their eyes homed in on Wang as they drew closer.

"It's probably not Ra," Wang said, waving politely and heading into C Ring to pick up Corridor 6 and progress to the Mall Entrance of the Pentagon. When some distance was behind him, his returned to the conversation. "More likely the Eye of Providence, without the triangle."

"The All-Seeing Eye? Like on the dollar bill?"

Wang thought about it. "The symbol represents the eye of God as he watches over humanity. EyePoint Applications uses the icon in its corporate logo. And EyePoint secured its IT and security systems and master services contracts through the Phoenix Consortium and RMG Global Solutions. Also EyePoint has direct contracts with WMATA and the GSA at St. Elizabeths. I found line-item budget references to the Navy and the Pentagon."

"So Barnes used this EyePoint Applications as his vehicle to get around security protocols?"

Wang frowned. "Who's Barnes?"

"I'll tell you about him after you get the general's attention."

The call ended.

Wang waited in a small lobby that fronted several executive offices until a uniformed major came out to escort him into the office of Major General James Davidson.

In his dress uniform, the general stood behind a large corner desk and gazed out a west window, into the orange glow of an emerging sunset.

As Wang stood at attention, he scanned the broad office. Blue carpets. A flag stand with the U.S. and Army flags. Four pictures: the President, the Vice President, the Secretary of Defense, the Chief of Staff of the Army. Casework displaying a series of antique swords.

"Thank you for seeing me, General," Wang said.

No acknowledgement was given, the senior officer making it clear the courtesy of a meeting was extended only because of their common bond—Army.

Wang stood in silence for half a minute, then said, "I have news on your daughter, sir."

The general's head turned.

When the superior officer faced him, Wang saluted.

"At ease, Colonel," Davidson said, obviously burdened. "I'm not at liberty to discuss whatever the NSA and CYBERCOM are after. So I doubt I can do anything for you."

"Understood, sir." Wang walked to the other end of his office, placed his cell phone on a small conference table, and looked out a window at the sunset. "Your operations are visually compromised. If you play your situation forward, everything is terminal. Congressional inquiries, GAO audits, federal investigations will destroy all your work."

"Are you threatening me?" the general asked.

"No, sir." Wang took a breath and stepped closer. "Some of us are called to operate in the gray areas. Conduct our business on behalf of our beloved nation in dark, uncomfortable shadows. I'm not here to judge. My visit is as a neutral broker. It's not about what you can do for me as much as what I can do for you."

The general nodded for him to continue.

Wang picked up his cell phone. "You can be reunited with your wife and daughter. All we have to do is place a call."

Northwest of Dupont Circle, Washington, DC

Kate Morgan felt the familiar surge of adrenaline fill her bloodstream when the phone rang.

Sitting in an ornate study, she snacked on canned ham and crackers. Behind an executive-style solid wood desk, Pratt had kicked up her boots on the desk's edge and finished off slices of salami. Neither had eaten since before the morning commute.

Pratt tapped the phone's speaker button then licked her fingers to get the meat residue off of them.

"Special Agent Katherine Morgan, FBI," Kate said, her hand spinning an ornate old-world globe in a stand.

"Morgan, this is Army Colonel Randall Wang," he said on the other end of the call. "General Davidson is here with me."

Kate glanced over at Pratt, whose nerves suddenly made her look a shade paler.

"General," Kate said, clearing her throat loudly. "I don't know how to say this, so I'll just get on with it. Captain Rachel Pratt died of injuries sustained during an explosion at Soldiers' Home. She lost her life trying to save others. Law enforcement, including the bureau, also lost personnel."

"How'd she die?" the general asked.

She hadn't expected the question and rolled her eyes in thought. Pratt pointed to her chest.

"Penetrating chest trauma." Kate sighed so the general could hear her. "I'm a doctor, specializing in forensics. From the placement of her thoracic wounds I would say shrapnel severed her aorta. She wasn't wearing any protective gear. Probably died instantly."

After a pause, the general said, "Pratt was an excellent soldier."

Pratt let the corner of her mouth lift in a smile.

"Yes, sir, she was" Kate said. "You may not know this, but she was one of the first responders after the WMATA bombing. While she didn't exactly save my life, she made a difference. Demonstrated grit and valor. Helped rescue a mother and child. Jumped into harm's way and put others ahead of herself."

Pratt arched an eyebrow at the sentiments.

Kate almost grinned. "Phillip Logan Barnes murdered her. And so many others. Good people. People with families and children. He's the terrorist at large, the perpetrator of these heinous murders. From the clues that he's provided, we know he was one of your lab rats, and I've had the horrific experience of engaging him personally."

"Agent," the general said, "Barnes hasn't been part of the U.S. Armed Forces in years. Official records document him as deceased. I'm shocked as anyone to hear he's alive and learn about his involvement."

Kate bobbed her head in mock agreement. "Well, he seems quite the resurrection story—like a lot of people lately. Sir, in his last communication, Phillip Barnes directed me to contact you. Unfortunately, I couldn't do that until now."

"I have nothing to contribute or discuss. I'm sorry you've wasted your time."

She rapped the hardwood desk with her finger. "Barnes demands a trade: you for your daughter. I've seen video footage. Frances is alive. If you decline this offer, she'll be executed. Shot once through the heart. I was told you'd understand that significance. If you accept, a time and location for the exchange will be provided. He said you sacrificed Navy Lieutenant Martin Carpenter and a squad of Army Rangers searching for him. He asked for no more blood to be shed. No more lives lost. No more secrets. It seems his final stop in this premeditated insanity ends with the three of us: you, me, and him."

"When do I have to provide an answer?"

Kate shrugged. "Pretty much now." She exhaled another heavy breath, loud enough to be heard over the phone. "The bureau took your wife, Mary, in for additional questioning. I can get her released. That's the easy part. But you need to understand that Frances is lying in an open grave. It's getting dark. Your daughter won't survive until morning. Barnes will kill her."

With no immediate answer, she pressed. "What's your answer, General? Willing to risk your life to be a hero?"

The general's response was like that of a defeated man. "When and where?"

57
BACKPACKS

Alice Watson studied the solutions revealed in SCRABBLE tiles.

Game over. We're coming for you, Phillip Logan Barnes.

Beside her, Will Shortz stroked his chin. "1 ACROSS. A fifteener. A word-phrase that spans the grid and defines boundaries."

She admired his eclectic mind, how he saw associations, relationships. His efficiency under pressure mimicked that of a chess grandmaster who crushed the clock during the five minutes of blitz play.

1 ACROSS—FOUNDATION STONE—seemed linked to the symbol in the lower left-hand corner of the photographed skin. Its crude Lego-like representation supported two building blocks. Without context, though, looking for a solution was like searching for a single grain of sand hidden on the long Virginia Beach oceanfront. Physical stones? Washington, DC, was full of monuments built of stone: granite, sandstone, and marble. Impossible to track down a single stone in the nation's capital without tripping over another.

Yet Morgan had figured out the related wordplay.

A photo, only seen by a mother, hinted that her daughter occupied a shallow grave surrounded by broken stones. Discarded stones. Tombstones.

Relics from the past, hidden in plain sight: the Capitol Stones in Rock Creek Park.

Watson agreed to give Morgan the latitude to find the victim and one set of clues without backup or additional fanfare.

1 ACROSS was kept off all networks. For now.

With her heart pounding, Watson knew this gambit would end her career if anything went awry. Everything hinged on Morgan's plan, and only if she didn't get herself killed by taking unnecessary risks.

Watson returned to the puzzle. Shortz had delivered the remaining four solutions for these as well.

31 DOWN was SATORI, a Zen Buddhist expression with Japanese origins used in several Asian cultures: Chinese, Korean, Vietnamese, and Japanese. Comprehension. Understanding. Seeing into one's true nature. It proved a theme for the latest solutions and reinforced the intersecting abbreviation in 53 ACROSS. ABI's initials fit a Pentagon program called the Advanced Biogenetics Initiative.

Through secondary sources, they'd learned ABI's principal investigator (PI) and director was none other than Major General James Davidson himself.

Enlightenment personified. Davidson and his team created 40 DOWN: IGOR. Known to the world as Phillip Logan Barnes. The nation's latest domestic terrorist and the FBI's newest public enemy number one.

The word THRALL in 55 ACROSS intersected the T in TUES and the L in SHELTER. Not too far of a stretch was the notion that Barnes had considered himself a slave. Disillusioned with Davidson's genetic research, the mass murderer was hell-bent on destroying everyone from his past, including FBI Special Agent Katherine Morgan.

Shortz picked OAK as the best possibility for 50 DOWN and SLEEPS IS SEED—a solution with a potential association to the destination.

Morgan had solved 38 DOWN: ELK PASS. Field agents had been dispatched to the small coal mining town in West Virginia, a place that had made national news because of a catastrophic mine explosion that killed seventeen miners and the town's doctor. Katherine Morgan had been on a rural exchange from Johns Hopkins and was the only doctor available to treat the injured.

A technician handed Watson two objects: a briefcase and a small backpack.

Watson held them up to Shortz, her mind dressing him with the latest in bureau-provided, GPS-tracked accessories. "What do you think, professor? The backpack?"

He shrugged. "Do I look like Dora the Explorer?"

"You jest," she said, "but I bet logistics can find you a purple version."

He slung it over one shoulder. "This one works just fine."

Her expression turned somber. "I can always find someone else."

Shortz shook his head. "I'll be okay." He slid his other arm into the remaining strap and cinched both shoulder straps up. "I'll pick up the evidence and return in a couple of hours. How hard can that be?"

58
A WALK IN THE PARK

5:20 PM, Rock Creek Park, Washington, DC

Kate hated deferring to others but went with Pratt's Ranger experience and instincts because they'd proven invaluable. On short notice, U.S Park Rangers had closed the park to get the public out of harm's way, shut off utility power to the area, and fired up a series of smudge pots. That last step was critical to their plan.

Pratt pulled her government-issued van into a thickening haze and parked. From the maintenance circle, they'd walk to the stones.

Through the front windshield, gray tree trunks looked like phantom fingers reaching up to a filtered canopy.

Kate stepped out into thick, still air. Her nostrils detected the fumes of kerosene, with a bitter accent of motor oil mixed with tree sap. Pratt had provided the infrared-light-limiting recipe, and in record time the Park Service maintenance crews had constructed makeshift smudge pots and cordoned off boundaries around the Capitol Stones.

The oily smoke stung Kate's eyes and forced her to take shorter breaths to avoid hacking and coughing.

A phone conversation with Wang on the drive over had offered insights into how the terrorist was pulling off his Eye of God observations—EyePoint Applications. The company had top secret, real-time, ultra-high definition satellite surveillance access. Because of its vital importance, the nation's capital had three dedicated geo-synchronous orbit (GEO) satellites, with another in final commissioning stages, dedicated to watching a little over a hundred square miles.

And Phillip Barnes had patched directly into those secured platforms.

"This going to work?" Kate asked, unloading first aid containers from the van.

"Our goal is to hide from infrared and passive infrared, thermal imaging. Those systems have inherent weaknesses that we're exploiting. Similar defensive techniques have been used in war to mask assets and protect targets." Pratt clipped an M4 carbine with a grenade launcher onto her vest. "Sunrise. Sunset. A twice-daily thermal crossover range. Those slip-through windows can be tight depending on the season. Smudging extends our time beyond an hour. The smog blanket will raise the ambient temperature a few degrees."

Smudging: a low-tech solution to thwart intrusive satellite surveillance. Kate knew about the non-EPA compliant smudge pots from their use in orchards to protect fruit from frost damage. She'd presumed Pratt knew her craft well and how to use smudging during war as well.

"Put this on." All business, Pratt tossed Kate a silver poncho.

"So how much of a genetically modified super soldier are you?" Kate asked, sliding the poncho over her clothing. The one-size-all, tent-like fit was cinched tight by a pair of straps.

"I was never given a percentage versus what remained from original donor material." Oblivious to personal space and boundaries, Pratt pulled up Kate's hood. Her brown eyes seemed to soak her up, as if trying to decide if she was a charity case or a threat that required elimination. "Consider me one hundred percent lethal."

Kate smiled thinly. "If Barnes is genius smart and strong, what powers do you have?"

"He was never as strong as me, and he knew it." Pratt flashed a maniacal grin and tapped her left breast. "My body can regulate and increase cellular regeneration, anything from controlling the production of proteins and white blood cells to accelerated fibroplasia and granulation tissue formation. The technical term is rapid cellular regeneration, RCR. I self-heal."

"So that's how you survived." A chill ran down Kate's spine. The movie *Gattaca* had explored this quandary in perfecting genetic engineering. It began with a quotation from Willard Gaylin, M.D.: "I not only think that we will tamper with Mother Nature, I think Mother wants us to." Humans hadn't waited for an invitation.

Pratt slid on her poncho. "Dig out the bullet, keep oxygen and blood flowing during surgery, add some internal and external sutures, and I get a better than a 50-50 chance of surviving. That's why Davidson shot me instead of Barnes. He wanted to keep both of us."

Kate refused to accept that premise, at least fully. "You told me Barnes questioned the program, authority. He spoke his mind. You probably kept your thoughts in check, never spoke out of turn."

Pratt whispered in her ear. "You think you know me?"

Kate extended her arm to maintain distance. "Just making observations, Rachel."

Pratt glared at her with incredulous, challenging eyes.

Kate smiled inwardly. Super soldiers were probably a hotheaded lot, just itching for a fight. Pratt fit that mold sure enough. Her test tube generation of warriors were FOUNDATION STONES. Years earlier, before the public declaration of Dolly the cloned sheep, rumors had circulated about scientists in government think tanks working on manipulating the human genome and enhancing human DNA using gene splicing. Genetically modified "test tube" babies needed incubators, and public fears rose that the government would sponsor neomortuaries.

Kate thought of her last investigation and its illegal test subjects.

Neomortuaries were wards set aside for incapacitated or recently deceased women to be kept alive by artificial means so their uteruses could host implanted embryos. When the babies reached term, C-sections would be performed and the hosts discarded. Congress responded to neomortuary and genetic testing fears with closed door hearings. In the end, the rumors were determined to be false. Neomortuaries and genetic testing did not exist, at least from the government's public point of view.

But such scientific thirsts could be quenched in one way only—proof of concepts.

It was never a matter of if but rather when.

A Chinese researcher named Jiankui dared to publically announce his use of a gene-editing tool called clustered regularly interspaced short palindromic repeats—CRISPR. His genetically tailored babies ushered in a new era.

Unknown to Jiankui, the human evolution genie had been free of the bottle well before his test tube gymnastics.

Advancing human evolution was an ominous reality.

During a morning commute, a WMATA train was bombed. The vile act of terrorism announced to the world that designer humans, perfect people, were stepping out of the shadows and into the light.

Northwest of Dupont Circle, Washington, DC

Will Shortz stepped through a bricked breezeway and ducked into the alley behind a historic three-story brownstone situated on a residential street corner. A wooden gate led to a rear patio. He found a door key beneath a flower pot just as directed. He unlocked the back door, entered the home, and typed in the four-digit code provided to disable the home's alarm.

He'd been told to get in, pick up the package, and get out.

No one was home, but that didn't mean he could linger.

Adrenaline surged as he darted inside. His heartbeat kept a steady rhythm, while his gaze swept back rooms, a kitchen, and down a narrow corridor. He stepped into a dining room and slowed his gait. An elegant hardwood table held a series of soft-sided equipment bags. A shotgun and a sniper's rifle were set beside the equipment bags.

Shortz swallowed. Volunteering to be Watson's pickup service might not have been the wisest of ideas. Perhaps he should have stayed in the SIOC and worked the clues as they came in.

He forced himself to stay focused. *Get in, get out.* Those were his directions.

Crossing a large foyer, he found his destination: a large corner study. Drapes covered windows that looked over an intersection of residential streets. Bookcases on two walls held vintage hardbacks. An ornate desk with a rosary stretched across it stood behind a brass telescope and a replica old world globe in a cradle.

Shortz was tempted to peruse the shelves. He loved books, especially those about world history and culture. Perhaps the FBI could let him come back, later.

Shortz turned to the globe. Its circular base was an inset compass face that racked bottles of distilled amber liquids neatly in a circle.

He grinned; this was a prop straight out of a spy movie.

Unclasping the northern hemisphere, he found a cavity inside the globe. Diamond cut whiskey tumblers surrounded a rolled parchment resting in a gold-plated ice cube tray.

Setting his backpack on the desk, he readied himself to make the transfer.

A faint tread of footsteps interrupted his thoughts and made him glance up.

He wasn't alone.

Standing in the doorway was a woman holding a gun.

Rock Creek Park, Washington, DC

Ambush.

Kate desperately wanted to avoid plummeting through another series of trap doors. Her Thelma and Louise partnership with Pratt was reassuring, and Kate doubted it was something Barnes could have expected.

That gave them an edge.

But a newly formed sisterhood didn't mean Kate trusted her soldier companion. Too many secrets, lies, and half-trusts to figure out. And she wasn't sure how she'd handle Pratt when the opportunity arose to gun down Barnes. The mass murderer, regardless of his genetic makeup, deserved a day in court. It was his right to be judged on his crimes.

Kate kept pace behind Pratt as they hiked through the smoky forest. They passed tree trunks stripped of limbs, like ghostly pillars of distrust and danger. The smudge pot smoke made her reflect on the train bombing. She could almost see faces of the dead inside the confines of twisted metal. The dense trunks seemed to shift past her like apparitions. Thick air brushed her checks and she could feel the side effects of wearing Pratt's protective poncho. Inside the heat-signature reducing blanket, she was smoldering, sweating profusely. Much longer and she'd boil from the inside out. Another disadvantage of the space-age poncho was that it crinkled and crunched like the rocks in the trail beneath her boots.

Pratt pushed forward, her outline and M4 clearing the way.

The main trail ebbed and flowed as it snaked its ladder rung-like path from one north-south rail to the next.

Ahead, Pratt took a knee and tinkered with an earpiece. The gadget in her hand pinged sound waves outside the range of human hearing. The technique worked like sonar, but Pratt assured Kate that no sonic attacks would occur this time. In the tunnels, Barnes had used trip wires to set off explosives that collapsed the tunnels and severed sewer lines.

Following the device's guidance, Pratt moved south of the main trail, up a slight embankment. The former Ranger crouched forward.

The path changed from being beaten down by regular foot traffic, thinning out and narrowing. Shallow tree roots cut across a narrow footpath, and Kate had to lift her feet higher to keep from tripping.

Breaking through a wall of gray, a stone outcropping emerged.

The Capitol Stones.

A park ranger had provided a brief history: in the late 1950s, the Architect of the Capitol and the Speaker of the House conspired to expand the U.S. Capitol's eastern front and replace its old sandstone façade with Georgian White marble. Eventually, the discarded Aquia Creek sandstone made its way to the park. But the ownership of the abandoned materials never actually had transferred over to the U.S. Park Service. Instead, the custody of the construction waste passed to the House and Senate Office building commissions, where occasionally the U.S. Capitol Historical Society—through the Speaker of the House—would authorize an allotment of the stones to be cut down and sold off as bookends.

FOUNDATION STONES. Kate wondered what liberties Barnes had taken with this solution. What connected those abstract ideas together: setting, victims, the advanced biogenetics initiative, advancing human evolution, and the House Speaker's office.

"Stop here," Pratt said. From a bag she pulled out a signal jammer and switched it on. She passed the device to Kate and told her it was same tech employed by the Secret Service to protect POTUS during motorcade movements. It would disrupt cellular signals that could be used by bombers to trigger remote devices.

Kate duct-taped the gadget with stubby antennas to the closest tree trunk.

Ahead, the squared end of the stones looked ominous, lurking behind a veil of gray smoke.

Kate fell back in behind Pratt as she meticulously worked closer, checking her sensors for any dangers or traps that lay in wait.

59
PARASITES

In a small breakout room, Alice Watson huddled with computer and network experts from the bureau's Cyber and IT Infrastructure Divisions. A wall monitor showed multiple camera shots of a dark-haired man in a suit among busy passengers who came and went from the WMATA Foggy Bottom-GWU station. None of the photos offered clear views of his face. Enhanced filtering had mocked up several potential appearances. The terrorist had proved deceptively elusive to CCTV. Photos of a blonde-haired man in his twenties were placed beside the others.

"Phillip Logan Barnes," she said, shifting a mouse pointer between photos, "was his birth name. He's got to be using an alias now. Most of his Army records are classified, which we're working on securing, but we did discover a psychological assessment on him. Recruiters documented his intelligent with a battery of aptitude tests. He's got a 160 IQ."

"So he's a damn smart terrorist," the tech from cyber said.

Watson shrugged. "That's an understatement." She withheld pertinent facts in the next part. "Under Army governance, Barnes was assigned to a special research program. He dropped out of training after an altercation. He died shortly after that being discharged."

- 283 -

"What kind of altercation?" the IT infrastructure tech asked.

"I'm not at liberty to say, but off the record, someone died."

"So he's a smart murderer," said the IT tech.

Watson sighed. "Today he's a super intelligent mass murderer who's experienced with hacking security networks and explosives."

"What do we know about him after the Army?" the cyber tech asked.

Watson displayed transcripts from MIT on the screen. Class grades listed all As. "The name on his college application is Isaac Smith from Water Island, U.S. Virgin Islands. We know that's false because he grew up in Elk Pass, West Virginia. His education was self-funded and he fast-tracked dual masters: mechanical engineering and computer science with an emphasis in theoretical computer science. Open-source code modules he wrote during college are still used in multiple surveillance system platforms, including U.S. spy satellites."

"He wrote code for spy satellites?" the cyber tech asked.

Watson nodded. "That's the part of his biography we know about. Barnes is brilliant and versatile enough to circumvent WMATA security systems. That's how he planted the IEDs on the train tracks undetected. To make him super lethal, he obtained at least one military-built EMP cannon." She hesitated before hitting her colleagues with the real gut punch. "But, worst of all, we believe Barnes has hacked into secured bureau networks and satellite systems. He's been plugged into our every move."

The IT infrastructure tech cursed.

The cyber tech shook his head. "Not possible. Firewalls and security protocols prohibit outside access to classified networks."

Watson slammed an open palm against the table. "It doesn't matter what you believe. Consider it fact until disproven. And what I care about is discovering how Phillip Logan Barnes has hacked our networks."

60
OUT THE WINDOW

Northwest of Dupont Circle, Washington, DC

Shortz took a nervous breath and raised his hands. His day of firsts had continued, much to his surprise. Staring at the barrel of a gun was a foreign if not a completely out-of-body experience. On this particular Monday perhaps he should have stayed in New York, rather than get caught up in terrorism investigations and volunteering to run errands for the FBI.

"Sorry for the intrusion. I was told no one would be home," he said, realizing that his statement sounded like an incompetent burglar's admission. "I was sent to pick this up."

"Who are you?" asked the woman. Her frazzled dark hair was painted with thick strands of silver. She glanced at the globe, which was hinged open like a hollow Easter egg.

An appropriate question, considering he'd never been invited into the home. Against a twinge of better judgment, Shortz deferred answering her question as he probed his eclectic memory. The woman looked familiar. Especially her face. He had seen her before.

Then it came to him. During the FBI's monastery stop, her picture was on the SIOC's big board. In the photo, Mary Davidson stood next to her uniformed husband, an Army general. The couple appeared to have been attending some red carpet gala. A shawl had covered her shoulders and she wore a black evening dress.

"You're the FOUNDATION STONE," he blurted. The epiphany fueled a rush through his veins. It was why he loved solving puzzles so damn much. Beyond clues and solutions, themes and destinations, secrets and research, he'd been exposed to enough of the core investigation to comprehend its grander picture. Bombings. Crimes. Secret labs. Victims. Suspects. Bizarre interrelationships. "This is as much about you as it is your husband."

Mary Davidson wore her poker mask well. "You law enforcement?"

"No. I work... puzzles." Shortz lowered his arms, but kept his hands close to his waist. If he'd stayed in New York, he'd have missed this deeper clue. History was the teacher here. No matter what a person believed or how they viewed Jesus of Nazareth's claim on divinity, the Son of God wouldn't exist without his birthmother. Mary. A patron saint. Saint Mary of the Angels. Portiuncula Chapel. The first church of Saint Francis. The symbolic birthplace of the Franciscan Order. The line BE MINDFUL OF ORIGINS pinged in his mind. The woman holding a gun was a reflection, the symbolic birthmother of this new breed of genetically created super soldiers.

The woman entered the study, keeping the weapon's sights on Shortz. Her attention was drawn to the globe like a compass needle seeking true north.

Gesturing at the parchment of skin, she asked, "Does that belong to my daughter?"

"I don't know, Dr. Davidson," he said, going with a presumptive title rather than her name. "I assume the FBI needs to run DNA analysis on it before making any determinations."

She lowered her weapon. "My father loved his study. When I was a child, this was his sanctuary. I know this old house is my family home, but I'm unsure how we got here." She swallowed hard. "Frances will always be my oldest. My baby. But Phillip holds a special place in my heart as my firstborn."

"Agents are searching for your daughter. I know that for a fact."

Davidson turned to the window and wrenched back its drapes. Outside, darkness began to crease through the historic neighborhood.

"It won't matter. By morning, my children will be dead."

The coldness of her words hit him in the gut. "Perhaps you should talk with someone."

She shook her head. "Hatred and vengeance are manifestations of the monster that I've created. Soon, my achievements will be gone. My husband. My daughter. My work."

Reading people was not Shortz's best strength, but he saw that Mary Davidson was scarred on the inside and outside. "I don't know about your husband, but the FBI believes your daughter is alive."

She faced him. "In her current state, Frances is dead to me." She waved the gun at the open globe. "Take what you came for."

He wasn't exactly sure how to absorb the newsflash. In the SIOC, agents had discussed the medical conditions of the victims, how they'd been maimed and skinned and put into unconscious states similar to comas. "What's wrong with your daughter?"

Her eyes narrowed. "Ask Agent Morgan what happened in Princeton and why its lead researcher cannot be revived." She took a breath. "I thought if I went along with his scheme, displayed faith and waited in the monastery, Phillip would spare my daughter. When I saw that researcher in the tiny church I knew I was wrong. Phillip's victims are trapped inside their own bodies. He destroyed their work by silencing their minds."

Shortz snatched up the parchment of skin and a canning jar containing black dirt. The killer's treasures went into his backpack, which he slung over his shoulder.

He left the study, leaving Mary Davidson standing in the window.

Instead of backtracking through the house, he let himself out the front door and navigated red brick steps to the street.

Glancing back, he saw Mary Davidson in the window. She raised her arm as if she was about to wave. The flash of light and a startling gunshot caused him to stumble. He lowered his gaze for a second to the sidewalk as he regained his balance.

When Will Shortz looked up again, Mary Davidson was nowhere in sight.

.

61
STONES

Rock Creek Park, Washington, DC

Kate's arms quivered as she pulled against the fiberglass handle of a pick-axe, its point wedged between slab and foundation.

Darkness had seized the smoke-filled forest more rapidly than Pratt expected, further complicating their search and rescue efforts. But sure enough, they found a makeshift crypt inside an alley of stacked, lichen covered sandstone blocks. Eerily, the setting was nothing like what Mary Davidson had described. Besides a hazy envelope of darkness, their problem was a six-inch thick stone slab. Under ultraviolet light, the Eye of Providence marked the stone. Between stone lid and its underlayment was a gap wide enough to spy through. Flashlight beams revealed an earthly coffin with one occupant: Frances Davidson.

Before they even focused on the grave, Pratt was adamant about clearing the scene of hazards: trip wires, pressure-plate explosives, or other IEDs. Nothing was found. No booby traps. No explosives. And since they were well past Pratt's targeted thermal crossover for satellites, they had shed their sweltering ponchos in favor of the night air. Every movement they made was visible to surveillance satellites that ran infrared scans.

Drenched in sweat, Kate shivered and repositioned herself around the axe.

Pratt's eyes were wild in the glow of a flashlight. "You doing anything useful?" She grunted and heaved on a long pry bar wedged between the rocks, trying to shift the slab sideways.

Across the slab, Kate dug her boots in and jerked on her tool's handle again. "What happened to you? Where'd all your muscles go?" She took several panting breaths. "I expected a soldier of your genetic caliber to damn near be able to fly."

Pratt snapped at her. "You want to miss some front teeth?"

Kate threw her hands up and backed away, trying to slow her breathing in the thick air.

"Grab that axe!"

Kate shook her head. "This isn't working!"

"You going to let her die like you did Navy Lieutenant Martin Carpenter?"

"I tried—"

"To save him? You were a coward. I would've gone in."

The verbal jab hurt. "And you would've died."

Pratt dropped her pry bar and broadened her shoulders.

Kate brushed a palm against her chin and snatched up a flashlight, turning her back to the soldier. Sweeping the beam across the landscape of stacked rocks and cast aside stonework, something hit her. It was something Pratt had said earlier.

She hit the soldier with the spotlight. "You really stronger than Barnes?"

Pratt cracked a smile and her brown face radiated her thoughts. "That was never in doubt."

Kate dropped to her stomach, lying flat against the dirt. She squeezed a spray of light into the makeshift crypt. Past the naked, incapacitated figure, she spotted a dark hole up by the head.

"We're going about this the wrong way," Kate said, hopping to her feet and scampering over stones that were stacked like hardened firewood. She dropped into a hole on the other side of the discarded pile of rock and disappeared. She called back, "Over here."

Pratt did a half leap, leaving her torso balancing on the top of the stone wall, her own flashlight brightening up the crypt.

Kate held up a palm full of granulated dirt. "It's fresh from digging. He tunneled under the slab and the wall to make a burial chamber. Mary Davidson saw this side of the wall in the photo, not the other."

The perspiration in her clothes held the cold and made her shiver.

Pratt's expression seemed to dare her to mole her way underground.

"Wish me luck," Kate said, resenting the accusation that she'd been a coward.

"Rangers don't operate on luck."

"Or emotion," Kate countered, wanting desperately to repay the dig. "Hey, make yourself useful. Toss down those ponchos and some rope."

Earthy aromas filled her nostrils. Behind the beam of the flashlight, she determined the tunnel's length to be no longer than ten feet. It was hand-carved, rounded and large enough to slither through. There was no way she was getting back out two at a time.

The deeper she squirmed on her elbows, the tighter the tunnel got, contracting around her. Fears of getting stuck crept into her mind. Tight, small spaces terrified her, including elevators, which was why she always took the stairs. MRIs freaked her out too. She chastised herself. She'd swam the channel in the Pit of Misery and survived—it was probably that or die. This was a shorter version of that test. Pushing ahead, she broke into the burial chamber and had to climb over the comatose Frances Davidson to get turned around.

"I made it," she called up through the cracks beneath the immovable stone lid. Kate thrust her fingers into the victim's neck to detect a pulse from a carotid artery. It was faint but present. "She's alive."

Kate sprayed the illumination down the length of the woman's body. Same as the other victims. The skin on her left breast had been replaced with an artificial patch. Scanning from her neck to navel, Kate saw freckles covering Frances's torso like stars in the Milky Way. In her hands, she held another set of clues. Leaning across the woman, Kate performed a sternum rub and got no response to painful stimuli.

Pratt stuffed rope and ponchos through the gaps. Kate used the coverings to cocoon Frances Davidson and bind her feet. There was only one safe way out, and that was feet first while Kate trailed behind her to keep Frances's head from dragging the ground.

62
THE VAN

Fort Totten, Washington, DC

Takoma Park Police Sergeant Clinton Jones turned his patrol car onto Brookland Ave NE and idled his vehicle through Fort Totten Park. Working two hand-held flashlights, one pointed through each side window, he scanned his assigned quadrant north of Soldiers' Home.

With his windows down, lingering smoke from the bombing made its way into his nostrils. When Jones had learned of the cowardly attack, he volunteered to extend his shift. In times of need, the law enforcement community rallied together as family. Washington, DC, had been battered. And the FBI, MPDC, and WMATA had taken some big hits.

The throw of his tactical-style flashlights pierced through the trees to about 500 feet. Swiveling his head, he peered past the trunks of dormant trees. The park setting had the usual squatters and homeless with their tents and bags of worldly possessions. A couple of guilty-in-their-eyes young men turned toward him. From the dancing cherries in the air, they were smoking something. One of the boys raised a hand with a middle finger extended, a universal sign of peace, love, and keep moving, cop.

Jones shrugged at the gesture. This was hardly time for community outreach.

Returning to his pass-through survey, his lights illuminated more treed landscape. He turned the steering wheel with his knees and guided his patrol car around a curve. He tapped the brakes when he approached a gravel turnaround, which obviously had been used by the aggregate company on the adjacent property.

Something in the distance caught his attention.

A black van.

It was a transit style vehicle with an extended top for storage.

And that fit a description from the FBI.

Strategical Information & Operations Center (SIOC), FBI Headquarters, Washington, DC

"Do not approach the vehicle," Alice Watson directed the Takoma Park Police officer over a phone. In the front of the ops center, one screen was dedicated solely to Phillip Logan Barnes. The other screens coordinated response and real-time satellite telemetry at Ft. Totten. As the satellite zoomed in, vehicle headlights illuminated a black van tucked beneath a tree. "Officer Jones, great job on finding it. Hold your position. Consider the vehicle booby-trapped. Our bomb squad and SWAT teams are en route."

"SWAT has an ETA of five minutes by air," a logistics tech announced. "Bomb squad is mobilizing from Soldiers' Home—they'll be there in just over five. ATF is sending agents as well—they track ten minutes out."

"Watson," a technician shouted, "you have a call on line two. He said to tell you he ran into a complication."

Complication? That grabbed her attention.

"Someone take over coordination with Officer Jones," she said, before switching over to line two. Avoiding a speaker phone, she wanted their conversation to stay out of earshot of other parties. "Professor," she said, "is everything okay?"

A concerned voice came across the line. "Mary Davidson is dead."

"Dead?" Watson took a seat. "How? No, wait. Are you injured?"

"No. Suicide. I think." Shortz took a breath. "She was at the house. It was her family home."

Watson frowned, unsure how to interpret the news. An FBI check of the property listed it in the Clark Family Trust. Mary Davidson's maiden name must've been Clark.

"She's 1 ACROSS. The FOUNDATION STONE. I missed the clues from the monastery. Dr. Davidson led the original research efforts, not her husband. This is merely interpretation, but I think Frances Davidson was just following in her mother's footsteps."

"Who else knows about this?"

"Just you and me." He cleared his throat. "There's two more aspects to our conversation."

"Go ahead."

"She said, 'By morning, my children will be dead.' I suspect that includes her daughter, along with her genetic creations. Her super soldiers. And she seemed resigned to the fact that something was going to happen."

"Did she provide specifics?" she asked.

"No."

"Besides her biological and chemically created offspring, what's the second thing?"

He exhaled over the phone. "No one can wake her daughter. When I asked what was wrong with her, she directed me to Agent Morgan. Something about Princeton. A researcher there who can't wake up. I'm a bit short on the conversational context for that riddle."

Watson shivered. "She said Princeton?"

"Yes," he confirmed. "Dr. Davidson said Phillip Barnes is trapping his victims inside their own bodies, silencing their minds."

Watson dropped her head against a desk and spoke beneath her breath. "Princeton ties this back to the White House."

That bothered her.

FOUNDATIONSTONE
O O L
RP MURDER XII
LA II S
Y H I
LAB A O
EUGENICS SEVEN
A
ELIZABETHS S
LOGTHETOURS H
K O ET R HOME
P R ABI THRALL
A I U K T
S O E E
STIGMA SAPPER

63
HEED THIS PROCLAMATION

6:45 PM, George Washington University Hospital (GWU), Washington, DC

Kate Morgan rode with Frances Davidson in the ambulance to the hospital, returning to the very place where her Monday-from-hell had started. Beside her, an EMT tended to the incapacitated woman and set an IV line to administer fluids and compensate for dehydration.

The ambulance driver chirped his siren and sped through a traffic light, forcing her and the EMT to rebalance and ride out the constant shifting of the vehicle's momentum.

"Give me some room," Kate said, sliding on sterile gloves. Pulling back the sheet covering the victim's torso, she laid the latest patch containing clues over the artificial replacement. She smoothed it out so that seams and edges matched up.

"What the hell are you doing?" the EMT asked.

"Nothing you're allowed to discuss with anyone," Kate said. "Unless, of course, you want to go to federal prison for a very long time."

The skin tones and textures varied. And this patch was stretched as if it belonged to another female victim. The tally was two men and two women out of seven, and all worked with scientific research initiatives. She studied the inked message.

KATHERINE, PROVIDENCE'S LIGHT EXPOSES WHAT IS DONE IN DARKNESS. THE MINDS OF TYRANTS ARE CAPABLE OF CREATING HEAVEN OF HELL AND HELL OF HEAVEN, SO ANGELS MUST LOOK HOMEWARD.

DOWN

2	LINK	24	BEHOLD
4	FLESHY FRUIT WITH STONE	36	ABBR: NASA RESEARCH
		39	ABBR: DARKEN
6	WELKIN	67	ABBR: PERIHELION PASSAGE
12	DAGGER OF DAYAK PEOPLE		

Eight clues.

All down.

Her head flooded with questions she did not have answers to and she let her finger trace the symbol of a sun.

The next destination. The next stop in a journey of terror.

She reread the madman's prologue.

PROVIDENCE'S LIGHT EXPOSES WHAT IS DONE IN DARKNESS.

It was a proclamation. Barnes' Eye of PROVIDENCE sought to expose dark secrets, his version of HELL. She reflected on what Pratt had said about Soldiers' Home. Her personalized version classified as HELL on Earth in a multitude of ways.

Her gaze gravitated to the last line: SO ANGELS MUST LOOK HOMEWARD. Themes for this stop were along the lines of sky, heaven, or space. She stayed with HEAVEN.

Taking a breath, Kate realized that a shocked face was watching her. She had forgotten about the EMT.

"Pass me one of those," Kate said, pointing to the tissue-like box holding biohazard bags.

She lifted the patch of skin off the slumbering Frances Davidson and slid it into the plastic waste bag for protection. After stripping off her gloves, she covered the victim again. A reflex spurred her to take the woman's limp hand. She thought of Mary Davidson and the conversation they'd shared in the monastery.

At least Kate had kept her promise and found Mary's daughter. It was a small victory in a day mired in failures.

Their ride made several turns and the ambulance driver radioed into the hospital.

Reflecting on the clues, Kate realized the only one she could solve without additional homework was 24 DOWN. LOOK or SEE made the most sense.

The ambulance made more turns before swinging into an ambulance bay.

Kate took one last look at the unconscious woman and squeezed her hand, as if to say it would be all right. The hollow gesture was more about wishes than substance. Nothing about this madness or how Frances Davidson had been tortured and violated would ever be all right. The woman, close to her own age, had been scarred for life.

Their transport stopped and the rear doors flung open.

ER personnel greeted them, anxiously awaiting their patient. Kate let go of the victim's hand and stepped out, making room for the EMT and hospital personnel.

"You Katherine Morgan?" a voice asked.

Looking back, she found a man holding a backpack. He wore an FBI contractor's badge on a lanyard.

He extended his hand and they shook. "Will Shortz."

Kate handed him a biohazard bag. "Walk with me, Mr. Shortz," she said.

He felt the weight of the flat object contained in plastic. She'd done the same thing the first time around. His eyes told her that he understood what was inside the bag.

They entered the ER Department, where a hospital staff member badged them into a restricted elevator, which they rode up alone.

"Alice Watson directed me to tell you—" He looked uneasy while he searched for words. "Mary Davidson is dead."

She turned to him. "How?"

His gaze came across as genuine, mournful. "Suicide."

Kate's stomach felt heavy with guilt. She'd failed to save both mother and daughter. Her promise felt like an empty gesture.

Shortz replayed what had happened at the home, what was said, and the revelation that Dr. Mary Davidson was the FOUNDATION STONE. "And there's more."

Stunned, she swore as the elevator doors opened. She hadn't expected that twist.

Dr. Mary Davidson was the creator of 40 DOWN, IGOR, a descendant of Norse Gods.

"Hold those thoughts, Mr. Shortz," she said, flashing her badge to the MPDC officer standing watch over the floor.

After signing in, she guided Shortz past the nurses' station and into the closest patient room. Two beds were racked into a single-bed patient room. Kate recognized both slumbering patients: one was the man found at St. Elizabeths, the other the woman at the monastery. Both were medical researchers in the fields of genetics and DNA transformations.

Snatching two pairs of sterile gloves, she handed one set to Shortz before asking him to continue. While he donned the gloves, she took out the Capitol Stones clues and set them atop the biohazard bag.

Shortz eyes widened as he studied the clues.

Performing rounds, a nurse popped into the room.

Kate held up her badge. "FBI. This is a confidential conversation. We require a few minutes alone, but while we're discussing business, I need to track down your head of neurology. I need him *stat*."

The nurse frowned, obviously considering a stranger's blunt directions rude, but she left them alone.

Shortz flattened out the patch of skin and studied its eight clues. Next to it he placed a sheet of paper that had grid lines and solutions worked out. His work was sketched out in pencil and several eraser smudges showed where solutions and grid numbers had been re-worked. Scratch work listed potential words and abbreviations. He had worked out several answers ahead of the dispensed clues. His 1 ACROSS cornerstone word phrase was FOUNDATION STONE. ELISION anchored the word at 8 DOWN.

Her eyes found the word that had started it all: 13 ACROSS, where MURDER was impossible to miss.

"What else did you need to tell me?" she asked, interrupting his thoughts.

He'd already filled in 24 DOWN with SEE.

"I solved that one," she added, wanting to make sure he noticed her contribution. "This theme is to look skyward. Toward HEAVEN."

He pointed to the inverse silhouette of a sun embedded in a circle. "39 DOWN is LO, solved by the pairing of ELIZABETHS and LOG THE TOURS. LO is an old-fashioned way of starting an announcement, saying listen up, heed this proclamation. The ab-breviation of LO is something along the lines of LIGHTS OUT. SKY is 6 DOWN. WELKIN is taken from Shakespeare's *King John*: 'The sun of heaven methought was loath to set, but stay'd and made the western WELKIN blush.'"

She eyed him closely. "LO, you're avoiding my question. What else do you need to tell me?"

Shortz took a tired breath, put aside his pencil, and faced her. "When I asked Mary Davidson what was wrong with her daughter, she said, 'Ask Agent Morgan what happened in Princeton and why its lead researcher cannot be revived.'"

Kate's blood went cold as she understood the inquiry.

"Who else have you told?" she asked, not really wanting to hear the answer.

"Alice Watson," he said.

Suddenly Kate felt alone, her heart burdened by a dark secret she didn't want to acknowledge. Mary Davidson was calling her out on it, even in death.

Her legs felt weak, unsteady.

Excusing herself, Kate fled into the corridor. Near breathless and full of panic, she asked at the nurses' station for the nearest toilet.

The directions led to a unisex restroom. Ducking inside, she locked the door behind her and sat on the tiled floor. Kate placed her head between her knees, her jaw clenched shut, aching and burning as it tried to hold in a scream.

Breaths came hard and frantic.

Phillip Barnes had deliberately placed his victims into comas to silence their minds.

Keep secrets.

She'd been thinking of Thomas Parker throughout the day. She missed him, missed spending time with him. Their jaunt to the Grand Caymans had allowed them to decompress from a shared experience inside a research lab. Similar to St. Elizabeths, the Advanced Neurological and Cybernetic Research Institute was a place where horrors and atrocities were justified in the name of science. Its lead researcher had sacrificed his own daughter. Kidnapped human subjects underwent inhumane experimentation. The whole series of events had started with the abduction and murder of a U.S. Senator.

What people in power did to protect secrets.

While Mary Davidson hadn't mentioned Thomas by name, she implied his involvement. Thomas had been one of the last people to see that lead researcher conscious. There was a reason that man could not be revived.

It was a secret she avoided asking about.

Deep inside, Kate didn't want to know what had happened to Stewart Richards.

Her time with Thomas had refreshed her. A thousand tiny moments had nurtured her soul. They made love, walked barefoot on sandy beaches, dove for pretend treasures at the bottom of the ocean, and sailed open water to chase sunsets. The Grand Caymans had been the perfect escape.

Their time together offered plenty of chances to ask, but she was afraid of the answer—fearful she would think less of Thomas Parker.

He'd avoided sharing his final moments with a madman. And that was okay. The maniacal researcher deserved to experience his own monstrous contraction, regardless of the debilitating outcome.

Somehow, Mary Davidson, and perhaps even Phillip Barnes, had learned what Thomas had done. Facts and detailed events she herself didn't want to know.

That was no longer an option. She needed to know, even if the disclosure destroyed her relationship with Thomas Parker.

64
WATCH THE DRONES CLOSELY

Strategic Information & Operations Center (SIOC), FBI Headquarters, Washington, DC

Long-overdue breaks in the investigations were coming their way at last.

And time for the FBI to unveil a few tricks of its own.

Alice Watson fought down the anxiety swelling inside her and stared at the broad screens fronting the ops center. She set a cup of coffee down and folded her arms. On screen, drones like a group of crows encircled a black van, splashing it with bright LED light and capturing the vehicle's every angle through digital cameras. SIOC saw the same video as the techs on the ground.

Running with lights, the drones had shorter flight time, their batteries rapidly draining.

That mattered little. They were merely pawns. Diversions.

Out of picture, the real advance team waited. The retasked satellite image only zoomed in on the van. Peripheral movements further out from the van in Ft. Totten Park had been deliberately left off of the screens.

"No anomalies, radiation, or heat signatures detected," a technician said. "Registering no power surges."

Across an open intercom a voice said, "Drone One, execute your scan."

On screen, One's camera zoomed through a front windshield to peer into the vehicle. In the back of the van, racks of equipment came into focus. Bulky boxes and bundled cabling ran everywhere.

"The license plate is bogus," another tech announced.

The drone task manager said, "One, stand down and park. Two and Three, front and center." He paused while flight formations were reworked. The screen revealed two drones staring head on to the vehicle. "In position. Commencing the breach in three. Ready. Three. Two. One. Go. Go. Go."

The two drones discharged projectiles that penetrated the van's front windshield, carving out precision golf ball-sized holes. The recoil of the discharges caused the drones to swoop backward before autocorrect flight systems kicked in to continue their advance. From each drone, tubes telescoped forward and penetrated the holes in the windshield. About the size of TV-viewed lottery balls, the drones dispensed mini sphere robots into the vehicle.

New images appeared on the screens as the ball-style robots rolled over a dashboard and bounced to the floor of the van. One mini bot scanned the lower area, the other the ceiling, which showed a tubular device mounted in a turret.

East of the Washington Navy Yard, Washington, DC

The next move was his.

It seemed inevitable that one of his autonomous vehicles would fall prey to authorities, but Barnes had hoped it wouldn't be this vehicle. He still needed it.

On a set of screens, he watched the unfolding drama. Curiosity had captivated him from the moment the uniformed officer located his van in Ft. Totten Park to the arrival of the FBI bomb squad. Their approach and the deployment of gizmos and gadgets, drones and robot spheres intrigued him. Clearly, the FBI had learned not to storm a situation with valued capital. Now law enforcement kept agents and K9 teams out of harm's way until the scene was secured.

They were buying time, stalling, while their tiny robots surveyed the interior of his van. He saw the inside of the vehicle appear on another set of screens, mirrored feeds from the FBI's own systems.

He knew everything they were up to.

Barnes chuckled. When would the FBI catch on that he'd hacked their network via his gateway installation embedded in the servers of the mobile command center parked outside the Foggy Bottom Metro station? That was their network vulnerability. Even if they figured it out, midnight would strike and the world would be stunned by the discoveries exposed in dawn's early light.

It was time to begin his finale.

He wished Katherine Morgan had survived Soldiers' Home. From FBI internal memos, he gleaned she'd been killed along with many others. Her name had been withheld from public announcements until her next of kin could be notified. He knew she had no surviving family. No parents. No siblings. Nobody to mourn for her except a lover in Princeton.

This challenge had been constructed just for her.

More stops remained and those mattered—Rachel would continue the challenge until the end—and the world had to know what they were.

On a keyboard, he entered the commands to charge the EMP cannon mounted high in the ceiling of the van. A complete charge required two minutes.

He was concerned with only one thing: salvaging this asset and keeping it in play.

Strategic Information & Operations Center (SIOC), FBI Headquarters, Washington, DC

Watson stepped closer to the array of screens. Ft. Totten Park on-site operations were entirely out of her control. In HQ, everyone was a bystander.

Coordination directives came across intercom speakers.

"We have a power spike," a tech announced. "Magnetic fields are building. The EMP cannon is charging."

"Roger that," the on-site agent in charge responded. "Start the countdown. Wait for my signal."

"Confirmed," the tech said. "Countdown started."

Watson took a nervous breath. On screen drones still buzzed around the van, like flies surrounding a dead carcass. Inside the van, mini sphere bots communicated images. Lights and consoles were alive with activity. The belly of the beast was waking from its slumber and ready to feed on unsuspecting travelers.

"Peripheral systems power off," the special agent in charge said. "All personnel take shelter. Breachers, ready your assets. Time to go dark, people. All comms drop off, except for tech and drones. On three. Three. Two. One."

"The power spike is increasing," the tech said.

"Confirmed," the special agent in charge said. "We only get one shot at this."

Satellite imaging went dark, as did perimeter imaging.

The spherical bots' camera feeds shook as if to signal an earthquake was imminent.

Watson took a uneven breath. *Here it comes.*

"Power down drones," the special agent in charge directed. "All comms off. Everything off. Protective measures."

Drone feeds went dark, leaving only the mini bots inside the van active.

Silence lurked in the ops center. No one spoke, their collective gaze fixated onto a single screen: the spherical cameras riding out the storm behind enemy lines.

A thundering reverberation resonated and the satellite feed glazed over, a large flash consuming the screen before it went blank. The mini bots inside the van went dark and died.

Watson's eyes caught the countdown on a red LED clock.

She gave an order to restrict distribution of the video feeds of the bureau's bomb squad and advanced team in Ft. Totten Park. Only SIOC personnel could view what had transpired.

Ten seconds ticked off and audio systems crackled as they came back online.

"Comms active," the special agent in charge directed. "Breachers, advance your bots."

"Two drones are unresponsive," a tech announced. "Two operational."

The satellite feed cycled through synchronizing checks and refocused its camera. Video shots from the remaining drones, highlighted by LED lighting, showed that tracked robots had torched holes through the side of the van. Behind those breaching robots snaked large tubes. Through the cut holes, the tubes had been inserted into the vehicle like needles into a patient's arm.

The tubing on the ground inflated, swelling at the seams.

One of the drones took up position at the van's front windshield. Its camera revealed a swelling expanse of high-pressure, liquid ballistics gel flooding into the cavity of the vehicle.

East of the Washington Navy Yard, Washington, DC

Barnes stared in disbelief at the readouts on the screen in front of him. Video feeds from FBI networks went blank.

He was blind.

There was no way of discerning the amount of damage done by the EMP, but the lack of active feeds revealed the FBI might be onto him. It was a possibility.

He wanted to wait for his own satellite mapping to reset, its fuzzy picture slowly returning to clarity. Nighttime images showed no movement. Thermal imaging picked up a ring of figures holding back at a safe distance to the vehicle.

Barnes' jaw went tight. Seconds mattered and only one option remained: destruction of the vehicle. Time to sacrifice a pawn.

He swore and launched his remaining countermeasure.

His satellite imaging cleared up and caught the faintest of flashes, like a sunburst swelling radially away from its dark core, which was as black as the night itself.

Barnes stumbled backward, stunned by what he was seeing.

The explosives had detonated, but the devices were nowhere close to producing the intended blast. Somehow, either the explosives had failed to detonate or the FBI managed to mitigate the explosive energy.

The second scenario seemed unlikely, but plausible. He took a breath and paced, considering his next move.

Deliberation didn't take long. Without Katherine Morgan invested in the puzzle, some of his taste for revenge had faded. The FBI would try and solve the clues, but the preordained solutions and stops on a map seemed less important. A deep-seated emptiness, even loneliness, nudged him. This entire pageant was meant to be shared.

The seeds of revelation had been planted at each stop, except the last two.

Now it was time bring the day to closure, and give Rachel a goodbye.

65
PARADISE LOST

George Washington University Hospital (GWU), Washington, DC

After relinquishing the physical canvases to an FBI evidence technician, Will Shortz set up shop in a dictation room, down the hall from victims, while he waited for Agent Morgan to finish a meeting with one of the hospital's Chairs of Neurology.

Working off a loaner laptop, he parsed clues and solutions, scribbling notes on a tablet and again on reprinted photos, one of which was a snapshot of his SCRABBLE layout from the SIOC conference room.

Since he worked mostly from home, he enjoyed the freedom it provided for editing puzzles and tweaking clues. The comforts of his New York home gave him everything needed for daily exercises that stimulated his mind.

He thought about Mary Davidson and her family home—a godlike creator who'd been challenged, personally attacked by her very own creation. The madman's quest to broadcast his version of truth had destroyed lives beyond his creators and his seven victims.

Shortz's senses tingled when he glanced at a photo of the latest clues.

Paradise Lost.

The killer's prelude was a mirror moment from John Milton's epic poem—the Fall of Man account extended beyond Adam and Eve and their expulsion from paradise. It was also the tale of Satan, the once powerful angel who'd rebelled against God. The consequences of Satan's actions were expulsion from heaven and he was cast into hell. Satan argued that God was the tyrant, and all angelic hosts should rule as gods.

The mind is its own place, and in itself can make a heaven of hell, a hell of heaven. Satan's words were mockingly similar to those of a mass murderer, where in his narrative the tyrant was Mary Davidson and Providence's light was his own.

ANGELS MUST LOOK HOMEWARD.

Directions to remember where he came from: HEAVEN.

After some Internet searching, 12 DOWN translated to PISAU, a knife.

4 DOWN didn't target a specific fruit, but rather category in botany. It stood for a skin covered fruit that contained a central pit or seed inside. A five-letter word. DRUPE. Its U intersected the U in MURDER. DRUPE served as a metaphor, either for the victims or for the treasure hunt itself.

Input from the FBI's SIOC team ran down NASA abbreviations, which he arranged to focus on space or heavens or gazing. 36 DOWN was an abbreviation for Earth & Space Research, ESR.

The themes paired with the tattooed image of a sun or star screamed "observatory" or "planetarium." Inside the boundaries of Washington, DC, he tracked down three matches: Rock Creek Park Nature Center and Planetarium, the National Air & Space Museum, and the United States Naval Observatory.

He ruled out Rock Creek Park, since Frances Davidson had been rescued there.

That left either the Air & Space or the Naval Observatory.

66
THE SWITCH OF CONSCIOUSNESS

George Washington University Hospital (GWU).

Right place. Right time. Right experts. And secrets.

Kate fumed as she listened to doctors present findings from a landmark case involving a patient with epilepsy. She was mad at herself, not the doctors, for not asking Thomas Parker what had happened in the final hour inside a research lab over a month ago.

Secrets.

In her case, ignorance was not bliss.

The doctors demonstrated insights on the thin span of grey matter underneath the inner part of the neocortex called the claustrum. The thin sheet of neurons functioned as a gateway of sorts, and had a nickname: the on-off switch for human consciousness. Their medical experiments involved implanting electrodes into a female patient's brain. When the woman's claustrum was stimulated with micro-electrical currents, she stopped conscious functions: no speech, no motor skills, and no memory of the events. The electrical signals had triggered unconsciousness or at least disrupted neural functions such that consciousness was disengaged from the brain.

It was as if their patient had been frozen in time.

On a wall at the end of a table, a pair of screens posted side-by-side MRI scans, one for each victim: St. Elizabeths and the monastery. Frances Davidson was still in the Emergency department, before being sent to imaging. Labels flagged the claustrum regions of each brain, where pea-sized areas were clouded over as if the areas had been hit by a stroke.

She doubted coincidences.

Frances Davidson's MRI scans would disprove coincidences.

A genetically created mass murderer taunted her with LOG THE TOURS.

Her day of horror-filled destinations had been orchestrated madness, filled with themes of vindication that sought to justify a killer's actions. Incremental steps, deep-seated doubt, and guilt had led her to talk with one of the chairs in GWU's Neuroscience Institute. This was a momentary side path to discovery as well.

The brains of his hand-picked victims, more specifically their claustrum regions, the tiny crescent landscapes buried inside a walnut shaped organ, had been deliberately destroyed.

Secrets.

Some had been malevolently disclosed, while others locked away out of reach.

Her last case had accidentally exposed her to deep, dark secrets—the Frontier, a madman's neurological quest to unhinge the human mind—callous and inhumane work that sought to uncover secrets.

Thomas Parker was the first neuroscientist she'd met with such deep and comprehensive understanding of brain anatomy, its vast and hidden secrets, and neurological functions that made the Frontier a reality.

Thomas had exposed her to secrets she'd never imagined.

Somehow, Mary Davidson and Barnes knew about Parker's work.

Pandora's jar had been opened, its vile contents released into the world.

And Barnes had access to knowledge that empowered him to render victims permanently unconscious, imprisoning them within their own bodies. Each victim had been condemned to a moment of time and isolation.

By silencing their minds, disrupting their ability to regain consciousness, a mass murderer had sealed off their secrets from the rest of the world.

In each victim, the Spirit of Hope remained trapped and out of reach.

Nausea swelled inside her. Bile rumbled inside her stomach and sought a way out.

Bolting from the room, Kate dashed down hospital corridors, pushing past doctors and nurses until she reached a stairwell. She descended to the street level and burst through metal doors.

Outside, the night air washed over her. She staggered down an empty 23rd Street NW. Her feet carried her past the I Street pedestrian breezeway, still populated with FBI situation tents, and down another block to police barriers at H Street.

She felt small and scared, as if none of her actions had mattered.

Barnes' twisted aspirations and vile acts of murder and mutilation only worked to tear down her life, strip her naked like his victims, and destroy what she thought mattered most.

She doubted anyone other than Rachel Pratt would blame her if she just took a seat on the sidelines and watched the rest of the madness play on without her. The stroke of midnight would come whether she participated in the game or not.

67
BAD NEWS

East of the Washington Navy Yard, Washington, DC

The news stunned Barnes. And setbacks just kept coming.

First, his EMP-equipped van was lost to the FBI and its bomb squad. Now this.

The monitors in his operations center prominently displayed an internal FBI memo. He reread its contents, which confirmed what he already knew about Katherine Morgan. Her untimely death was tragic. But Rachel? The memo clearly listed Army Captain Rachel Pratt among the deceased. Rachel wasn't supposed to die this early. Not at Soldiers' Home—a place she'd despise with her very last breath.

She was a self-healer but not invincible or immortal. Regardless of her genetic enhancements, her body still possessed physiological limitations.

Yet Rachel's death hurt.

After Morgan, Rachel had been the main reason for the challenge to continue.

Her death stung him more than expected. He'd loved her, even though he knew Rachel would seek closure. She'd need to face him behind the sights of a gun. That's how she was wired. Since the hospital, he'd fantasized about staring into her eyes, wanting, longing to see if she'd pull the trigger.

He wouldn't hesitate in the slightest.

That was the fate she deserved, not a premature death at Soldiers' Home.

Concern ticked through his mind, prompting him to push away from the consoles.

13 ACROSS was his promise to the world—a revelation.

Seven stops. Seven parchments. A race against time.

The journey required completion, even if the road to enlightenment was littered with casualties.

The seven victims caught in this web deserved their fates. They were chosen. They were required sacrifices. None were random selections. None were innocent, and each had either served a purpose or were his hybrid cousins.

In the end, only history would be the judge.

Barnes would be remembered for courageous actions against those committed to reshaping the human species.

Some would see him as a hero, others as the devil. But all would see him as the Adam of a new creation of mankind nonetheless.

His resolve was to breach the castle, tear down its gates, and expose secrets. Others would storm the castle grounds: the media, the court of public opinion, and even Congress itself. The Perfect People Initiative was on life support, and nothing the Department of Defense, the Vice President, or the Speaker of the House did could defend it.

In Morgan's absence, the *New York Times* crossword puzzle editor had become the *de facto* standard bearer. This puzzle revealed a story that needed to be told. Will Shortz alone was the best reason for the challenge to continue.

Only one essential death remained—that of Army General James Davidson.

68
WHAT THE FILE SAYS

The Pentagon, U.S. Department of Defense, Virginia

Randy Wang reflected on an old adage: *when armed only with a stick, don't poke the sleeping bear.* Two-star James Davidson was the bear. He, on the other hand, was the lower ranking fool with the stick.

That was especially true in this case.

But he owed Morgan, even if he risked damaging his career and sustaining a political mauling.

While Pentagon leadership had sought to marginalize Major General James Davidson by shuffling him sideways into a Joint Rapid Cell team under USD R&E, that didn't mean the Department of Defense would abandon its advanced biogenetics initiatives. Top brass saw a greater reward in protecting the gains of DNA research and secretive genetic improvements. Translation: Davidson was a dangerous man, especially to a colonel asking all the wrong questions.

Wang returned to the NSA SCIF and logged onto a vacant terminal.

Morgan's conversation with the general provided confirmation of old intel and added new information. Morgan seemed invested in playing out her own dangerous game, one that involved luring Davidson out into the open and using both of them as bait.

Before the Central Security Service (CSS) and NSA, Wang had initiated similar games during his years with Army intelligence, mostly with the Chinese, Russians, and Turks. One lesson he'd learned the hard way was that state-sponsored actors often played to the bitter end, even if that meant innocent people would die.

Phillip Barnes, a former Davidson lab rat, ex-soldier, and domestic terrorist, would be no different. His desire involved killing until all means were exhausted, and then some more while life still filled his beating heart.

And clearly, that meant Morgan was in over her head.

Wang understood that law enforcement would track their mass murderer down traditional paths, but his unique advantage could squeeze Barnes on a different front. Flush him out into the open where law enforcement could take him down.

Thriving as a spy meant understanding your foe before stepping onto the field of battle. In order to do that, Wang needed Barnes' personnel records.

On his terminal, Wang queried Barnes' basic combat training (BCT) and Advanced Individual Training (AIT) files. An associated AIT unit code did not line up with the Army's standard schools; indicating that Davidson had grabbed Barnes straight out of basic. Three years later, a week before Barnes was scheduled to attend the Army's Basic Leadership Course, the soldier had died of injuries sustained during a combat training exercise. At the time of Barnes' death, his enlisted rank was E-4. Not an abnormality. But links to two nine-digit Army job codes provided immediate red flags.

Military command could not function without three things: competent if not sterling leadership, dedicated and driven soldiers, and job codes. Every enlisted soldier had a job.

Barnes had mastered two within three years. Unusual. His first military occupational specialties (MOS) code was 12B for a combat engineer, an Army Sapper, assigned to the 35th Engineering Battalion. The second was 89D, belonging to an explosive ordnance disposal (EOD) specialist.

And no station records listed Barnes as ever having been assigned AIT training at Ft. Leonard Wood, Missouri, for combat engineering or Ft. Lee, Virginia, for explosive ordinance disposal training.

Anomalies, to say the least. Highly irregular, but not impossible for special situations.

Those were deviations that required high-level Pentagon approvals. If Barnes had received his combat engineer and explosives training outside traditional AIT schools, that meant Davidson's ghost programs were tailored for small, tactical incursions.

Those basic job skills alone made Phillip Barnes extremely dangerous.

69
NETWORK BREACHES

23rd Street SW at the Foggy Bottom—GWU Station, Washington, DC

FBI Computer Scientist Elizabeth Price hated the service technician aspect of her job, but it was impossible to refuse an order from headquarters. With DC investigations consuming resources at an alarming rate, she'd been pulled out of the Norfolk Field Office for field support. Her task was a simple one: evaluate network solutions in a bureau mobile command center.

The two-tone gray rig was hard to miss, taking up a fair share of the curbside on the blocked-off street.

She rapped her fist against the door.

A second later, it opened and she went inside. Tired-looking agents and technicians ate Chinese takeout and worked at laptop terminals.

"Someone fixed the antenna this morning," a technician said, slurping broth from a noodle bowl. "Everything's worked just fine since then."

She frowned, uninterested in antennas and work orders that hadn't been logged in the bureau's IT resource system. The last IT Infrastructure Division work order was a month ago, after the big rig returned from crime scene support in Pittsburgh.

She'd been briefed on her assignment on the ride up from Virginia. Headquarters suspected classified and non-classified network breaches.

"What was wrong with your antenna?" she asked, making her way to the back of the mobile unit. In a dedicated closet next to the toilet, she accessed the network server racks. A year earlier, the NSA had developed portable, plug-and-play network resource and protocol evaluation tools. She plugged the micro-computer into a server port and synced with the server rack. "I never saw his service report. It was a guy, right?"

"Some fella from ITID," an agent said of the bureau's IT Infrastructure Division as he looked up from his chicken and shrimp bowl. Price assumed he was the on-scene logistics coordinator. "He had the antenna array online in about five minutes."

"That fast, huh?" The device in her hand blinked green as it ran checks and diagnostics before flashing a steady stream of red lights. "You catch his name?"

Red lights meant trouble. Serious trouble.

Price patched in a laptop and brought up listed network activities. The log flagged multiple threats and destination protocol violations.

Headquarters was right: bureau networks had been hacked, from the inside and behind firewalls. Outgoing communications had been mirrored and scattered to at least a dozen unapproved IP addresses. The web destinations were numerical and required a deeper forensics investigation.

Spinning around, she scrutinized the men in the rig. They were all men. And there was no telling if one was the culprit, a mole for a black hat hacker, or an inside ghost working computer support.

Since people and relationships weren't her strong suit, Elizabeth Price left her diagnostic equipment connected to the network, stepped out of the rig, and placed a call to her superior.

70
BASEBALL

Strategic Information & Operations Center (SIOC), FBI Headquarters, Washington, DC

Two strikes. Three base hits. And the bases were loaded.

At a terminal, Alice Watson scanned shipping manifests from a Pennsylvania explosives manufacturer. Forensics testing of trace explosives found at the WMATA bombing site led to the single supplier of RDX. And since the shipping of hazardous materials fell under the Alcohol Tobacco and Firearm (ATF) and Department of Transportation (DOT), their coordinated court orders had been used to track down invoices and sales records.

All customers had accounted for their RDX materials, except one: HC Industrials in Anchorage, Alaska.

ATF had gotten search warrants in record time. Its raid of the company's headquarters turned up an empty warehouse. The property owner indicated the tenant had paid in cash, two years in advance. IRS records showed a single tax filing for a company with no employees and a deceased Native Alaskan owner. The RDX had been shipped there, then moved elsewhere.

Strike one.

They'd tracked the sonic device used in the attack at St. Elizabeths to Lithium Secure Electronics, or LISE—a company with no tax filings and no IRS records. None. Its home base warehouse in Baltimore had been repurposed and remodeled into urban, loft-style housing. LISE had no physical footprint and no traceable existence.

Strike two.

Neither phantom company revealed any connection to Phillip Barnes.

He'd proved to be a bomb-making, ex-soldier, terrorist with no shadow. Because of those labels, the team focused on three aspects: his micro-footprint, his security clearance access, and his hypothesized genetic existence. Even if the genius-level psychopath proved to be one of General Davidson's rogue laboratory experiments, Barnes still needed deep-pocket financing. And that funding had to come from somewhere. Finance investigators were building a money trail, but getting nowhere.

That troubled Watson. Barnes needed tens of millions to finance his terrorist activities—a great deal of money for a man with a micro-footprint.

Their first base hit: agents had already met with professors at MIT to start building a biography on Barnes.

The second base hit: Facial Analysis, Comparison and Evaluation (FACE) in the Biometrics Services Division had constructed preliminary facial recognition (FR) models. Eventually they'd be able to track down his presence.

The last hit to load the bases were the remnants of the van and its nearly intact EMP cannon, a massively destructive device stolen from the U.S. Naval Research Laboratory in Washington, DC.

Unlike Davidson's Army colleagues, the Secretary of the Navy had permitted agents to accompany NCIS officers in their searches of base weapons' storage and research areas. Reciprocating the gesture, the FBI Director invited Navy investigators to observe bureau technicians and staff as they dissected the van and evaluated the EMP cannon in the FBI lab at Quantico.

Watson doubted the loaded bases translated into runs before midnight. Unlike baseball, their clock was ticking and not enough hours remained, leaving potential scores stranded on base. The bureau needed the next set of solutions from Morgan and Shortz. Fast.

71
THE ENDGAME DRAWS NEAR

East of the Washington Navy Yard, Washington, DC

Barnes had wondered how long it would take authorities to start figuring things out.

Now he knew.

The FBI had gone on the offensive. Finding his hardware in the FBI's mobile command center had given them hope. The bureau white hats would start pinging IP addresses in an effort to track down his location. Mirrored addresses, cloned gateways, and redirected extra wide area networks would challenge their efforts.

Even the best in the business would be tested, but sooner or later, even the most persistent got lucky.

His Soldiers' Home van was gone now. Beyond an inconvenience, it was a technical handicap. But the asset's loss was a recoverable event. Of course, law enforcement would have actions and intelligence not visible from his end. By now, they knew his birth name and the name used during his enlistment with the Army. They'd probably even located his college transcripts. They probably suspected he possessed satellite capabilities, without the foggiest idea how he was pulling off the intrusion.

Beyond the captured EMP cannon, they would eventually trace the origins of his sonic weapon and the explosives used in the Metro bombing, but both of those paths would prove fruitless. The bombing method and arsenal employed at Soldiers' Home were his own invention, and offered no avenues for tracking him through material components or physical evidence.

The trail of bread crumbs kept the challenge close, interesting. The series of maps, symbols, wordplay, and clue-filled parchments from his victims forced law enforcement to focus on a final destination.

The endgame was near. The hands of the clock circled closer to midnight.

And now General James Davidson had been forced into play.

72
STREETSIDE

23rd Street NW at the Foggy Bottom—GWU Station, Washington, DC

Circling back on 23rd Street, Kate Morgan walked the barricaded streets and tried to suppress her anger at the thought that Thomas Parker had put someone into a permanent coma. No matter his justifications, Thomas' actions were unethical, criminal. And her participation in the destruction of the facility's supercomputers had concealed a potential crime. It would be virtually impossible for prosecutors to prove assault, whether accidental or premediated.

Her actions had made her an accomplice. Chalk that up as one more thing the Senate could grill her on when she eventually testified.

Deep inside, a voice told her to steer clear of Thomas Parker—her life, a career with the bureau, and a medical license counted on never seeing Thomas again.

Another clever dig from Barnes. A deeper layer to his sick and twisted game.

Kate sighed and took in the night air. She strolled past parked law enforcement vehicles, their lights still flashing and pulsing between university buildings and the hospital.

Thrusting her hands into her pockets, she watched a growing commotion outside the FBI's mobile command center, the rig.

A K9 agent and her dog conducted a sweep around the vehicle. Agents armed with HK MP5s escorted other agents and technicians outside and across the street to be patted down and searched. IDs were checked. Kate vaguely recognized one of the agents from the morning.

What had Barnes done now?

A shoulder bump drew her attention.

"You weren't supposed to come here," Kate said to Rachel Pratt.

Pratt shrugged. "Cops were visiting Davidson's home, which wrecked my plans to lay low there."

Kate exhaled. "After Mary Davidson was released from questioning, she shot herself."

"Does the general know?" Pratt asked.

Kate shook her head. "Not sure."

"If he decides to bail because his wife is dead, that wrecks your plan."

Kate turned to her. "Did you kill that nurse?"

Pratt's face clouded over. "You shouldn't have to ask." Her voice softened. "I was strapped to the bed the entire time. Barnes set me up."

"Says the woman who's wanted in connection to a murder," Kate said. "And it sounds like you're MPDC's only suspect."

"Agent Morgan," a man called.

Both turned to see Will Shortz hurrying toward them.

Kate lifted a stiff finger to her lips. He picked up on her cue.

"I have the next stop," he said, slightly out of breath. "Well, one of two locations: the Smithsonian Air and Space Museum or the Naval Observatory." He presented the solutions and tied the key word phrases to the star on the fragment of skin. "Those are the most logical."

Pratt shook her head. "How do we pick between them?"

Kate wrinkled her nose. "This all started when we referenced links from District Fallout and a 1965 Community Shelter Plan. That's how we ended up at St. Elizabeths and the monastery. Both the Smithsonian campus and the Naval Observatory will have basements that function as fallout shelters."

"There's no time to do both." Pratt pressed her hands against her hips.

Kate's mind foraged the events of her day. She turned toward the Metro entrance. Her morning commute seemed so long ago.

Pratt snapped her fingers. "You know who lives at the observatory, don't you?"

Kate shrugged.

"The Vice President," Will Shortz said. "Number One Observatory Circle. Rockefeller passed on living in the Admiral's House as Vice President, but every VP since Mondale has lived there."

"Okay, so what's the deeper meaning?" Kate asked. "You guys saying the Vice President is involved?"

Pratt retrieved a CAC card from her shirt pocket and held it up. "Guess who I spoke with on the phone this morning? The VP implied that Davidson had been reassigned. He told me to stand down. That was before a bombing landed me in the hospital and killed six Rangers." She let her statement sink in, then flipped the card over. A small yellow sticky note read: ADMIRAL'S HOUSE ACCESS. "This was a gift."

"Gift? That's an odd take." Kate's thoughts crystallized as a knot formed in her stomach. She grabbed Pratt's arm and moved away from Shortz. "Pratt, you're not going to kill the Vice President, are you?"

"I told you, Barnes is my mark." Her eyes passed on a different message entirely. Something else was implied. Pratt would take out the Vice President if she believed the man had authorized a hit on the soldiers who had accompanied her to St. Elizabeths. The VP and the general seemed to be playing for different objectives.

Kate folded her arms. "Why do you think Davidson gave you access to the VP's house?"

"Maybe the general knew we'd go there?"

Kate ground her teeth. "That implies Davidson knew about Barnes's plan and locations ahead of time. You have an explanation for that?"

Pratt started to walk away. "You coming, agent?"

Kate hustled over to Will Shortz, who looked both confused and annoyed. He was trying to process their conversation, and Kate wasn't sure that was a good thing.

"Mr. Shortz," she said, "I've had a rough day. Actually, a horrible day. And I'm not sure I've actually thanked you for your assistance. I couldn't have solved these clues on my own. Your contributions have made a difference."

He raised an eyebrow. "You're welcome—I guess?"

Kate smiled thinly. "Right now, we're going to a place where both the Navy and the Secret Service operate. Based on current events, their security forces could have mighty tight trigger fingers. You know, shoot first, ask questions later. So it wouldn't be wise for you to go there with us."

Disappointment flashed in Shortz's eyes. His cloak-and-dagger role had grown on him.

"Sorry, I've got to go before Pratt leaves without me," she said, considering an alternative for him that did not involve sonic assault, bombings, falling through trap doors, or crawling through make-shift graves. Taking out a pen, she took his hand and scrawled her sat phone number on his palm. "Al Tiramisu. It's Italian. Northeast of here. Meet me there. One hour. Maybe longer. We'll work on the next stop. And call me if anything comes up. You have my number."

73
THE STRING GAME

NSA SCIF, The Pentagon, U.S. Department of Defense, Virginia

Adrenaline flooded into Randy Wang's bloodstream.

The jackpot had been found following points along a string.

He'd never lost his thirst for intelligence, especially the dark side, which became rarer as his career got longer. On most days, he consulted inside the Department of Defense and worked with deskbound cyberwarriors at the NSA. That was intellectually stimulating, but nothing like battling a dangerous rival on the street.

And when he was given the freedom to run his own ops, that counted.

Phillip Barnes was as good as dead.

Progressing from get-to-know-you personnel records, Wang circled back to connections to RMG Global Solutions and EyePoint Applications. He stumbled on a Defense Contract Management Agency (DCMA) purchase order for material and installation of one mile of 12-strand SMFO cable. The base was the Washington Navy Yard. The general contractor and installer was RMG. The final integrator was EyePoint Applications. The funding source for the work was a joint-venture federal user research group for a covert program called SpaceKey.

Wang frowned. Funding priorities required the NSA to pass on the geosynchronous orbit (GEO) SpaceKey platform. In the NSA's wake, the National Reconnaissance Office took over as the lead agency.

SpaceKey was a prototype next generation, super high definition spy satellite. And ahead of the Vandenberg Air Force Base launch window, the SMFO cable had been installed linking the Navy base's CNIC headquarters, Building 111, to a dedicated operations complex east of I-695. After mission launch, the SpaceKey program had been shelved due to catastrophic systems failures.

SpaceKey was a spy satellite that didn't spy, or so everyone thought.

Wang bet Barnes and EyePoint were behind the malfunctions.

And that meant Phillip Barnes controlled the world's newest and most advanced spy satellite.

Wang left his SCIF station and walked out into a common corridor to place a call.

74
DEPARTURES

East of the Washington Navy Yard, Washington, DC

Barnes knew his anonymity was ending as midnight approached.

But his obligation, his role in the challenge, required addressing inevitable facts before the clock ticked through its movements.

History proved *obsolete classes would not voluntarily abdicate the stage of history*; they needed to be forcibly driven from it. Education and exposure were his weapons to weaken untouchable institutions and reveal their secrets. Revenge was the sweetener. Years of planning had created a stockpile of disclosures.

As his anticipation rose and the game unfolded, however, Barnes felt unfulfilled, wanting.

Katherine Morgan was dead.

Rachel Pratt was dead.

Soon James Davidson and his ABI program would be dead, along with their offspring.

Barnes considered his remaining course, the charted actions that lay ahead. The end of his musical movement was nigh, his stretto closer.

The time had come to finish what he'd started.

The FBI network connection had been severed, his inside news source gone. The direct fiber tie-ins with the Washington Navy Yard would follow. Eventually, authorities would discover his control of a dormant advanced systems satellite known as SpaceKey.

In his command center, Barnes distributed operational controls to mobile systems and powered down his main consoles. The final two victims, naked and terminally asleep, were loaded into different autonomous vehicles and driven ahead to their final destinations. His remaining fleet had been parked along intercept points where the vehicles waited to strike.

Barnes strolled past the cages where seven imprisoned and tortured victims once lay, and past a cluster of modular rooms where brutal experiments had been performed. He stopped at the front door of the metal building and spun around to admire what he'd built.

He'd come far since Elk Pass, where he'd witnessed the murders of his father, uncle, and brother. A foster family. People who understood him. People who gave him a home. With her death, Katherine Morgan, M.D., had paid for her incompetence. It was that moment of being orphaned that sent him down the path of being conscripted into the Perfect People Initiative and its applications program, the Advanced Biogenetics Initiative.

Destroying James Davidson and tearing down ABI were his primary objectives. Killing Morgan was secondary. And killing Rachel was a benefit by association.

Barnes took a thoughtful breath before arming the self-destruct explosives that protected his operations base from the inevitable invasion. The number of explosives in place would leave mere fragments of his ghost-like existence.

In the parking lot, Barnes climbed into an automated Ford Explorer and drove out the facility's front gate, heading for the Circle.

75
LOOKING FOR STARS

8:05 PM, South Gate, Naval Support Facility, US Naval Observatory (USNO), Washington, DC

Kate found herself limiting the flow of information to both Rachel Pratt and Alice Watson. Davidson's gift to Pratt was troubling, his trump card put into play before other moves had been made. The Vice President had become a role player as no different than 11 ACROSS. His involvement was perplexing. How was the VP of the United States of America associated with Barnes' absurd scheme? Why was he at odds with Davidson?

Elements were missing from a bigger picture.

Either the general had inside information on Barnes' grand plan or someone was manipulating him. Why else would the general have given Pratt that card?

Kate's prior case had revealed White House and State Department sponsorship of illegal and unethical research trials. Emails traced consent back to White House staff and the Secretary of State. After the death of a U.S. Senator from Oklahoma, Congress was gunning for the President himself.

Now it was the Pentagon's turn. The Advanced Biogenetics Initiative and Advancing Human Evolution project would be marquee targets. The staging of a crime set on a site that connected these projects to both the Navy and the Vice President would amplify the scrutiny.

Genius, really. Barnes had set everyone up.

Including her.

And Kate understood the Observatory was a federal enclave, a constitutionally-protected area of exclusive federal jurisdiction. At the Observatory, the FBI had no legal authority; Congress and the Department of Defense protected the site. Taking matters into her own hands equated to career suicide, and her career already dangled by the proverbial thread.

So before climbing into Pratt's van, Kate called the SIOC and spoke with Alice Watson.

Watson told her that the Secretary of the Navy had approved bureau engagement at other Navy sites. He was amenable to authorizing the escapade, as long as it was constrained within boundaries and time.

One hour. Not a minute more.

Kate took the offer.

As Pratt drove, Kate called a professor and astronomer who'd been a one-time date. He provided a briefing about the Observatory and its campus on the fly and directed them to the South Gate—the access point used by employees, staff, and researchers. Based on his descriptions, Kate decided to start with the library building.

Pratt drove to the end of Observatory Circle, set back from Massachusetts Avenue past the British and New Zealand embassies. An island guard station stood behind flush-payment vehicle barricades.

Pratt used the ID provided by Davidson. The security officer checked it with a hand-held scanner and asked about their business.

"Observatory walk with the astrometry department," Pratt said.

The officer returned the ID and waved them through.

Pratt parked at the concrete building that housed the government's atomic clocks, and they walked to the main building. Pratt carried her backpack, crammed with gadgets she'd used to detect booby traps in Rock Creek Park.

Above them trillions of tiny lights, faint stars fought through the urban light pollution and haze of Washington, DC. A picturesque lawn and helicopter pad fronted the original observatory and library building. Lighting was kept low to aid the telescopes. The stars and stripes flew from a tall, Navy-white flag pole. Below Old Glory, the right side of the mast hoisted four nautical flags while its left posted a single white flag with two stars. Kate figured the stars matched the site's ranking officer, a two-star admiral.

Stopping, Kate allowed Pratt to extend her pace.

Someone was watching. Glancing in each direction, Kate imagined Navy Security Forces lurking in the protective darkness of distant tree lines, their night scopes and sights locked onto their approach. She sensed at least one of the security forces snipers was sighting her down. Understandable, considering they were trespassing.

Pratt turned around. "What are you doing?"

Kate pointed in different directions. "The shutter doors are opened for the telescopes. Astronomers have started work for the evening."

Pratt cocked an annoyed glance at each of the domed structures. "So?"

Kate walked to catch up. "What? You don't like the stars?"

Pratt kept moving. "Do I look like an astronaut? No. Stars aren't my thing. That's what Barnes was bred for. He was the future space traveler in our group."

Kate recognized that the observatory compound represented a working site, a secured circular campus with a national archive of atomic clocks, telescopes, and more astronomers than its limited set of mirrors and refractors could support.

As they approached the library building, she noticed it was unattended, even though a few lights had been left on inside. The raised observatory was located in the west wing, its famous library displaying notes from Copernicus, Galileo and Newton in the east section.

"Where do we start?" Pratt asked, walking into the grand entrance.

They stood inside a wide entry with glossed floors and an old telescope corded off with velvet robes and brass stands. The vintage building had a school-museum feel to it. Clothed tables flanked the entry. Pictures of planetary bodies populated the walls. Ahead, hallways spread to the east and west.

"You think this is the place?" Kate asked in a library whisper, more as reassurance than an actual question. "Wouldn't Barnes rather visit the Air and Space Museum? You said he was an astronaut prototype."

"No. This is it."

Kate closed the main door. "How do you think Barnes accesses these sites?"

"He has a security clearance, obviously."

"Right." Kate arbitrarily gestured down the east corridor, away from any physicists or astronomers working the night shift.

Pratt marched down the hall. "Let's start at one end. Work our way through the building."

Kate took a breath and followed. They passed a series of closed doors and stepped into the circular, two-story open library. High perimeter windows filtered starlight into the room and lower inset windows marked the hour positions of a clock. A centerpiece fountain bubbled water.

Pratt broke out a flashlight. Kate opted for the black light she'd picked up at the monastery.

Framed cases displayed old books. Tables and chairs were arranged for reading. Hard-surfaced, white specked flooring had silver circular seams. Books were cataloged like a traditional library.

With hard flooring, it was difficult to see how a body could be stashed beneath the library.

Other than smudges and a few prints, the UV light illuminated nothing.

Pratt searched low.

Kate went high, taking one of the spiral staircases to a book balcony. Waving her black light, she noticed nothing of importance. The shelving was packed with books on navigation, astronomy, and physics.

Flustered, Kate whipped around, facing the circular room below.

The fountain below bubbled in a faint splash of light that streamed in from the upper band of windows. She reflected on the message that accompanied her last clues: PROVIDENCE'S LIGHT EXPOSES WHAT IS DONE IN DARKNESS.

Her exposure to the stars on the bottom of the well under Stanley Hall Chapel sparked a series of neurons to fire wildly in her mind.

The message was hidden in the centerpiece fountain.

Metal spiral stairs rumbled under foot as Kate descended and ran to the central concaved bowl perched above a pond-like octagon base. She cast her black light over the structure. Coins littered the both the top and bottom portions of the fountain. A set of coins in both basins glowed purple.

Bingo.

"You should do this." Kate swallowed hard before turning to Pratt. "I did it last time. Times two. The altar and the makeshift gravesite. Well, actually three if you include the little church. You weren't there for that one, but I did it without you."

Pratt looked unconvinced.

Kate panned the black light over the fountain again. In the upper basin, the spread of coins beneath the water's surface appeared random with an asymmetric pattern of seven glowing coins placed on top of the others. Nothing was random. In the bottom basin, the coins formed a circle.

Pratt studied the fountain for booby traps before reaching out with her hand.

"Wait." Kate jerked Pratt's arm back. Pulling out her sat phone, she snapped photos of the coin placements. "The upper cluster looks like the Big Dipper."

Pratt looked unconvinced. "Can I collect the loose change now?"

Kate counted the tiny shapes. "Stars. They're stars. Seven stars in the big dipper. Seven coins for seven stops. The bottom marks the hour placements on a clock."

Pratt pinched up the coins, keeping the upper and lower currencies in different hands, and carried them to a glass-covered table. She slapped them down on the clear surface and water pooled beneath her palm.

"Don't mix them up," Kate said.

Pratt cast a hard glare her way.

Eight old texts rested below the spread of water and coins. Pratt flipped the upper bowl's wet mixed coins over to reveal single letters painted in violet. She worked the pennies, nickels, and dimes into a random wordplay: SOAR LIP. She turned the lower bowl's coins face up to see their markings: mostly numbers, two dots, and a dash or line.

Kate smiled. The challenge was in the form of an anagram. Nudging Pratt aside, she reordered the letters: POLARIS.

"The North Star," she said. "It's the guiding star in the northern horizon. The Earth's axis points to it and other star systems rotate about it. Polaris symbolizes balance, focus, truth. It's a unique phenomenon."

"Aren't you little Miss Star Club?"

"The astronomy club." Kate felt a chill. Barnes knew of her childhood passion for stargazing. It could have been as simple as tracking down her high school yearbook, which had photos of her as club president working with telescopes. The mass murdering ex-super soldier probably knew more about her than anyone.

The library was another test, but not the destination.

Troubling.

Uncomfortably, Kate moved to the twelve coins. All quarters. Letters were marked on heads, numbers on tails. She skipped the math and numbers to focus on the anagram. Flipping over the quarters, she revealed the letters: CICEROHITLIN. A quick separation showed CICERO HIT LIN. Well, that didn't make sense. She tried CIRCLE HIT ONE. Glancing back to the fountain, she assumed the answer would be related to POLARIS. From the Earth's point of view, stars moved about the North Star, a center of truth. She rearranged the quarters and settled on HELIOCENTRIC. It was the astronomical model in which planets in the solar system revolved around the sun, rather than the flawed geocentric models promoted by Plato, Aristotle, and others.

Kate stared harder at the wordplay and realized just beneath it, past protective glass, rested a copy of *de revolutionibus orbi um coelestium*, On the Revolutions of Heavenly Spheres, by Nicolai Copernici Torinensis. Nicholas Copernicus, a Renaissance-era astronomer and mathematician. Page markers held the rare book, written in Latin, open to his famous heliocentric sketch. Extending past an edge of the page was a blue piece of paper with a typed number: 1236.

Exhilaration coursed through her. She'd figured it out.

"You got a pocket knife?" she asked, searching the display case for a lock and a hinged door. Instincts pushed her to consider mashing the glass, but she feared damaging the books.

She found the lock on a side panel. Pratt handed her a multi-tool.

Wedging a thin dagger-like blade into the lock, Kate wrenched hard, shearing the latch assembly and breaking the lock. Digging up the blue matting, she slowly reeled out the books, stopping at *de revolutionibus orbi um coelestium*. Gently she lifted the book away from the others and returned the blue mat to the display case. At a reading stand, she peeled open the book to the marked page and panned over it with her UV light.

Nothing.

Pratt clicked on a flashlight to reveal a message on the bookmark: ORIGINAL THOUGHT IS SOMETIMES RESTATED SENTIMENT FROM PREDECESSORS.

Pratt scrunched up her forehead. "What does that mean?"

Kate grinned. "There's a claim that Copernicus didn't conceive the heliocentric theory. Someone else did." She flipped the bookmark over. The backside revealed a library catalogue number and a book title: *The Sand Reckoner*.

She followed the books along the curved walls until she located a thin hardback reprint. Sliding it off the shelf, she noted the book's cover was wider than its printed pages.

Archimedis Syracusani arenarius et dimensio circuli, a Latin translation from original Greek. Handwritten notes marked margins. The book's title was translated as *The Sand Reckoner by Archimedes*. It was filled with mathematic citations she couldn't understand.

"Who's Archimedes?" Pratt asked impatiently.

Kate glanced around. "He's Greek," she said. "Someone who wrote about the stars."

Inside the thin book, taped to a blue bookmark tag, was a Band-Aid-like rubber fingerprint. A breadth of Latin text had been highlighted and translated: *In 225 BCE a mathematician named Aristarchus of Samos hypothesized that the sun remains unmoved, that the earth revolves about the sun in the circumference of a circle.* 225 BCE came well before the Middle Ages and time of Copernicus. Barnes was saying he Renaissance scientist expanded on someone else's theory and took credit for it.

Handwritten in the footer was: THE GRIM SHADOW OF THE PUPPETEER'S EVIL LIES UNCHALLENGED WHERE STARLIGHT AND INQUISITIVE THOUGHT CANNOT SHINE. BATTLELINES CREATED FROM ASHES AND DIRT EXPOSE WHAT IS NOT GOD'S DOING.

Pratt rolled her eyes. "What's this mean?"

Studying the latex-like fingerprint, Kate processed the translation.

"Leave the books," she said, sprinting out of the library. "And bring our change."

76
THE IMPORTANCE OF A CALL

Strategic Information & Operations Center (SIOC), FBI Headquarters, Washington, DC

Alice Watson needed to take this call in private.

In the executive conference room attached to the ops center, she closed the door and listened to the man at the other end of the speaker phone.

"Where is Morgan?" asked the man, who identified himself as Army Colonel Randal Wang. "Dispense with the pretenses, because I know she's not dead. And I know about St. Elizabeths."

Watson considered her response and lied. "I don't know."

"You don't know, or you won't say?"

Her bluff had been called awfully fast. Watson knew where Morgan and Pratt were, having talked with both Shortz and Morgan before making a personal request of the Secretary of the Navy. Morgan had been granted one-hour access and latitude within reason to the Naval Observatory grounds under tight surveillance. The greatest of these conditions was that they were not to trespass onto the Vice President's side of the circular property.

She glanced up at a digital clock on the wall. Morgan was thirty minutes into her hour.

"I need thirty minutes before I can answer your question," she said.

"Then I won't tell you where Phillip Barnes operates from."

That statement got her attention. "You go first, Colonel."

There was a thoughtful pause. "His base of operations is east of the Navy Yard," Wang said. "Now where's Morgan?"

"The Naval Observatory."

"The observatory?"

Watson cleared her throat. "I don't know where Morgan's headed next, but we've concluded based on Barnes' prior actions that two more locations are in play. There's a consultant supporting the disclosure of solutions as they materialize. That's where the thirty minutes factors in."

"Regardless what you may know of his biological enhancements, Barnes is beyond dangerous. He's trained in combat engineering and explosive ordinances. He excels at munitions. The Metro and Soldiers' Home were child's play. He can do a lot more damage. And somewhere along the way, he secured absolute control of a satellite."

"A satellite?" Watson frowned. "Under the name Isaac Smith, Barnes attended MIT and completed advanced degrees in mechanical engineering and computer science with an emphasis in theoretical computer science. In college, he wrote essential code for satellite systems."

"That fills in some gaps." Wang sighed heavily. "The asset he controls is called SpaceKey. It's *the* next generation reconnaissance GEO satellite. It's powerful. Game changing. It was decommissioned while its dead-as-a-rock platform was evaluated for catastrophic, systemic anomalies. I don't think the asset is very dead. Barnes has been monitoring and watching the whole time."

Watson had to ask. "Can you shut down this SpaceKey?"

"No. But with assistance from the Navy, we can terminate fiber optic communications between his base of operations and the Navy Yard. That will cripple his network, but won't kill his operations. SpaceKey remains operational."

"Can we shoot the satellite down?"

"You want to start a war?" Wang laughed. "The Chinese and Russians might consider ground-to-orbit intervention a prelude to war. They have sensitive assets to protect, even if we don't like their birds watching us. And if the United States had the technology to intercept spacecraft—which I'm not allowed to disclose—you'd require launch authorization from both the President and the Secretary of Defense. I don't see that happening. Do you?"

"Colonel," Watson said with a sigh, "what are your intentions when I tell you where Morgan will be next?"

Wang's response was crystal clear. "As law enforcement, you don't want to know that answer."

77
HOLD FAST

US Naval Observatory (USNO), Washington, DC

Kate sprinted into the hallway outside the library and appraised ascending and descending options. Beside stairs leading up, a painted white door was marked BASEMENT.

Kate clutched the brass handle. It was locked. Pratt caught up to her, lugging her backpack and awkwardly stuffing the coins from the fountain into her pants pockets.

Kate stepped back and nodded.

Pratt's face went stone-like as she kicked in the door, splintering it from the jamb. Flicking on lights, Pratt headed down as Kate trailed. Painted wooden stairs led to a utilitarian basement. Storage identifiers marked the rooms.

Using the UV light, Kate panned over doors along the way. The door they sought was not hard to find, branded in UV markings: the Eye of Providence and a number, 1261830.

Inset from the rest of the corridor, the gray metal door was mated to a reinforced masonry block wall. Beside the door was dual-input access control: a fingerprint biometric reader and a numerical keypad. A domed security camera watched them from above.

Kate ignored the camera and knew there was no kicking in this door, no matter how much super-strength Pratt possessed. The space behind the door could probably be classified as a bunker, something far superior to a fallout shelter.

Barnes had led them here for a reason.

"Get out your gadgets," Kate said. She slid the manufactured fingerprint over her index finger, pressed it against the biometrics reader, and typed in the number from the door.

The latches clicked.

Pratt had a hand-held scanner active and ready when Kate swung open the door.

A long gray corridor stretched as far as the eye could see. LED lights, piping, and conduits were racked overhead.

Pratt took point as Kate waved the UV light from side to side.

"I didn't ask this earlier," Kate asked. "Do those devices of yours protect people against sonic warfare?"

"Sonic what?"

Kate grunted. "This morning, Barnes introduced himself with telepathic outreach. My entire skull hurt. And I can still hear his voice. Creepy. Very creepy."

Pratt laughed. "Sounds like cheap CIA tech."

"Yeah, well, it was painful. Had a headache for hours."

"This lifesaver detects a variety of sound and infrared waves, light refractions from laser sensors, and sends out a band of its own sound waves to resonate with trip wires. Barnes used trip wires at St. Elizabeths."

Morgan frowned. "You still love him?"

"Really. You're asking that question now?" Pratt kept marching. "Yeah, I love him enough to rip his heart out of his chest."

"And most girls just want to break a guy's heart."

Pratt held up her hand. "Shut up and keep up."

Kate looked down the tunnel. "Slow down. We don't want to end up in the Vice President's residence, where I'm sure Secret Service is waiting."

Pratt gestured at a large steel door fixed flush into the tunnel wall—a blast door to a hardened shelter. Above it was stenciled UNITED STATES NAVAL OBSERVATORY. A brass plate was mounted next to the door with only square indentation visible. Here were no biometrics, no keypad.

Kate waved the black light. The door lit up like Christmas. A circular serpent appeared in violet neon. Its body was sculpted out of woven rope as the reptile consumed its own tail—an ouroboros symbol. HOLD FAST was written inside the circle.

"How do we get in?" Pratt asked, poking her fingertip into the square. "You got a key?"

They exchanged looks.

The bone shaft from the jar of coal dust found at Soldiers' Home.

Kate dug into her pocket as Pratt washed her hands with a flashlight.

The rectangular object was etched and carved. Its shaft was the same shape and size as the square hole in the plate. It was a blocked key like none she'd ever seen before.

"Here goes nothing," she said, sliding it into the key reader.

The locks on the door hummed. Spiral gears retracted locking bolts.

Pratt aimed her devices at the crease between the door and its frame. Nothing showed on her sensors.

A pull on a small catch at the bottom of the blast door allowed it to pivot. The enormous door glided open effortlessly. A faint breeze brushed their faces as oxygen seemed to purge the room and drive out stale air. LED lighting blinked on automatically.

"This was locked down," Pratt said. "How'd Barnes ever get in here?"

Kate frowned. "Security clearances. And he wants to prove how smart he is."

Before them, an elongated bunker was structured as a series of gray compartments that linked to each other. Uniquely Navy. The first was a command and control room with a central table, prepped and ready for emergency operations. Blank monitors and screens populated both sides of the room. Digital clocks logged 24-hour time in different parts of the world.

Sensing the bunker would be difficult to booby trap, Kate pushed ahead of Pratt and moved deeper into the ship-like berths, sweeping her UV light side-to-side. Communications room. Common area and storage. Finally sleeping bunks, with curtains drawn. Unisex toilets announced a dead end.

Pratt shrugged. "What now?"

Kate studied the bunk arrangement. Sleeping cubicles were stacked three high in columns of three along each side. The bunker had been designed to hold eighteen inhabitants.

They jerked back curtains.

Pratt found the bunk they sought: a man, his naked figure covered by a simple white sheet. He was stone-cold, out like the others. If his eyes had been open, he'd be staring up at the patch of skin taped directly above him.

Kate frowned. His face looked familiar. She remembered seeing him at inauguration ceremonies. It was the Vice President's son.

"Freeze!" a voice bellowed from the bunker's entry.

They spun sideways and saw four Navy security force officers in split high-low stances. Automatic weapons sighted them down as eager young men and women waited for an excuse to pull triggers.

Pratt whispered to Kate, "You're right. We should've toured the air and space museum."

Kate raised her arms and nudged Pratt to do the same.

"Get a medic," Kate said, nodding at one of the sleeping bunks.

"I don't care!" one of the officers shouted. "I will not repeat myself! Turn around! Get on your knees! Place your hands on your head!" He lowered his voice to over-enunciate his next words. "Or we will open fire and drag your corpses out of here."

78
DROPPING POWER

EyePoint Applications Facility, East of the Washington Navy Yard, Washington, DC

On Water Street SE, FBI Special Agent Jack Wright had a front row seat to a strip of Navy-owned industrial property. As the lone FBI representative, he stood beside heavily armed Navy security forces. His observation role had come as a direct request from the Secretary of the Navy—something Randy Wang had engineered. MPDC supported the exercise by evacuating the marinas and barricading both ends of Water Street. Potomac Electrical Power Company (PEPCO) dropped utility power from a vault down the street, sending the entire riverfront into darkness. Incoming fiber optic lines and phone lines had been cut, including a dedicated fiber line from the Washington Navy Yard.

Leaning against a Humvee, Wright watched from the standoff distance and the calculated blast radius for standard munitions. A theoretical blast radius. Anything associated with Phillip Logan Barnes had proven lethal.

No one was taking chances after Soldiers' Home. They assumed the property was booby-trapped—fact until proven otherwise.

On the phone, the five-star admiral made it clear this was a Navy security forces enforcement exercise. Nothing more. Unlike what was portrayed in movies and TV shows, U.S. law restricted military operations on American soil. Security force actions were an exception, as long as these actions were conducted on or within the federal territorial boundaries. Since the Navy owned the industrial property and EyePoint Applications was its civilian user group, the Navy had the authority to conduct safety and security operations without notifying the Department of Defense.

The last thing the bureau wanted was to tip off the Pentagon or General James Davidson. That was the plan, anyway.

Without utility power, the site's emergency generators kicked on.

A Navy security forces sniper straddled the perimeter fencing and fired consecutive shots into the cooling radiators of the generators. Everyone waited.

An unmistakable heavy thrum broke the night air. Pinpointing the direction of the oncoming noises was hard. Wright sensed the invasion force came from the Potomac River.

Lights approached on a dark horizon, low and over the water.

A pair of Sikorsky helicopters from Little Creek, Virginia, broke a tight formation. One deployed Navy SEALs just inside the river's fencing line. The second chopper dropped SEALs onto the main structure's roof.

Wright had been told that this SEAL platoon carried demolition and explosives experts. They had trained for urban missions just like this one.

Holes were torched into the roof and concussion grenades were dropped inside. SEALs rappelled inward, out of sight. Trailing lines from the choppers went slack. The aircraft retreated to the river and hovered over the water at a safe distance.

Overheating, the emergency generators dropped offline right on cue, plunging the set of structures on the property into complete darkness.

From the street side, security bypassed the hydraulic actuators to the front gate, slid it open, and edged Humvees just onto the property boundary. Two young men stood behind M2 Browning .50 caliber machine guns mounted onto the vehicles.

Wright listened to a radio placed on the hood of the Humvee.

"Mermaid, this is LandShark One," a SEAL announced. "We're in. Off leash. Over."

"Roger that."

"Light green det cord spotted," the SEAL continued. "Charges are placed below the roofline and at building columns. One thing is clear—this bastard wants to blow a hole to the center of the Earth. Over."

"Don't take unnecessary risks, LandSharks."

"Acknowledge that, Mermaid. No feedback loop is installed on the charges. This shack is strictly blow and go. A brick and pin approach. Cutting cord as we go. The detonation sequence will be controlled from a central location. Scanning for power sources and controllers. Over."

"Roger that."

Wright glanced around at the tense faces of the security personnel standing with him. Young sailors itching for a chance to jump into the fray. He'd been one of them once, but on the Army intelligence side. That was a long time ago, before his time with the bureau.

Wright thought about Kate and regretted ever involving her in field work. In Princeton, he'd put her life at risk. Her suspension and Congressional inquiry were the result of combined actions: hers, his, Wang's. He'd convinced the Director to get her Office of Professional Responsibility hearing frozen, get her reassigned, and have her Senate subpoena vacated. But a domestic terrorist had pulled her back into harm's way.

Kate was ill-prepared for this day of hell. And that was his fault.

Crossword grid

- 1. FOUNDATIONSTONE
- 9. P R O ... K O L
- 11. R 12. P 13. MURDER 16. R Y 17. XII
- I 20. PLA I I S
- 22. S E Y 23. H 24. S I
- 25. LAB 26. H E O
- 29. EUGENICS 32. SEVEN
- 34. A 35. 36. E
- 38. ELIZABETHS 45. S
- 46. LOGTHETOURS H
- K O E T 48. R 49. HOME
- P R 53. A 54. B I 55. THRALL
- A I 58. U K T
- S O E 67. T N E
- 69. STIGMA 70. SAPPER

79
ARRIVAL OF CIRCLES

9:10 PM, Naval Support Facility, US Naval Observatory (USNO), Washington, DC

Kate sat shackled to a wooden chair as a no-nonsense Navy security officer stood beside a closed door, gripping his automatic weapon and watching her. They'd separated her from Pratt and brought her to a room that was part museum, part antique repair shop.

Her gaze strafed the room, taking in a series of naval instruments: bronze sextants, telescopes, pendulum clocks, a device tagged as a bond chronometer. Two wooden boxes were dedicated for instruments, incoming and outgoing. She could hear movement in the outside hallway and a vintage clock ticking off the seconds.

Anxiety rose. While the clock was ticking, she'd been put in a timeout. And the Navy seemed to have its own timetable.

She'd demanded to speak with the top officer on duty. The only word that seemed to have any impact was "medic."

Security forces had manhandled her at gunpoint into a women's toilet, where a female officer got extremely intimate with her body search. The roughhouse tactics were part of the intimidation factor—don't mess with the U.S. Navy.

The door opened and a two-star admiral entered carrying a box. He gestured to the officer at the door to uncuff her and leave the room.

"A Judge Advocate General reminded me that trespassing and destruction of federal property over a value of one-thousand dollars carry a jail term of up to eleven years combined," the admiral said. "The display case and basement door were antiques. A lot of things at the observatory are historical artifacts. Some say that includes me."

He set the box on a work bench and motioned for her to join him.

"You two were solid bad guys tonight," he said with a grin. "Security forces prepare damn hard and their exercises drive us nuts. They get tired of substituting one of their own as stand-in threats. Having fresh meat and solid captures made their day."

Kate exhaled. "Admiral, I'm real tired of being the bait."

She peered into the box. It held almost everything, including her Glock and the parchment of flesh. Missing was the key to the bunker's blast doors—no sense in returning that, she supposed, or even acknowledging it existed.

The admiral picked up the synthetic fingertip. "No more than twenty people have access to that bunker or those tunnels." He contemplated his question before asking it. "Who will we find when this is processed?"

The severity of the security breach didn't escape her. "I presume the Vice President."

He sighed. "Well, that's going to be a challenging conversation to have with his staff."

Kate shook her head. "Any more than telling the VP his son was a victim of a kidnapping and is in a coma for the rest of his life?" She holstered her sidearm and collected the rest of her treasures.

"I guess not." He inhaled deeply. "I've been asked to hand you over to bureau personnel. They arrive in five minutes."

Kate extracted the parchment of skin, laid it on the table, and snapped several pictures of it with her sat phone. She hit the send button and forwarded the photos.

He leaned close to study it. "What the hell is that?"

"The reason you need to let me leave with Captain Pratt." Kate gave him the reader's digest version, leaving out the parts about her killing a murderer's family and an army general in charge of creating test tube children and experimenting with human genes. "It's critical that we riddle it out. And I cannot do that if I'm parked at headquarters playing it safe."

The admiral eyed her as if she was insane, then ducked out into the hallway to converse with security forces personnel.

She studied the inked message.

KATHERINE, AS BLACK POWDER'S ARRIVAL CHANGED GEOPOLITCAL LANDSCAPES, THE INCREASE OF SOPHISTICATED DECEPTION CREATES POPULATIONS THAT BELIEVE IN NOTHING OR FANATICAL HALF-TRUTHS, SUCH THAT PEOPLE SEEK TO DESTORY OTHERS AND PERPETUATE THE FRACTURED THOUGHTS OF CLASS-PROPAGANDA.

ACROSS

9   ABBR: THRESHOLD
20   INTERSECTING FORUMS
22   MORTALITY
34   CONSUMPTION
48   ABBR: WATERCRAFT
58   ABBR: RESISTANCE

DOWN

3   ABBR: OSTENSIBLE
16   CARRIAGE REPLACEMENT
26   IRRATIONAL QUANTITY
33   TRANSITION IN ROUTE
35   ABBR: NODE CONVEYANCE
51   ABBR: SACROCMERE CENTER
56   ABBR: SECRET GOV PROCESS

Her heart was weary, numb to the killer's intimate soliloquies, written to rationalize his actions and explain away murder. Her mind worked through words, line by line. BLACK POWDER, no different than other game-changing technologies, had changed how wars were fought. A race of genetically enhanced super soldiers, super astronauts, super spies would change the world, and perhaps not for the better. Barnes had asserted views on how Davidson and his team thrived unchecked in the shadows with no regard for the ethical questions, creating a superior race of humans. Political discord and the absence of ethical accountability were paving the way for this non-evolutionary, artificially created breed of super humans.

She thought of Dolly's clan of sheep and the CRISPR babies. Those initiatives hadn't been the first efforts, only the first that were publicly disclosed. Those scientists played god, daring to redraw boundaries of evolution.

No different from Davidson and his team, she supposed.

She returned to the parchment. The open circle reminded her of the serpent eating its tail painted on the underground blast door. Ouroboros. Circles carried numerous meanings: life-death, marriage, beginning-end, inclusion, wholeness. As a forensics investigator, she knew the snake and dragon version from street gangs: ouroboros stood for unification and renewal. The all-is-one symbol had ties to Egypt, alchemy, witchcraft, Gnosticism, and Indian lore. Following the train of thought for destinations in DC, circles were abundant. Even the observatory grounds were a circle. Famous landmarks bounded by circles would include the Lincoln, Jefferson, and Washington Memorials, the Capitol, and even the White House. Many of those would have fallout shelters or bunkers.

But Barnes had avoided highly visible locations, preferring to focus on locations tied to people or deeper meanings.

Every stop played a role in a broader story.

Kate looked at the clues and grinned. It was about time her medical degree contributed.

51 DOWN lined up with M LINE or A BAND CENTER. Since it was an abbreviation, her bet was MLINE. She texted the solutions to the same number as the photos.

The Admiral returned. "So your team breaks down puzzle clues and you race off to find the next victim? It's concerning that your fifth set of clues led you here."

She almost smiled. "The story of my day."

"How many did law enforcement lose at Soldiers' Home?" he asked.

She sighed. "HQ never gave me numbers, but it's bad. And one agent is too many."

The admiral's jaw went tense. "And what's the role of the Vice President in this? And why is his son involved?"

Kate shrugged. "This is speculation. Unfounded. But I think when every angle is evaluated, we'll learn the VP greased research skids. And through his political connections he put his son, who holds a Ph.D. in Biogenetics and DNA modifications, in the program's lead role. Phillip Barnes targeted select researchers as a way to expose secrets."

The Admiral nodded thoughtfully. "You can't leave in the vehicle you arrived in. Security forces inspected it and discovered weapons and stolen license plates." He took a breath. "The Navy will hold an investigation on how you managed to escape from our custody. I won't cover for you, but I do suggest a bathroom break. Unsupervised. Use the west gate. Go on foot. A car will be waiting for you. Don't converse with the driver."

Kate saw Pratt being escorted outside in the hallway doorway.

She smiled. "Thank you."

The admiral shrugged. "Catch this terrorist and I can wash over your little lapse here." He pointed to her remaining personal items in the box. "The change from the fountain and the key you found stay with me. That's not negotiable."

"Who do we owe for the ride?" she asked, scooping up her possessions including the parchment.

"The Brits across the street owed me a favor. It's a one-time use." He paused. "No one knows except you and me."

Kate glanced at a clock. Minutes counted. Breaking into the hallway, she noticed the only person in sight was the admiral.

"Godspeed, Agent Morgan," he said, nodding toward a door.

She ducked into the women's toilet. Inside, Pratt waited at a double-hinged window, which was slid up and open.

"You have friends in mighty high places," Pratt said with a crooked smile.

They climbed out the window. The night sky was sprinkled with stars. The air was cooler, crisper than Kate remembered it. Sprinting, their feet left solid asphalt and they reached the spread of grass just outside the main observatory dome. Ducking into a band of trees, they connected to an access drive. The unattended west service gate was open enough for someone to slip through. Racing through the gap, they broke into an alley between buildings.

Out of breath, Kate stopped to put her hands on her hips and saw that Pratt wasn't the slightest bit winded. Her gaze moved to Wisconsin Avenue south. A band of men loitered on the sidewalk a couple of shops down, between a sushi restaurant and a Rite Aid.

Across the street, fronting red-bricked condos, a man in a black suit stood next to a black sedan. He caught her gaze and held up a coin.

As they approached, his steely gaze was sharp, appraising. He spotted the semi-automatic holstered on Kate's hip. Beneath the suit he seemed fit, even muscular. Kate sensed he could handle himself and assumed he was either a British operative or one of their security officers.

He said nothing but held the coin, a quarter, in his open palm.

Kate dug out her UV light from her pants pocket.

The quarter glowed violet. It was a coin from the library fountain at the observatory.

Clever. The admiral knew the perfect non-spoken password.

She snatched up the coin and the driver opened the rear doors.

Sliding into the sedan's backseat, she said, "Al Tiramisu."

80
EXPLOSIVE CIRCLES

Al Tiramisu, West of Dupont Circle, Washington, DC

Two blocks west of Dupont Circle, Will Shortz discussed his situation with a server, who provided a table in the back. The service and food were outstanding and it was clear why celebrities and politicians had frequented the restaurant and posed in pictures with Chef Luigi. He ordered *risotto del giorno* and sipped water while tweaking the solutions that remained.

Pausing from his list of solutions on a notepad, he glanced at his watch for the tenth time.

Morgan should have called already.

"May I join you?" an Asian man asked, making himself at home across the table before Shortz could reply. The uninvited man wore a sportcoat and a collared shirt. His inquisitive brown eyes studied Shortz's puzzle and its solutions. "So that's the puzzle?"

Shortz placed a napkin over his work. "Can I help you?"

"Doubt it." The man appraised a menu. "Morgan reached out to me on other affairs. I was told she going to meet you here."

"And you are?"

Shortz's phone pinged with an incoming text. Nervously, he glanced at the device and saw the message had attachments. It was from FBI Agent Katherine Morgan.

The man leaned across the table and whispered, "I work for the federal government."

Shortz presented his best poker face, despite an adrenaline surge. The man avoided the question, which gave him the hunch that some branch of national intelligence had gotten involved. Not overly surprising given super soldiers and the events of the day. The man across from him looked experienced at deception and seeking ways to elicit responses.

Standing, the man revealed a phone of his own with a mirrored text and attachments.

"I'll be outside doing some reading, Mr. Shortz," he said. "Let's chat when you have these clues solved."

Shortz watched the mystery man leave the restaurant. What had just happened? Did his phone get hacked right in front of him? Another addition to his day of firsts. He made a mental note to re-place his phone in the morning, then looked at the texts.

Another patch of skin provided fresh clues and a companion prologue. This set included no sophisticated graphics, merely a cir-cle. Symbols had defined destinations. The circle meant something, directed them to the next stop.

Shortz transferred content to his notepad and matched clues to known solutions and open spaces in the puzzle. He wrote down Morgan's hint at 51 DOWN and focused on the low-hanging fruit.

20 ACROSS was rather simple: PLAZAS. 34 ACROSS was RATE.

With Morgan's contribution to 51 DOWN as MLINE since the phrase intersected with the words HOME and THRALL, 22 ACROSS and CONSUMPTION could be a variety of solutions so he skipped that clue. 16 DOWN, CARRIAGE REPLACEMENT, seemed to imply mass transit, trains, subways, bus lines.

The developing theme seemed transit-related. A toll booth or subway, perhaps.

He noticed that 30 DOWN had been omitted. That was perplex-ing. Unless he missed it, the word or phrase was CRET. Nothing in the puzzle was by accident. The absence of the word was deliberate. A quick web search on CRET came up with root forms linking to discharge or generate and a shortlist of abbreviations, including Cretan. Cret was also an architect who had a list of achievements, buildings and bridges in the DC area. Since the connection and significance escaped him, Shortz moved onto other clues.

He brought a wide view of Washington DC up on his laptop. This destination was tied to circles. The shapes were everywhere. Traffic circles. Monuments. Buildings. Roads. Ponds. Too many locations to sort through. And he imagined many of the locations had fallout shelters.

His gaze drifted back to the clues and 58 ACROSS. ABBR: RESISTANCE. He penciled in UG as the solution. The circle was UNDERGROUND.

Now his mind was split, one part wanting to track down subways and rail terminals and the other simpler traffic circles. A generic theme provided a wider array of possible destinations.

The wordplay this time out seemed more elementary. Convenient. 26 DOWN and IRRATIONAL QUANTITY fit a saying he'd heard. PI was labeled the "irrational number" because its numerical sequence didn't repeat. Its value was unknowable found in nature, DNA, the universe. PI was essential to life and circles.

This prize was in the associations.

He needed to narrow the field.

A quick Internet search listed thirty-four traffic circles in Washington.

He backtracked to 35 DOWN. ABBR: NODE CONVEYANCE.

Based on his puzzle's layout, it was a four-letter phrase.

Transportation hub. T-HUB. He jotted it down.

He backtracked to the note preceding the clues. The mention of BLACK POWDER and its ARRIVAL was relevant, perhaps more so than the sentiment expressed in the terrorist's digression into social and political discourse.

BLACK POWDER was the central clue.

And that had something to do with an underground transportation circle.

81
THE FRESH BREATH OF RESURRECTION

Phillip Barnes felt a jolt in his heart.

They'd fooled him. They were alive.

From the darkness of an alley, as he returned to one of his autonomous vans parked at the curb on P Street, he spotted a black car as it stopped. Katherine Morgan and Rachel Pratt left the vehicle and jaywalked to a restaurant, Al Tiramisu.

He hunkered close to a building, cutting off lines of sight. The thrill of the challenge surged back into his veins.

Both women had played dead to buy themselves time, secretly following clues but not yet discovering the destination of the circle. Barnes wondered if Rachel had solved the clues he'd written on her palm in the hospital.

Together. Wow. More than he could have hoped for. They were resurrection stories, if only for a moment.

Breathless with anticipation, he unconsciously stepped onto the sidewalk, using his van as cover. Opening its side door, he leaned across its front seat and watched them as they met an Asian man outside a restaurant. They spoke, then entered Al Tiramisu.

Barnes smiled, feeling the same rush he'd experienced on the Metro platform before the train bombing.

Katherine Morgan had survived her trials and stayed the course.

Damn impressive.

As for Rachel, this was her last stop. The island finale only had room for Morgan.

82
NO PLAN B

Kate followed Pratt and Wang to a table in the back of the restaurant. The mini reunion seemed to have caught Will Shortz by surprise. Pratt sat next to the puzzle master, Wang across from him.

Shortz offered an awkward smile and a look that said, "What am I doing here?"

"Have you two met?" Kate asked, taking a seat.

Shortz gave an uncomfortable shrug.

Wang smiled. "We chatted, briefly."

Kate caught the tension. "Be nice, Colonel, and stop reading his emails. Mr. Shortz, Wang here works for the NSA. He has some unique skills we need."

Shortz pushed his laptop across the table. His fifteen-by-fifteen crossword puzzle was nearly complete, with only a few squares unsolved.

Pratt pressed forward on her elbows, scanning for words.

Kate studied the solution, a side tabulation column of wordplay dedicated to this stop.

"If BLACK POWDER is the key," Shortz said rubbing his forehead, "then Dupont Circle is your destination. If it's misdirection, I don't have a plan B."

Kate forced a smile. "Shocking. No plan B?"

Shortz laid out his logic, connecting Éleuthère Irénée du Pont de Nemours to the founding of an American gunpowder manufacturer that later became an international conglomerate, the Du Pont

Company. Originally named Pacific Circle, the roundabout and town center was renamed after Samuel Francis Du Pont, a Civil War naval admiral. Beneath the circle was an old transportation hub, a trolley and streetcar station, which had served as a community fallout shelter for quite a while.

"It's the best match, unless I'm missing deeper meanings," Shortz said. "A cultural non-profit called Dupont Underground uses a portion of the subterranean spaces for urban art galleries, concerts, theater. That leaves large sections of the underground spaces abandoned."

Kate bit her lip. "Abandoned?"

Pratt glanced at her palm, which was painted over with smudges.

From the corner of her eye, Kate caught Wang studying Pratt.

Cocking her head, she asked, "Ever train there?"

Pratt shook her head. "Sounds like another trap." Pratt's fingers migrated to specific portions of the puzzle, touching MLINE and 51 DOWN, then a void in the puzzle. "Given any thought to 60 ACROSS?"

Shortz shook his head. "That word phrase isn't in play. Is there something I missed?"

Pratt arched her shoulders. "Keep an eye out for that clue."

"Care to share, Captain?" Kate asked. "Now's not the time to withhold information."

Pratt almost laughed. "You know what I know."

Kate turned to Wang. "Okay. I think it's time to call the general, don't you think?"

83
SPACEKEY

EyePoint Applications Facility, East of the Washington Navy Yard, Washington, DC

Without tripping sensors, the SEAL platoon had bypassed battery systems and cut out the primary and secondary controllers to the explosive charges. Barnes had rigged everything on the property to blow. But this time, the good guys won without casualties.

Jack Wright watched the SEAL platoon pack up and Navy security forces complete their final sweeps of the EyePoint site. It would take days, if not weeks, and a barrage of forensic specialists to break down the extent of Barnes's network infiltration, dig into his clandestine empire, and figure how he'd managed take control of a decommissioned spy satellite.

The fallout from Barnes' domestic espionage activities would take months to uncover, and heads would roll across multiple agencies.

A car pulled to a stop outside the property gate. A man in a suit got out. Navy security forces checked his credentials and allowed him to pass.

"You have my permission to shoot this guy," Wright whispered to the security forces officer standing closest to him.

"I don't work for you, sir," the young man said.

Wright grinned. "He doesn't know that."

Introductions were made. The National Reconnaissance Office (NRO) had sent their Principal Deputy Director to perform damage control.

Wright got to the point. "What can you tell me about SpaceKey? And how the hell did Barnes and EyePoint get control of it?"

The PDD shuffled nervously. "It's a prototype, superior platform on multiple levels. The asset demonstrated catastrophic systems failures immediately after GEO deployment. It's an extremely rare outcome, but mathematically possible. SpaceKey was a dead rock in space. Or so we thought. When our in-house team could not re-engage and reinitialize the satellite, the NRO outsourced this effort to EyePoint."

"My bet is that Barnes had control of your asset the entire time." Wright shook his head in frustration. "What are the full capabilities of this satellite?"

"I'm not at liberty to discuss that."

Wright turned to the soldier that he'd spoke with earlier. "Shoot him, sailor."

The security forces officer's face went stone-like and he drew his side arm. "Where do you want me to aim, sir?"

Wright chuckled. "Last month, I got shot in the chest. No lie. And it hurt like hell. Start there. If he survives that wound, go for the head and see if that does the trick. He's a civilian, so it won't be hard for the NRO to replace him."

A second security forces officer stepped in behind the PDD, blocking the man's retreat.

The officer with the sidearm raised his weapon.

Wright doubled down on the charade. "What are the capabilities of SpaceKey? I won't ask a third time."

Concern, if not fear, showed in the administrator's eyes. "It's a dual function platform. Ultra-high-definition, real-time imaging combined with interactive high-precision GPS systems for autonomous vehicles. We developed it for deployment over Russia and China."

"What's so secret about that?" Wright asked.

The PDD swallowed hard. "The autonomous systems it can control include first strike protocols."

"First strike?" A troubling development.

The PDD exhaled. "SpaceKey has the capabilities to control autonomous vehicles. Think of it as commanding a swarm of remote assassins on wheels. Long-distance weapons on foreign soil without human assets on the ground. Cheaper than launching missiles. A fleet of vehicles packed with explosives can be deployed like battering rams or used as single strike measures. SpaceKey was built to execute long-distance regime change."

Wright's head was swimming. "Gentlemen, stand down." The security force officers stepped back. "Any chance to hack back into SpaceKey and shut it down?"

The PDD shook his head. "We tried that and had no success."

Wright turned and sprinted toward his car. He needed to warn SIOC that Barnes had a drone army on wheels at his disposal.

84
TUNNELS

For an instant, Kate Morgan felt as if time had stopped.

Beside her was a fountain adorned with figurines. Water flowed from the upper bowl and poured into a large circular basin. People sat on benches and the grass enjoying the evening under the night sky as if nothing was about to happen.

Dupont Circle was a different stop—an urban setting—an historic neighborhood that functioned as a convergence of businesses, embassies, hotels, restaurants, and residences.

No one knew what lay in the maze of subterranean spaces beneath the circle.

Kate studied the faces of people around her. If she met Barnes, she might not even recognize him. That was a troubling thought. Her vision tracked down Rachel Pratt, who jogged across the street and ducked into the Dupont Circle Hotel. Pratt would know what Barnes looked like. And since the police were looking for her, it was best for her to remain out of sight. Kate focused on Will Shortz as he accompanied Pratt into the hotel's Doyle Bar.

Without the puzzle master, Kate doubted she'd be standing in Dupont Circle. Now all they had to do was locate the X marks the spot on a map and the next secret bunker.

During the walk from Al Tiramisu, she coordinated logistics with Alice Watson. SIOC had dispatched rapid response law enforcement and utility crews. If the underground was rigged to blow, an entire three-block radius was at risk.

In the distance, Kate could see Washington Metropolitan Police Department (MPDC) erected barricades, redirecting and restricting vehicle traffic. PEPCO trucks stood ready to drop power in its underground transformer vaults. Beneath her, Dupont Circle Station and the metro had remained closed since the morning's bombing. Its transit tunnel paralleled Connecticut Ave and cut below the circle.

The chaotic, multi-colored brilliance of vehicle emergency lights reflected in jarring flashes between buildings as MPDC and FBI WFO SWAT teams arrived at the same time.

Kate's pulse quickened.

"Morgan," said the WFO SWAT Unit Chief, "I bet you'd trade this day for that Congressional hearing you missed."

Nervous civilians watched the massing of helmeted and heavily armed agents. Kate remembered how her day started, with Dix Martinez and his tactical unit. They'd be missed.

"I don't know about that," she said. "Congress can get pretty ruthless."

She shook hands with each agent and provided the Cliff Notes version, knowing full well command wasn't going to let her freelance this time. MPDC's SWAT team joined the growing crowd at the fountain. Because of its urban setting, this stop was a "by the book" situation where SWAT called the shots.

Agents and MPDC officers ushered the concerned civilians out of the park, leaving Kate alone with the SWAT Unit Chief.

"We've got this," he said. "If Barnes is here, we'll track him down. I'll call you in when we locate Barnes or the victim."

Kate swallowed her pride. "Understood."

His face darkened with concern and she sensed he was keenly aware of the lives lost at Soldiers' Home. "Tell me what we can expect."

Kate laid out Barnes's MO and what they'd learned since the Metro bombing. It wasn't anything he hadn't heard before, but rather confirmation. Booby traps. Explosives. High-tech gadgets and EMP weapons. Trap doors. And two victims remaining to be found.

A man in a hardhat interrupted their conversation and introduced himself as the Director for Public Works. He unrolled a set of blue-tinted drawings on the brim of the fountain's basin and lit up the hand-drawn plans with a flashlight.

"I know you're going to ask," the Public Works Director said, "so I'll just come out with it. We don't have a lot on the old tunnels. We've progressed to the Digital Age. Some plans were lost or discarded before materials were archived. Below us are at least seventy-five thousand square feet of tunnels and passages. Additional hand-dug spaces date back before the turn of the century. As in the late 1800s, turn of the century."

The SWAT Unit Chief swore. "Okay. We'll methodically work through tunnels even if it takes all night."

Kate shook her head. "We don't have all night. Barnes implied that everything ends at midnight. And there's one stop after Dupont Circle. Someplace not identified yet."

"Midnight?" The SWAT Unit Chief looked as if he'd been smacked with a baseball bat. He glanced at his wristwatch, silently doing math in his mind. "We don't cut corners here. We'll use small teams. Move fast. Push through what we can." He snatched the drawings and regrouped the WFO and MPDC teams.

Kate tried to picture the underground labyrinth of tunnels, trying to fathom the spread of hidden passageways from eras long gone. No wonder Barnes had chosen Dupont Circle as a stop. Even without the risk of booby traps, it'd be challenging for law enforcement to locate the victim in time.

85
SEATS AT THE BAR

Bar Dupont, The Dupont Hotel, Washington, DC

Through exterior windows, Will Shortz watched police begin the chaotic task of clearing people from the streets. Likewise, the bar staff had relocated patrons sitting at the windows and an outside patio to an interior dining area where they could continue their cocktails, along with a round of drinks on the house.

While he waited for Morgan, he set up shop at the bar.

Randy Wang grabbed a chair beside him, the man's attention split between Shortz and the restaurant's entrance. Shortz had listened to bits and pieces of conversation during the walk from Al Tiramisu—something about the man being an Army Colonel with the Central Security Service, which worked with the NSA and the Pentagon. He couldn't fathom how the man, who was out of uniform and off-duty, was connected to the FBI and Katherine Morgan. Their trial-tested bond seemed strong in an obscure way.

"I hear you've contributed quite a bit," Wang said. "Thank you."

"Glad to help." Shortz shifted in his bar chair. "But this experience is foreign to me. Sometimes it feels like I'd never solved a puzzle before in my life."

Wang grinned. "Alice Watson says you're pretty good at SCRABBLE, too."

Shortz forced a smile. It was clear he was talking to some kind of experienced, if not lethal cyber spy. He couldn't know what were sincere compliments and what was conversational politeness meant to extract additional information. The man was harder to read than any puzzle clue.

Shortz shrugged. "Working with the tiles freed my mind to consider other possibilities."

Wang looked away and Shortz turned to follow what had snatched the man's attention. Just an empty corridor. No one was in sight, not even restaurant staff.

Wang whispered into his ear. "Stay sharp, puzzle master."

Shortz internalized the statement, trying to decide if it was a challenge or warning.

The cyber spy got up and started to walk away, before turning back.

"Hey, back at the Italian restaurant," Wang said, "Captain Pratt glanced at her palm? Right before asking you a question. Her palm was smudged. The ink spot looked like blurred handwriting."

Shortz flipped his hand over, remembering the phone number Morgan had written down.

Wang continued. "Who else writes on skin? Coincidence?" He rapped the bar with his fingers. "You'd best figure out what Pratt asked about. 60 ACROSS."

Wang left the bar, leaving Shortz pulling open his notepad to scour his notes.

86
THE SANCTUARY IN A CIRCLE

Below Dupont Circle, Washington, DC

Barnes strode down a long path of arched-ceiling tunnels with the last of his supplies. Above on P Street, across from Al Tiramisu, he'd left an autonomous van marked with utility company decals parked over a manhole. Utility cones dotted the vehicle's four corners. A removable panel in the van's floor provided access to the manhole, which in turn led to a grated vault and a heavy steel door.

He'd first learned of the tunnels from congressional transcripts. In 1924, House Speaker Frederick Gillett was concerned over newspaper reports about secret tunnels dug by Harrison Dyar, an entomologist, bigamist, and Bahá'í faith disciple. Discovered by accident, Dyar's mysterious tunnels fueled public speculation. Found inside were German newspapers printed during World War One that highlighted the value of unrestricted submarine warfare and success of the U-boat campaign. Congressional directives commissioned surveys to map the tunnels. Gillett's committee reports had been declassified after the House Committee on Un-American Activities was restructured. The original hand-sketched survey maps were lost in the Library of Congress archives until Barnes himself had dug them up.

For Barnes, learning about the original tunnels was like striking gold.

The surveys disclosed extensive tunneling, far more than the newspapers of the time had revealed. Construction activities for Dupont Circle's trolley station provided fortuitous extensions to Dyar's original tunnels. In his explorations, Barnes had discovered a hollowed-out space, vertically deeper than any underground segment, including the Dupont Circle Metro station and tunnels. He suspected the unmarked room was originally built to function as a deep underground nuclear bomb shelter to protect key embassy officials.

The refuge had been named Dictaen, after the Psychro Caves in Crete, thought to be the birthplace of Zeus.

This central cavern was round with a domed ceiling. A circle. A sanctuary-style room had no true beginning or end, representative of origins and endings.

Six equally-spaced openings cut into the walls, which Barnes had altered to make all but one invisible. Visitors entered in a predicable manner, their eyes taking in the sanctuary from a specific point of view. Central to the sanctuary was a round altar, built from discarded Capitol stones and the unwanted relics at Rock Creek Park.

On the altar lay a man, stripped down to his fleshen shell, his bare figure unable to hide any more secrets. A brother of sorts, the unconscious man was another bastard child of science. Naked. Unaware of his surroundings. The ranks of humans who were neither created by God nor the natural biological offspring of the human race had dwindled down to three. Soon only one would survive. The Perfect People lineage ended in this sanctuary.

Adjacent to the altar was a basin of water, its pump overflowing the bowl and circulating excess water into pockets carved within the solid rock floor. Spread across the ceiling were luminescent stars and heavenly markings. The circular walls were marked with luminescent symbols and inscriptions essential to the Bahá'í faith, symbols and inscriptions.

The sentiment Barnes was most proud of encircled the room, written high on the walls in a single line of text. A MIND AND BODY BRED INTO THE BONDS OF SLAVERY CANNOT SEIZE

THE OPPORTUNITY OF FREEDOM. KNOWLEDGE WITH ACTION IS REQUIRED TO CONFRONT THOSE WHO AFFORD THE OPPRESSED NO CHOICE.

The statement was over-the-top, but aligned with the Bahá'í guiding principle on slavery.

The Dictaen sanctuary was an ouroboros circle, representing rebirth and renewal.

His clan of Perfect People had been bred for one thing: to change the course of human history. A generation of soldiers and astronauts for a distant journey across the stars.

Their enslavement ended at the circle.

87
DISCUSSIONS

Office of the Vice President, Eisenhower Executive Office Building, Washington, DC

In his second-floor office, the Vice President gazed out the windows over the grounds of the White House. Troubled, he knew his actions and support of ambiguous research activities had put the President right into the media's crosshairs.

First Princeton, now Washington.

His son Andrew, a brilliant and award-winning biogenetics researcher, had pushed for greater latitude in legislation, a radical extension of semi-dormant scientific pursuits, and funding appropriations—the Perfect People Initiative was the sentinel program—which had become the Advanced Biogenetics Initiative and Advancing Human Evolution. A post-core program called the Human Genetics Operations Application led to the nation's secret creation of test-tube super soldiers. And now Andrew had fallen victim to malice and hatred.

The door opened behind him, and the Vice President turned to greet his guest.

The Speaker of the House stood before him pale, ghost-like, weary. The Vice President's Secret Service detail retreated into the main corridor and closed the door. They were alone.

"Is it true?" the Speaker asked.

"Yes," the Vice President said, his voice heavy. He avoided specifics, not wanting to add fuel to the media frenzy if this olive-branch negotiation went south. "Andrew was found not far from my residence. He's in a coma, but alive."

The Speaker looked grim. "And my niece? Will she be in the same condition?"

"We won't know until we find Lelia," the Vice President said. He couldn't make life or death statements until Dr. Lelia Maddox, the Speaker's niece, had been located. Alive. "I assure you, this terrorist will not see the light of day, and his corpse won't even find the solace of a potter's field. As we speak, someone on the inside is in position to bring us closure, and justice."

The Speaker's eyes closed. "I want Phillip Barnes dead."

"As do I." He'd avoided speaking the terrorist's name and wondered how much the Speaker actually knew. That knowledge likely had come from sanitized FBI debriefings.

The Speaker of the House gave him a look that promised vengeance. "Is there any hope for recovery?"

The Vice President took a breath and nodded. "A plan is being developed that might allow for a reversal of their medical conditions. Our aim will be full recovery." He paused to let a sliver of hope sink in. "Provided I get assurances."

The Speaker blinked, waiting for the rest.

The Vice President turned his back on the Speaker and cast his gaze out the windows to the White House. "After the immediacy of this madness is dealt with and the media storms subside, both houses of Congress must prove loyal and shelter both myself and the President. That is not negotiable."

The Speaker sighed. "If my niece is found alive—and if she recovers from this condition she's been given—Congress will be in your corner."

The Vice President smiled for the first time in days.

88
SUDDEN IMPACT

Near Navy Yard, Washington, DC

Racing north on 11th Street SE, FBI Special Agent Jack Wright floored his accelerator to clear the light at M Street. With the gas pedal mashed to the floor, his Lincoln felt like a luxury thoroughbred streaking past slower vehicles.

Connected wirelessly to the car's speakers, he briefed a SIOC field coordination tech while Alice Watson supported operations at Dupont Circle.

"Tell Watson," he shouted over the car's engine, "that Barnes has full access to SpaceKey and a fleet of autonomous vehicles. He has the capability to—"

His peripheral vision caught a blur. Fast. Westbound down M Street.

Wright cocked his head and braced himself, his eyes flashing wide with fear.

The front grill of a large boxed bed utility truck with no visible driver exploded into the side of his Lincoln. The impact was deafening as fragments of glass, plastic, and crumpling metal consumed Wright's vision, thrusting him into the driver's side door.

Airbags erupted around him in an underwhelming attempt to arrest the violent collision and cushion the effects of the impact.

Skidding and bouncing off the asphalt, Wright's Lincoln flipped wildly side over side as the box truck continued its attack, like a raging rhinoceros barreling down on a wounded lion. Both vehicles cleared a curb, sheared off a fire hydrant, and plowed through a spread of chain-link fencing.

The Lincoln came to rest upside down on scraped-off property with the box truck centered high on top, as a spray of water from the hydrant soaked both vehicles.

As he hung upside down, Jack Wright's vision faded to blackness.

89
ALLIANCES

Hotel Dupont, Washington, DC

Rachel Pratt loitered near the hotel's main entry. A man in casual attire walked past her to the elevators. She paid General James Davidson no attention, allowing him a head start. The elevator dinged. Doors opened, then closed. Pratt glanced back to watch the elevator's travel indicator and a floor number: B. The general had gone to the basement.

The next elevator arrived. A couple got out.

Pratt strolled into the bar area. She made eye contact with the CSS/NSA spy standing beside the *Times* crossword puzzle editor. She allowed her gaze to linger, sending an invitation.

Returning to the available elevator, she pressed the down button.

Wang stepped beside her.

"Davidson," she said without looking at him, "just arrived."

The elevator's doors opened and she stepped inside.

Wang was trying to get a read on her. Typical for a spy.

"The general wants to talk alone before meeting with Morgan," Pratt said.

Wang nodded, and reluctantly got into the elevator.

As the doors closed, Pratt moved fast.

A heel kick to Wang's knee sent the shorter man buckling. He groaned in pain. The move was crippling. Grabbing the back of his head, she drove him face first into the elevator's hand railing. He countered with an elbow to her face and a roundhouse fist that caught her in the top of the head.

He had some skills, and that made her smile.

Pratt allowed a baiting strike zone to develop between them. An opponent was most vulnerable when committing to the offensive act of punching or kicking.

Wang made his move. He went low.

Pratt kept her pace and rhythm, sliding the advance with a block and engaging a roundhouse of her own. Her counterstrike created a pause. She delivered an uppercut that arched Wang backwards.

Rather than protecting himself further, he changed tactics and reached for a weapon. A semi-automatic appeared.

Pratt stomped a boot to an exposed throat. Cartilage buckled.

The weapon clattered to the floor of the elevator. After driving a full-weighted knee into his stomach, she delivered the knockout blow to Wang's face. The spy fell limp.

The elevator doors opened to reveal Davidson.

Pratt snatched Wang's limp body and weapon off the elevator's floor, hauled him over her shoulder and dumped him into a housekeeping linen cart. She covered him with a sheet and handed the weapon to Davidson.

"Is it true that Mary's dead?" Davidson asked.

"Cops were at your home, making it unsafe for me to return there," she said. "The guy with the *Times* said she shot herself."

He took a solemn breath. "And my daughter?"

"In a coma." Pratt produced an antique dagger, the *pisau* collected from his daughter's body at Rock Creek Park. She sensed a life force connection with the weapon, a bond she couldn't explain. She worked the dagger in her hand, testing its balance. "At George Washington in a private ward."

"And my daughter's condition is permanent?"

"Morgan thinks so."

He processed the news. "What do you propose to do with Agent Morgan once we've dispensed with Barnes?"

Staring at the dagger in her hand, her eyes swelled with malice. "Barnes has waged war on my humanity. He built this delusional scavenger hunt for her. And played us like pawns. Pride, cleverness, and revenge inspired this delusion." She snorted. "We used this blade during our training together. That's why he placed it with the clues. Before Phillip Barnes takes his last breath, I plan to use this dagger to carve Katherine Morgan's heart out. And I intend to make him watch. I want him to understand my face will be the last one either of them sees before they die."

90
BAD NEWS

Strategic Information & Operations Center (SIOC), FBI Headquarters, Washington, DC

Alice Watson never imagined the day would unfold as it had, in a domestic terrorist's fixation with intricate revenge. Innocent victims had been maimed and murdered in a Metro bombing, a cold-blooded event meant to make headlines and grab media attention. Agents had given their lives in service to the country.

The day's exhaustion wore like empty words spoken at a funeral. In the SIOC, no one had left after their shifts, committed to seeing the crisis through.

Spirits were strong nonetheless.

Yet everyone felt the pressure of time.

Wall-mounted digital clocks ticked off closer to midnight.

At the front of the ops center, the big board displayed active crime scene locations across the city. The bureau had assigned a dedicated investigative detail to each site. On a group of monitors, files listed data on Phillip Logan Barnes. Animation modelers and the FACE Services Unit had constructed imaging profiles to feed into Next Generation Identification facial recognition systems. If Barnes stepped in front of any of the accessible FR cameras placed in the city, the FBI would know about it.

Dupont Circle was moved to the middle four screens.

Real-time satellite images showed SWAT teams on the move. SIOC had assigned a logistics agent to interface between the SAC, SWAT, ATF, MPDC, and utility crews.

"Watson," one of the technicians announced, "a MPDC report just came in. One of ours was involved in a two-car accident near Navy Yard."

Watson frowned. "Do we have a name?" She knew of the Navy-led operation at the waterfront. It was need-to-know. It had something to do with Barnes' unworldly access to encrypted satellite systems and taking down a site controlled by EyePoint Applications. "Any details?"

"Jack Wright." The technician listened to a barrage of incoming information and rose from his seat. "He's in critical condition. EMS is treating in transit. The driver of the other vehicle has not been located."

Her colleagues stared at each other.

Watson knew what they were thinking: autonomous cars. There was a real possibility no one was driving the other vehicle.

Watson swore beneath her breath. "Okay, people. We have a new problem to add to the list. Make some calls. Notify Wright's family if he has any. Make sure we have an agent at the hospital talking to doctors. And get me that Admiral with Navy. I want to know what the hell the Navy found at EyePoint."

91
ON THE SIDELINES

Dupont Circle, Washington, DC

Kate understood the neighborhood was under siege. The circle had been cleared of civilians. Overhead, helicopters circled and swept the streets with searchlights. Drones flashed and buzzed to fill in surveillance gaps not covered by high-level air support. Armored vehicles. Tiered roadblocks. Heavily armed law enforcement in fatigues. Snipers perched on rooftops.

The bureau was showing force on a massive scale.

No one was underestimating Phillip Barnes this time.

And this was as close as she was getting to the action. Orders from the Director himself.

Kate couldn't blame anyone for benching her. Again. At least they hadn't cuffed her or locked her up. Handcuffs made her think of the observatory. She wondered what the admiral had told bureau leadership—trespassing? Damage of federal property?

She fingered the quarter collected from their British driver, one of the coins collected from the Observatory's fountain. While she flipped it over in her hand, she panned her gaze across the neighborhood. The vehicle emergency lights had given the night an eerie feeling, like an urban war zone.

It was a war zone. Exactly what Barnes wanted.

What clues had Barnes left for her to find at Dupont Circle? Hard to figure that out when she was sidelined.

Kate watched SWAT teams come and go from underground spaces, starting with the art venue known as Dupont Underground. All told, eight trolley station stairways dotted the circle, their entrances opened. PEPCO utility crews had disconnected power to underground vaults and cut power to street lighting. The entire circle was dark except the fountain area. Except for the circle's eye, the neighborhood was a dark hole in the city surrounded by the lights of neighboring buildings.

Taking proactive measures, fire trucks and ambulances parked a hundred yards back from the circle's spokes. Connecticut Avenue had been closed, since it ran directly beneath the circle and utilized portions of the old trolley tunnels. Cellular communication jammers blocked phone signals while the neighborhood and underground spaces were systematically searched.

The radio chatter among FBI, MPDC, and ATF teams played out smoother than she expected. All of the force multipliers were deployed this time around: robots, throw bots, and drones for advanced deployment searches. K9 teams cleared both above-grade and underground spaces. Bomb squad teams waited beside their vehicles. The underground circle had been divided into quadrants as SWAT teams progressed from east to west, supplemented by city engineering teams.

Kate checked her sat phone and the time.

U.S. Army General James Davidson was late.

Pratt had agreed to convince the general into showing up, as a way to draw out Barnes, should the maniac be watching the festivities from hacked security camera feeds or his surveillance resources in the sky. If Barnes was a no-show, Kate was intent on taking in the general as a person of interest, something they couldn't do while he was hiding out at the Pentagon. Besides need-to-know secrets and classified research, the man had a great deal to account for beyond coerced involvement and management of illicit research.

Kate repositioned herself outside the Dupont Hotel. Spying through windows, she watched CSS/NSA Colonel Randy Wang and Will Shortz at the bar.

She chuckled. Wang was not a good influence on anyone. Nonverbal cues hinted something was going on between them.

Wang's attention locked onto something she couldn't see. He walked away from the puzzle master and headed toward the lobby.

That was probably best for Will Shortz.

Through the windows, she watched Shortz return to his work, studying his computer and writing tablet. His pencil was in motion. His intense, inquisitive expression revealed he was onto the final clues.

For a moment, he glanced her way, past the windows, scanning for solutions that only his mind could see. It was as if he stared straight through her. She turned around. Shortz was looking in the direction of the fountain, the circle's center, its origin.

Kate stepped out of his line of sight. Voyeurism wasn't one of her hobbies.

From the corner of her eye, she spotted James Davidson and Rachel Pratt walk out of the hotel. Together. After getting their bearings, they headed down 19th Street, straight toward her.

Something wasn't right.

Kate whirled behind the trunk of the tree.

The cops manning the barricades at the Dupont Underground entrance asked for credentials, which Davidson and Pratt provided. After the visual check, the pair cut across the Connecticut Ave overpass and walked along the frontage side of the street.

Alarm bells blared in Kate's mind.

The general and captain were working together.

And they were headed somewhere.

92
THE INVASION

Basement, Dupont Hotel, Dupont Circle, Washington, DC

Nothing happening outside was good or good for business. The hotel staff called the events an invasion. Jennie Hodges, a night-shift housekeeper, was frightened. Even for a Monday, Dupont Circle could be hopping, but not like tonight. Tonight, things were crazy.

Outside, helicopters circled like vultures. Drones skimmed the rooftops. Law enforcement from every agency imaginable carried automatic weapons. Armored personnel vehicles blocked off intersections. Dogs and handlers scoured storage areas. Unattended cars were towed away to clear the streets. And even to an untrained eye, law enforcement seemed most concerned about underground spaces and old tunnels beneath the neighborhood.

Terrorism had struck the city. Again.

Workers gossiped about bombs hidden in the hotel and buried in the old trolley station.

To alleviate staff fears, the manager asked maintenance staff to sweep the hotel's basement and first floor. They found no bombs.

But that did little to alleviate Jennie Hodges' fears. And regardless of the disarray outside, hotel bookings for the night actually increased.

Seizing the moment, hotel management did backflips to accommodate and relocate guests amidst the chaos. It was shocking how many stupid people wanted the upper rooms with balconies just so they could have better views.

That meant her staff had to bust ass to make last-minute rooms available.

Jennie Hodges returned a full cart to the dirty linen room and grabbed the handle of a cart in the empty queue. The handle she grasped jerked her shoulder, and she realized the cart had not been emptied from a previous shift. The cart was heavier than expected.

The damn maintenance staff. They'd thrown their crap into a housekeeping cart. Not the first time for that nonsense.

Wrenching back the cart's top sheets, Jennie Hodges screamed.

An Asian man was in the bottom of the linen cart. And he wasn't moving.

93
DEEPER UNDERGROUND

20th Street NW & Q Street NW, Dupont Circle Metro Station, Washington, DC

Walking north on Connecticut Avenue, Kate tracked Pratt and Davidson with the greatest possible lag without losing them. Ahead, PEPCO crews worked over a flush-grade transformer vault and appeared to be controlling power to the area. At the Q Street intersection, MPDC had barricaded the street. Avoiding the cops, Pratt and Davidson dodged left by the PEPCO crews. Kate jogged hard to make up ground and spotted them showing credentials to the WMATA officers standing outside the Dupont Circle Metro station's north escalators.

She assessed the situation and made a decision. The two of them were engaged in a different game. Who would've thought?

And they had to know something no one else did: the next stop.

Kate leaned against the large bowl's railing and peered downward as Pratt and Davidson disappeared underground. Sprinting around the rim, she flashed her badge to the WMATA officers. She thought about saying something about surviving the Metro earlier, but kept the sarcasm to herself. The escalators were powered off, so she took two steps at a time.

An outer body sensation flashed over her—the day was coming full circle. Intentional. The ouroboros. The snake eating its own tail.

The Metro entrance fit that description too—a circle leading to the bowels of the Earth.

The solutions for RAIL and PLAZAS pinged in her mind, sending a chill down her spine. This was the UG, the underground, match in the puzzle.

She glanced up as she ran lower into the ground, the stars and the night sky disappearing from view. The escalator dropped forever, as if taking her deep into the bowels of hell. Vaguely she remembered hearing about electrical fires and smoke that had closed the Red Line sometime back. That day would have paled in comparison to her morning commute.

She reached the payment kiosks. WMATA had kept the lights on. Keeping her eyes moving, Kate drew her Glock and hastened her pace.

She hopped over the ticketing turnstiles and jogged toward the station platforms, scanning the empty station. Dupont Circle had architecture similar to Foggy Bottom: pocketed and arched ceilings, hexagon floor tiling, and the Red Line tracks ran through the middle of a split platform.

A caustic, metallic taste filled Kate's mouth and stimulated a wave of panic. Her heartbeat thundered to a crescendo as a rumbling train bore down on her. For an instant, she imagined being transported to the tracks. Her feet were fused into the rails. Blinding blue lights and reflections raged closer as thunder penetrated her chest. She gasped for a ragged breath and clutched her weapon in her right hand. The Orange Line struck her and sucked her straight into a mangled and overturn passenger car. Panicked faces appeared from a distorted tapestry of smoke and haze. Everywhere she turned she saw death and bodies. Her nostrils were overwhelmed with the burning odors of plastic and grease. Surrounding her, fire approached and personified death.

Kate forced herself to take purging breaths and clear the vision.

Part of her had died on the train along with those who couldn't escape.

Lifting her chin, she caught sight of silhouettes at the other end of the platform.

Pratt and Davidson stepped around the restriction railing and headed down the blue-tinted rail tunnel. From her prior glance at the city engineer maps, Kate understood the Metro had been constructed long after the original trolley station and much deeper and slightly offset. The Metro didn't run directly beneath the fountain of Dupont Circle.

Kate sprinted to the station platform and pushed herself to hasten the pace. She ignored the NO TRESSPASSING sign and hopped around the swing gate.

Barnes' puzzle solutions hinted at an ultimate destination, but not a precise point. She wasn't sure where the labyrinth led, but Pratt and Davidson knew exactly where they were going. And that wasn't good.

The extended intervals of interior lighting dotted the tunnel and provided enough light.

A wave of déjà vu washed over her again. She forced her tired mind to focus on the narrow pedestrian path. She'd allowed too much distance between herself and her quarry and was grateful to hear the sound of scraping metal and rusted hinges. The unmuffled sounds echoed in the tunnel.

Kate raised her hands a bit higher and made sure her pistol led the way, rather than walking with her weapon aimed at the concrete floor.

The steel hatchway wasn't hard to find, the only one visible. After a reassuring breath, she grabbed the door's handle. Training her weapon at the latch side, she cracked open the door and prayed its hinges wouldn't groan. The heavy steel door clunked open, making only the most modest of sounds. Yet any sound was loud in a nowhere-to-run space. Cool dampness filled her nostrils. An earthen odor filled the stale air.

The old power cable path was dark and seemed to run forever.

Kate fumbled for her flashlight before shutting the hatch behind her. Cupping it in her hand, a muted beam penetrated her palm and made her fingers glow red. The diminished spray of light was enough to pass through absolute darkness without totally giving her away.

The tunnel was a narrow passage. Grit crunched beneath her boots when she walked. She sensed the direction headed away from the Metro, due west and at a slight incline. Impossible to know for sure without matching the routes against street layouts.

Moving forward, she realized Pratt and Davidson had nowhere to veer off to. Their only path of travel was straight ahead.

She might be walking into a trap, but they didn't know she was following them. If she went back for reinforcements, the bureau would miss the mole meeting entirely.

She'd come too far to not see it through. She was staying the course.

Kate risked broader flashes of light by uncupping her palm from the flashlight to confirm she wasn't missing any intersections or manholes going vertical.

The grit beneath her boots gave way to the sounds of water flowing. The old power cable route linked to a broader platform. The depth of the water painting the concrete floor was about a sole width of her boot. Leaking drainage piping above proved to be the source of the water. The quick beam of her flashlight located a vertical ladder dropping to another platform.

Kate held up at the ladder, thinking of the pit and tunnels beneath the chapel at Soldiers' Home.

Welcome to the Pit of Misery where your corpse will never be found. Ever.

From higher ground, she detected a faint beacon light on a level below her. Pratt and Davidson seemed oblivious to her presence.

Kate wanted to keep it that way.

94
A FOUNTAIN OF STARS

Doyle Bar, The Dupont Hotel, Dupont Circle, Washington, DC

No clues were needed this time.

Will Shortz spun away from the bar counter, where he drafted the puzzle's final solutions. Looking through the windows facing the circle, he allowed the sequence of words and phrases to form in his mind. Outside emergency lights bristled and crackled splashes of disjointed illumination in the night. But inside his mind, the puzzle's luminescence formed a spectrum of clearly refined colors.

The wordplay was far from elegant, yet appeared effortlessly. Since this puzzle allowed two-letter abbreviations, it was possible to be delinquent a few combinations but nothing more.

1 DOWN, the left edge anchor word, was FERRULE. It stood for the endcap attached to a shaft; the object's function was to keep the shaft from splitting or its assembly from coming apart. For golfers, the ferrule on the club mated the club head to the shaft. On a military spear, the ferrule was the cuplike portion of the spear's tip. A weapon, Shortz deduced.

REST IN PEACE was abbreviated to RIP in 18 ACROSS. Easy. The terrorist intended to kill again, or kill Morgan in the end. That fatality had been implied earlier. 21 DOWN shed light on how that might happen with an ICY END. The location was a PARK in 52

ACROSS where Morgan was going to run into 66 ACROSS and EOT for END OF TIME. MIDNIGHT.

That left one last clue of significance. Rachel Pratt had asked about it in Al Tiramisu.

60 ACROSS. SWAP SPOT.

Dupont Circle was the SWAP SPOT in a PARK.

Shortz left his computer, notepad, and pencil to occupy a seat at the bar counter and headed outside.

He flashed his FBI contractor credentials to MPDC officers securing the circle and made his way to the historic neighborhood's center.

From the beginning, the terrorist, now identified as Phillip Barnes, had revealed his backstory and its connection with the human heart. Regardless of what lay in the maze of underground spaces, the heart of Dupont Circle was its centerpiece fountain.

A clue was the fountain.

During his research, Shortz had read that the original bronze statue of Admiral Du Pont had been moved to Delaware. For a fitting replacement, the Du Pont family had commissioned the Lincoln Memorial's sculptor and architect to construct a fountain.

With the circle barricaded off, Shortz had the park setting to himself except for the band of law enforcement working a perimeter and those helping the FBI search teams access the subterranean spaces under his feet. Ringed light poles lit up the urban circle, and its steps matched the radials of the main streets intersecting the wider traffic circle. From three spouts, water flowed from an upper bowl and into the foot basin. Three marble-sculpted figures adorned the shaft: Sea, Wind, and Stars. Perhaps another thematic tie back to the Naval Observatory. Beyond battle prowess, Shortz realized, a Civil War era admiral would be required to master each aspect of ocean navigation.

Shortz studied the first embodiment of ancient seafaring mastery: a long-haired feminine personification of the Sea. She gazed across the water and cradled a boat in her arm. Her free hand soothed a seagull perched on her shoulder. A dolphin swam at her feet. Nothing symbolic in this journey had focused on the sea, so he moved to the next allegorical representation. Wind was a chiseled-featured, nude man half-draped in the billowing sail of a ship that he stood over. The man clutched a conch shell, ready to use it as a horn. His gaze angled down, as if he was watching seafarers from the sky. Wind hadn't been a focus, either.

Shortz shifted to the last figurine. Stars stood past the spread of her robe as her bare figure and hand embraced a globe tight to her left breast. She watched over the Earth. Stars dotted the heavens behind her. Stars' right hand was turned above her shoulders to fluff out her long-flowing hair, and held the end of a spear. The spear shaft stretched across her naked figure, its blade anchored into the gown covering one of her feet.

Shortz edged closer for a better view. Something wasn't right about Stars. He dropped his gaze to her feet and found the source of his concern.

Stars held her spear pointed down, not up. Its tip was a small trident endcap.

And a FERRULE bonded the trident to the weapon's shaft.

Shortz grinned, pleased with his old-fashioned detective work. Stepping over the basin's rim, he waded into chilly knee-high water. An icy cold bonded to his legs. His shoes slipped against the fountain's bottom and forced him to shorten his steps. As Shortz stood before her, Stars gazed at him as if she was looking straight through his soul, her eight-foot Greek goddess-like figure perched on top of a pedestal that rose above the water by another three feet.

Since the spear's end was equal to her earlobe, it was impossible to reach.

With little choice, Shortz latched onto the trident itself that pinned down her gown.

Officers shouted and booted footsteps followed.

Shortz ignored the voices ordering him to stop. Due to the height of the marble statue, he was forced to lean forward, completely off balance. With a tight grip, he jerked. The trident barely budged. He repositioned his feet and yanked again. The weapon slipped its position, slightly. Angling to his right, Shortz pulled diagonal and the trident tip spear broke loose, scraping against white marble.

"Wow!" he shouted, catching his breath and shuffling his feet in the pond to keep his balance. "Damn, I did it!"

The police officers partially encircled the fountain with their guns drawn.

"Drop the weapon!"

There was more shouting than he could process. It dawned on Shortz that he should have explained himself before wading into the water.

Another first for his day: trespassing into a cold fountain, staring at cops with weapons drawn, immediately after defacing a historical monument. But what the hell—he possessed the weapon of Poseidon, a trident!

This moment was worth it. *Priceless.*

Hoisting up his lanyard, Shortz called out, "I'm helping the FBI. On the investigations." He was about to say something like he did this kind of thing all of the time, but decided against injecting untimely humor. He took a prideful breath. The faces glaring back at him were ready to shoot him. "Come on, give me a break."

An officer waved for him to hand over the weapon.

After stepping out of the fountain, Shortz surrendered the trident and pointed back to Stars. "That's not part of the fountain. It was an addition. A clue for law enforcement to find."

95
MIND THE GAP

Below and West of Dupont Circle, Washington, DC

Kate risked spraying the ladder with a beam from her flashlight. Just a quick pass of illumination to allow for locating the top rail and vertical handles. Negotiating the cool railing of the ladder, she dropped down to a larger open area.

When her feet reached concrete, she shielded the flashlight's beam and saw that she stood in an enormous storm basin.

Ahead of her in the dark passage, Pratt and Davidson had not deviated from their original direction.

She forced herself to envision where the two of them were headed. This was too far down to be going anywhere.

The only answer, the only solution that made sense was a meeting with Barnes.

Kate kept moving, her Glock in one hand and palm-covered flashlight in the other.

Reaching a crevice, she saw a plank that bridged roughly a ten-foot gap between two sections of tunnel. She risked a full spray of the situation with her flashlight. The crevice was manmade concrete and formed a drainage channel.

Kate tested the plank with her weight, knowing this was the only path Pratt and the general could have traveled. They had nowhere to go except forward. The wood plank held without much give and she took a broader stride. She took another. On her third step, her boot caught something. It felt like a swipe of a hand.

Crashing forward, Kate made the decision to catch herself instead of plummeting into a deeper unknown. Discarding her flashlight and pistol, she flailed for the plank. Wood smacked her face and stars brightened the darkness. Her balance shifted toward the void below. She kicked, propelling herself and lunging for possible handholds in the dark.

One set of fingertips latched onto a concrete ledge while the other kept a tenuous hold of the planks.

Hanging in midair, Kate screamed as the concrete edge under her fingertips broke loose. Her body dropped, but did not fall.

Someone had grabbed a fistful of hair and yanked, upward.

Pain seared her scalp and dancing spots clouded her vision. Kate felt almost buoyant, as if she were floating. More hands grasped the back of her collar and jerked.

In the dark, it was impossible to tell how she ended up cartwheeling heels-over-head. Concrete slammed against her back, driving air from her lungs. Her head struck hard. She tried to gasp for breath, but her body wouldn't cooperate.

A flashlight clicked on, blinding her.

Kate didn't catch the sight of a pair of knuckles until it was too late.

"Let me just kill her," Rachel Pratt said. "It simplifies matters moving forward."

"No." Davidson washed the unconscious FBI agent with illumination from the flashlight. He turned and walked further down the tunnel. "She can be a bargaining chip. She dies after Barnes is dealt with."

Pratt huffed and latched onto a boot, dragging Kate Morgan feet first, head banging and scraping across the concrete bottom of the passageway.

Davidson turned and hit Pratt with illumination from his flashlight. "Barnes will be disappointed if he receives damaged goods. Pick her up, Captain. That's an order."

96
REWARDS

Dupont Circle, Washington, DC

Rewards. It was all about rewards.

Will Shortz stared at the trident, which one of the officers held while another checked his credentials. The trident was a reward based on an earned action. Video game developers used multiple reward types to keep players engaged. Beyond the killer's unfolding puzzle, a physical reward tapped into the human psyche—the brain's socially conditioned, psychological gratification mechanisms.

It was like Pavlov's dog: ring the bell, get a treat. Do well in school, get a gold star. Solve a sadistic crossword puzzle from a mass murderer, save someone's life, and advance to the next stop.

The fountain functioned as a treasure chest.

Swiping his hand across the water in the fountain, Shortz splashed his face to stimulate his alertness. He looked up at the nautical figurines. Stars had provided his reward.

He moved to the next figure, Wind. A masculine, bare-featured god drove the wind through a sail of a ship that he stood over. The conch in his hand was one of the many voices of the sea, a means to communicate. Tucked behind Wind in the fold of his robe was a white knapsack, its color naturally blending into the marble. Near impossible to notice, a person could easily consider it part of the sculpture.

"I need to borrow this," Shortz said with a smile. He took the trident back from the officer holding it.

Hooking the knapsack with the tip of the trident, Shortz plucked it from behind Wind and dropped it into the stunned officer's hands.

Next, he studied Sea. She was semi-clothed, unlike her siblings. Shortz's eyes tracked from the seagull perched on her shoulder across her bosom to the boat cradled in her arm. A smaller white mound filled the cavity of the boat. From ground level, the small mound looked like a tarp. It took several attempts and different angles before Shortz snagged the rim of the sack and swung it out.

He anchored the heel of the trident's shaft and did his best Aquaman impersonation. The faces staring at him didn't get the reference.

"Never mind," he said.

The officers sorted through the two sacks, breaking out antique navigation instruments: compass, sextant, spy glass, divider, and rope.

Hidden in plain sight: tools of a seafaring explorer. Instruments for travel, by ship, by sea.

Shortz processed the associations, homing in on meanings connected to the last wordplay.

"Your cleverness has made you worthy," a woman's voice said. "You hold the trident."

His gaze drifted until he found someone he knew to be dead.

Mary Davidson. The general's wife. 1 ACROSS. The FOUNDATION STONE.

"No small feat for a boy from Indiana," she added with a smile.

"You're not—?"

"Dead?" She shook her head. "A magician's illusion. You saw what you wanted to see. My deception served a purpose." She strolled around the fountain, taking in its sculpted features. "If you would, do me a favor and retrieve the necklace from the goddess of the Sea."

The law enforcement officers watched, but did not object.

"What does all this mean?" Shortz finally asked.

"The necklace?"

"By all means," Shortz said as he stepped back into the fountain, slid a tine of the trident beneath a stone white necklace, and plucked it off the statue. He swung it over to Mary Davidson's waiting hands.

She inspected it, then clasped it around her neck. After patting the necklace down on her bosom, she said, "Thank you. It was a gift from my father. I gave it to Phillip."

Shortz frowned. Stepping out of the fountain, he shook off his wet pants legs. "What's special about the necklace?"

Mary Davidson laughed. "Phillip was going to give it to Rachel when they graduated from the program. He was heartbroken when she—"

He gestured to the fountain. "Why would Barnes leave these objects here for us to find? Are they tools for the final stop?"

"No. This is a shrine for Phillip." She waved her hands. "He was the most superstitious of the original twelve. I doubt he intended for you to find these trinkets. They're offerings to the gods for a safe voyage, a safe passage."

"Where's he going?"

"Come, walk with me. And bring the trident if you wish."

Shortz hesitated, thinking he was ill-prepared to go to war with a pitchfork. Walking fast to catch up, he asked, "Dr. Davidson, why fake your death?"

"James drove me away. Pushed me out of the very research that I started." She led him across the circle and down P Street. "Since I was a medical researcher, he was concerned I'd take his program in a different direction. He was concerned I was humanizing the process."

"Why?" Shortz asked.

"Political compromises were required to keep our *Most Important Product* funded. Several political insiders saw the Perfect People Initiative as unethical because we were playing God, but our diehard supporters understood the revolution. To buffer us from the critics, our research was shifted to the Pentagon. And rather than breeding a new race of humans, we focused on breeding super soldiers."

Shortz glanced behind them, wondering if Mary Davidson was disclosing national secrets that he shouldn't be exposed to. If that was the case, he didn't want anyone following.

They crossed 20th Street NW and walked past another set of MPDC barricades.

"We're not new kids on the block," she said. "Matter of fact, the Perfect People Initiative started under Truman. Kennedy learned about our work the week before his trip to Dallas. He wasn't a fan. Oswald did us a favor. Back then, our work was crude compared to today's approaches. We explored every angle. Radical ideas. We injected embryos with foreign genetic material to stimulate cellular re-integration and grafted in structural changes to fetuses, providing them with gills and wings. We explored creating a race that could swim and fly. Live well past a hundred years. Live in oxygen-deprived environments. There were some live births, but none of our offspring survived. Some even killed their hosts."

Shortz's ears perked up. "You know, some interpretations say Frankenstein's creation was never the true monster."

Mary Davidson chuckled and led him to the north side of P Street. "The human genome project launched in 1990. The secret side of that research gave our Perfect People Initiative a jumpstart on steroids. We cloned human embryos three years before the Scottish sheep. Our proof of concept was essential to gene-sequencing modifications and gene-editing. Phillip Barnes was our first live birth. His enhanced traits were extreme intelligence combined with a warrior's mindset. NASA wanted to artificially gestate a future galaxy-traveling astronaut. Their vision was to expand the human race to the stars. That's why you found the trident with the goddess of the stars. Rachel is three months younger than Phillip—she's a pure warrior. Mortality rates of alpha embryos to term were high. In total, twelve alphas were born."

He couldn't help himself from saying, "You're playing God."

"Yes," she said, unapologetically. "And I'll continue to do so. But without James. I'm raising our next generation of children without him. And out of the Pentagon's reach."

Shortz felt short of breath as he did mental laps. The Perfect People Initiative was personified madness from its creator to its creations.

"Why are you telling me this?" he asked.

"In case events don't work out, I wanted someone to know my side of the story. I knew long ago our world needs different children to extend our future." Mary Davidson fixed her gaze onto his. "It's time to call in your law enforcement friends." She put a hand on the PEPCO van parked over the sidewalk. Orange utility cones had been placed around it. "Tell them not to enter the vehicle. It'll be rigged to blow everyone to hell. I know my Phillip."

She smiled politely, got onto her knees, and disappeared under the van.

Shortz crouched and watched Mary Davidson slip into an open manhole.

97
THE GATHERING

The Circle, Below and West of Dupont Circle, Washington, DC

"That's close enough," Phillip Barnes said, stepping past a concealing panel in the wall. He snapped his fingers and lights sparked on.

The final show had begun.

The circular room glowed like a shrine, its centerpiece being the dark-skinned, naked man on a round sandstone altar. Unlit candles circled his slumbering body and a square patch of lighter-colored parchment with writing on it rested on the man's bare chest.

The altar was strategically situated between Barnes and his guests.

He assessed their postures, knowing each had well-rehearsed poker faces. Their expressions would give away few clues. The general's stance showed nervousness. Clearly, he was out of his element. Rachel Pratt's brown eyes studied the situation before rolling the FBI agent that she carried on her shoulder onto the floor. The unconscious body thudded cheek down in a thin glaze of water.

Rachel finally looked at him. If she noticed his semi-automatic aimed at her chest, she showed no concern.

Rachel was one cool customer. There was no need to escalate the situation, provoke an untimely response. She was assessing how quickly she could draw her own pistol and shoot him first.

He grinned. There'd be time for that inevitable exchange, later. They both knew that.

Barnes sensed the grandness of the moment had yet to register in their psyches. This was a station stop. Perhaps the end of their line.

"Rachel," he said, "I've missed you."

She exhaled. "I can't say the same."

He glanced to Davidson, while keeping his weapon on Rachel. "That's because he poisoned your mind. Erased memories. Rewrote your past. Conditioned you into being a trustworthy slave."

Davidson shook his head and widened his arc, drawing closer to the altar and the man arranged like a sacrifice on the slab. His face cracked with a hint of emotion. One of his precious soldiers had been stripped bare and put out on display.

"What have you done to them?" Davidson asked.

Barnes shrugged. "Silenced dangerous minds."

"Dangerous?" Davidson asked. "Who did these people threaten? You?"

"The future."

Davidson laughed. "No. I'm in charge of our future." He cleared his throat and gestured to the round room. "I argued against creating smart soldiers. Preliminary research signaled cognitive instability, paranoia. An Army is built with doers, not philosophers. This parade of yours is delusional. And no matter how hard you try to prove you're smarter than the rest of us, you're still just playing catch-up."

Barnes ground his teeth. "Rachel, I presume you've brought the *pisau*. Slowly. No sudden movements. Hand it to me."

With two fingers, Rachel slowly plucked a dagger from her vest pocket, its ivory handle tainted blue like a beacon of light. She reached across the altar to pass it to him.

He took the dagger blade first. "I know you wanted to use this in a different manner."

Rachel shifted her balance, getting ready to draw a firearm. Her dominant hand hovered near her waist, fingers slightly widened.

In a quick, circular movement, Barnes thrust the blade of the dagger deep into the chest of the naked man, pinning the parchment of skin to a now-dead body.

Rachel snatched her weapon.

Barnes glided sideways to his left, keeping his semi-automatic on her.

"That soldier was unarmed," Davidson barked. "You're a coward, Barnes."

"Pull the trigger, Rachel." Barnes said. "That's what the general wants. Go ahead. Let's find out who walks out of here alive."

"There was no need to kill him," Rachel said, her lips twitching slightly. "You didn't have to kill any of them."

"Oh, you're blaming me for those Rangers this morning." He nodded. "I understand it, but that wasn't me. That's the executive branch cleaning up the general's mess. Ask him if that's true."

Barnes had outright dared Rachel to pull the trigger. She didn't. Something held her back. It wasn't the threat of getting shot or dying. Rachel sought answers as much as he did.

"Barnes," Davidson said, "you blame the wrong people for your slights. Come up with the wrong conclusions. Your life was never yours. Blaming doctors is convenient, trite. Your scheme of revelation is... misguided. I killed your pretend family. They were merely stand-ins, placeholders, until the time came for you to grow in a different direction. The mine and railway explosions in Elk Pass created clean slates. Change. In one night, both of you were freed from the childhood bonds of family. Great soldiers don't have the chains of sentimentality holding them back. That's why intimacy was treated harshly. There is no place in your hearts for love. The punishment you received served to realign your focus. The Perfect People Initiative ensures the survival of the human race. Its mission is grander than all of us."

A blink in Rachel's eyes showed she'd processed the newsflash. Her family had died as a result of those accidents. Davidson had orphaned both them, leaving them in need of a replacement family—the *Perfect People Initiative*.

Barnes took a tense breath. "Mary, I know you're there. Come out and join us."

To Rachel's left, Mary Davidson stepped past a camouflaged entry.

"Stand next to Rachel, if you would."

Rachel glanced sideways, breaking her focus. The creator's presence shocked her. The FOUNDATION STONE had arrived. Even the general seemed surprised.

"Phillip, I'm fine right where I'm at," Mary said, her tone defiant.

"Mary, leave," Davidson said. "This business will be over shortly."

"He's right," Pratt said. "You shouldn't be here. You need to leave."

Barnes laughed maniacally. "Concern for her wellbeing is admirable. I didn't know either of you have that kind of sentimentality in you."

During ABI's training and trials, Mary Davidson was the only one to show compassion and understanding, even the smallest glimmer of love. Never, not once, had she held a weapon or participated in the combat aspects of their training. She seemed unarmed, so Barnes permitted her to stand where she was. Obviously, Mary was concerned about getting caught in the crossfire.

"Phillip," Mary Davidson said, "the killing has to stop. Please. Let's take a different path."

Barnes shook his head. "Your secrets have been drawn into the light only because there's been death."

"Listen to Mary," Davidson said, his tone changing. "She's right. There's common ground here. It's time to stand down, soldier. Time for a different path."

98
THE ROUND ROOM

Kate awoke tasting grit and blood. Her cheek lay in water, deep enough to trickle into her mouth and nostrils. Her vision blurred as her mind struggled to catch up with current events. Her head pounded and a stiff neck made it difficult to turn her head.

Around her people were talking, their voices garbed.

Her body ached. The simple act of breathing was painful. Taking in a snort of air and she caught a whiff of a familiar, almost everyday fragrance.

Her mind struggled to categorize the smell.

Then it registered: hand sanitizer. Alcohol-enriched gel used every day in forensics labs and all through medical school. Was she in a hospital?

The faint recollection of the odor unlocked the physical world for her mind.

Kate blinked her eyes to focus. The voices were clearer now, coming into mid-argument.

"Barnes," Davidson said, his tone indifferent and direct, "we delivered the FBI agent. Now end your game and deliver the Speaker's niece."

"Once again, you're missing the picture, General."

A pain shot down her spine as Kate lifted her head to take in the situation.

"End this, Phillip," Mary Davidson said, like a scolding parent.

Kate recognized everyone in the circular room.

Gray rectangles on the walls shimmered like clouded-over portraits. Lights lit up a round altar like a shrine. Kate thought of the little stone church at the monastery. Candles were set up on the table. A fountain overflowed and pools of water painted the floor in large square pockets.

Barnes stood on a dry spot beside a stone altar that displayed the body of a man. A dagger had been driven through the victim's chest. Confidently, Barnes pointed a semi-automatic pistol at Rachel Pratt, aiming for her chest. Eight feet away, Pratt mirrored his actions with a similar pistol pointed back at Barnes. Davidson stood clear, near the feet of the man on the altar. Mary Davidson stood in front of a shimmering panel.

Davidson shook his head. "Soldier, this path has no unobtainable outcome. Life and our work are not black or white as you've depicted. The greater good is served in our research. A new race of soldiers. Needed soldiers. A new generation of astronauts. Men and women who will establish colonies across the stars. The Perfect People Initiative cannot be blackmailed into nonexistence, no matter how hard you attempt to derail it. Rejoin us and be part of it again."

Barnes did not avert his gaze from Pratt. "*The world changed, never to be the same. A few laughed. A few cried. Most were silent.* Those were Oppenheimer's sentiments when recalling the detonation of the atomic bomb." His focus on Pratt intensified. "Genetic alterations create an advanced evolutionary footprint that will forever trample out a percentage of the human species. We had a chance for love. And it was taken away. This is my time and place to act, not be silent."

Kate slid her hand alongside her hip and felt an empty holster. She vaguely recalled losing her firearm and the flashlight during her fall at the crevice.

"So this is what it comes down to?" Davidson asked, unctuous and cruel. He produced a nickel-plated semi-automatic and aimed it at Barnes. Two against one.

Barnes raised his free hand to show off a controller of some sort, his thumb pressing a red trigger. "General, this was never a negotiation. It was a stop. Your death was preordained, absolute. Beyond the abuse, the torture, your sin was you stole love from us. This circle is Rachel's test. Love over obligation and alliances?"

Kate took a painful breath. The smell of hand sanitizer signaled trouble in the dark recesses of her brain. An inferno was coming. Barnes was going to ignite the place and kill everyone. That was the reason he was standing on the room's only dry landing.

Summoning inner strength, Kate staggered to her feet. She looked around the circle, trying to decide where the hell to run. The death trap had one way out—behind her.

Pratt glanced at Davidson, while leaving her weapon trained on Barnes. "If the Rangers had killed Phillip this morning, did their secondary directives include terminating me as well?"

Davidson chuckled. "Soldier, I'm in charge of protecting our total assets. The Advanced Biogenetics Initiative is too valuable to fold up shop, disappear. Barnes's delusional grandeur has exposed a great deal of our work. Blame him for making you expendable. Not me. You're an asset with a shelf life. Nothing more. And your mission still stands. Kill this—"

"FOOD FOR POWDER," Barnes snapped.

Pratt swung her arm. A loud retort resonated in the confined chamber. Her pistol fired once, striking its intended target. Davidson collapsed to the floor, his face landing in a spread of water. His eyes were fixed open in glass-like states.

Pratt moved her weapon shoulder high, pointed at the ceiling and away from any target.

Barnes never shifted his aim, targeting her heart.

"Phillip, I remember what I so desperately wanted to forget." She spoke the words like a curse. "I did love you. Once. A long time ago. Shangri-La, as much as I fantasized about it, was no destination for us. We're bred for specific reasons. My loyalty is with our creator. Once torn and shattered, my heart could never be anyone's. She's the one who made me whole again."

His voice fell distant. "Then your circle is complete."

Pratt lowered her weapon.

Barnes closed his eyes. The muzzle flash from his gun was unexpected. A single shot struck Pratt in the chest. She staggered, her face shocked. A superhuman effort kept her standing as she aimed her pistol.

Mary Davidson yelled. "No!"

"Run, Katherine!" Barnes shouted. His thumb left the trigger of the controller he clutched.

The room plunged into darkness.

Blinding fire and flames sparked like exploding stars against a black tapestry. White hot flashes expelled torrid waves of heat. Sizzling sounds radiated from every direction. Snakes of fire zipped at Kate's feet. Blue and green pools of water churned up smoke.

Kate ran, distancing herself from the kaleidoscope of spreading explosions. Heat washed the back of her neck and painted her cheeks.

Risking a glance back, she saw a fusillade of muzzle shots pulsing among Barnes, Pratt, and Mary Davidson. The room vibrated in a reign of fire beyond the pyrotechnic display created by Barnes.

It was impossible for anyone to survive a duel at such close distances.

But the shots kept coming.

Sheltering her eyes, Kate scampered further back as blue and green flames chased her footsteps. Slamming into a wall, she flailed for the only opening she'd seen, and spun out of the consuming inferno.

Smoke and brilliant, pulsing waves of light and heat ripped through the doorway. The disjointed flashes illuminated the passageway in which she stood.

Kate caught her breath and leaned against cold concrete. Her heart pounded in her chest. Her knees felt weak. The crescendo of insanity waned. The cool underground air penetrated her clothes and tingled her skin, making her realize everything she wore was soaked with whatever Barnes had poured onto the floor of his circle sanctuary. Based on the grandness of his fireworks display, she guessed it was a mix of insoluble alcohol-based flammables poured over water.

A single gunshot rang out.

Kate pushed her haggard mind through mental gymnastics: unarmed, no flashlight, dark passageways, fatal crevice. Certain death. Even if she groped her way through dark passageways, she could walk forever and never find a way out.

She took a breath. She'd face whoever survived the circle's gauntlet.

After swearing inwardly, she peered around the door opening.

The combustibles had spent most of their fuel. Ankle-high blue and green flames lingered in pools carved into the flooring. The cavern was thick with smoke. The light from the remaining fire flickered and diminished. Lit candles encircled a charred body on the altar.

Three figures lay motionless on the floor.

Kate moved quickly.

Sprinting into the circle, she noticed the glowing pocketed floor had highpoints, almost like a hopscotch path. In stride, her boots hit the dead spots between the flames until she reached Rachel Pratt.

Pratt still gripped her semi-automatic, its slide locked back, its magazine spent. Dwindling blue flames tickled the edges of her body, making bullet wounds visible. Three holes marked the shirt over her left breast and one centered her forehead.

Difficult wounds to self-heal.

No sense in checking for a pulse, so Kate found the flashlight Rachel carried instead. Clicking it on, she swept light across the circle.

The general was down, a single and fatal bullet to his temple. Kate leapt for his nickel-plated firearm. Pain caused her to wince and gasp for a breath. Pivoting, she searched for Barnes. Steadying the acquired pistol, she gathered her strength and crawled to the other side of the round altar, clearing that part of the circle.

Barnes had vanished. Only blood pooled where he once stood.

Kate moved the beam of the flashlight.

In shock, Mary Davidson sat slumped against a curtained door-way that was camouflaged into the walls. A pearl necklace she wore was splattered in blood. She'd been shot in the chest and abdomen. The woman twitched and wheezed when she breathed. Her eyes harbored disbelief and confusion.

She struggled to comprehend how Mary Davidson had found the circle, much less knowingly stepped into gunfire. A loosely gripped pistol was in her hand.

Questions and answers would have to wait.

Kate slid Mary onto her back and applied pressure to seal her chest wound. The more threatening wound was in her abdomen. Gunshot wounds were essentially violent puncture wounds. Instincts told Kate that Mary had only minutes to live.

Suddenly, Mary reminded her of the woman with gold braclets on her wrists sitting beside her on the Orange line train—a place where her whirlwind day had started—a place she wanted to forget but knew she never would.

Mary tried to lean up. "I thought I could save them both."

Kate pressed her back down. "Save your strength."

The woman glanced at the altar, then to the people on the floor. "Rachel?"

Kate shook her head. "She's gone."

The woman gasped. "You have to stop him."

She mustered a fake smile. "Mary, you weren't truthful with me at the monastery."

"I never lied to you."

"You withheld information. You knew Phillip Barnes was the terrorist, the bomber. You knew his name. Who he was."

"He'll be waiting for you."

Kate nodded. "At the last stop. Before midnight."

"I'm cold." Mary shivered and coughed. "Thank you for saving Frances. Now I need you to wake her. For the children. Wake Frances."

She fought back a tear. "The children? What children? I'm not following."

Mary took a pained breath. "I chip my children. Use the patches. Find Phillip. Maybe those can help somehow. T6."

"T6?"

"I'm cold." Mary's eyelids grew heavy and she shivered again. "Wake my daughter."

"I don't know how to do that." Kate took a ragged breath as a wave of emotions hit her.

"Thomas Parker will." Mary's mouth bubbled up more blood and her body went still.

Kate gasped and turned away. Tears flooded her eyes and she cried.

What was Mary saying? Thomas? Frances? Children?

Nothing made sense.

Red dots swarmed the room. Haze from the smoke revealed the tails of laser sights. Shouting and screaming followed as the red dots singled out the only person alive in the room.

Kate moved her hands slowly, placing them where they could be seen.

"Damn it, Morgan!" the WFO SWAT Unit Chief shouted. "What the hell are you doing down here?"

99
FRESH AIR

West of Dupont Circle, Washington, DC

Phillip Barnes' fury burned. He'd prepared for contingencies, but none included getting shot. That scenario happened to everyone else. That was the plan.

Before Mary Davidson shot him, twice: his dominant hand and right shoulder. The two wounds didn't feel life-threatening, but at the same time, beyond the pain, something inside him didn't feel right. And he doubted her marksmanship was deliberate but its crippling nature was effective enough.

Adrenaline charged through his system as he backtracked through tunnels, fleeing in a different manner than originally intended to bypass FBI SWAT agents storming his subterranean circle. His flashlight lit up the dirt path beneath his feet and he kept his right arm and hand clutched tight to his chest. His chest felt tight and caused him to cough.

Mary Davidson was the FOUNDATION STONE, the creator, the brilliance and brains behind the *Perfect People Initiative*. It had never been enough to kill James Davidson as the program's director and principal investigator. The general managed. Others created. With five of the seven victims parked in terminal dormancies, Mary Davidson remained the last part of the research equation to zero out.

Mary Davidson's invitation to the circle was about closure: ouroboros.

He just hadn't expected Rachel to choose being a slave to the creator over love.

Perhaps Rachel felt indebted to their creator for saving her life after then-Lieutenant Colonel James Davidson shot and killed Rachel at Soldiers Home. Mary Davidson had come to the circle to save Rachel one more time. In the end, no one was saved.

Rachel could have walked away, but she'd chosen poorly.

The near-invisible, bullet-proof micro-armor mesh deployed between himself and Rachel made all the difference. Rachel Pratt was an excellent marksman, outstanding at all distances. She never missed her mark. But unknown to Rachel, their confrontation had been one-sided. Dramatically so. Exactly how he'd planned it.

Tripping on a rock, he banged his wounded shoulder against the tunnel wall. He grimaced, knowing medical attention would have to wait a bit longer. All he had to do was fight through the pain, stop the bleeding, and minimize blood loss. His ten-million-dollar cash paid-in-advance, call-when-needed, and discreet trauma surgeon and triage team waited for him in Virginia.

He came to a stop in the tunnels. Above him was a red-bricked structure with wooden flooring.

Barnes unlocked a floor panel in the old Dupont Circle ticket office above. Gritting his teeth, he climbed with his good arm, pulling himself up a ladder until he was in the basement of the building. The tunnel hatch was closed. From a metal locker, he extracted a field trauma kit and inside that he tracked down a pair of scissors. Grimacing, he cut off his shirt.

Blood painted his torso. One bullet had shattered his right shoulder blade. The wound looked worse than first imagined.

He'd trained to endure and tolerate pain, but these wounds were pushing his thresholds.

His arm and shoulder were useless. His hand told a similar story. Bloodied fingers were knocked out of alignment where a bullet had penetrated his palm. His shooting hand was now a useless tool. And both injuries would require surgery and extensive rehabs. Army combat training had prepared him for the self-dressing of wounds sustained during combat. His six-step medic training kicked in: clean the wounds, stop bleeding, elevate when necessary, manage pain, immobilize limbs, and dress the wounds. With his good hand, he skipped to the fourth step and unwrapped two transmucosal fentanyl citrate lollipops. He shoveled the berry-flavored suckers into his mouth. The stick lozenges delivered pain meds to the blood-stream faster than injections. He skipped cleaning the wounds. No time for that. After applying QuikClot combat dressing, with one hand, he did his best to wrap his shoulder. It was a lousy job but was close enough. His shattered hand was easier to bandage.

Barnes skipped putting on a shirt and awkwardly slid on a construction worker's jacket that had been stashed with the med kit. From a field bag, he grabbed a brimmed hardhat, safety glasses, and walkie-talkie, then put on a bright yellow safety vest. The last accessory snatched up was an ID badge: Howard Watt, DC Capital Construction Services, Civil Engineering Department.

The double dose of pain meds started to take the edge off. He made his way upstairs and exited through the front door of the old single-story trolley ticket office. The night air was welcomed and he took several deep breaths to gather himself and make sure he comprehended the collective situation.

Directly ahead of him, heavily armed MPDC SWAT officers stood over an old trolley stairway leading down into the abandoned Dupont Circle Trolley Station. They glanced his way. Instinctively he raised his good hand and tapped the side of his hard hat.

One of the rules for blending in was knowing the necessary role and playing the part. He snatched the walkie-talkie off his belt.

"Dispatch, we're going to need those assessment reports," Barnes said, keying his radio and acting out his end of a fake communica-tion. "I found nothing over here."

He looked across Dupont Circle and studied the frenzy. Every federal agency imaginable was represented. The disjoined brilliance of flashing lights on a myriad of vehicles lit up the night. On the surface, the chaos felt somewhat organized.

He peered down P Street. Several blocks down, armored vehicles surrounded the autonomous van that he'd used to enter the tunnels. That would've been the same entrance Mary Davidson had used to enter the circle.

He put the latest events behind him and walked toward Massachusetts Avenue, moving past the crowds that had gathered around the final set of police barricades. He removed his helmet and sighed as if he was ending his shift. Just above Q Street, along 21st he climbed into another autonomous vehicle, an SUV marked with DC Construction Services logos on its doors and fake government license plates.

He had strategically parked six autonomous vehicles in the neighborhoods around Dupont Circle. At first glance, he'd only lost the van parked across Al Tiramisu. Not bad.

He gave a voice command and the vehicle started, its auto-pilot taking charge. Slumping into the driver's seat, he closed his eyes and the vehicle merged into traffic.

His mind drifted, compliments of the pain killers.

He wondered about Rachel, if her true broken heart had experienced the sting of death. His sentiment for her grew distant, almost lost in the erosion of time. After targeting her heart, he'd stepped around his protective screen and shot Rachel once between the eyes, making sure to lay her self-healing genetic abilities to rest with a bullet to her brain.

During the barrage of gunfire and stream of distracting fireworks, he'd forgotten about Katherine Morgan, vaguely remembering he'd even yelled for her to run.

She'd heeded his directions and sought refuge.

The island was where Morgan would find closure to her circle.

1 F	O	2 U	3 N	4 D	A	5 T	I	O	N	6 S	T	O	7 N	8 E
		9 P	O	R		O				K			10 O	L
11 R	12 P		13 M	U	14 R	D	15 E	16 R		Y		17 X	I	I
18	I	19		20 P	L	A	Z	A	S		21 I	I		S
22 U	S	A	G	E		Y		I		23 H			24 S	I
25 L	A	B			26 P			L		27 A			28 E	O
29 E	U	G	E	N	I	30 C	31 S			32 S	E	33 V	E	N
						34 R	A	35 T	36 E		37	I		
38 E	39 L	40 I	41 Z	42 A	43 B	E	T	H	S		44	A		45 S
46 L	O	G	T	H	E	T	O	U	R	S				H
K		O		47 E	T		48 R	B			49 H	50 O	51 M	E
52 P		R			53 A	54 B	I		55 T	56 H	R	A	L	L
A				57		I			58 U	G		59 K	I	T
60 S	61	62	63		64	O	65		66 E	O	67 T		68 N	E
69 S	T	I	G	M	A				70 S	A	P	P	E	R

100
THE AFTERMATH OF CARNAGE

The Circle, Below and West of Dupont Circle, Washington, DC

Kate stiffly rose to her feet. SWAT agents brushed past her to secure the scene and check on the victims. Her entire body ached when she moved. Muscles she didn't remember having seemed to scream at her. Her battered mind struggled to catch up, some of the events appearing dream-like in her consciousness. The hazy, smoke-filled room matched her clouded-over psyche. Barnes had hidden entries and exits, limiting the dissipation of the fumes and smoke from the fireworks show.

"You're stupid and reckless!" the FBI SWAT Unit Chief shouted. "And you've got a real bad death wish, Morgan."

The insults were warranted. He wasn't wrong.

The agents clicked on flashlights to illuminate the circular cavern.

"Everyone's dead," she mumbled.

One of the agents asked, "What the hell went on down here?"

She ignored the question. Rhetorical. She fell silent as agents checked for pulses: Pratt, Mary Davidson, and the general.

Barnes had lured everyone into this death trap.

She scanned the floor, hoping to see him gasping for a last breath. Barnes had vanished. Moved on. Her vision backtracked to where he last stood. Small splashes of blood dotted the floor. He'd been wounded. On the floor in front of where Barnes had stood was a crumpled screen. Wires stretched from the floor to the ceiling. She crouched and felt its fabric. Smooth, Teflon-like but see-through. The bullet-proof, near invisible fabric had the thickness of a sail.

Barnes had used the magic screen to protect himself. Rachel Pratt never stood a chance. Her O.K. Corral moment was one-sided. Mary Davidson had caught him off guard and shot him from the side.

As Kate's mind limped into action, she turned to the altar.

This madness wasn't over. There was one more stop. The last stop.

A charred shell of a man lay on a round sandstone centerpiece. The sight was horrifying. His skin was encapsulated in a burnt, hardened resin. The handle of a dagger protruded from the victim's chest, nailing down the last parchment of clues. The lit candles surrounding him gave the repulsive placement a shrine-like feel.

Bile rose in Kate's throat. As a forensics investigator she saw death every day. Senseless brutality and carnage came in numerous forms. But never like this.

Matted to the victim's chest was the last set of clues, pristine, and unfazed by fire and flame. The dagger stabbing him through the chest was done as a statement, to drive home a point.

Kate spun back to the lifeless Mary Davidson, the FOUNDATION STONE. The woman had turned her head in the direction of Rachel Pratt, something she didn't notice at the time Mary had taken her last breath. The woman never saw her creations as soldiers but rather an evolution of the human race.

Mary had mentioned children, her daughter Frances, and Thomas Parker.

Thomas. What was Thomas to her? Something opposite to how she'd felt before the Metro bombing. That was how Phillip Barnes wanted her to feel. Confused. Torn between love and duty. Questioning her own morality and ethics.

Everything was so messed up. And Kate had mixed feelings about Rachel Pratt. A test tube creation. Accomplished soldier. A hero. A twisted psychopath's ex-girlfriend. Twice a victim. Someone who'd played multiple angles in a deadly game.

Pratt didn't deserve her fate.

None of them did.

Well, the general did. He probably deserved worse than he'd received. His instantaneous death was an easy out. If the *Perfect People Initiative* survived, the Pentagon would replace him with another bureaucrat and continue its test subject atrocities.

An idea stirred in Kate's mind. If she could somehow capture Barnes, force him to testify, public pressure would force the Pentagon's hand. Force the shutdown of the *Perfect People Initiative* and end the Advanced Biogenetics Initiative. In order for that to happen, she needed Barnes alive.

A revolting thought.

She studied Pratt's bullet wounds, and touched the soldier's chest above her heart. She remembered what the friar had told her: "that kind of evil resides in a hardened heart. *For where one's treasure is, there will your heart be also.* A corrupted heart and mind can possess a great deal of evil." The skin over a heart was more than a way to reveal a treasure. Barnes had removed his victim's flesh as a distorted way to tell a story: his, Rachel's, Mary's, the general's. Barnes had murdered Pratt because she shunned him.

With her hands still laid on Pratt, Kate realized that her hands were bloodstained and sticky. The blood had come from Mary Davidson.

No one was blameless in this interwoven set of broken relationships and broken people.

The odd senseless feeling ran counter to her beliefs as a physician. Part of her wanted to avenge their deaths.

Mary's voice returned to her mind: "You have to stop him."

Kate took a steadying breath and glanced at the altar.

One more stop.

Returning to the altar, she studied the parchment. Removing her sat phone, she snapped pictures of the message, the altar, and statement on slavery marked high on the walls above.

The last inked message read:

KATHERINE, IF THIS IS YOURS, YOU UNDERSTAND THE
PENANCE REQUIRED FOR PEACE IN HEAVEN AND EARTH.
WHAT CAN BE AVOIDED WHOSE END IS PURPOSED BY THE
GODS? WHAT TRADE PAYS AMBITION'S DEBT? THE WORLD'S
A STAGE AND YOUR EXIT IS CAST.

ACROSS		DOWN	
18	DEATH'S MARK	1	STAFF'S CAP
37	ABBR: COIN	18	ABBR: STOW SIZEABLE COLT
44	BLACK FATE DOTH DEPEND	21	GLACIAL FINALLY
52	ADD POLICEMAN & GIRL	57	ABBR: UNIT'S CHARGED VIGIL
60	MARKED EXCHANGE	65	ABBR: BIG STICK RIDER
66	ABBR: CLOCK'S TERM		

There wasn't time to debate crime scene preservation, so Kate
snatched the parchment off the charred victim and scrolled it backwards, placing the dagger on the backside of the material.

Walking to the closest SWAT agent, Kate said, "Please escort me
out of here."

101
T6

Kate put her mind in neutral to let it go silent. Zombie-like, she trudged behind an agent leading her out of the tunnels, his flashlight showing the way.

Everything in her body hurt. The pressure inside her skull made it seem like her brain was going to explode. She was so tired it was hard to lift her boots as she walked across the grit of a dirt floor tunnel. All she wanted to do was close her eyes and sleep. For days.

Against her chest, she clutched the parchment wrapped around the dagger. They were tools for her to use. She just didn't know what to do with them.

Discarded plastic canisters left on the side of the tunnel caught her eye.

Kate stopped. Rather than turning her neck to look, she pivoted her entire body.

"Wait," she said to the agent. "Bring your light over here."

The agent returned. "What's all this?"

She pointed. "I know how Barnes staged his magic show."

Kate snatched the light out of his hands and crouched in front of the containers. She illuminated the discarded materials and wrappings. Twisting off the cap to one of the industrial-sized tubs of clinical gel hand sanitizer, she swabbed her fingers around the rim of the container and applied the ethyl alcohol-based solution to a gash in the back of her scalp.

"Holy sh—" Kate screamed, forcing her fingers to massage the antiseptic deeper into her wound. "That's a wake-up."

The escorting agent wasn't exactly following her.

She rifled through the discarded tubs, materials, and packaging. Everything used in his magic show: petroleum gels, alcohol gels, magnesium ribbons, strontium, copper, and sodium compounds. Petroleum-based fuels, metal fuels and oxidizers.

Fireworks chemistry. Destructive chemistry.

The chemistry assortment made her think of Thomas Parker.

Barnes's magic show was for effects. A startling distraction. Meant to provide an edge during the real firefight. That was why the coward stood in the only dry spot in the room—high ground—while everyone else was ready to be lit up.

She took a whiff of her clothes. She reeked of fumes and chemicals.

Glancing down the tunnel, she could see the glow lights from inside Barnes' circular sanctuary.

She had to go back.

After unwrapping the dagger from the parchment, she handed the agent the inked skin and returned his flashlight.

"Run that up to Will Shortz," she said. "He'll know what to do with it. Just don't tell him we took it off a dead guy. That might gross him out. Also, we're on the clock."

Snatching up an empty tub of clinical gel hand sanitizer, Kate trudged back to the light.

Kate returned to the den of insanity. Barnes' twisted chamber of enlightenment. To her right, Mary Davidson lay on the floor. Pratt and the general were across the room. The crime scene detail had arrived to document the scene. Kate set her contraband, the dagger, on the altar and pinched out the still burning flames on the candles.

"Morgan," the SWAT Unit Chief said, "you need to leave."

"I'm not done yet." Kate shook the empty tub of hand sanitizer, sloshing the residual leftovers to the cap-side of the container. After scooping out the contents, she sanitized her hands. "Make yourself useful and take off your work gloves. You need to get your hands dirty."

"What?"

She glanced to his name badge. Uhrback. Even outside, before the circle, they'd never really exchanged greetings or names. Their brief conversations had been one way. His way. That was about to change.

The victim's hardened, crusted skin revealed he'd been slathered in a chemical mixture that burned. Burned hot. She thought of the sailor found in the Grant Building. Barnes had blown up the building before the bureau could reach him. She suspected his motives were the same here. This victim must have been one of the program's remaining super soldiers.

Kate snatched up an extra pair of gloves from a box provided by the crime scene detail. After snapping them on past her wrists, she swept the altar with ultraviolet light from her black light. It lit up like the communion table in Stanley Hall at Soldiers' Home.

Neon violet illumination highlighted an ouroboros crushing a compass. Encircling the ouroboros was the line: IN A TIME OF DECEIT TELLING THE TRUTH IS A REVOLUTIONARY ACT.

It sounded like something George Orwell would say. Barnes used the reference to justify his actions.

"Morgan, what's going on?" Uhrback asked.

She shrugged. "If I told you in advance, you'd stop me. So it's best if you just roll with this experience." His expression darkened. "Have one of your guys go back through the tunnels. Out that door." She pointed. "They'll find a drainage channel where I dropped my Glock and a flashlight. I'm going to need those."

Uhrback made the call on the radio.

"And while you're at it, you got a multi-tool on you?"

His jaw fell open as he retrieved the bureau's version of a Swiss Army knife.

She pointed to the floor. "Cut those cables and roll up the fabric."

"What is this?" he asked, severing the thin cables that ran floor to ceiling. With its rollup line gone, the sail-like fabric came free of the floor.

"I suspect it's a see-through, bullet-resistant fabric." She recapped how the exchange of gunfire went down—at least her version of it. "Barnes used the invisible shield to protect himself in front, but he never counted on Mary Davidson shooting at him from the side."

She tossed Uhrback a pair of blue gloves.

"What are we doing?" he asked with a nervous look.

"Grab his feet."

Holding the victim's shoulders firm, she turned him onto his side. Uhrback pivoted feet. She moved the dagger along the man's spine and stopped at the T6 vertebrae. The spot was right between the shoulder blades. Using its blade, she cut back skin and dug against bone. Faint edges defined an object fused to bone. Using the dagger's blade, she peeled off the object like peeling off the meaty skin of an apple.

Out came a bloodied stamp-sized chip.

"What the hell is that?"

"A GPS-RFID tracking device." She shrugged. "Mary Davidson chipped her children."

"Chipped? Like pets?" He froze when saw Kate kneel beside Pratt on the floor. "No, Morgan. I'm not doing this to her."

Kate shot him a stern glare. "Why, because she's a woman? She's dead. Trust me. I spent part of the day with her. Rachel Pratt won't give a damn what we do to her corpse as long as it leads to hunting down the man who killed her."

She waited for Uhrback to lend a hand. Repeating the process, Kate turned Pratt sideways then cut off her shirt and sports bra to locate T6. Digging below Pratt's skin, Kate peeled out another bloody chip.

Kate handed Uhrback the bloody tiny flexible patch taken from the man on the altar.

He studied it apprehensively.

"If you want to follow me," she said, "have a lab tech lock onto its GPS or RFID signature."

102
THE TEMPEST

P Street NW, Dupont Circle, Washington, DC

Outside the rear gates of the Embassy of Portugal, Will Shortz worked in a semi-sterile white tent erected next to a bus stop. Agents armed with assault rifles stood watch outside the tent.

LED lights beamed above him. They'd asked him to wear gloves while handling evidence. His hands sweated inside the plastic gloves. The parchment of clues was spread out on a plastic mat on a plastic table. Beside him, FBI crime scene technicians examined the nautical instruments he'd extracted from the fountain.

He studied the inked words.

These last solutions troubled him as much as the first set.

This human tapestry was an affirmation of a madman's promise. A finale for death. Outside, he'd heard agents mention the shootings underground: Dr. Mary Davidson, Army Captain Rachel Pratt, and Army General James Davidson. While he hadn't really known them, their deaths bothered him. It wasn't his kind of day at the office.

The associated wordplay sparked neurons in his mind. He thought of Shakespeare's *The Tempest*. A remote island with threads of magic, deception, plots of murder and revenge, and marriage. At the end of the play, Prospero, the magician central to the story, hints that he will bury magic and drown his book of spells if the audience frees him from the island with applause. The applause is a form of payment and respect. Beneath the surface, Phillip Barnes showed similar desires, except the payment required was a penance of death and sacrifice. His blended prologue preceding the clues was an amalgamation of Shakespearian lines: HEAVEN AND EARTH, PURPOSED BY THE GODS, AMBITION'S DEBT, and WHAT TRADE were extracted from *Julius Caesar*; THE WORLD'S A STAGE from *As You Like It*.

Barnes had recited Shakespeare earlier, but here the reference was closer to what Prospero required in *The Tempest*.

The payment here was Katherine Morgan's life. 18 ACROSS. Rest in Peace.

Neither the last sentiment nor its solutions identified physical locations. And for some reason, *The Tempest* kept creeping back into his mind, even though the play was not a reference.

He remembered one of the puzzle's prior associations. ELISION. Mary Davidson had mentioned it to Morgan. The merging of abstract ideas.

The location brightened his thoughts, like the first rays of sunrise beaming across a meadow. 65 DOWN. The abbreviation of a BIG STICK RIDER. TR. Theodore Roosevelt. Prior to his presidency, Roosevelt had organized the Rough Riders to fight in the Spanish-American War. As President, his foreign policy actions were backed by the bullying mindset of "speak softly and carry a big stick, you will go far." And just inside the boundary of Washington, DC, in the Potomac River, was a spot of land named Theodore Roosevelt Island.

His eyes found the icon at the bottom left-hand portion of the clues: an odd hourglass set of parallel lines surrounded by a circle.

Shortz nudged the crime scene technician closest to him. "If this was a symbol on a park map, hiking, walking, what does it look like to you?"

The technician scrunched up his nose. After a moment, he said, "A bridge?"

Shortz smiled. The symbol implied a bridge to an island.

103
PREPARATIONS

Kate was nearly in tears and the walk and climb out of the tunnels had been grueling. Every inch of her body hurt. Escorted down the sidewalk, she entered the white tent with the FBI Special Agent in Charge (SAC) Charles Murray and the SWAT Unit Chief Bruno Uhrback on her heels.

Will Shortz glanced up from a map displayed on a computer. He was studying Theodore Roosevelt Island. The last stop.

"This is not how the FBI conducts its business," Murray said following her into the tent.

"And it's suicide," Uhrback added.

Kate spun toward them. "All day I've been *the* bait. Chase this spot on a map. Now go there. Jump. No jump higher. Wacked like a mole when it was convenient. Dropped into in dungeons and pits. Hell, even the U.S. Navy used me as bait in a training exercise. Now, really, this is just an extension of that insanity."

Murray folded his arms. "What happens when Barnes puts a bullet through your head?"

"I will see this through."

"Even if it kills you?"

Kate shot both men glares. "I need a helmet with night vision and thermal imaging, a second Glock, and no bullshit. You can have me fired tomorrow, but right now, make a choice."

"All right, fellas, give Morgan space," Murray said, ushering others out.

Kate sat on a chair and unlaced her boots. "Mr. Shortz, stay. Please."

Shortz lingered by the door.

"So Barnes intends to kill me," she said as a statement and not a question. She unbuckled her holster and set her Glock aside. She emptied everything out of her pockets, including the dagger taken from the circle and her letters from the Director. "Rest in Peace."

"At the monastery, he inserted a line from Horace. Its translation from Latin was *Love and hope won't save us from death.*" He shrugged. "I'm not a profiler, but this is too long of a prelude to lead anywhere else."

She nodded. "Point taken."

Shortz glanced away as Kate peeled off her chemically soiled shirt, stripping down to her bra, and discarded the shirt into a yellow hazardous waste bin. Stiff and sore, she moved slowly. Every part of her body ached. Scanning her arms and torso, the black and blue welts and abrasions covering her skin were more than she could count. Signs of a rough day. From a bag with her name on it, she retrieved a multi-sleeved top and two thin, lightweight ballistic plates.

"Need some help, if you don't mind?"

Shortz snuck a peek her way. "Sure."

She tossed him the black top, turned her back to him, and raised her hands.

There was a long pause. She imaged he was studying the vast spread of bruising that had accumulated. She said nothing and allowed the moment to pass.

He touched her arm, his touch light, tentative. Her skin tingled. She winced when he slid her arms into the sleeves of the ballistic compression top, pulled it over her head, and flattened it down around her waist.

"Thank you," she said, grimacing.

"You going to be all right?"

She chuckled. "Ask me at midnight." She handed him one of the polyethylene ballistic plates, then slid the form-fitted one she held into the sleeved chest pocket of her soft body armor. "That goes in the back."

After Shortz slid the plate into place, she put on an untucked long-sleeve, tan work shirt over everything. Adding to her accessories, she put a ballistic camo vest on over everything and cinched down its straps. Instinctively, she tapped the gold FBI logo centering the vest.

She turned around. "You said Barnes quoted Shakespeare. Let me guess: *Midsummer's Night Dream, Romeo and Juliet*?"

Shortz smiled thinly. "*Julius Caesar* and *As You Like It*."

She frowned. "Caesar? He was assassinated."

He pointed to the dagger on the table. "Struck first by a guy named Servilius Casca."

Kate slid off her soiled pants, pulled on a clean pair of cargo pants, and dumped her old pants into the hazmat bin. Her belongings on the table went back into pockets, including the dagger and one of Mary Davidson's tracking microchips. She glanced at the letters given to her by Martinez earlier in the morning, and decided on leaving those behind.

"What navigation tools did you find?" she asked as she strapped on her Glock.

Shortz led her to a plastic bin used by the Evidence and Response Team. Items were recorded and tagged. A compass, sextant, collapsible spy glass, divider, and rope.

He pointed to a corner of the tent. Standing vertical was the trident. "He left that too."

"Barnes must be a fan of Aquaman."

"At least someone gets the reference."

Kate grabbed a sack and stuffed the compass, spy glass, and rope inside.

She turned to Shortz. "Thank you. I couldn't have done this without you."

1 F	O	2 U	3 N	4 D	A	5 T	I	O	N	6 S	T	O	7 N	8 E
E		9 P	O	R		O				K			10 O	L
11 R	12 P		13 M	U	14 R	D	15 E	16 R		Y		17 X	I	I
18 R	I	19 P		20 P	L	A	Z	A	S		21 I	I		S
22 U	S	A	G	E		Y		I		23 H	C		24 S	I
25 L	A	B			26 P			L		27 A	Y		28 E	O
29 E	U	G	E	N	I	30 C	31 S			32 S	E	33 V	E	N
						34 R	A	35 T	36 E		37 N	I		
38 E	39 L	40 I	41 Z	42 A	43 B	E	T	H	S		44 D	A	Y	45 S
46 L	O	G	T	H	E	T	O	U	R	S				H
K		O		47 E	T		48 R	B			49 H	50 O	51 M	E
52 P	A	R	K		53 A	54 B	I		55 T	56 H	R	A	L	L
A				57 E		I			58 U	G		59 K	I	T
60 S	61 W	62 A	63 P	S	64 P	O	65 T		66 E	O	67 T		68 N	E
69 S	T	I	G	M	A		R		70 S	A	P	P	E	R

104
CONTINGENCY PLANS

Strategic Information & Operations Center (SIOC), FBI Headquarters, Washington, DC

Waiting to pounce.

Alice Watson sensed Phillip Logan Barnes had boxed himself in.

His final stop was a foolish destination—an easy trap for law enforcement to set.

She scrutinized the big board's center monitors that displayed darkened satellite imagery on the site known as Theodore Roosevelt Island National Memorial. The darkness of night dramatically reduced visibility. National Park Service Rangers were patched into ongoing conference calls. The Park Service had closed the site and its footbridge, and provided logistical and historical insight. Before it was a national monument, the island had been a patch of farmland inside the boundaries of the District of Columbia.

Not taking chances, more agents had been dispatched to the Library of Congress to rifle through archives for historical maps—a lesson learned from the missing records of the underground tunnels at Dupont Circle.

Law enforcement secured every conceivable boundary.

Local and state police, SWAT teams, and snipers took up positions on both sides of the Potomac. Trails and freeways had been closed. Bridges from the Key Bridge to the 14th Street Bridge were closed. The U.S. Coast Guard restricted watercraft usage north of the I-495 Bridge. Harbors and marinas north of that crossing and up to Fletchers Cove were closed. And in case Barnes went into the river, suited Coast Guard and Navy divers waited aboard fast-approach incident response boats and intercepting watercraft just downstream of the 14th Street Bridge.

While a straight-line path existed between Rosslyn and Foggy Bottom-GWU Metro stations, the actual underground Metro tunnels for the Orange, Gray, and Blue Lines ran up and around the island. That took the Metro lines out of play. Taking no chances, additional WMATA officers secured those stations just in case law enforcement had missed an access route.

Reagan National Airport was closed to air traffic. Helicopters with snipers circled at a half-mile perimeter. The Aviation Division with its drone teams had set up positions on the Theodore Roosevelt Bridge and prepared to launch their birds.

If Phillip Logan Barnes was on the island, he was not getting off it.

Profilers reminded the team that since Barnes had left token nautical instruments in the fountain at Dupont Circle, there was a strong possibility that his escape plans reflected this theme. Knowing Barnes had lived under the alias of Isaac Smith on Water Island in the U.S. Virgin Islands reinforced this theory. At some point before or after college, he would have been exposed to seamanship, open water sailing, and old-fashioned navigation.

There was no escape. Not this time.

The only question was whether Kate Morgan could pull off her meeting with Barnes without getting herself killed. The longshot approach was to get Barnes to surrender and save the victim. On the Virginia side of the river, HRT was ready to strike if she failed.

105
HEADING TO THE SWAP SPOT

11:05 PM, I-66 Approaching Theodore Roosevelt Island, Washington, DC

Kate had gambled her life on a hunch, and it wasn't even midnight yet.

It felt right, even if she struggled to articulate her instincts.

If Barnes wanted her dead, she'd be dead—that was fact. Or was Barnes like the wild beast that kept its prey alive to play with as entertainment before killing it for dinner?

Yeah, that summed her up too—the dinner companion who was also the main course.

Before he'd kill her, though, he'd allow her to speak. That was her hunch.

It is during our darkest moments that we must focus to see the light. A quote from Aristotle. During the day, she'd survived the grueling darkness, not knowing if her survival was sheer luck, skill and wit and determination, or bizarre benevolence from Phillip Barnes.

All roads lead to Rome. That proverb had meaning here.

All the events had led to Theodore Roosevelt Island—the last stop on a tour of madness.

She knew the island not as a park, but rather as a place to jog on the weekends. Its eighty-plus acres were accessible only by a footbridge from Virginia. Trails and footpaths were beat down and easy to navigate. An odd spot for a last stop.

It was her wild idea to hijack the autonomous van marked with energy company logos parked over the manhole on P Street. Barnes couldn't say no to the house call. His ego drew him to be an accomplice in his own demise. The vehicle's cameras had been left active but the bomb squad had deactivated all self-destruct circuits. Due to time, the RDX explosives lodged into frame of the vehicle had been left in place. Through the front windshield, she could see an MPDC police escort and flashing lights.

Sitting in the back of the van, she was all geared up—helmet with night vision binoculars, a second Glock holstered in the small of her back, and an itchy trigger finger waiting to grab the Glock holstered on her hip. Generous road noise and the sound of tires passing over expansion joints and pavement along I-66 filled the back of the windowless van with a hypnotic cadence. Under normal circumstances, she would have fallen asleep, but her veins were charged with a fresh surge of adrenaline.

The curves of the freeway announced the island was close.

Someplace up ahead Barnes was waiting.

And she didn't want to disappoint him.

During her academy training at Quantico, new agent trainees dissected real-life case studies, life or death situations. One case in particular was a scenario in Belvedere, Ohio. A female agent investigated leads on a serial killer. She'd entered the suspect's house. Events evolved differently than expected. Alone, the agent followed the suspect into a basement, where she could hear one of his victims screaming. Power was turned off in the house, plunging it into darkness, leaving the agent at a severe disadvantage. An exchange of gunfire ensued. The suspect fired one shot. The agent fired four. One hit the suspect in the chest and killed him. Split-second instincts and hours of training had saved that agent's life.

Kate wanted to believe that skill and instincts had gotten her through the day. That wasn't the complete truth. Part of her survival had been sheer luck.

Barnes was an intelligent, premeditated pathological killer who blamed her for the deaths of his family. His thirst for vengeance fueled this maniacal scavenger hunt. From his perspective, his motives were justifiable.

The human collateral was not a concern. The grand premeditation of events had brought General James Davidson to his gallows. The general believed his secret weapon, Rachel Pratt, would defend him, complying with her obligation as a soldier, an officer. Rachel chose differently. Barnes showed jealousy after being shunned, and shot Rachel for rejecting him. It wasn't clear if Barnes had planned for Mary Davidson to be present. If he didn't call her in, someone else had sent her to stop Barnes. Mary turned out to be kryptonite. The creator he didn't blame for creating him. His forced servitude to Davidson and the program's mandates had been the source of his underlying resentment. Barnes was the slave who sought freedom.

As she died, Mary Davidson had charged her with stopping Barnes, awakening her daughter Frances, and saving the children. Kate had no idea who "the children" were. Frances was in a permanent vegetative state. Stopping Barnes, that was counter to what she was now thinking.

The world needed Barnes to tell his story. That only happened if he was alive.

This madness was unlike any case study or training exercise.

Barnes was an anomaly: a trained killer with exceptional intelligence and knowledge of explosives and satellite systems, even if being a genetically created super soldier proved to be only a minor biological enhancement compared to the other standard-bearers of the human race.

The rev of engines caused Kate to peer through the front windshield.

Officers sprinted to the sides of the four-lane bridge. Patrol cars moved from their blockade arrangement. In the distance she could see the dark outline of the treed island. Out the front side windows, two vans pulled beside the one she was riding in. Escort vehicles without drivers.

Not reassuring.

The trio of autonomous vehicles cleared the MPDC blockade. The Potomac River ran below them. Passing streetlights painted the bridge with splashes of light.

The vehicles slowed to a stop over the island. The door to the van automatically opened.

Kate jumped as her heart thundered in her chest. She got out, bringing her bag of treasures from the fountain with her.

Distant booms echoed. The bridge beneath her feet rumbled.

She stepped away from the vehicles and the overhead highway spanning both sides of the bridge, fearing it would collapse.

Barnes was blowing gaps in the bridge.

Cannon-like explosions thundered. Gritting her teeth, Kate watched as sections of the bridge in both directions buckled and twisted. Bridge supports had been targeted. Spans of concrete and steel groaned and broke away, falling into the river below. Streetlights went out casting the center span of bridge into darkness.

Theodore Roosevelt Island had turned into an isolated black hole in the Potomac.

In the distance, emergency lights from vehicles parked along connected spans of freeways twinkled and flashed against a background of city lights. Glancing up, she was stunned by the clarity of the night sky and stars above.

A last moment under the stars. Part of Barnes's twisted plan.

She patted her pants pocket and felt the stamp-sized GPS-RFID tracking patches she'd carved out of Rachel Pratt. HRT was tuned into those signals and tracking her. Maybe they'd get lucky and Barnes would be chipped to the same frequency as well.

After a nervous breath, Kate flipped down the night vision binoculars on her helmet and drew her Glock. Everything in her vision glowed shades of green and black. Approaching the north bridge railing, she glanced in both directions. The downed bridge had dammed up the river. to the south Barnes was separating her from anyone who could offer immediate backup.

Secured to the top of the railing was an extension ladder.

Peering over the edge, she targeted the ground below with her Glock. It looked only to be twenty feet down. A sloped hillside brushed up to this section of the bridge and offered an easy transition to the island. The terrain was thick with overgrowth.

Time was running out.

Kate was ready to face him, no matter the consequences.

106
ISLAND WATCH

Strategic Information & Operations Center (SIOC), FBI Headquarters, Washington, DC

Nothing else in the nation's capital seemed to matter. The big board displayed video and real-time imagery of Theodore Roosevelt Island. Camera and surveillance feeds from every angle possible were patched into the collage of screens.

Alice Watson and the ops team watched demolition charges take out supports for the I-66/I-50 bridge. Large spans of concrete and steel crashed into the Potomac.

Barnes had made the first move. Now it was law enforcement's turn.

Helicopters carrying snipers and circling at a half-mile out closed on the shorelines. Drones were put into play above the island itself. On the ground, snipers established forward positions at the closest remaining sections of the bridge. The U.S. Coast Guard motored upriver to the Arlington Memorial Bridge.

On the board, high-definition images showed Morgan going over the railing and descending into a forested landscape. Her GPS-RFID tracker marked her position on satellite imagery. Snipers tracked her movements.

On the ground, Morgan had ten minutes to pull off her miraculous stunt.

After ten minutes, the island would be as densely populated with law enforcement as the National Mall on the Fourth of July.

107
THE GIFT OF FIRE

Theodore Roosevelt Island, Washington, DC

Kate fought through soreness, climbed down the ladder, and traversed the overgrowth on the downslope that spread away from the bridge. The night vision binoculars on her helmet showed the darkness in shades of green and black. Its integral thermal imaging picked up nothing. She was grateful for the night vision. It freed up both hands and allowed her to better grip her Glock. The backpack she carried held the nautical treasures from the fountain.

She tried to be mindful about where she stepped; debris, leaves, and branches littered the ground made it impossible not to make noise.

Her heart thundered in her chest. Anyone could hear her coming. She listened to distant noises, helicopters, drones, and traffic.

At the bottom of the slope, Kate found a chain link gate open. Behind her Glock, she moved to the bridge. The Park Service had stated that the original mansion's foundation had been infilled. The 1965 Community Shelter Plan only listed one fallout shelter, on the east shore of the Potomac: the ramp off the Theodore Roosevelt Bridge.

No other bunkers or shelters or basements existed on the island.

Simple deduction drew her to the bridge.

Standing below the west span of steel and concrete, her gaze through night vision spotted urban markings. Graffiti. Gang signs. Across the river, bridge supports towered above the water like apparitions. Spans of the bridge lay half-in, half-out of the river. Beyond, the Virginia shoreline was dotted with emergency lights from vehicles.

Concentrating on the bridge, she noted its steel structure was about thirty feet off the ground. Too high to access. There were no doors, secret entrances, or manholes. She moved south through a gap in chain-link fencing. More uneven ground and thick brush. The paths here were barely wide enough to walk.

On the east side, the remnants of the bridge above revealed different construction. Its arched cavern-like span of concrete and foundation walls reminded her of the hardened bunker beneath St. Elizabeths.

This was the place. The final stop.

An inset door caught her attention—an entrance to a dungeon, a place where murderous trolls and psychopathic mass murderers probably lived.

Using her black light, she sprayed the door and concrete columns with ultraviolet light.

Invisible graffiti emerged. A message just for her.

A STOLEN TORCH AND THE SPARK FROM THE SUN'S CHARIOT WERE THE GOD'S CRIME DELIVERED AS A GIFT. THE GREAT JUPITER GREW ANGRY AND AFRAID. MAN WAS NO LONGER A SLAVE OR BOUND TO DARKNESS OR FEARFUL OF THUNDER. FIRE WAS FREEDOM.

Kate scoured her mind for mythology stories. Roman. Greek. Jupiter was essentially Zeus. Prometheus stole fire from Olympus and gave it to humanity. The advancement allowed humankind to evolve. Light dispelled darkness. For his treachery, Zeus chained Prometheus to a rock, where each day an eagle tormented the benefactor of man by pecking out his liver.

Barnes compared his murderous actions to the gift of fire—he was a modern Prometheus.

Mary Shelley had given *Frankenstein* the subtitle of *The Modern Prometheus*. There was irony in that thought. Barnes was the test tube monster created by Mary Davidson.

Studying the bunker door, Kate saw it had a numerical padlock. Four digits.

Fingering the tumblers, she dialed 1236. The sequence had worked all day.

The lock's shackle disengaged. Freed from the lock, the door swung inward. Kate forced the muzzle of her Glock into a dark inner chamber. A single heat signature glowed orange and yellow against a mask of green under thermal imaging. Using the edge of the doorway for protection, she targeted a standing figure.

"Are you alone?" a man's voice asked, echoing in the vast open space.

Kate heard a vague hum in the distance. The sound of a portable generator.

"F-B-I," Kate called, praying for her voice not to shake. "Phillip Barnes, also known as Isaac Smith, you are under arrest."

The resounding echo of laughter made her feel small, not in control.

"Barnes, I have a proposition." She took a calming breath. "And you need to hear me out."

Lights inside the bunker flashed on, blinding her through the night vision goggles.

Whirling out of the doorway, Kate flipped up the binoculars and blinked, trying to regain normal vision. Bobbing her head in and out of the door, she snuck peeks of the bunker. Illuminated by LED lighting, the vast cavern was half the size of a football field. Thirty feet inside the room, an unconscious woman dressed in a thin, blood-smeared robe was strapped to a vertical backboard. Bare tanned legs touched the floor. Bound arms raised above her head. Her robe was parted to reveal an edge of replacement skin.

Barnes was nowhere to be seen.

Kate swallowed hard, knowing that if she had fired the victim would be dead.

"So you want to talk?" The voice echoed, and she couldn't get a bearing on its source.

Leaning through the doorway, using its frame for protection, she sighted down the victim. The coward hid behind her. The only explanation. If she fired shots just above the woman's shoulders, Barnes might drop. But she was nowhere near that good a shot, at any range.

From her backpack, Kate retrieved the nautical compass and hurled it at the feet of the victim.

"Before she died," she shouted, "Mary told me to track your radio frequencies. You have a tracking implant inside you." She didn't know if that statement was a lie or true. But Barnes didn't either. The ruse was to make him believe he had carried a tracking chip. "The creator always knew where you were. She never lost track of you. It's attached to your spine. The T6 vertebrae. Now every law enforcement agency is locked onto you because I gave them the frequencies. There's nowhere in the world you can hide. It's over."

"Come inside. Close the door."

Kate knew compliance translated to suicide. Once inside, the bunker would block her own RFID-GPS tracking and no one could find her.

From her pants pocket, Kate extracted the extra tracking stamp she'd collected at the circle and dropped the electronic bread crumb on the ground outside. At least HRT and SWAT would know to come to the door.

After she shut it, automatic locking bolts engaged.

She saw a digital timer mounted on the ceiling above her. Numbers blinked on and counted down from five minutes.

Kate's breath stalled in her chest.

She'd just activated a bomb. And now she was trapped in a tomb with a madman.

18 ACROSS. REST IN PEACE.

108
GROUND MOVEMENTS

Strategic Information & Operations Center (SIOC), FBI Headquarters, Washington, DC

Six minutes and counting. That was how much time Morgan had for freelancing remaining.

Alice Watson listened to the communications. The ops center buzzed with conversations. Tactical movements. Strategic placements. Emergency response. Satellite imaging had tracked the agent as she looped around the remaining bridge structures. On the bridge's east side, the RFID-GPS stamp that Morgan carried winked in and out of tracking.

The bridge's mass and structure had interfered with signals.

And whatever was happening took place under the bridge.

Northeast of Morgan's position, a drone hovered over the marsh. Its HD camera zoomed in on the agent as she stepped through a metal doorway and disappeared. Fortunately, she'd dropped her tracking stamp outside the doorway before it closed.

The signal was given.

HRT and SWAT teams moved in.

109
NO ESCAPE

Theodore Roosevelt Island, Washington, DC

Above, brick-style explosives were anchored to the concrete ceiling. Kate ignored the digital countdown and the explosives, took an active shooting stance, and sighted down the victim.

Barnes' intentions were obvious: bury everyone at the last stop.

"Your reign of terror has ended," she called. "And you need to hear me out."

Barnes stepped out from behind the victim and targeted the woman's temple with a semi-automatic. He stood on the woman's right, with the pistol in his left hand.

Kate's mind was overwhelmed with things she wanted to scream at the monster. The devil himself stood before her, daring her to pull the trigger. Barnes looked different from what she remembered in the circle. Out in public, Barnes could pass for an accountant or lawyer. Normal. Every day normal. Nothing like the monster she knew or imagined. But Barnes was a terrorist, a mass murderer.

As suspected, he was injured. His bloody right shoulder slumped. His pale right arm was clutched tight to his chest. Blood spotted his midsection. His face looked ashen. His features shimmered as if it were his ghost standing before her.

Ghost. That summed him up. She curled her lips at the corners. Mary Davidson had almost slain her monster.

"LOG THE TOURS," he said, struggling for a deeper breath.

Despite his wounds, clever eyes, intelligent eyes, stared back at her. Evil lurked behind Barnes' gaze, even though she couldn't see its current manifestation.

"No more puzzles," she said.

Adjusting the notch and post sights of her Glock, Kate targeted his chest. She channeled her focus, drawing shallow breaths, not wanting to break a rhythm when she pulled the trigger.

"Phillip," she said, resisting the urge to scream, "you don't look so well."

"ELK PASS," he said flatly, as if it were a programmed statement. "You didn't kill my family. I know that now."

A stunning revelation. "But you still blame me for their deaths."

"Katherine, say what you must. Time is fleeting."

He wasn't wrong. The trap she'd entered was checkmate.

"The Speaker's niece doesn't deserve to die," Kate said, knowing there was no changing his mind. No one deserved to die. "This is your SWAP SPOT. Let her live. Take me instead. I'm all yours."

He blinked. The offer was unexpected.

Kate holstered her Glock and unbuckled her helmet, tossing it aside. She stepped closer, daring him to pull the trigger.

"Stop!"

She pointed to his injured arm. "Phillip, the bullet in the shoulder tore up your medial clavicle. Pale skin on your injured arm and in your face is a sign of vascular complications. Your subclavian artery is either pinched or torn. Blood has to go somewhere. Right now, it's pooling up inside you, putting pressure on your lungs and internal organs. Natural coagulation will create blood clots. You need medical attention now. And I need you to live. To tell your story. About the LAB. About ELIZABETH'S LAB."

"Only one of us can leave." He tilted his head.

Kate risked a glance.

On the south wall was an iron bulkhead. It had a ship's wheel on it and large bolts anchoring it in place. Beside the door was an orange plastic bin.

He took a labored breath. "Tell my story. People will listen to you."

She shook her head. "The Perfect People Initiative. Advanced Biogenetics Initiative. Advancing Human Evolution. SAINT ELIZABETHS. That's your story. So tell it."

Barnes moved to the other side of the victim, pressed his cheek against hers, and put his pistol on the opposite side of his temple.

He intended to kill them both by blowing their brains out.

"Wait!" Kate screamed, inching closer. Her hand gripped her Glock's handle. "Phillip, don't this!"

"I'm counting to three." Distant, lifeless eyes stared at her now. The monster now looked tired, alone. This wasn't the end he'd planned, but one he'd accept. "Katherine, you need to leave."

She ground her teeth together. "No. All of us leave, or none of us. Please."

"One."

Kate felt her chest tighten. "I wish I was a better doctor. I wish I could've saved your father and brother and uncle. And Rachel's family. And the others. After they died, I felt like I could never help anyone again. I wanted them to live."

"I know. Two." A tear broke away from his eyes and streaked down his face.

He'd made peace where he hadn't expected to. This was an acceptable endgame.

Kate drew her Glock and fired.

Barnes' head jerked back, the bullet striking him in the right eye. His ability to stay standing seemed superhuman. His head lolled forward. He readjusted the aim of his semi-automatic.

Closing the distance, Kate advanced and fired three more times.

Bullets tore into his chest. Barnes collapsed backward, his left eye glassed over and staring at the bomb-populated ceiling above them.

Kate swung around and located the countdown clock. One minute, thirty-five seconds. She had no idea of how to disarm bombs and doubted there was a retreat the way she'd entered.

Barnes was a planner. Meticulous in his stops. The iron bulkhead had been his way out all along.

Holstering her Glock, she retrieved the dagger used in the circle and cut the victim free. Folding the woman over her shoulders in a fireman's carry, Kate trudged to the bulkhead door.

Collapsing to the ground, she rolled the victim aside, unclasped the orange box and wrenched it open. Inside was a SCUBA apparatus, but not like one she'd ever seen; a bag of tools; a medical kit; plastic bags; and duct tape.

She cursed at Barnes. "Really, you were going to swim off the island?"

Turning the wheel on the bulkhead door, she opened it and faced steps leading down to a narrow pool of water. Another underground tunnel, this one submerged.

"Damn you, Barnes." Images of the wells beneath Stanley Hall and Soldiers' Home flooded her mind.

Kate dragged the victim and the plastic box into the water-filled passage. The metal door was dialed closed. Cold water swallowed her body past her hips. Using her flashlight, she lit up the confined space. The escape tunnel wasn't completely submerged, leaving a foot gap between the water surface and its concrete ceiling. At some point she reckoned that gap approached zero.

Propping the victim upright against the wall gave Kate freedom to shed her ballistic vest and the backpack with Barnes' remaining nautical instruments.

The chilling shock of greenish-brown water felt painful. ICY END came to mind. Perhaps the solution was in Barnes' original plan—a solution that drowned her in the tunnel.

With the tunnel offering a way out, her spontaneous tryst to the Cayman Islands with Thomas Parker had proved a blessing. That was where she'd learned to scuba dive.

From the box, Kate retrieved its buoyance control device (BCD). The equipment was tagged as an emergency deployment BCD. The slimmed down, compact BCD came with a mini tank, gauges, and two regulators. She strapped it on and snatched up plastic bags and duct tape.

Even though she couldn't see the clock, she felt the seconds counting down.

Time was up.

A deafening explosion rocked the tunnel.

Kate snatched the ballistic vest and dove over the victim. Shards of concrete and dust fell from the tunnel's ceiling. From the other side of the bulkhead, she could hear chunks of concrete slam into steel, buckling a door that swung outward.

With the flashlight she assessed the tunnel. Its concrete walls and ceiling had jagged cracks. Murky water migrated into their chamber, adding to the water level.

Swimming out was the only option. If they stayed put, they drowned.

Kate turned to the victim and realized she'd never called the woman by her name. Lelia Maddox was the Speaker of the House's niece, the last of SEVEN.

"Lelia, apologies in advance if I suffocate you," she said, knowing there would be no response, "but we can't stay here."

Kate slid double-lined plastic bags over Lelia's head, wrapped the bags tight around the second regulator, and duct-taped everything around the woman's neck, careful not to constrict her airway. Unconscious, a person had a low breathing rate. Without exertion Lelia stood a chance, as long as the makeshift bubble helmet retained air. They couldn't submerge to any depth, but they could float. Kate dialed open the regulator and manually inflated the plastic bag about halfway.

Spitting into a mask, Kate sealed it over her face.

After testing her own regulator, Kate snatched up the flashlight and edged them into the cold silt-filled water, pulling Lelia with her.

Keeping Lelia's head up, she goosed the regulator to add extra air and off they floated.

The submerged tunnel angled down, decreasing the air gap between the water and the tunnel's ceiling. Leveling off, the air gap remained at about two inches and shrinking.

Water pressure shrunk Lelia's makeshift helmet. Clicking the regulator from time to time, Kate added air to keep it inflated. Bobbing and pulling, she dragged them through the water-filled tunnel, staying as close to the ceiling as possible without dragging Lelia against any surfaces.

She lost track of distance and time.

Through the brownish river water, a bulkhead door materialized. It looked identical to the one they'd used to escape the island. The door was underwater, about four feet down from the tunnel's ceiling. Kate kicked its locking wheel. Nothing budged. Kate let go of Lelia so she could grab the lever with two hands. Using her legs, she applied the needed leverage to break it free.

Glancing back, she noticed Lelia had drifted away into the murky fog. Snatching the woman's hand, she reeled her past the door.

They floated into a small chamber with another door. It took moment for Kate to realize what they were in: an equalization space. Closing and locking the door they entered, she focused on the remaining door. Its handle wrenched, the door swung violently open. Powerful forces clutched their bodies as a torrent swept them away, like the feeling of surfing a water slide. Tumbling and rolling, the wave offered no options but to ride the movement as water drained into a dry adjacent tunnel.

Collapsing onto hard concrete, Kate groaned as more pain streaked through her body. She'd tumbled, rolled, and been beaten more in one day than ever expected in an entire lifetime. Crawling on all fours, she ripped the regulator mouthpiece away and rolled Lelia onto her back. Tearing open the bag covering the woman's head, she exposed the woman to the cool, damp air of a tunnel. Kate checked for a pulse, a clear airway, and listened for breathing.

Lelia Maddox was alive.

Disconnecting her BCD, Kate lay on the tunnel's cold concrete floor and caught her breath. She stared at gray concrete, then looked in both directions. The long tunnel appeared to cross below the Potomac. Twenty feet away was a van, parked in the direction she suspected was Washington, DC.

Glancing to the unconscious Lelia Maddox, Kate said, "Remind me to never do this again. Ever."

110
NO SHOT AVAILABLE

Rosslyn, Virginia

Manea had taken the spec hit because it paid one hundred thousand for showing up and five million per drop. There were two drops. And since she happened to be in the neighborhood casing a future assignment, it was worth collecting the show up fee.

International freelance work paid well, even at the sacrifice of family. Her children were grown and caught up in their own lives. Her ex-husband and a pair of lovers were dead. Her high-dollar shrink had been permanently retired.

She had no immediate obligations and nothing but time to kill.

This hit had seemed like the perfect get-in/get-out kind of side job, by personal invitation from a person who had the number to her secured satellite phone.

The Vice President of the United States was one of the few people who had an encrypted password and the ability to reach her.

It was a favor. A good score. A deposit to her account told her that the hundred thousand-dollar good faith payment had made its way to a bank in the Caribbean.

From her vantage point, an upper floor vacant office in the tallest commercial office building overlooking the Potomac and Roosevelt Island, Manea understood the nest was terrible. The setup had limited sightlines and narrow windows for a shot. And outside, there were federal authorities and cops on both sides of the Potomac. The invasion forces left little room for error, even if she had a shot to take. It would be a tough escape.

Ten million and a hundred thousand did her no good dead or in custody.

Without the benefit of details, she understood that this hit had something to do with the Metro bombing and perhaps the one at Soldiers' Home. Blatant attacks on the fabric of democracy. And somehow the Vice President was connected to those events.

She stared out the windows at the action below. The I-66 bridge had been taken out by parties unknown. Drones and helicopters circled. Watercraft approached from the north and south. HRT and SWAT teams moved closer.

One object of interest had climbed off the north side of the bridge and down to the island below. It was a manageable distance.

Her modular .308 long rifle semi-auto 10+1 rifle with suppressor mounted to a stand easily handled the 2,100 feet shot at a down angle of 21 degrees.

Manea had made contact at distances much greater than that and under duress.

But there was no shot to take. Not tonight.

Earlier, she'd considered the Kennedy Center rooftop but that was too exposed and without a height advantage. It was Rosslyn behind glass or nothing at all.

Two photos had been provided. A former Army soldier named Phillip Barnes was the primary target. FBI Special Agent Katherine Morgan was secondary. Both were marked as threats. She didn't know Barnes. Only met Morgan twice. If she'd shot Morgan in Princeton when she had the chance, she'd be out one-hundred thousand for this job. The VP had set three conditions to the hit: Barnes first, Morgan second, and no harm to the hostage. The hostage's name had been withheld, but a secondary source confirmed the victim to be none other than the Speaker of the House's niece, Dr. Lelia Maddox.

Through the scope of her sniper's rifle, Debra Ford had tracked the FBI agent as she navigated a ladder and disappeared into thick brush and natural forest.

If it weren't for the first condition of the contract, Katherine Morgan would have never stepped off the bridge.

Manea smiled. There was always next time.

111
NEW RACKETS AND BEDSIDE MOMENTS

The Dupont Hotel, Washington, DC

On a wall-mounted television, Will Shortz watched the endless news recaps while he sat at the bar. Alice Morgan called and told him to stay put. She was in transit to personally execute an out-briefing and collect his contractor's ID badge.

The good news was Katherine Morgan had made it and the terrorist had died on Theodore Roosevelt Island. Everything else was just follow-up.

The hotel provided rounds on the house. He rarely drank, except on special occasions with close friends. Tonight though, it was too hard to turn down a beer. This moment was special. He'd made a difference.

Exhausted, his mind felt clouded, his body sluggish, drained, but he grinned, knowing he'd held the trident.

A woman sat next to him. He didn't glance over until he noticed a table tennis racket sliding his way.

Alice Watson smiled. "I hear you have an active streak of days played still going."

He nodded. "Something like that."

"I'm off duty and it's not midnight yet."

He gripped the racket. "I haven't heard that line before." He grabbed his things and tipped the bartender for the free beer. "Where's our table?"

Watson guided him away from the bar. "The Director placed a call. The Washington DC Table Tennis Center, if that works. They're staying open after hours just for us. And he's arranged an escort to get us there before midnight."

Shortz grinned. "I think my evening calendar just freed up."

GWU Medical Center, Washington, DC

Three hours later. Tuesday.

Kate had given a debrief to Case Agents, showered, and changed into hospital scrubs. Medical staff had treated her various lacerations and abrasions and gave her a tetanus booster. Randy Wang was on a ventilator in the intensive care unit. She visited him after his emergency surgery. The CSS/NSA officer might need to learn how to use his voice again. The attack had done significant damage to his larynx. In a long loop through the hospital, she stopped to see Barnes' surviving victims, including Lelia Maddox.

Five individuals who'd been scarred for life and would never recover from their eternal slumbers.

None of them deserved their fates. They were stops on a map in a madman's game.

Wearing hospital-provided socks, Kate traipsed back into Jack Wright's ICU room. He too had spent time in surgery: punctured lung, broken ribs, lacerated kidney. Battered and beaten. A nasal cannula looped beneath his nose delivering O_2. As a precaution, he was sedated for the night.

Sitting bedside, Kate held Jack's hand and wondered what their lives would be like if they'd stayed together. He had an itch that always needed scratching. She'd known their relationship had a limited longevity. He was the kind of guy who needed figurative options. Not a one-gal man. Right now, though, Jack had no living relatives. She was the closest thing to family and planned to stay as long as he needed her. No commitments.

Jack was so different from Thomas Parker. Her day had started with thoughts of Thomas, but ended with no phone call made to him. Their time spent island hopping, sailing, making love and enjoying sunsets seemed so long ago now.

Mixed-up feelings made her feel guilty, as if she wasn't worthy of either man.

Yet Mary Davidson had implied Thomas was the secret to reviving the victims.

He was a brilliant neuroscientist. Kate didn't know if she could face him given her recent enlightenment. Perhaps they were both flawed and made biased decisions, taken actions into their own hands when another path had been available.

Movement caught Kate's attention. The Director entered and tucked a tiny teddy bear in Wright's arm, a stand-in animal spirit. The Director had made a point to visit each agent and staff member who'd been injured while on duty. He was an agent's director. Someone who gave a damn about the frontline troops, less bureaucrat and more beat cop.

"Why did Jack fake his death?" she asked.

"Jack almost died pulling off his stunt," the Director said.

"You're avoiding my question."

The Director took a breath. "Jack feared word might get out if he survived. He's going after Debra Ford. Manea. The woman has alliances, people in the State Department and Congress who will shelter her. Legacy connections that go back to her father, when he worked at State. We think she's in possession of Parker's university research tech and has plans to assassinate a diplomat. Someone here in the States."

From his suit pocket, he extracted two crumpled and stained pieces of paper. Dix Martinez had given those to her earlier in the day—her reinstatement and congressional waiver letters. She had discarded them before setting out to Theodore Roosevelt Island and her show down with Barnes. He set them on the side table beside her.

"Barnes made me choose." She took a ragged breath. "Part of me wanted to kill him. Part of me wanted to bring him in alive."

The Director exhaled through his nose. "From your debriefing, Barnes had the chance to kill all three of you. He made a different choice. Perhaps when he finally reached the SWAP SPOT, he'd discovered some semblance of peace. By that time, maybe his outcome was not absolute: either you or him." The Director thought for a long moment. "It's best that Barnes did not survive."

She shrugged and sensed the Director understood she didn't want to dive deeper into loose ends and unresolved associations. Her haggard mind was too tired to think about the madness of a killer, children or waking victims, or thin connections to the Vice President.

"Thank you for your service, Agent." The Director walked to the ICU doorway and stopped. "When you're ready, stop by my office. I have an assignment. It involves returning to Princeton."

THE END

THE SINGULARITY TRANSFER

A new novel coming in late 2019.

Chapters 1 and 2

Dan Grant

The genie is free of the lamp. Pandora's box is open. A radical technology threatens to change the world forever. Princeton Neurosurgeon Thomas Parker and FBI Kate Morgan are back in the fray, fighting against overwhelming odds. Stewart Richards, the madman of a secret lab is resurrected, brought back from the dead, and poses Parkers' greatest challenge yet. Teaming up, Parker and Kate must track down a series of secret experiments that are building to become the foundation for creating super spies. These spies will be programmed to change the global world stage and redraw the political boundaries of the world as we know it.

Learn more by visiting www.DanGrantBooks.com.

MindScape Press, Inc.
www.MindScapePress.com

CHAPTER 1
SLEEPING BEAUTY AWAITS

Undisclosed Hospital Location, New York

Dr. Rikona Tanaka considered raising a man from near death an intriguing concept, but the man before her was the last person on earth who deserved such a chance.

Standing at the foot of a hospital bed, she loathed the unconscious man in it.

Stewart Richards didn't deserve a second chance, at anything.

A month earlier, she escaped the executions of scientists. Colleagues. Friends. The mass house cleaning eliminated anyone who knew the dark secrets about the Advanced Neurological and Cybernetic Research Institute (ANCRI).

The urban landscape of New York City had been the perfect place to disappear, or so she hoped. But she'd been tracked down for a singular reason: as a neurobiologist, she had proven to be a talented green thumb—a biological creator of life. That's what the Phoenix Consortium wanted from her—to resurrect this man from his eternal slumber—to wake Sleeping Beauty.

Vaguely, Tanaka knew the Biblical stories of Jesus raising Lazarus and two others, whether from deep sleeps or still-hearted deaths. Now she was asked to apply modern science and perform a similar miracle.

The decision before her was a moot one.

1

Tanaka didn't fear for her own life but that of her daughter's.

Across the hospital room, a muscular-framed man in a suit held a cell phone where she could see it. The device carried a live image of a Japanese college-aged girl. Bound and gagged. A handgun pointed at her temple.

It was obvious what she'd do next.

Save her daughter.

And do whatever was required to resurrect a cold-blooded killer from a neurological state of limbo, his eternal slumber, his physiological imprisonment.

CHAPTER 2
TROUBLE AT HOME

Princeton, New Jersey

Two weeks later. Thomas Parker jolted awake from a bone-deep sleep, and it took him a half-breath to remember where he was. His newly installed home alarm blared in the darkness, obliterating the usual stillness of his colonial-style house. He had dreamt of Kate Morgan and their excursion to the Grand Caymans. On Starfish Point, incoming surf crashed over a pair of footprints impressed in white sand, washing away traces of their time spent together and pulling him back to reality. Two days after there return, she stopped calling and hadn't returned his messages. That was troubling since they seemed to be such a good fit together.

His heart stammered in his chest as his bare feet met the wood floor of his bedroom.

Through his panic, he knew what was happening—someone had broken into his house.

Stumbling, he groped through the darkness not daring to switch on a light.

His mind grew charged and fully alert, adrenaline fueling clarity.

They were coming for him. The Phoenix Consortium. It had been a possibility. Four weeks in the Caribbean gave him time to reflect on his actions. He destroyed their research and technology,

3

and for all intents and purposes killed their research lead, Stewart Richards.

His actions had exposed radical secrets to the world.

His home alarm fell silent, its sound replaced by the echoing tread of footsteps on hundred-year-old floors.

Parker peered into the hallway and detected movement approaching fast, coming from downstairs. Retreating to his master bedroom, he quietly shut its door and jammed the back of a chair beneath its knob.

He heard the door's knob turn, slowly at first then more robustly.

A thump signaled that a shoulder had engaged the other side of the door.

The improvised doorstop wouldn't hold long.

Parker grabbed a pair of sneakers and slid up the double hung window, which made enough noise to announce his intentions.

The bedroom door shuddered violently from an obvious boot strike.

The battering ram motion continued. Illuminated by moonlight streaming through the open window, the chair brace against the knob slipped a fraction of an inch.

Parker launched himself at the screen covering his window, awkwardly clearing the windowsill and leaving himself dangling hanging half-in, half-out of his two-story home. His sneakers slipped out of his grasp as his gaze panned his backyard below before returning to his tenuous grip on the window ledge. Fingertips and palms ached as he fought for better handholds.

Even though he knew it was coming, the sound of his bedroom door coming unhinged shook him to the core.

A crisp red laser dot grazed the window frame above his head, its lethal splash seeking a target. A firsthand experience over a month ago, when he stumbled into hired killers, reminded him encountering laser sights led to getting shot.

He took several rapid breaths and knew he needed to move.

Instead of dropping twelve feet and perhaps twisting an ankle, Parker scaled sideways to a drainpipe at the corner of his house. His toes dug against exterior siding for any measure of grip while his hands did most of the work. Fingers latched onto thin layers of trim. Muscles ached and they felt as if they were on fire. Pushing himself, he navigated out of view of his bedroom window and lunged at another second story windowsill.

"Outside!" a voice snapped, its frustration-etched sentiment hung ominously in the air. "The doc's outside. Over."

Parker sought a better grip and forced his toes to dig onto of the lip of the first floor window's trim immediately below him. His exposed position offered a tenuous balance at best, while gravity's clutch tried to bring him down to earth.

He felt the acute sting of the night's chill. Even if he managed to jump without injury, being barefoot didn't help matters. He wouldn't last long if people were trying to hunt him down.

His mind played through limited options and he picked one.

Head up, not down.

Hooking the crook of his elbow into the windowsill, he used his freehand and knuckles to poke out the glass near the latch in the sliding window. The announcement of breaking of glass was more than he could bear, but he didn't hesitate to thumb over the internal latch and shove up the window.

Parker climbed in and rolled past where he thought shards of glass might lay. The master bathroom and house remained dark, which was a disadvantage if his pursuers came equipped with night vision. His hand felt wet and he wrapped it in a hand towel. There was no time to inspect a glass cut, and he'd rather die moving than to die out of caution or inaction.

Unarmed, his only advantage was his house.

Dark or not, he knew its layout and contents best.

Parker moved on the balls of his feet and progressed back into his master bedroom. He slid on a change of clothing and tied up hiking boots before stepping into the upstairs hallway and readying himself for a fight.

He had gotten lucky.

Peering over the stair railing, he heard two voices below. One sounded agitated, the other dismissive. Through the darkness, he discerned movement and the closing of his back door.

One of the intruders had left to join the others looking for him outside, leaving one intruder remaining inside.

If he wanted to stay among the living, the moment was now.

Beyond rudimentary cooking utensils and a wood-block knife set from Bed Bath & Beyond, the only weapon he possessed resided on the wall in the bedroom adjacent to his master. He passed his unbandaged fingers across the etched brass inscription beneath a childhood gift from his archeological parents before their untimely deaths: "There are but few important events in the affairs of men brought about by their own choice." Ulysses S. Grant's words rang hollow, knowing Grant himself rarely wore a sword much less a proper Army uniform before his promotion to brigadier general of the volunteers. He wrenched the weapon from its mount and gripped it in two hands.

He took a calming breath and let the vintage Calvary war sword lead the way.

Creeping low, he avoided moonlight breaking past draperies and headed downstairs.

The intruders seemed to be looking for something.

It didn't take much to figure out what the Phoenix Consortium and its hired gunmen wanted. His research—a working neurological interface to the human mind. A dangerous technology that offered the ability to change global and political landscapes. He knew it as neurological singularity. Science's last great Frontier. Previously, the Phoenix Consortium or their competitors had tried to acquire his research and ransacked his home looking for his prototype inter-face. His hermit-like abode still displayed much of that ransacking.

He knew firsthand that ANCRI and its governing Phoenix Consortium would kill anyone to secure his work.

That was an outcome worth avoiding.

The remaining intruder rifled through papers on his desk. His back was turned and he loosely held a submachine gun in his hand.

Parker came in low and reached up to twist the man's weapon away, thrusting the blunt pommel of the sword upward. Aged steel contacted chin and bone. The man's balance shifted to his heels. Jerking the weapon from the man's grasp. In a single motion, he swept the man's leg with his foot and dropped him hard to the floor.

The body crashing against the floor fractured any quietness.

Parker struck the man's face with the butt of the sword again, and the man never screamed as his body went limp.

Removing the man's tactical wireless communications, he patted down the body until a phone and a wallet were located, then snatched up the submachine gun.

Now he had a gun, which went a long way toward evening the odds.

It wouldn't take the remaining intruders long to figure out one of theirs was down.

They'd return with a vengeance.

He deposited the sword in a wicker umbrella stand, then rolled the unconscious man beneath his desk, out of sight.

Parker inserted the earpiece to the man's comms and clipped the radio to the waist of his own pants.

Using the man's cell phone, he dialed 911 from the emergency call option.

The 911 operator came on the line with a no-nonsense kind of manner.

He raised his voice an octave and laid on his best Jersey accent for the recording. "I'm mindin' my own business, but I got to report this. Men with machine guns broke into my neighbor's home and set off his alarm." He gave his address. The operator started asking questions and he cut her off. "Sneaking around the bushes, there's no way they're cops. Criminals. Dangerous criminals. Oh, I think they saw me. Get the cops out here."

Clicking off the phone, he tossed it under his desk where the unconscious man lay.

Parker sensed he needed to pick up his pace just as the back door of the house cracked open. Multiple footsteps approached quickly.

He gripped the newly acquired weapon tight in his hands and moved through a pair of French doors to duck behind a hutch packed with books.

The comms' piece in his ear sparked alive. A woman's voice. Assertive. Confident. Their leader. "Arkansas, did you locate the schematics or solid state drives yet?"

Movement progressed past him and gathered in his study.

She was back on comms. "Arkansas, report your location. Over." She waited for a response that never came then said, "Arkansas, report in. Over."

Parker beamed a grin. *Check back with Arkansas later.*

"Georgia and Mississippi," she said, not using the comms, "tear apart the upstairs. Find his tech. Damn it, we're on a clock here. And if you two reconvene with Arkansas, secure him. I'll teach the man not to wander off and go silent." She clicked on the comms again. "Texas and Missouri, return to the house. The good doctor has a limited means to remain off the radar. He can't hide. We'll secure him by another means. Over."

"Understood. Tex and The Real Deal Miss returning to the house," another voice said.

He counted five states from the conversation—codenames. The leader rounded out the group at six intruders.

They wanted his tech from ANCRI. That made sense.

Parker felt an unexpected pulse surge through him and risked a glance. Two large and armed shadows presumed to be Georgia and Mississippi headed upstairs, leaving their female boss to pillage his study.

Seizing the moment, Parker dashed in the opposite direction.

He cracked open the basement door and ducked into its narrow stairs. He didn't risk turning on lights and felt along the wall to keep his balance. Unfinished stair treads creaked under his weight— nothing he could do about that.

Where are the police? Anytime now.

At the bottom, in total darkness, he hugged the walls and moved with purpose.

Parker slammed into something around his knees and the sounds of secondhand research equipment that he'd been meaning to pick up clattered onto the basement's plywood subfloor—its clamor resonating like thunder. He imagined the noise had reached the rest of the house as well.

From the floor above, movement paused and the house fell eerily still.

"Texas and Missouri, search the basement again," the woman's voice said over the comms. "Check everything, including crawl spaces. Make sure there's nowhere to hide. Over."

Watch for *The Singularity Transfer* in late 2019.

Learn more by visiting www.DanGrantBooks.com.

ACKNOWLEDGEMENTS

As usual, there are numerous people to thank, more than this small snapshot can cover.

After *The Singularity Witness* and during extensive rewrites (which included a new puzzle, settings and destinations, and characters), I knew Kate Morgan needed help. She had to be freed up to tackle the stops as they unfolded. From there a new character was born, a subject matter expert in crossword puzzles. During research of puzzle history, its pop culture and lore, I realized that this character could be real. So the first person I must thank is Will Shortz for allowing me the opportunity to fictionalize him as the case's grand puzzle master. Will was gracious and gave a wide latitude for his character. It was fun and quite the challenge to find ways to put him in play, place him in mild harms' way, and get creative with his character's contribution to the story. Any flaws that exist in his presence, actions, or personal reflections are clearly mine.

Christian Jaeger, my roommate in college, gave me a copy of the article *Our Most Important Product*, by Dr. George J. Annas. Nothing in his article was new, but Dr. Annas did structure his narrative in a way that told its own story. The points he made resonated with me and I knew that I had to work similar concepts into a story of my own. In some ways, the Perfect People Initiative worked as a fictional extension of Annas' narrative and gave Phillip Barnes fuel, purpose, and a history.

Also, I want to thank agents from the Federal Bureau of Investigation for their time, insight, and input on how certain aspects of the bureau operate. Any narrative discrepancies that don't match actual FBI procedural or operational parameters were done either deliberately or for the consolidation of characters and time. Any inaccuracies or misrepresentations are mine.

Thanks to my editor Ellen Clair Lamb for her contribution, skill, and insight, and help in making *Thirteen Across* better; and thanks to Caitlin Berve for the follow up support.

And finally, my wife Leslie is always my first reader and sounding board. She asks questions and quizzes me on characters and concepts. I'm grateful for her input, patience, and encouragement. She's given me the support and freedom to tell stories and take chances.

BACKGROUND

In 2018, *The Singularity Witness* was released. That science-fiction/science-medical style thriller featured two main characters: Thomas Parker and Kate Morgan. In that tale, both characters are co-heroes with their own quests; the story requires a contribution from each of them.

In the late 1990s, the first drafts of *Thirteen Across* and a crossword puzzle were written (then called *Thirteen Across Spells Murder*). That puzzle visited vastly different locations in the nation's capital. And like *The Singularity Witness*, its original manuscript found itself locked inside drawers while my engineering career took off.

Thirteen Across is a research-based, cross-genre, parallel story to a core Singularity Series and fits a more traditional style catch-me-if-you-can thriller. This story is not different from *The Singularity Witness* because there's less science or that it focuses on Kate Morgan or merges a crossword puzzle into the tale as a plot device, but more so because it reveals aspects and areas of cutting edge science breakthroughs through the villain's backstory. It's a puzzle in a puzzle—a story inside a story. My idea to infuse a crossword puzzle into the story came from the graphics inside *Jurassic Park*. I'm not the first to bring crossword puzzles and crossword creators/editors into stories, but *Thirteen Across* should be unique from other stories in how the puzzle is woven and layered into a catch-me-if-you-can/treasure map scenario and how it unfolds to reveal character's backstories.

Drawing on the article *Our Most Important Product*, Barnes is a super soldier who became a disenfranchised, heart-broken slave. In many ways, Kate Morgan and Phillip Barnes wrote this story and I was only along for the ride. The scavenger hunt quest and locations in the story matter—at least to Barnes. It was fun visiting and researching lesser known locations in Washington, DC., and seeking ways to bring them alive in different contexts.

Learn more about *Thirteen Across*, its background, and read about some of the research mentioned, visit
https://DanGrantBooks.com/Thirteen-Across

ABOUT THE AUTHOR

Dan loves stories, especially intriguing tales that weave science, medicine, technology, or history into the fabric of the story. *Thirteen Across* does that and adds locations to the mix as well.

He's a licensed professional engineer with degrees from Northern Arizona University: a bachelor's in electrical engineering and masters' in college education and English with an emphasis in creative writing. His engineering endeavors have provided opportunities to work with a variety of medical and technological applications, and get behind the scenes of military facilities. Besides engineering, he has taught college English and computer programming, worked as a technical writer, and presented writing workshops. He lives in Colorado with his wife, two boys, and two dogs.

Dan is working on his next thriller—Thomas Parker and Kate Morgan will be back in *The Singularity Transfer*. Kate will return in a sequel to *Thirteen Across*, which has yet to be titled... and we shall see what puzzles and quandaries lay in wait for her.

To find out more, read author notes, and see some of the background material, go to www.DanGrantBooks.com.

CPSIA information can be obtained
at www.ICGtesting.com
Printed in the USA
LVHW081454141119
637370LV00010B/235/P